BLOOD MEMORY

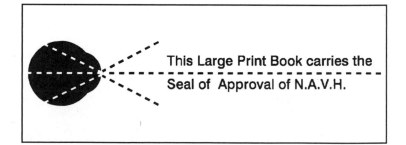

This Large Print Book carries the
Seal of Approval of N.A.V.H.

BLOOD MEMORY

MARGARET COEL

THORNDIKE PRESS
A part of Gale, Cengage Learning

GALE
CENGAGE Learning™

Detroit • New York • San Francisco • New Haven, Conn • Waterville, Maine • London

GALE
CENGAGE Learning™

Thorndike Press® Large Print Core.
The text of this Large Print edition is unabridged.
Other aspects of the book may vary from the original edition.
Set in 16 pt. Plantin.
Printed on permanent paper.

LIBRARY OF CONGRESS CATALOGING-IN-PUBLICATION DATA

Coel, Margaret, 1937–
    Blood memory / by Margaret Coel.
        p. cm. — (Thorndike Press large print core)
    ISBN-13: 978-1-4104-1204-1 (hardcover : alk. paper)
    ISBN-10: 1-4104-1204-0 (hardcover : alk. paper)
    1. Women journalists—Fiction. 2. Denver (Colo.)—Fiction. 3. Indians of North America—Land tenure—Fiction. 4. Large type books. I. Title.
    PS3553.O347B55 2009
    813'.54—dc22   2008038792

Published in 2009 by arrangement with The Berkley Publishing Group, a member of Penguin Group (USA) Inc.

Printed in the United States of America
1 2 3 4 5 6 7 12 11 10 09 08

In memory of my parents,
Margaret and Sam.

ACKNOWLEDGMENTS

I am indebted to many people for walking me through various details of this novel. Special thanks to such knowledgeable friends as David F. Halaas, Ph.D., former chief historian, Colorado Historical Society, now director of the Center for the French and Indian War at Pittsburgh's Senator John Heinz History Center, and coauthor (along with Andrew Masich) of *Halfbreed;* Karen Cotton, features/entertainment reporter, *Wyoming Tribune-Eagle* in Cheyenne; Fred Walker, firearms expert; Mike Fiori, retired detective, Denver Police Department; Ann Ripley, author of the Louise Eldridge mystery series, including *Death in the Orchid Garden.*

And to my knowledgeable family members: son-in-law, Tom Harrison; brother, Clay Speas; niece and nephew, Denise and Sean Saxon.

I also want to thank Holly Heineman,

former title company official, and the many helpful folks at the Colorado Secretary of State's office and at the Boulder County Clerk's office who cheerfully explained the arcane matters relating to nineteenth-century property titles.

And, as always, a tip of my hat to the dear friends who read parts or all of the manuscript and made insightful suggestions: Bev Carrigan, Sheila Carrigan, and Karen Gilleland. And of course to my husband, George.

The blood means nothing; the spirit, the ghost of the land moves in the blood, moves the blood.

— WILLIAM CARLOS WILLIAMS

1

The August night was perfect. A full moon hanging low in a silver sky, just enough hint of a cool breeze to banish the day's heat. An automobile rumbling along a street somewhere and a squirrel scampering up a tree broke into the quiet. She watched her shadow fall around the golden retriever's as he plunged ahead, straining against the leash. They were alone in the moon-filled night that wrapped around them.

They had reached an understanding, she and Rex, a kind of compromise. He would stay in the dog run at the side of the town house while she was at work. And she would take him on a mile-long walk around the neighborhood — good for both of them, she told herself — when she got home in the evenings. She'd gotten home later than usual tonight. It must be close to midnight. It was hard to get a look at her watch with the dog pulling her down the sidewalk.

Flattened behind the shadows on both sides of the street were townhomes that looked much like her own, fake adobe façades and red-tiled roofs reminiscent of Mexico or Italy, unlike the redbrick Denver bungalows that had occupied the neighborhood for the past hundred years. An enterprising developer, who happened to be her ex-husband, had bought up four blocks of bungalows and called out the wrecking crew before the historic preservationists could force a change in plans. Before anyone realized what was happening, a new neighborhood had been plunked down amid the old. "Upscale" is how the brochures termed the town houses, "green" for the young professionals who cared about such things, minimal landscaping that consisted of a few strategically placed trees and bushes arranged around neat patches of groomed gravel.

They crossed the street and started down the next block, the dog still pulling ahead. She could feel the strength in his muscles transported along the rayon fibers of the leash. They had already made two swings around the periphery of the neighborhood, and she was beginning to relax, the tension of the day melting out of her muscles and sinews. Ahead, something moved in the shadows in front of one of the town houses. Her heart took a little jump. She gave a yank on the leash and closed the gap with the dog, not taking her eyes from the spot where she'd caught the movement, so slight it might have been her imagination. It wasn't there now.

A shadow adjusting itself in the moonlight, she told herself. Everything looked different at night, moved differently, even the spindle-like trees swaying in the breeze. Besides, the neighborhood was safe — perfectly safe, her ex-husband had assured her — the type of neighborhood a professional woman on her own, such as herself, could be comfortable in. She and her neighbors would have similar interests. And those interests would be — she gave the leash a little slack, watching the dog bolt ahead, shoulders rounded in the task — a total dedication to career, whatever the career might be, so total there was no space for anything else. Which explained the appeal of "green" gravelly yards, hardly the kind where children would be found playing.

A friendly neighborhood, he had said. That was funny, thinking about it now. Almost a year in the town house and she didn't know a single neighbor, probably wouldn't recognize a neighbor if she bumped into one at the deli. The sum of exchanges with the neighbors amounted to occasional eye contact across identical yards, nods and muted "Morning"s as they backed their respective cars out of upscale garages and down upscale driveways. But that was her fault, she knew. She had preferred to bury herself in her work, staying late, working weekends. The neighborhood passed for okay, and it was close to the *Journal* building. And Rex helped. A friend waiting at home when she finally got there. Her life was her career now. A journalist at the daily newspaper read by everyone who cared about what was going on in Denver. Even if there weren't many newspapers left on the driveways, she suspected that her neighbors probably read her byline on the Internet in the mornings. The townhome was an interim place — a place to spend the night.

There was a scraping noise on the sidewalk behind her.

She pulled on the leash and wheeled around. Nothing except patches of shadow and moonlight. The sidewalk and street were empty, melting into the darkness down the block. She was imagining things in the night that weren't there. Still she felt jittery. Such a distinctive sound, the scrape of boots on concrete. She searched the shadows again, then turned and started walking fast toward the corner ahead, giving the leash a lot of slack. Her townhome was around the corner and halfway down the block. She was five minutes from home.

She heard the sound again. The footsteps tapped out a brisk rhythm that matched her own. Someone was following her. A jumble of thoughts clanged in her head. She felt her body tense, a thousand electrical impulses set to fire. Rex must have sensed the tension, because he was now walking beside her. She made herself keep the same pace — yes, that was what she must do. Not change her pace and tip him off that she *knew* he was there. It was a man, she was certain, the footsteps heavy and definite. She slipped her hand into her jeans pocket, pulled out her house key, and closed her fist around the metal so that the sharp point protruded between her middle fingers.

She kept her head straight ahead, her eyes sweeping over the street and sidewalk and yards. Lights glowed in the upstairs windows of the town house at the corner. He wouldn't close on her there, grab her from behind and try to pull her into the bushes. She tried to think the way he would think, a man planning to tackle and rape her, beat

15

her. He would wait until she walked in front of a town house swallowed by the night. Until then, he had to think that she thought everything was normal. She was simply out enjoying a walk with her dog.

She reached the corner, turned past the thin slice of light on the sidewalk from the town house window, and glanced around. She saw him then, a tall, large figure all in black, shoulders hunched inside a bulky jacket, hands jammed into the pockets, elbows sticking out like those of a wrestler strutting into the ring. He was close, not more than two houses behind, backlit by the moonlight. She thought about running to the door with the lights on upstairs, then dismissed the idea. By the time anyone came down the stairs and opened the door, he would be on her, and he would be strong. She could almost feel the clasp of a fleshy hand over her mouth, the arms dragging her off to the side while someone leaned outside, looking around, seeing nothing, except for a dog barking and growling near the bushes, frantic. *Go home! Go home! Damn people, why don't they keep their dogs locked up?* The door would slam shut, and she would be alone with him. At best, the person might call the police. The police would come, but it would be too late.

16

She was half a block from home.

She kept going at the same steady pace, keeping the dark figure in her peripheral vision. The instant she passed the corner of the town house, out of his sight, she broke into a full-out run, running as fast as she could, pulling Rex along. "Come on! Come on!" she managed to order in between gulps of air crashing into her lungs. Her heart was hammering. She glanced back as she turned up her own sidewalk. He had just rounded the corner, and in the way he hesitated, turning his head side to side, she knew that she had only a moment before he started running after her. She lunged for the door, jammed the key into the lock, and slipped inside, holding the dog by his collar now, bringing him with her. She closed the door quietly, not wanting to signal where she was, and pushed the bolt. She had to lean against the door a moment to catch her breath. Her lungs were on fire, her heart exploding in her chest. The dog rubbed against her legs and emitted little whimpering noises, as if he grasped that whatever was wrong, they were in it together.

She removed the leash, then flattened herself against the door and peered through the tiny view hole. He had passed her house, and now he stood on the sidewalk in front of the neighbor's, looking up and down the street. He had on a black ski hat, pulled low over his forehead. His face was distorted, filled with angry frustration, the face of a creature with a long nose and tight lips, half man, half monster. She watched until he moved down the sidewalk and into the shadows.

She'd left the light on upstairs, and a thin stream of light ran down the stairs and across the tile floor in front of the door. A Dave Brubeck CD was playing softly. She didn't turn on any other light. There could be no changes, nothing to catch his attention and bring him to her town house. She went into the kitchen and threw the bolt on the back door. There were narrow alleys of gravel between the clusters of townhomes. The dog run was on the south side. But he might take one of the other alleys, come through the backyards. There were no fences, thanks to the homeowners' association, which had decreed that the tiny yards should flow like a dry, gravel river along the back of the townhomes and create an illusion of space and privacy. It had practically taken an act of God to get the dog run approved, that and a phone call to the association president from her ex-husband.

She stared at the window. Moonlight

18

winked in the black glass. She hadn't pulled the blinds — God, why hadn't she pulled the blinds? He could see her moving about in the faint light. She started to pull down the blind, then stopped. No changes. Her saliva tasted like acid.

She opened a cabinet, took out a bottle of Wild Turkey, and sloshed an inch or so into a juice glass next to the sink. She took a long drink, then backed across the kitchen, picked up the phone, and tapped out Maury's number. She cradled the phone against her ear, finished off the bourbon, and concentrated on the buzzing noise of the ringing phone.

"Yeah? Who is it?" His voice was sleep clogged and tentative, as if he were coming out of a dream and trying to adjust to a new reality.

"Maury, it's me," she said. "A man followed me home."

"What?" He was Maury now, divorce attorney with a client he'd befriended after her divorce. "Where were you?"

"Out walking."

"Now? You know what time it is? You shouldn't be walking alone at this hour."

"Rex was with me."

"Yeah, right. Rex. You lock your doors?"

"Yes." She swallowed back the acid erupting in her throat and threw a glance across the kitchen. She'd intended to bolt the doors, but now she couldn't say for certain what she'd done. "He's still out there somewhere," she said.

"Jesus. Some pervert. I'm on my way over," Maury said. "Hang up and call the police."

Of course she should call the cops. She should have called the cops first thing. "Right," she said, but she was talking to a bleeping noise. The CD had ended. The house was quiet.

She pressed the off key, then dialed 911, on automatic now, following directions as if she'd already done all she could to save herself and there was nothing else she had the presence of mind to do on her own.

"What is your emergency?" The woman on the line sounded as if she were at the end of a long shift. She told her that a man had followed her home.

"Did you get into your house?"

"Yes."

"Is the man still outside?"

"I think so." She could feel him outside, somewhere close. A pervert, Maury had called him. A pervert who had targeted a woman who happened to be walking her dog too late at night. He would still be looking for her. She tried to catch her breath, but it was like trying to breathe past a tightening noose.

"Where are you?"

She managed to spit out her address, then she heard the routine calmness washing through the woman's voice: a police car was on the way. She should lock her doors and not go outside.

She hung up and, feeling disembodied, floating somewhere above herself, went back into the living room and sank onto the tile floor in the corner away from the window. She pulled her knees to her chest and crossed her arms around her legs. She could feel her muscles twitching, as if they were twitching in someone else's body. God, she needed another drink. She pushed the idea away. She had to keep her mind clear, she had to think. She heard herself whispering, calling Rex. The dog skittered over, slid down beside her, and tried to fit his muzzle beneath her chin. She patted his head. "Good boy," she said. "Maury's coming."

She wasn't sure how long she sat there. A week, a month. Time had stopped. Probably no more than five minutes, she realized. Maury lived only a few blocks away in a Denver bungalow with a swing on the front porch and two strips of green lawn on either side of the walkway, all of it sloping down to the sidewalk under the shade of a big oak tree. He'd pull on a pair of jeans, stick his feet into the worn docksiders, wake up Philip to say he'd be back soon, and drive over. Six, seven minutes at the most. She could picture him running up her walk, dark hair tousled, face puffy from sleep, the tee shirt he'd been sleeping in smashed against his chest.

Outside a car door slammed, followed by the scuff of footsteps.

She uncurled from the corner and threw herself at the door, barely aware of Rex barking and jumping about. Her hand grasped the bolt, but she stopped herself from slamming it back. She peered into the tiny circle of glass. Maury was coming up the walk, his face expanding as he got closer. He looked as she'd imagined, except for the determined look in his eyes and rictus of resolve in the muscles of his jaw.

She pushed the bolt back and yanked open the door. "Thank God," she said in the instant before everything exploded. It happened so fast that, even later when she tried to place the events in the order in which they occurred, she couldn't be certain what had happened first. Maury had started to come inside, and she'd stepped back,

22

pulling the door with her. Yes, that was how it went. Except that Maury had burst inside, as if he'd been shot from a cannon. Or had that happened first and then — with the shock of it — the door slammed back? The man dressed in black blurred like a shadow flitting across her vision and threw himself against Maury. Maury toppled like an oak felled in a field. The sound of Rex barking came from far away, background noise as Maury rolled over, jumped to his feet, and swung a thick arm against the figure dancing about, a grotesque marionette, swinging and dodging Maury's fists.

Then they were locked together, stumbling about the living room, breathing hard. The coffee table crashed onto its side, a chair toppled backward. She staggered toward them, looking for something to grab, some weapon. She spotted the lamp on the side table, but before she could reach it, they crashed into the table and the lamp fell, shattering into minuscule pieces of glass that spilled marbles across the tile. Rex was circling about, barking and yelping. Finally Maury wrenched himself out of the man's grasp. He rocked backward before he threw a fist into the man's chest.

Then the man rocked backward. Yes, that was how it happened. There had been a moment when she'd thought that it was over, that the intruder would collapse. He staggered about, throwing his head around, and that must have been what she was watching because she hadn't seen him pull the gun out of the pocket of his bulky jacket. Yet he was pointing the black gun at Maury. Maury moved backward, both arms thrust out, as if he could have deflected the bullet that exploded in his chest. She blinked at the deadened report of the gunshot, when she had expected an explosion like an accumulation of all the noise in the world. Maury fell backward, head and shoulders hitting the floor in the doorway to the kitchen, blood blossoming across the front of his white tee shirt, running across the tile.

She pressed herself down behind the upturned table near the foot of the stairs and held her breath, terrified that the sound of her breathing would lead him to her. She could hear the small noise of Rex's whimpers coming from the corner where they'd waited for Maury. Her eyes were glued to the man standing over Maury, head cocked to one side, the knitted cap pushed up into a peak. At first she thought he was looking for her, then she heard the sirens and realized that he was listening. He glanced around, and she moved back into the shadows along the wall, still holding her breath. She felt as if a stone were crushing her chest.

A door slammed somewhere, followed by a cacophony of voices, neighbors yelling across the yards: "What's going on?" "You hear that?" And against the cacophony, the swelling noise of sirens.

The intruder swung about and ran through the front door.

She crawled around the table and across the cold tile to Maury. The black hole in his chest was like a crater sucking everything into it: tee shirt and blood and life, as if Maury himself would disappear into the crater. And yet it was his blood and life that were pouring out, turning the white tee shirt black.

She tried to find a pulse in his neck, her fingers as numb as dried twigs quivering against his warm skin. She was barely aware of Rex crouching next to her, or of the black boots and dark trousers of police officers moving toward them.

2

My name is Catherine McLeod.

I'm thirty-nine years old.

Divorced. Married six years, divorced ten months.

What do I do? I've been an investigative reporter for the Journal *the last three years.*

Maury Beekner is my friend. He came to help me. God, don't let him die.

I don't know the intruder.

I don't know why he followed me. How would I know why he followed me?

I have no idea why anyone would want to kill me.

"Catherine? Are you okay?"

Catherine shifted her weight on the hard seat and looked across the metal table at the man with black hair cropped short over his ears, silver at the temples. "Detective Bustamante," he'd said when he met her in the lobby at Denver Police Headquarters.

"Nick Bustamante." He had held out a large hand that could probably wrap around a basketball. "I'm handling the investigation into last night's shooting."

There was some comfort in that. She had felt the strength and determination in his grip.

"I'm okay," she managed. They were in a cubicle not much larger than a closet with a one-way glass panel behind Bustamante and a door that led into the wide corridor they had traversed after they had stepped out of the elevator. Someone on the other side of the glass would videotape the interview, Bustamante had explained. She had a prickly sense of invisible eyes moving over her.

Bustamante opened a file folder and stared at a printed sheet. Filtering into the quiet were angry, insistent male voices moving along the corridor.

"I told the officers everything last night," she said. Nick Bustamante was handsome in an unaware way. Dark eyes, the hint of a shadow along his jaw. "Can we finish up here? I have to check in at work and get back to the hospital."

The sun was rising when she had left Denver Health. Layers of golds, tangerines, and magentas filled the eastern sky and cast a blood-red hue over the skyscrapers in the distance. She had hurried across the parking lot to her silver convertible and, somehow, had found her way through the empty streets back to her town house, but she couldn't have retraced the route she'd taken. She remembered gripping the steering wheel, barely aware of the parking lots, gas stations, and stores, and finally the residential neighborhoods that blurred past.

She'd had to duck under the yellow police tape to get into the town house, ignoring the words Do Not Cross. She had forced herself to look away from the dark brown smears on the tile as she'd walked through the kitchen and out the back door to check on Rex in the dog run. Refilling the water dish, shaking dried food out of the bag into his pan, patting his head, going through the morning routine on automatic, as if everything were normal.

Back inside, she had climbed the stairs and fallen into an exhausted and jerky half sleep for about an hour, she guessed, although time had stood still since Maury was shot, as if everything had coalesced into that moment. She had felt groggy and half-sick as she'd dragged herself to her feet, showered, pulled on a sleeveless dress and sandals, and tried to do something with her makeup so that the woman staring back in the bathroom mirror didn't resemble a drawn, blanched character in a horror movie. She had run her fingers through her black, shoulder-length hair and pushed back the shorter pieces that fell about her face, then made her way down the stairs — *don't look, don't look.* Then she had driven downtown to police headquarters, still on automatic, following the instructions of the police officer last night, as if she no longer had any control over her own life.

"I'm sorry to put you through it again," Bustamante said, his attention still on the sheet of paper. He wore a white shirt, opened at the neck, and a summer-weight, tweedy brown jacket that, she guessed, he'd pulled on for the interview, judging by the uneasy way it rode across his broad shoulders. He would never be mistaken for a banker, she thought.

He looked up at her. "I need your statement today as well. You would be surprised how many details victims recall after the shock begins to wear off." A flickering of sympathetic light in his dark eyes. "You must still be in shock after seeing your friend shot."

"I don't know if he's going to make it," Catherine said, and with that, the hard knots of anxiety and fear she'd been struggling to swallow back began pouring out. The interview room and the man on the other side of the metal table were a watery blur. She ran her palm across her cheeks in a not very successful attempt to wipe away the warm tears that kept coming, barely aware of the white square that Nick Bustamante held out to her. She took the handkerchief, mopped at the moisture, and blew her nose.

"Philip and I were at the hospital the rest of the night," she said, closing her fist around the damp handkerchief. She felt as if she were still in the ICU waiting room, she and Philip sitting side by side, two plastic statues molded to the plastic chairs, and all the time she had felt the resentment and anger blowing off Philip like smoke. Every time the metal door had swung open and a green-clad doctor walked through, they had jumped up and asked about Maury. The answer was always the same — no change — and always delivered in a flat, neutral tone. As if it weren't Maury they were talking about — big, smiling, bearlike Maury — but some anonymous gunshot victim brought in from the street.

She went on: "They refused to let me see him. Family only, they said, which is crazy because he doesn't have any family. We're his family."

"I see," Bustamante said, as if he'd just framed a picture in his mind. He leaned back against his chair. "Is that why you called Maury after you spotted the man following you last night?"

"No, you don't see. We're not in a relationship, if that's what you're thinking. Maury and I are good friends, that's all." She could see by the way his features rearranged themselves around some new idea that it was exactly what he had been thinking. "It's not sexual. Maury's gay." God, what did this have to do with anything? Silence filtered between them a moment. "They should have let us see him. What if he should die? He will have died alone, and we . . ." The tears started again. She rolled up the moist handkerchief and dabbed at her eyes.

"Philip would be . . ." Bustamante clasped his hands on the table.

"Philip Case," she said. "They even refused to let him see Maury at first. He'd had to go home and get Maury's power of attorney and all the other legal papers."

"So Philip Case and Maury are . . ." He let the rest of it drift.

"Married," she said, "even if the law

31

doesn't say so. Maury is my good friend. We're very close."

"I know somebody in hospital administration," Bustamante said. "I'll call her. Perhaps she can arrange to relax the rules in this case, if Philip agrees. No promises."

"Thank you."

He went back to the file folder, thumbed through the thin stack of papers, and pushed one toward her. It was a map of her neighborhood, enlarged from a map of Denver. A thick red line had been drawn around the town house development. "Show me where you first spotted the attacker," he said.

Catherine pulled the map closer and set her index finger on the spot a block and a half from her townhome. "Here," she said. "He may have started following me earlier." Then she told him how she thought she'd heard footsteps behind her, but when she had turned around, no one was there. It struck her now that the man hadn't wanted her to see him at that point, yet a few yards later, he had been confident enough not to care. The idea sent a chill through her. At that moment, he had been confident there was nothing she could do.

She hunched forward, clasped her arms against the chill, and told him the rest of it. How she had kept walking at the same steady pace, how she had waited until she was out of sight around the corner before she broke into a run and got inside her townhome. She had called Maury before she'd called the police.

She felt the pressure of the tears forming again. She pressed the handkerchief against her eyes. "The bastard crashed through the door with Maury and shot him," she said. "I never should have called him. This wouldn't have happened." Her mouth felt dry, bitter tasting. She wished she had a drink — bourbon or a glass of wine.

She had to look away. Beyond the glass, a camera was videotaping everything; officers were watching and listening. There was no hiding from the truth: she had sacrificed Maury for her own safety. The realization made her feel sick to her stomach. What had she been thinking? That Maury could protect her from a man with a gun? And yet, she hadn't known the man had a gun. She hadn't wanted to be alone, that was all, and she knew Maury would have stayed until the police found the man or morning arrived, whichever came first, and she could forget the whole nightmare of it — the hunter coming down the moonlit sidewalk, stalking her.

"You said he's your friend. Wouldn't he

have wanted you to call him?" Bustamante set his elbows on the table and regarded her over clasped hands. Something new had come into his eyes, as if he had been observing her under a microscope and found something unexpectedly interesting. "If the attacker was lurking outside when Maury Beekner arrived . . ."

"What do you mean, *if?*" Catherine stared at him. "Obviously he was waiting outside." She'd covered enough criminal cases for the *Journal* to know how investigations went: Everything was on the table. No account of what had occurred was ever taken at face value. Stories were always layered, like plaster on a wall. Peel back the top coat and you got a different design, a whole different wall.

"What about the gunshot?" Bustamante's voice sliced into her thoughts. "What did it sound like?"

"A dull thud," she said. She could see the black tube attached to the gun. "He used a silencer."

"You know guns?"

"My dad used to take me target shooting when I was growing up. He taught me a little about guns."

"That would explain why the neighbors heard the commotion, but nobody recognized the gunshot," Bustamante said. His voice was neutral. "Describe him for me. Anything familiar about him?" A distant look came into his eyes. He was still peeling back the layers, and she had the sickening sense that he expected to find something else.

"You think I've made this up?" she said. "You think I called Maury and shot him when he arrived?"

The detective didn't say anything.

"My God!" Catherine started to get to her feet, then sat down hard. She could feel the flush of anger in her face. "The man who shot Maury was six feet tall." She kept her voice steady and certain. "He had on a bulky jacket that made him seem bigger than he might have been. He seemed slim, wiry, with a big jacket on. He was dressed all in black — black pants, black jacket, black knit hat. He wore black gloves." She didn't know why she remembered the gloves, except that, closing her eyes, trying to remember every detail, she could see the image of him lasered on the back of her eyelids. "He looked like a monster."

Bustamante took a moment, as if he were starting to believe her. "Not anyone you think you might know?" he said.

She opened her eyes. "He's a rapist. He

was trolling for a woman out alone. He happened in my neighborhood and zeroed in on me, that's all. It could have been any woman."

"It's possible . . ." he began.

"Now what are you saying?" Catherine had the sense that he was probing yet another layer that she hadn't realized existed. "That I was his target? He was after me? That's ridiculous. I told you, I don't know why anyone would want to harm me. There's a rapist in the Washington Park area, right? He hasn't been arrested yet."

"Washington Park's three miles away. No reports of intruders in your neighborhood. Last year there was a domestic disturbance call, and a couple of months ago, one of the neighbors backed out of his driveway and scraped the side of the car parked across the street. You live in a safe neighborhood." Bustamante spread his large hands. Wisps of black hair curled over the edge of his jacket sleeves. "He used a gun with a silencer, he wore gloves. Isn't it possible he was a man with a specific mission and he came prepared?"

"To kill me?"

He gave her a long, searching look. "Tell me about yourself," he said. "Problems with any neighbors?"

Catherine shook her head, and he went on. "Any repairmen in your townhome lately?"

"No."

"Altercations with other drivers?"

"No," she said again.

"Anything out of the ordinary at all? Angry encounters with anyone in a store or restaurant?"

Catherine was quiet a moment. "Not exactly," she said.

"Tell me."

"About ten days ago, I was having coffee at a shop around the corner from the *Journal.* I realized I didn't have my purse. I went back to the counter and the clerk gave it to me. Said someone had just turned it in. I must have set it down while I was ordering. Nothing was missing. It didn't look as if anything inside had been disturbed."

Bustamante took a moment before he said, "Family problems?"

"Oh, God." She looked away. Where was this going? All this probing, and what good would it do? Her mouth had gone dry. She needed something to drink. "I happened to be in the wrong place at the wrong time, that's all."

He didn't say anything, and Catherine understood he was waiting for her to go on.

"I don't have much of a family," she said. "I was adopted when I was five years old. Now it's just my mother, Marie, and me. I've always called her Marie." Why was she going on like this? What did this matter? "My father died when I was a teenager. No brothers or sisters. Maury's like a brother."

"Ex-boyfriends?"

"Who want to kill me?" She forced a little laugh that sounded like the rasp of a death cough. "None who might care that much," she said, folding her hands in her lap, avoiding his eyes. She felt like a schoolgirl called into the principal's office for breaking some rule she didn't know existed. "I haven't been in a serious relationship" — she shrugged — "since my divorce."

"Which brings us to your ex-husband. Lawrence Stern, part of the prominent Stern family, correct?"

She studied the metal table: the file folder and the printed map with the thick, red lines, the stream of light reflected from the fluorescent fixture overhead. Detective Bustamante had done his homework. "There would be no reason for Lawrence to want me killed, if that's what you're implying."

"I'm not implying anything," Bustamante said. "I want to nail the guy that followed you home last night and shot Maury

Beekner. I don't want him out walking the streets, so why don't you just tell me about your relationship with Lawrence Stern."

"There is no relationship." This was complicated, she was thinking. She hurried on: "We parted on friendly terms, irreconcilable differences, or some such. It wasn't a big deal."

Bustamante's eyebrows arched. "Six years? No big deal?"

"We wanted different things, different lives." She paused for a moment, trying to gather her thoughts into a logical sequence that would make sense to this stranger probing into her life. "We came from different backgrounds," she said. "I grew up on the northwest side, not quite the right side, an adopted girl with no background, and Lawrence — well, he came from a pioneer Colorado family, the Denver Country Club and all that. He was Harvard; I was Metro State. He was WASP in capital letters, a real blueblood, a Denver aristocrat." She paused. "And I don't really know who I am."

That had stopped him, she thought. She tried for a smile to let him know that it was all right. It was just the way things were. When he didn't say anything, she said, "You might say that my genealogy is mixed. I'm part Indian, Arapaho, maybe, but it wasn't something that was ever discussed. It was a miracle Lawrence and I ever met."

Bustamante had an annoying way of remaining absolutely quiet.

She went on: "I was a general assignment reporter at the *Journal,* occasionally covering social news. You know, who attended which fund-raising event and donated the most money, who wore tailored tuxedos and designer gowns and had the biggest hair, the best face-lifts, and the whitest smiles. Supposedly it was a temporary assignment until a position as investigative reporter opened up. It lasted three years. I didn't mind it all that much. I got to see another world, and I met interesting people."

"You met Lawrence?"

Catherine nodded. "I did a story on his engagement party. We ran photos of several guests and a photo of Lawrence holding his fiancée's hand. Very blond, very beautiful, and appropriate for him. He should have married her, but I remember that when the photographer snapped the picture, Lawrence was looking at me. He called the next day and invited me to lunch. I thought he was going to give me a scoop about the upcoming wedding. Instead, he told me they had agreed to call it off."

"How did it end, your marriage to Lawrence Stern? Large alimony he might want to stop paying?"

"You're out of line." She was beginning to feel an intense dislike for the man across from her.

He didn't blink or move. "I'm conducting an investigation. Most crimes are solved in the inner circle — family, friends."

She took a moment before she said, "I'll answer the question because you'll just keep asking until I do. Lawrence and I parted on good terms. There's no alimony. He gave me a town house, a car, and two hundred and fifty thousand dollars. We go to lunch occasionally. We're friends." *We sleep together once in a while,* she was thinking, but that wasn't any of Detective Bustamante's business.

"Two hundred and fifty thou from the Stern family?" Bustamante shook his head. "Didn't I just read your ex-husband built the hundred-million-dollar office and residential complex near Colorado Boulevard? Six years of marriage, seems like you could have gotten more."

"You sound like my divorce lawyer."

"Maury Beekner," he said. She imagined a hive of assistants bent over computers somewhere in the windowless cellars of the

41

Denver Police Headquarters, accessing her life.

She said, "I'm going to tell you what I told Maury. I didn't marry Lawrence for his money, and I didn't divorce him for his money. Is that understood?"

"Let's discuss your current position at the *Journal*," he said without missing a beat. "You've been there now for three years. You must have taken some time off."

She shrugged. "I stopped working for a while when I was married. Lawrence didn't really approve, and . . ." She tried to blink back the memories looming in front of her. ". . . there were so many obligations."

"I see. I've read some of your articles. I pulled a number of them this morning. You dig beneath the PR releases. Maybe you've stepped on somebody's toes."

"It wouldn't be the first time."

"Got somebody mad enough to send a killer after you?"

"I'm a reporter," she said. "I'm paid to do the research, gather the facts, and write the stories. I don't make up the stories."

Bustamante folded his elbows on the table and leaned toward her. "I want you to think very carefully. Anybody called or e-mailed you, taken issue with what you've written?"

"Every day," she said. "It's part of the

business. If I make a mistake, I retract it in the next issue."

"Threatened you?"

"You mean, called me too dumb to be a reporter, too biased toward the right or the left, too stubborn and pigheaded to see the truth?" Catherine shook her head. This wasn't the early decades of the last century when irate readers broke into the offices of the Denver newspapers and shot at the editors, wounding some of them. "It's part of the business. I report the facts as I find them."

"State treasurer charged with embezzlement. You came down pretty hard on that story. Went into his background, wrote about how he'd been fired from a job twenty years ago after accounting irregularities were discovered. And what about the Civic Center architectural plans? How many stories did you write on how the design had nothing to do with Denver's history and how it would destroy Civic Center? Seems to me your stories influenced the city council's vote. The architects folded their tent and went back to Boston or New York or wherever they came from."

"Boston," she said. "They have commissions around the world. The Civic Center makeover was a minor job. I hardly think they would send someone to shoot me."

"The point is, Catherine," he said, "you've taken on tough issues involving important people. Last couple of weeks you've written about how the Arapahos and Cheyennes have filed claims on twenty-seven million acres of Colorado."

"It's a developing story. The government has already settled the land claims. The tribes were paid $15 million in 1965. They're hoping Congress will reopen the agreement." She shrugged. "Look, the *Mirror* has been covering the same story. Nothing I've written would make someone want to kill me." Catherine started to lift herself to her feet. "Are we done here?"

Bustamante stood up, reached inside his sport coat, and pulled out a business card. He leaned over the table, scratched a number on the back side of the card, and handed it to her. "You can reach me on my cell at any time." Then he closed the file folder over the thin stack of papers and picked it up. "You should stay somewhere else for a while," he said.

"Somewhere else?" The town house was home. There wasn't anywhere else. She didn't want to camp out in some motel that allowed dogs. "Check your unsolved rape cases," she said.

"Whoever the guy is, he knows where you live." Bustamante kept his expression the same. He gripped the folder in one hand and opened the door with the other.

Catherine stood rooted to the floor. She felt as if he'd slapped her in the face with a wet towel. *He knows where you live.* She had been pushing the truth from her mind. She had to hold on to the edge of the table a moment before she trusted herself to cross the room and walk into the corridor. She had no idea where she and Rex could go.

3

Erik Bolton surveyed the array of guns and ammunition on the bedspread. The motel room smelled of cigarette smoke and stale food. Daylight filtered past the dingy curtains. He'd had to switch on the lamp by the bed to appreciate the subtle differences in his collection. He didn't need to carry the assortment with him — any one of them could handle the job, but he liked having them. The way they looked nestled in purple velvet inside the walnut case he'd had constructed. Businessmen carried laptops and files. He carried guns.

The Beretta, Model 21A. The little .22, excellent for close range, easily concealed. The semiautomatic Beretta, 92FS — a sentimental favorite. It was accurate. He could always count on it. He liked the Sig Sauer P220, which he considered the most accurate .45 out of the box. Decocking lever, automatic firing pin safety block that meant the pistol was always ready. A sentimental favorite; he'd been armed with one in the Army. Accurate, but loud. And it wasn't fitted for a silencer. He'd needed a silencer last night. He'd carried the Sig 226 Tactical, easy to control and threaded for a recoil reducer that screwed on the same as a silencer.

He slid along the edge of the bed, lifting each of the guns in turn, savoring the weight and the smooth feel of the metal. Power. Now this was power. He had on a white tee shirt and shorts, and the cheap, rough fabric of the red and black striped bedspread nipped at the back of his thighs. He had made an unfortunate move last night, but one unfortunate move wasn't the game. It was only the opening gambit. The job paid $50,000, which he made sure was deposited in his account in the Cayman Islands before he'd started the surveillance.

Enough money to stay in a fine hotel in downtown Denver. He had walked through the lobbies and listened with a distinct pleasure to the clack of his own boots on the marble floors glistening under the chandeliers. He'd wandered about, had a drink in the bars. The Ship Tavern at the Brown Palace, now that was a nice bar, wood paneling and Oriental carpets and all of it drenched in history. He could stay anywhere, pull out his wallet and slap the cash on the registration counter, but that wasn't his way. Stay anonymous, that was best. A seedy motel on Santa Fe Drive where the hungover clerk with a three-day-old stubble was used to taking cash, hadn't bothered to look at him, and would never pick him out of a police album filled with the faces of losers.

Erik Bolton was not a loser. He was a winner with, admittedly, a minor setback in the first move of the game. He picked up the Sig 226 Tactical and ran his index finger over the stainless steel frame and the soft rubber grip. He screwed on the silencer and lifted the gun, feeling again the familiar heft of it. He had chosen the correct weapon. No one would have recognized the gunshot for what it was, even if they had heard a noise. He could have shot her and been out of the town house in minutes.

The plan had been foolproof. He'd been watching Catherine McLeod for ten days. He had even managed to slip the wallet out of her purse in the coffee shop, copy down the credit card numbers. He'd handed the purse to the kid at the counter, said he'd found it on the floor. All before she had realized her purse was gone. He had called his contact at the credit card company, an old friend he'd worked with on two or three other assignments. The minute Catherine used her card, the friend would let him know.

How smoothly everything would work. He had even managed to steal a BlackBerry the day before, just lifted it out of the purse of a very stupid girl in line at another coffee shop. The cell phones that he kept on hand were another story. Cheap phones, purchased. The use-once-throw-away type. He smiled at the thought. Everything was in perfect order.

After the first few days, he'd known everything he needed to know about Catherine McLeod. Simple life, pared down to basics. She left her town house every morning at seven thirty, got into her silver Chrysler convertible, drove downtown with the top up, and parked in the lot next to the *Journal.* She walked inside a few minutes before eight. He had parked the brown sedan he'd rented a half block away and waited near the entrance, dressed in a suit, inconspicuous, a businessman checking his wristwatch. Sometimes he had parked in the lot across the street, waited for her to come out, and followed her.

She had come through the door a couple

of times each day, gotten into the convertible, and driven off. He had stayed two or three cars behind, a safe distance. Once she'd driven to a two-story Victorian house on the northwest side of town, and he had waited a discreet distance down the street. Interviewing someone for a story, he'd thought at first, but later, when he'd checked on the occupant, he had found that her mother lived in the house. Her adoptive mother. Name: Marie Lansing McLeod. He had added those pieces of information to everything else he had learned.

A couple of afternoons Catherine had emerged from the building and walked down the street. He'd followed her, staying a safe distance behind. She had gotten on the Sixteenth Street shuttle, and he had managed to jump on before it had pulled away. She had ridden to the end of the line at Civic Center, then walked to the Denver Public Library where, he'd discovered, she had spent several hours working in the Western History Department.

He had followed her to restaurants where she had met Maury Beekner, who looked like a gorilla, thick black hair, black hair spilling out of the V of his polo shirts. Another man had joined them — Philip Case, Maury's lover, he discovered. And that had been easy. He had followed one of Beekner's secretaries to a bar, bought her a drink, and got her chatting. He'd learned how much Maury Beekner cared about his clients, made friends with them, got involved in ways that, well, in her opinion — but no one ever asked her opinion — weren't smart.

Last Saturday morning he had followed Catherine McLeod to Confluence Park on the western edge of downtown. Maury and Philip were waiting on bikes, balanced on the seats, tipping water into their mouths out of plastic bottles. They looked ridiculous — tight, shiny bike shorts and shiny white shirts and sweat bands around their heads. There was a bike for Catherine waiting on the kick stand, and the three of them had started off. He decided against renting a bike and following. Let her enjoy her last Saturday, he'd thought.

Last week he had followed her to a café on Larimer Street where she had met a man with black hair and big shoulders, an Indian. They'd taken a table on the sidewalk and lingered over sandwiches and coffee, and all the time she had scribbled in a little note-pad next to her plate. In a way, it was a shame. All that effort for a story she would never live to write.

51

He had stayed with her when she went to the supermarket and the liquor store, where she had emerged with a brown bag cradled against her. So she liked to drink, and that was also good information. A drink or two when she got home at night. She would be less alert, a little cloudy.

Once, she had gone into a hair salon. He'd strolled across the street, keeping an eye on her through the plate glass window. Seated in a swivel chair wrapped in a white gown with a skinny, dark-haired man ruffling and blow-drying her black hair. He had followed her home each day, and he wasn't sure when he'd begun to — what was it? — connect with her. Whether it was the black hair flying about her head, so wild and free, or the quiet in her neighborhood. Most of the neighbors didn't even come home until late at night. And she walked the dog every night, no matter how late she got home. That was a bonus.

It had come over him gradually, the desire to have a little fun, walk behind her at night, scare her, then enjoy himself in the town house for a half hour or so, before he shot her. All the pieces of the plan fell together so neatly that he knew it was the way it should be. The other victims — they had been men. He had never killed a woman before, and that was what had tripped him up, he realized now, led to the unfortunate move. He'd never had the urge to do any of the other victims. But he had made a mistake. He should have expected her to call Maury Beekner. As it turned out, though, the gorilla had been an easy way into the town house. And what did he matter? Collateral damage.

The client had called his cell before six this morning. He had struggled upward out of a black well, sweeping his hand across the night table, knocking the cheap clock onto the floor. Working into his consciousness was the thought that it was Deborah, that something had happened, an accident, one of the kids in the emergency room. But it hadn't been Deborah's voice shouting in his ear. He had forced himself to the side of the bed, feet planted on the rough carpet, and explained. Everything was under control, he would take care of it. There wouldn't be any more glitches — he had refrained from calling what had happened last night a mistake.

He raised the Sig 226 and pointed it toward the door. He could blow out the lock. It would be easy. He was an expert, well-trained and experienced. He set the gun in its compartment in the case. After last night he had revised his plans. He knew Catherine McLeod. She would continue to go to the office for a day or two in an attempt to live her life as usual. He could crouch behind the half wall at the edge of the parking lot across the street, sight her in as she walked from the parking lot to the front door. He could take her out easily, but it would be risky. Other employees coming in and out, traffic lumbering past, which would make it difficult to drive away without some fool making him in the brown Ford that he had rented.

He could follow the original plan and kill her at home, but that was also risky now. The police would block off the house for a few days and step up patrol of the neighborhood. Nosy neighbors would start looking for any vehicle they hadn't noticed before.

In any case, as soon as she suspected that he was not a random intruder in the night, she would go into hiding. Stop going to work, stop living at home. He would have to finish the assignment before that happened, which gave him two days at the most, he figured. He knew her.

There was one place she was sure to go. Unless her gorilla friend died from the bullet he'd put in him, Catherine McLeod would go to Denver Health. He had checked on the parking lot this morning, the number of exits, the quickest way onto Speer Boulevard. He'd seen her come through the wide glass doors at the entrance, follow the sidewalk that bordered the lot, and walk between the parked cars to the convertible. She looked terrible: hair uncombed and matted, face pinched, shoulders hunched. He could have killed her then, but he hadn't yet mapped out the best escape route. People were coming out of the building and walking across the lot. There would always be people about, but he'd decided that the little groups hurrying to and from the hospital, consumed with their own worries, would work to his advantage. They wouldn't notice him. They wouldn't remember.

He would wait for her in the parking lot. When she came out of the hospital, he would be standing somewhere close to her car with the Sig 226 Tactical. He would use the silencer, of course. He would walk over, shoot her as she was about to get into the car, push her inside if necessary, and calmly walk away. He'd used that tactic once in a busy parking lot in St. Louis. It was three days before anyone had noticed the body in the front seat of the car.

At some point today, Catherine McLeod

would return to the hospital to see if the gorilla was still alive. He would be waiting.

4

Silence gripped the newsroom the instant Catherine came through the door. She could sense the vibrations in the air, as if the conversations had stopped on the same beat. The newsroom was half the size of a ballroom, a dozen reporters bent toward computer screens inside small cubicles separated by glass partitions. She started down an aisle, conscious of the eyes boring into her back. Then something extraordinary happened: A rhythmic clapping started up and gathered energy. Then applause and cheers swept around her.

Catherine stopped. She felt as if her breath had been knocked out of her. She glanced around at the familiar faces of her colleagues, all of them on their feet, clapping and smiling. There were times when they disagreed, when they got into heated arguments over the direction of a story; it was the nature of the business. They competed against one another, and they backed up one another. They went to the Denver Press Club on Friday nights for a drink. This morning they had read the brief article from the police reports that had probably made it into the last edition, or heard about what had happened on the radio. Now they were cheering her on, but the applause felt strange and out of place, like the applause at a funeral. It was as if they were cheering the fact that Maury had taken the bullet meant for her.

She was shaking her head, she realized, waving all of them back to work. Go back, go back. Let everything be normal. She swallowed the urge to burst into tears, hurried to her own cubicle at the end of the aisle, and set her bag in the lower desk drawer. A dull ache was invading her head. The applause began to fade away. Across the glass partition she saw her colleagues dropping onto their chairs. Chair legs scraped the tile floor, and there was the rapid-fire start-up of computer keys, like the riff in a jazz piece. She sank onto her own chair and jammed a fist against her mouth.

The little red light on the phone was blinking. She stared at it, reluctant to lift the receiver and listen to the messages —

anonymous voices of readers who read her articles and considered themselves her best friends. *So sorry to hear what happened. If there's anything I can do . . .*

And probably a message or two from the crackpots: *Hey! So somebody finally got mad enough to come after you. Surprised it didn't happen sooner.*

She looked away from the blinking light; she would listen to the messages when she was up to it, she thought, wondering how she would ever be up to it. Finally she squared herself in front of the desk and forced her attention on the computer, aware for the first time of the faint buzzing noise emanating from the base of the machine. It was probably always there, that noise, but she'd never noticed before. She felt raw and shaky, her nerves a jumble of live electric wires. The headache started to bore in. She had to concentrate hard in order to log into her e-mail. Still it took two tries before she had typed her password correctly and the long list of messages began to scroll down the screen.

"Everyone's glad to see you."

The voice behind her came like a gunshot. Catherine swung around, her heart pounding in her ears. Violet Henderson, the research assistant from an adjacent cubicle, stood in the doorway, medium height and about Catherine's age, with the slim, muscular figure of a biker, long, dark blond hair, and the freckled skin of a woman who spent a lot of time in the outdoors when she wasn't digging through archives and legal documents. "Marjorie's waiting in her office," she said.

Catherine turned back to the desk and rummaged through the clutter of the top drawer. She felt herself switching onto automatic. A summons had arrived from Marjorie Fennerman, managing editor and walking encyclopedia of facts, innuendos, and minutiae, which she spewed forth like voice mail in fast-forward mode. She never repeated herself for any reporter neglectful enough to enter the inner sanctuary without a pad and pen. Catherine had only made that mistake once.

She clipped a pen to the top of a small pad, gave Violet a half smile as she brushed past, and headed across the newsroom. All the sounds were familiar — keyboards clacking, phones ringing in various keys, a man's voice in one of the cubicles drilling questions at someone on the other end of a line. She rapped on the pebbly glass door that had a sheet of orange construction paper pasted in the middle. Someone had written in black marker: Stuff Stops Here.

She opened the door and stepped inside. Marjorie was bent over the computer on the small table set at a right angle to her desk, backlit by sunlight streaming through the window. Her light brown hair fell forward like a veil along her face. "You wanted to see me," Catherine said.

Marjorie swung sideways, got to her feet, and came around the desk. For an instant, Catherine felt herself enveloped in fleshy arms, then Marjorie stepped back and looked at her, as if she wanted to assure herself that Catherine was there. "You okay?" she said.

Catherine nodded. "Maury's in critical condition."

"I know, and I can't tell you how sorry all of us are. Sit down." She waved her to a chair in front of the desk. "Jason has the police report," she said. She had brown, bushy eyebrows that rose in arcs over deep-set brown eyes. "He's interviewed some of your neighbors. Didn't get much. Seems they heard the commotion and sirens, that's all."

Marjorie maneuvered herself around the desk and dropped back onto her chair. She took a moment — positioning her elbows on the desk, lacing her fingers together —

before she said, "We have a scoop here. One of our own, the primary witness. Jason needs to talk to you."

Catherine looked away. She let her gaze run over the rows of plaques and citations that lined the wall on her left: Best news story, best news photograph, best editorial. The name of Jason Metcalf, police reporter, had been engraved on three of the plaques. He was nothing if not thorough and persistent in running down witnesses, following them to their homes and offices, not giving up until he had the exclusive inside story at least one issue ahead of the *Mirror*. Marjorie Fennerman backed up her reporters. And wasn't that why Catherine had jumped at the chance to come back to work as an investigative reporter at the *Journal*? *Journal* reporters plumbed the depths; they went after the real news behind the stories. Lawrence had remained tight-lipped when she'd told him she had taken the job, but at that point, they both knew the marriage was over.

Jason Metcalf would want to plumb the depths of her story, she knew. And wouldn't she do the same? But this was different — this was Maury in ICU, maybe dying, and the idea of smearing the details across thousands of newspapers with large, black headlines that screamed at every stranger passing by newspaper stands on every downtown corner made her feel naked, stripped of her defenses, of everything normal that protected her.

"You're up to it, aren't you?" Marjorie said, and when Catherine didn't respond, she hurried on: "Jason could put off the interview for a couple hours, but we want the story for tomorrow's paper. You understand."

Catherine pried her eyes from the plaques on the wall and looked at the woman on the other side of the desk. It was her story, hers and Maury's, but it was also the intruder's, the monster who had shot Maury. And wasn't that what investigative journalism was all about — finding the kernel of truth that could bring a monster to justice?

"I understand," she said, but Marjorie's hand was already reaching for the phone. How well Marjorie knew her, Catherine thought. This was who she was, an investigative reporter. Maybe a story never told all of the truth, maybe there would always be questions and unproven suspicions and doubts, but it was the reporter's job to uncover as many of the jagged pieces of truth as possible and fit them into a story that made sense out of a small part of the world's madness.

Catherine was barely aware of Marjorie's voice, low and confidential, like the background purr of an engine. Marjorie set the phone back into the cradle. "You sure you're okay with this?" she said. "Want a cup of coffee or something?"

Catherine waved away the offer. She stopped herself from shouting out the truth: She was not okay. Maury could be dying and nothing was okay.

The door opened and Jason Metcalf crept into the office, like a cat stalking its prey. He was short and barrel shaped with a pink, balding scalp visible beneath the spray of brown hair. He pulled a side chair forward, sat down, and opened a laptop on the corner of the desk. Not until he'd tapped on the keys a moment and squinted at the screen did he look over. "Tough luck last night," he said, and she had the feeling that was what he always said on such occasions. Tough luck — to the murder witness, the victim's wife, husband, mother, the coroner up to his elbows at an autopsy, the police officer sucking on mints to get the smell of death out of his air passages. Real tough luck.

"I don't know what I can add to the police

report," she managed.

"Well, you never know." He gave her a mirthless grin that pulled his lips back over his upper teeth. "Maybe you remember something familiar about the shooter, now you had time to think about it."

"There was nothing familiar. What do you know about any recent rape cases in Denver? That's your story, Jason. That's what you should investigate."

"You telling me how to do my job?"

"How many unsolved rape cases are out there?" Catherine hurried on. "Half a dozen? A dozen? Ask Bustamante if he's working on that."

Jason Metcalf tapped on the computer keys a moment. Without looking up, he said, "Your common, deranged rapist, huh? How come he knew where you lived? Police report says you thought you got inside your town house while he was still looking for you. All those town houses look alike. How'd he know which one was yours?"

"I don't know."

"What happened after you got inside?"

"For godssakes, Jason. You read the report."

"Just tell him." Marjorie spread her hands on the desk. The thin gold chain at her

65

throat bounced over the neckline of her blue blouse.

Catherine set both elbows on the armrests and dipped her head into her hands. She rubbed her forehead with her fingertips, trying to massage away the headache blossoming behind her eyes. She had locked the door when she got inside, she said. Then she spilled out the rest of it, everything she'd told the officers last night and Bustamante this morning. All the details burned into her memory. There was nothing new.

When she had finished, he said, "You think it's possible the guy had a beef with you?"

"What?"

"You're a reporter," Marjorie said, and Catherine realized that she and Jason had already reached a conclusion that Jason simply wanted to confirm. "You've covered controversial issues; you've made people mad at you."

"The *Journal* has been making people mad for more than a hundred years. When was the last time a killer came after one of the reporters?" She glanced from Marjorie to the stocky man who had inched his way forward and was perched on the edge of the chair. "When was the last time a killer came after you, Jason? What about the illegal immigrant that shot the police officer last fall? Weren't you the reporter who found the cousin's house where he was hiding? He might have hidden out for a long time before he disappeared back into Mexico. Thanks to you, he's going to prison for life. Any relatives come after you?"

"Look, Catherine," Marjorie said. "Maybe you don't know that twenty-five, thirty years ago, a deranged lunatic shot and killed a Denver talk show host because he didn't like what he'd said. It's not impossible that you were the target."

Catherine felt the office walls closing in on her, the plaques leaping off the wall, the dark, engraved words dancing in front of her eyes. She closed her eyes. What they suggested was not true, she told herself. The intruder had nothing to do with her work, with her life. "It was a random attack," she heard herself say. She opened her eyes and made herself look at Jason Metcalf. "There's no evidence to suggest otherwise. You can quote me."

"Okay." Jason went back to tapping the keyboard. "So after he shot Maury Beekner, he ran out the front door. Tell me, why did he leave a witness still breathing? Why didn't he shoot you before he got out of there?"

"He had intended to rape me," Catherine

said. "He heard the sirens and ran off."
They had gotten to the truth now, she was
thinking, snapped the last random piece of
the puzzle into place. She felt a wave of ap-
preciation for the skills of the police reporter
leaning toward the laptop, keys clacking into
the silence. He had asked the key question
that brought the story into focus. Of course
that was the reason the intruder hadn't shot
her while she'd crouched under the table.
He had never intended to *shoot* her. He'd
shot Maury because Maury had tried to
subdue him. It made sense. It was as if Jason Metcalf had dug into the ground and
hit something hard and true.

She went back to massaging her forehead.
The headache entrenched now: the stress of
last night and the thought of Maury probably draped in white sheets with needles in
his arms and a tube jammed into his mouth
— all of it coalesced into a steel ball inside
her head. But there was something else,
something moving away from her grasp. She
could picture herself hiding in the darkness,
watching Maury and the intruder wrestling
about the room, the chairs and lamps crashing on the floor. She could see the gun in
the intruder's hand; she could almost hear
the shot. She tried to freeze the picture in
her head: The moment when he stood still,

looking around the room, and outside, the sirens blaring. He had run out then, but not for a long moment. He had taken the time to look around for her.

If he had seen her . . . She pushed away the thought. She was imagining things, she told herself. She'd been over the story so many times, scrutinizing the details. Maybe she was starting to make them up, give Jason Metcalf and Marjorie Fennerman and even Nick Bustamante the story they wanted — that the attack hadn't been a random act of violence, but a calculated and planned attack on her life.

"What is it?" Marjorie said. Jason glanced over the top of the computer screen, a look of hunger in his eyes, as if she might toss him a tasty morsel.

"Nothing. I need to get back to work."

Jason snapped the laptop shut at this and got to his feet. "I'm gonna be all over this story like superglue," he said. "Nobody's coming after one of our reporters without paying a big price, you hear me?"

"Thanks, Jason," Catherine managed, but she was talking to his back as he went through the door. She wasn't sure he'd heard her, or that it made any difference.

Marjorie jumped to her feet, closed the door, and leaned against it. "Until we know what this is all about, I don't think you should come in. I'll arrange an administrative leave of absence. I'll see that you're paid."

"Don't say that." Catherine got to her feet. Her legs felt numb and wobbly; she had to lean against the chair for support. "I need to work. I have to go on. He can't take that away from me." God, it was enough — it was too much — that he may have taken Maury. "Detective Bustamante is still investigating. There's no reason to think that it was anything other than a random attempt at rape."

Marjorie was gripping the doorknob hard. White knuckles popped in her reddened hand.

"Listen, Marjorie." Catherine pushed on. "I'm working on the story about the Arapaho and Cheyenne land claims. I want to stay on the story."

It was a moment before Marjorie said, "That story has a shelf life of a carton of milk. The tribes are going nowhere with their claims. They were settled forty years ago. The governor is on record opposing any further settlement. The entire story will wrap up in the next couple of weeks." She paused. "I suppose you could work on it from home."

Catherine shook her head. "That's funny, Marjorie. Bustamante told me to stay away from the town house, and now you're telling me to stay away from the paper. Just what am I supposed to do? Change my whole life? He's not coming back, not with the neighbors watching anybody walking through the neighborhood and the police patrolling the streets."

"What about your mother?" Marjorie said, still on her own track. "You could stay with her. What about friends? You could stay in a hotel."

Catherine squeezed her eyes shut a moment against the throbbing pain. She stopped herself from reminding Marjorie that she had a dog, that not every place might welcome Rex. It was too stupid to discuss. "I'll think about it." She stepped toward the door.

"Hold on." Marjorie went to the desk, picked up a brown envelope, and thrust it toward Catherine. "I had Violet pull your articles for the last month. Go through them, mark the names of anyone you interviewed who had been reluctant to talk or might be upset over what you wrote."

Catherine took the package. It was lighter than it looked. A month of her life wrapped in a brown envelope that a gust of wind could blow away. She had to tighten her fingers to keep it from sliding out of her hand. "It'll be a waste of time," she made herself say, because, she realized, the saying might make it true.

"Bustamante doesn't think so. Going back through the articles might trigger something."

"You've talked to Bustamante?"

"Of course. What do you think? He called an hour ago." Marjorie stepped back to the door and pulled it open. "He wants you to call him immediately if you find anything in the articles."

5

Catherine walked back into the noise of the newsroom — the ringing phones and jangling activity. She could feel Marjorie's eyes on her. Then she heard the door slam shut. She retraced her steps to the cubicle, ignoring the curiosity in the faces behind the glass panels. The red light on her phone was blinking furiously. More messages had come in. She pressed the message button and wrote the date at the top of the notepad.

"Sorry to hear about your troubles . . ." Catherine hit the delete button. There were seven or eight similar messages from other readers. Sorry, sorry, sorry. She deleted them all. She supposed she should be grateful that someone out there actually cared, but the messages left her feeling hollow inside, as if she were listening to eulogies at her own funeral.

"Honey, I'm so worried. Please call me right away." Catherine stared at the phone.

It was Marie's voice, strained and comforting at the same time. She picked up the receiver, dialed Marie's number, and listened to the noise of the phone ringing in the house in Highlands. Then Marie picked up: "Catherine?"

"I'm okay," Catherine said. "I don't want you to worry about me."

"Oh, my goodness, I've been so upset. The neighbors have been stopping by, and I didn't know what to tell them. Are you certain you weren't hurt?"

"No. No. I'm fine," she said. She let this hang between them a moment before she told her that Maury was in pretty bad shape.

"Who would do such a thing?" When Catherine didn't say anything, she went on: "You better come stay with me. Don't you think that would be a good idea? Rex can have the run of the yard."

"I'll let you know," she said. Then she made up an excuse about having to take another call, told her not to worry, and hung up. She probably should have said yes, yet the thought of leaving the town house, moving even a few of her things into the old redbrick house on top of the hill, settling into the upstairs bedroom that still had the pink bedspread and curtains, even for a few days, a week, a month — how long would it take Bustamante to arrest the man? — was crazy. She had built a new life; *he* would not take it away.

She pressed the message button again. "Catherine, it's me." Lawrence's voice. Even when weeks went by without hearing from her ex-husband, she could still summon his voice in her head. "I'm terribly worried about you. Call me right away and tell me you're all right." A faint click followed by the buzzing noise.

Catherine lifted the receiver again and called him back. He answered on the first ring. "Tell me you're not at work," he said, incredulity working through his voice.

"Where else should I be?" she said. "I can't sit at home. I'm not even supposed to be there."

"Of course not. You can't stay alone at the town house, not until they get the bastard. Who was he?"

"God, Lawrence. I have no idea."

"You're not hurt, right? He didn't hit you, or —" He stumbled over the thought.

"He didn't do anything to me. He shot Maury."

"The divorce lawyer."

Catherine didn't say anything.

"I've called Gilly at the ranch, told him to get the cottage ready for you. He'll stock the kitchen. You can stay as long as you like. You'll be safe there, Catherine, until they put that SOB in jail."

"I can't do that," she said. This was even worse than the idea of being drawn back into childhood. She would be drawn back into the wide net of security and comfort that Lawrence Stern and his family cast over everything and everyone they touched. "A detective is handling the case. He'll get the guy."

"Until that happens, you have to stay at the ranch." There was the authoritative note of a man used to being obeyed. "It's all arranged. You know the way."

"Did your grandmother agree to the invitation?" Catherine said. Elizabeth Stern, the matriarch of the family, had never agreed to the marriage. She had attended the wedding ceremony in the gothic apse of St. John's Episcopal Church where generations of Sterns had taken their marriage vows only because it would have created a scandal had she not been there. She stared narrow eyed out of the wedding photos, her face a powdery mask.

"Let me worry about Grandmother."

Catherine was quiet a moment before she said: "I just wanted you to know that I'm all right." Lawrence was saying something as she replaced the receiver. She deleted the rest of the phone messages — two more from readers, several from acquaintances. She couldn't call them friends. Friends had been hers and Lawrence's; they had remained his friends. She turned her attention to her e-mail, scrolling down the screen. The messages looked like more of the same: concerned readers, people with whom she exchanged pleasantries at the coffee shop or the deli.

The headache had developed fingers that stretched across the top of her skull. Halfway through the messages, she saw the name Norman Whitehorse. The subject: rally. Norman was the Arapaho who had alerted her to the fact that the Arapaho and Cheyenne tribes intended to file claims on half their ancestral lands, which amounted to twenty-seven million acres, nearly one-third of the state of Colorado. She'd gone to the Indian Center and interviewed Harold YellowBull, an Arapaho elder, and James Hunting, a Cheyenne elder. Norman had arranged the interview, an exclusive, he'd promised her. He had been waiting outside the glass door entrance, straight backed and slim in blue jeans and a plaid shirt, black hair pulled back in a ponytail and narrow black eyes. Smoke curled from the cigarette burned down to a stub in his fingers.

"Don't ask questions," he had told her. "Just be quiet and wait. The elders will want to check your heart first."

"What?" She'd stopped at the door and turned to him.

"Make sure you have a good heart before they talk to you. They know you're one of us."

She hadn't said anything to that. She looked Indian, black hair and dark complexion. Let them think she was Arapaho, if it meant getting the exclusive.

They had sat at a round table in a corner of the cafeteria, sipping black coffee out of white mugs. Other tables had been pushed toward the walls and a teenage girl with long, black hair was running a mop across the green linoleum floor. The old men had been reticent at first. Nodding, smiling, taking long draws of coffee.

Then they had begun talking. The black eyes looking out across the cafeteria toward some other time and place. This was their land, their place on the earth, they said. From the Continental Divide out across the plains, all the beautiful mountain slopes and prairies had belonged to the Arapaho and the Cheyenne. It was called the land between the two rivers, the Platte River on the north and the Arkansas River on the south. The government had sent commissioners out to Fort Laramie in 1851, Harold Yel-lowBull said, and James Hunting had nodded. *Yes, that was right.* And the commissioners had made a treaty with the tribes on sheets of paper. Oh, they had seen copies of this treaty. The treaty acknowledged that the land between the two rivers belonged to the tribes. A total of twenty-seven million acres.

Covered over by concrete highways and asphalt streets, Catherine had been thinking. And steel and glass skyscrapers and miles and miles of residential neighborhoods that constituted the city of Denver and the sprawling suburbs, and dozens of smaller cities, ranches, and farms, and close to three million people.

But there was something else they had spoken about, and this had made her glimpse the heart of the story, and she'd known that the story had legs. In the early dawn of November 29, 1864, the Third Colorado Regiment had attacked the Cheyenne and Arapaho camps at Sand Creek on the plains of southeastern Colorado. "So many of our people were killed there," Harold YellowBull said. "One hundred and sixty of 'em, mostly old men and women and children. The troops waited until the warriors had ridden out of camp to go hunting, get enough meat to feed the camp."

James Hunting had shifted forward, brown, knobby hands clasped around his mug. "Rest of the people, they were driven off our lands. They never came back to Colorado. Experts are calling that massacre at Sand Creek genocide, 'cause that's what it was. They tried to exterminate our people."

Catherine had understood right away. Despite the fact that the tribes had agreed to a $15 million settlement for their ancestral lands, this new claim — that the massacre at Sand Creek was an act of genocide — might erase any other settlements or agreements. It was possible that Congress might agree to reconsider the Arapaho and Cheyenne land claims. The tribes could never reclaim the old lands — the elders said they knew the truth — but they might get enough land to operate tribal ranches, raise cattle and horses, maybe even grow hay and barley. The ranches could provide a steady income for the people.

"Rally 3:00 p.m. this afternoon," the e-mail said. "Peter Arcott says he'll show." There was a map attached, and she hit the print key.

Peter Arcott. Catherine jotted down the name. She would check it on the Internet later. The printer next to her desk had spit out a map of black, blue, and red lines. The red lines outlined a rectangle on the plains east of Denver, near the airport. Five hundred acres of bare dirt and scrub brush, undeveloped and wild, the black line of I-70 running across the northern border.

She folded the map inside her notepad. She would have time to cover the rally and still get to the hospital this afternoon. She ran her eyes down the rest of the e-mail messages. More of the same: readers and acquaintances whose names she barely recognized.

Here was something different. She felt her stomach lurch. She didn't recognize the e-mail address. In the subject line were the words, "Last Night."

She clicked on the e-mail and watched the text appear on the screen. "Say good-bye, Catherine. Your friend, Erik."

Catherine took I-70 East, weaving around the semis and buses and jamming down on the gas pedal to pass the slower vehicles. She'd put the top down in the *Journal* parking lot, and the sun glinted on the dashboard and beat hard on her arms and hands. The sounds of Coltrane on the CD mixed with the noise of the wind. Through her dark sunglasses, the highway ahead looked bathed in shadows. Miles of squat buildings and warehouses — the industrial outcroppings of Denver — blurred past. In the rearview mirror, she could see a semi shimmering in the hazy heat, splashes of sunlight beaming on the metal bumper. The windshield looked like a black wall in the brightness, as if the semi were driving itself, some anonymous danger hurtling toward her. She pressed down on the gas pedal, passed a couple of cars, then settled into the outside lane ahead of a blue sedan. In the rearview mirror, she could see the cab of the semi looming over the line of vehicles. Beyond the semi, the front range of the Rocky Mountains, blue and streaked with snow, lifted into a perfect blue sky.

She took the exit that Whitehorse had marked on the map, and within a half mile, she was driving down an unpaved road that flung itself ahead like a yellow gash across the plains. There were scatterings of gray sagebrush and clusters of old cottonwood trees along the banks of dry creeks. The air smelled of dust and sage and the outdoors. The great wall of mountains curved in the distance. She could see Pikes Peak a hundred miles away. The white Teflon peaks of the airport roof glimmered in the rearview mirror. The roof was supposed to resemble the snowy peaks of the mountains, but she'd always thought that was wrong. The roof resembled the tipis of the villages that had once stood on the plains. Clouds of dust rolled behind her, and a gust of wind battered the side of the convertible and blew her hair about. She lifted her face into the sun a moment and let her hair blow free. Then she propped her elbow on the top of the door and held her hair back. She wasn't sure when she had lost the headache, but it had dropped somewhere behind. Each time she drove onto the plains, she had a sense of freedom.

The brown envelope that contained a month of stories rippled in the wind on the passenger seat. Somewhere in the articles was the reason that a man called Erik was determined to kill her. And somewhere inside her she had known it was true. She hadn't wanted it to be true. She hadn't wanted the truth to change her life the way she knew now that it would.

She'd called Bustamante, told him about the e-mail message, then forwarded it while he was still on the line. He'd remained silent a moment, considering the message, she knew, and she had gone on talking, rambling on about what she intended to do, not wanting Erik's words to fill up all of the silence. She would take Bustamante's advice, and everyone else's it seemed, and stay somewhere else until he'd arrested the man.

"You will find him," she'd said, trying to reassure herself.

"It's my every intention. I'll get a warrant right away on the Internet service provider. They'll have his name." He hesitated a moment. "Chances are he isn't using his real name. Where will you go?"

She'd told him she wasn't sure, and yet that wasn't the truth. Not only did Erik or whoever he was know where she lived, he knew where she worked. He knew *her.* There was every possibility that he knew where Marie lived. She couldn't put her mother in danger. But the Stern ranch was in the mountains, twenty miles from Denver, and it was private — a private retreat for the Stern family for more than a century. There were only a few people who even knew the family had a ranch, although, if anyone had taken the time to think about it, they would realize the family must have a ranch. Most of the old Denver families had ranches in the mountains where generations of wives and children had escaped the summer heat while the men built the buildings and houses, railroads, water systems, streets, and public transportation that turned a prairie settlement into a city.

Erik might know about the ranch; he was sure to know she'd been married to Lawrence Stern. Still, there was no address in a phone book, no signs on the road. A log fence ran around the periphery, and there were iron gates across the only entrance, with an intercom on the post. Gilly Mason guarded the property like a Marine sergeant. He opened the gates only for people who were expected. There were security cameras everywhere. If they detected any movement, Gilly dispensed a half dozen ranch hands, armed with rifles. She would be safe at the Stern ranch.

She'd told Bustamante that she had to go to the town house, get Rex, and pack a few things. She should call him first, he'd said. She shouldn't be alone. He'd have a patrol officer at the house.

She'd been reluctant to hang up, she remembered, as if the detective's voice at the other end meant that everything would be all right, that her life wouldn't change after all. Bustamante had been the one to end the call. She'd stared at the inert receiver a moment before she'd dropped it into the cradle. She'd started shivering then, as if a freezing wind had blown through the newsroom. The pain had exploded in her head. She'd had to force her attention back to the computer: Erik would not steal her life. She would not allow it.

She'd spent several minutes looking up Peter Arcott. She'd found numerous websites, the same information highlighted in bold, black type. Developer. Hotels. Restaurants. Resorts. Indian casinos in Alaska, Nevada, California.

It was then she'd understood what the rally was all about. This was what White-horse, her contact, a man she'd trusted, had done: He'd drawn her into a story about tribal claims for ancestral lands. He had known the elders would talk about an old massacre that nobody cared about, and he had taken the chance that she would care. She'd written an article on Sand Creek, the surprise attack, the lost lands, the injustice of it all. The article would pressure Congress to consider the new claims. The story would influence the people of Colorado to agree to an Indian casino on the plains — people who had voted seven times against any more casinos in the state. And she had written all of it without realizing what the story was about.

Little clouds of dust rose against the horizon ahead. Catherine spotted the rows of pickups and SUVs parked off-road in the bare dirt and the crowd beyond the vehicles. A platform had been erected, and dancers in Indian regalia — splashes of whites, yellows, blues, and reds against the brown backdrop of the plains — swayed to the rhythmic sound of drumbeats that pounded through the wind.

She turned off the road, bumped across the dirt past the rows of parked vehicles, and stopped next to a green pickup feathered with dust. People were walking toward the crowd in front of the platform, some of them pulling on ribboned shirts, beaded aprons, and feathered headdresses. Several men wore headdresses made of eagle feathers that draped down their backs, the kind of headdresses she'd seen in old photographs of the Plains Indians.

She went to find Norman Whitehorse.

6

Catherine spotted Norman next to the stage with a group of Indian men, all brown skinned and black haired, faces tilted up toward the dancers. A splash of color wove across the stage in rhythm to the steady beat of the drums. The feathers in the dancers' headdresses fluttered in the hot breeze. Norman wore a white shirt that stood out in relief against the dark plaid shirts of the others. His black hair, smoothed back and tied in a ponytail, shone silver in the sun.

She looked around for Marcus Henning, the *Journal* photographer. She'd called him before she'd left the office. He was on another assignment, but he'd promised to get here. There was no sign of him. Digging the notepad and pen out of the bag slung over her shoulder, she made her way through the crowd bunching in front of the stage. She found herself glancing about, searching the faces of the men, aware of the tightness in her muscles. Erik could be here.

Which didn't make any sense. There hadn't been any public announcements of the rally — nothing in the papers or on the radio or TV. If Norman hadn't e-mailed her, she wouldn't have known about it. How could *he* know she was here? And yet, there were two or three hundred Indians standing in a blistering sun that had dried the land to dust. Somebody had made a few phone calls, and news about the rally had passed around. That's how it was in the Indian community, she suspected. They had their own way of getting the news. Still it didn't mean Erik had found out, unless he happened to be Indian. She had to hold herself together, not fly into pieces.

She couldn't see Norman. He had disappeared into the hazy heat and the growing swell of the crowd. The thud of drums and the voices of singers filled the air and reverberated off the empty plains running into the distances. Then she spotted the white shirt on the makeshift steps at the side of the stage, the plaid shirts following in single line. The dancers had started dancing their way down the steps on the other side. She pushed through the crowd — excuse me, excuse me — and tried to ignore the startled and disapproving looks as the

Indian people moved aside to give her a clear path. She felt like a white woman — moving forward, not registering anything, going away from whatever was behind her. She waved her notebook like a flag to get the attention of the man in the white shirt striding across the stage.

It was then that she saw the television reporters and the photographers, black cameras hoisted on their shoulders, Channel 7 and Channel 4 and Channel 9 emblazoned on the backs of their shirts. On the far side of the TV crews were two photographers she recognized from the *Mirror,* and next to them, the *Mirror*'s front-page byline reporter, Dennis Newcomb, the long, gray braid trailing down the back of his blue shirt. Norman had made sure the press was here in force for the announcement of the real story — the story she had missed. The land claims were nothing but an attempt to get a casino.

The rest of the press had also missed the story, but she was the one who had interviewed the elders and written about the Sand Creek Massacre. Genocide, the elders had called it. Genocide changed everything. Genocide meant Congress might renegotiate the settlement made forty years ago. It meant the people in Colorado might welcome a casino.

Norman bent into the microphone and pulled it toward him at the same time. The drumbeats stopped, the voices of the singers died back. A high-pitched wail rose out of the microphone. He tapped at the mouthpiece, splitting the air with a deafening thump, then gripped the neck as if he might strangle out the noise. Silence fell over the crowd — the silence of the plains, she thought, the earth and the sky and the breeze all in perfect balance.

Catherine shouldered past the photographers and stationed herself at the foot of the stage. She could have reached out and touched Norman's black boots and the hem of his blue jeans, splattered with brown dust. He caught her eye a moment, then looked away — out over the crowd.

"I wanna thank everybody for coming out today." His voice boomed through the mic. "We're here to let people know — well, to let 'em know that Indian people are still here. Just like in the Old Time when this was the land of the Arapaho and Cheyenne. Now what do we see when we look across the plains?" he said, sweeping one hand to take in the four directions. "Off in the west, the skyscrapers of a big city."

Catherine found herself glancing around,

obeying the direction of his hand. The skyscrapers shimmered like a mirage. They looked disconnected, floating free against the backdrop of blue mountains.

"Suburbs creeping over the land in every direction," Norman said. "Highways crossing to the north and south, roads cut everywhere . . ."

A jet screamed overhead, so low that Catherine could see the row of small gray windows.

"Jets taking off and landing day and night at Denver International Airport. There's more people here than the ancestors could've ever imagined. They're still here, the ancestors, watching over us and guiding us, and they must think all the people in the world moved onto our lands. There might be skyscrapers and houses and all kinds of buildings and roads, but there are still tipi rings where our villages stood. You can walk over the plains and see the circles of stones that held the tipis down on the earth. There are fire pits, with the stones black from smoke. You'd think the women were cooking on the fires yesterday. The old stands of cottonwoods that had given 'em shade are still here."

He paused and stared off in the distance a moment, as if he wanted to confirm that the cottonwoods were there. Catherine followed his gaze. Cottonwoods not more than a hundred yards away, branches bent and gnarled, leaves gray with dust. They had always grown alongside the creeks, but the creeks had been tapped dry by irrigation pipes. Still the cottonwoods hung on, sucking out of the dry land whatever moisture was left.

"Our ancestors are buried here," Norman said. "The graves are everywhere. Every time they build another highway or excavate another building, they find the bones of our ancestors." He jammed his mouth against the mic. "The ancestors are still with us!"

He paused. His breathing sounded like a bellow through the microphone. "What're they telling us? That the earth is life itself. The earth gave us the buffalo, and that's how we lived, from the buffalo. The buffalo days are gone now. But the earth still gives us life. Now we're saying to the government, give us back our lands so we can live. The government says, you a bunch of crazy Indians? We say, this land is ours. But we're willing to trade all our ancestral lands for this parcel right here." He pounded his fist toward the ground. "Five hundred acres right here where we're standing. We're gonna build a first-rate resort. Hotel. Restaurants. Shops. Indian cultural center. And a casino. Casinos are the new buffalo."

The sound of a gunshot split the air. Catherine hunched forward, pulled in her arms, and curled around herself. Then she realized that someone in back had clapped, and now the rest of the crowd was joining in. The clapping rolled around her like the gusts of a firestorm, buffeting and enveloping her until she felt as if the wave of noise would smash her into the edge of the stage. She straightened herself, ignoring the glances thrown her way by the photographers. Her heart pounded in her ears.

Norman waited until the clapping had stopped and the quiet settled in again. "We had to make some hard decisions," he said, his tone low and serious, his mouth close to the mic. "The Treaty of Fort Laramie that our ancestors signed in 1851 said this is our land. All this land was covered with buffalo herds. The elders say the great herds looked like brown clouds hanging low on the plains. We could've lived here for generations if the gold seekers and homesteaders and farmers and all the other get-rich-quick settlers hadn't come and taken the land. By rights the government oughtta give all this land back to us."

He took another moment and ran his gaze

over the expanse of flat, open prairie, as if he expected to see the brown clouds of buffalo. His features might have been sculpted out of brown marble, Catherine thought: the prominent cheekbones, the cliff of a forehead that shadowed his dark eyes. She had the sense that he was summoning a memory from the edges of his consciousness, like a blood memory that could no more be forgotten than the memory of his own boyhood.

Then he cleared his throat, dropped his gaze, and surveyed the crowd before looking directly into the television cameras. "The government broke all the treaties and promises. They sent troops that attacked our people at Sand Creek, and we call that genocide. They killed our people, they drove us off our lands. The government says, we already settled with you Indians, but we got lawyers that say that genocide makes that settlement null and void. We're here today to demand that the government honor the treaty of 1851. This will be the site of the Arapaho-Cheyenne Casino!"

Catherine heard the roar rising around her again, the clapping and the shouting. Norman shouted into the noise: "We demand the government purchase five hundred acres and return that small part of our land to us. We will give up our claims to the rest of our ancestral lands. The Indian gaming law says that tribes can build a casino on any land that's part of a settlement for land claims. If Congress ignores our demand, we will fight for the title to the rest of our ancestral lands in federal court. Folks that think they own the lands will have to prove the titles belong to them. It's gonna mean years of litigation, but we're prepared to follow through. We say, it is time for justice."

The crowd was clapping and stomping. Catherine could feel the ground shaking, as if a herd of buffalo were approaching. Norman and the plaid shirts headed across the stage and down the left steps. Another dancing group whirled behind them, and the music started again, drums beating and singers screeching into the noise.

"Who's behind this?" Newcomb shouted as Catherine started past. "C'mon, Catherine. Let's work together." She waved him off and kept going. Norman stood on the last step, the plaid shirts piling up behind him. Newcomb pressed behind her and shouted at Norman: "What are the chances Congress will agree to your demands? How's the government gonna get possession of this land?"

"Every chance." Norman looked out over the crowd. "They can take the land the way they took it from us. 'Eminent domain,' they call it."

"You used me," Catherine said.

Norman regarded her for a long moment, then stepped down, forcing her to move to the side. She felt the weight of his hand on her upper arm steering her toward the rear of the stage. "Later," he called out, giving a backward wave to Newcomb and the television crews. The plaid shirts bunched together, and Norman led her across a patch of bare brown earth toward a semi with an empty flatbed parked parallel to the stage. They were at the rear of the flatbed before she felt him let go of her arm. He slipped a pack of cigarettes out of his shirt pocket, found a lighter somewhere, and bent his head toward the sputtering flame, cupping a broad hand around the lighter.

She had expected Newcomb and the TV reporters to push past the plaid shirts and follow Norman, shouting out questions, which was what she would have done. Instead she could see them circling the other Indians, scribbling in pocket-sized notebooks, backs curved into the task. One of the TV reporters thrust a microphone into the center of the circle. The cameras were all trained on the Indians.

"What are you talking about?" Norman said. He stuffed the lighter into the front pocket of his blue jeans. The stoic look about him made the anger swell inside her.

"This is about a casino!" She was shouting. Two of the men adjusting the electrical cords that ran from the loudspeakers on either side of the stage to the amplifier on the ground turned and stared at them a moment. "You handed me a story about an old massacre that would soften up the public and influence Congress so you can get a casino. Only you forgot to mention the casino part."

Norman lifted his chin and blinked into the sun. "We got a right to our lands," he said. His voice was calm. He took a long draw on the cigarette and blew the smoke out of the side of his mouth. Catherine had to glance away from the quiet confidence and self-possession shining through his features. "Seems like the government forgot what they did to us, but we never forgot. Peter Arcott can help us make things right."

"What! Build a casino?" She could hear her own voice, tense with anger. "The way he's built casinos for other tribes around the country? Found some loophole in the law so they could get title to part of their so-called ancestral lands. And what did he get for all of his trouble? The right to build and operate the casinos for a large share of the profits? Have I missed anything?"

She stopped. There was something else she'd missed. The tribes were also being used. If they went along with Arcott's plan, they would give up any legitimate land claims they might have for a few acres and a casino. She could picture the elders slumped in the plastic chairs at last week's interview. She could almost hear their voices talking about the Old Time and the beautiful prairie lands where the people had lived, and the horrible attack at Sand Creek. She'd been struck by the tones they'd used, tones of disinheritance and loss.

"When you gonna decide who you are?" Norman flicked the ash off the tip of his cigarette and stared at her out of eyes as black as agates.

"We're not talking about me."

"We're talking about Indian people getting justice," he said.

Catherine looked away. A new group of dancers was performing on the stage, the bright colors of their regalia twirling like pieces of glass in a kaleidoscope. The voices of the singers rose over the rhythmic thump of the drums.

Norman waited until the drumbeats had died back before he said, "We're talking about the ancestors that were thrown off our land. Your ancestors, too."

"I don't know anything about that," Catherine said, meeting his gaze.

"Maybe you oughtta look into your own story." For an instant, she thought he was about to twist his large frame around and walk off, but he seemed to think better of it. He stood still, as if he were rooted in the earth. "I seen your picture in the newspaper, and I could tell you were *Hi'nono eino,* Arapaho like me. I figured you'd understand. You'd want everybody to know what happened at Sand Creek. You'd want justice."

Catherine didn't say anything. He was wrong. What she had wanted was the story, the exclusive interview with the elders. Whatever had happened to her ancestors was far away and forgotten. No more a part of her than the blur of traffic moving along the highway in the distance. She hardly knew anything about the woman who had given her birth, nothing about the man who had fathered her, and she hadn't wanted to know. Her life had begun when she was five years old and went to live with Dad and Marie. They'd called her "squaw" in middle school, a couple of the girls, and she hadn't known what they were talking about because she'd never thought of herself as anything but white. She remembered going home and crying, though, because of the emptiness inside her and the effort it always seemed to take to belong.

"The elders didn't mention a casino," she said.

"They didn't make up their minds to give the okay until last week. Sure, Arcott met with some of us" — Norman poked the cigarette in the direction of the other Indians still encircled by the reporters — "and we thought it was the solution we'd been looking for. But it wasn't our decision until the elders agreed. It took a while before they admitted things were different now. We could fight Congress for years and hope to get enough land for ranches. But even the biggest spreads aren't gonna generate the income of a single casino, and our people need some security, something of our own, and we need it now." He didn't take his eyes from hers. Catherine had the sense that they were the only people in the vast emptiness of the plains.

"Do all the Arapahos and Cheyennes agree on this?" Norman had made it clear at the interview with the elders that the government had sent part of the tribes to

101

reservations in Oklahoma — reservations later sold back to the government — but the rest of the Arapahos had been sent to the Wind River Reservation in Wyoming, and the Cheyennes were in Lame Deer, Montana.

"Tribes had an election in Oklahoma. Big majority voted to go ahead with the land claims and settle for the casino."

"What about the Arapahos and Cheyennes in Wyoming and Montana?"

"Arcott's talking to 'em. They'll be on board. Senator Russell's gonna support us." He turned toward her. "Maybe you'd get behind your own people if you went to Sand Creek."

"What are you talking about?"

"Homecoming run coming up, week from Saturday. Arapaho kids gonna run in relays from Sand Creek across our Colorado lands and up to the Wind River Rez in Wyoming. They run every year to remember the dead at Sand Creek. You might wanna see the blessing ceremony before the run gets started. And see the place where the villages stood. After you see Sand Creek, you're never the same."

"I'll think about it," she said.

Norman was staring out across the crowd again, and she followed his gaze. A black

SUV was bouncing across the plains, balloons of dust spitting around the wheels. She thought about Senator George Russell, the senior U.S. senator from Colorado. He had just announced his intention to step down at the end of his current term.

A little group of Indians dragging folded chairs in the direction of the parking lot jumped aside as the SUV roared past. Then the SUV turned northward and came to a jerky stop on the left side of the stage. She expected Russell to emerge. Instead, a tall, angular man at least thirty years younger than Russell, dressed in dark slacks and a pinkish shirt with short sleeves, drew himself out of the front seat and clasped hands with several of the Indians crowding around.

The dancers seemed to have noticed him, too, because the lead dancer twirled about and headed down the steps on the other side. Two other men jumped out of the SUV, moved to either side of the steps, and waited while he worked his way through the crowd and bounded up the steps. He strode across the stage waving at the audience that was shouting and clapping. The other two men stood on the bottom step, arms straight at their sides like guards.

"My name's Peter Arcott." The voice boomed over the roar of noise. "I want to thank the elders for inviting me here today and for the wise decision they've made to bring the best possible future to the Arapaho and Cheyenne people." He took a moment, surveying the audience, arms raised, outstretched palms pressing against the noise. When it began to subside, he said, "I pledge to you that I will work with your elders to build the finest casino and resort in the state of Colorado. All at no expense to the people of this state, which will realize nearly a billion dollars in revenue in the first ten years. I'm talking about a couple thousand jobs, a lot of them for Indians, and $200 million annual cash flow for Arapahos and Cheyennes. But that's not all! We're also going to build a tribal museum along with the hotel and casino. We're gonna give the people back their dignity!"

The clapping started again, and with it the thud of boots stomping the dry ground. Horns blasted from the parking lot, and a jet descending toward DIA screamed overhead. Arcott gave a victory wave, arms lifted high overhead. The pinkish shirt stretched across the muscles of his back. There was something surreal about the scene, Catherine thought, the crowd worked into a frenzy, the brown, upturned faces, the eyes fastened on the white man on the stage but seeing a

104

casino, as if the steel and concrete had suddenly materialized out of the bare earth.

Catherine had to look away. Finally she turned back to Norman, who had the same transcendent expression on his face, the dark, shadowed eyes looking at something that wasn't there. "I want an interview with Arcott," she said.

Norman snapped his head around and blinked at her, as if he were trying to reconcile whatever images he'd been watching with the woman beside him. He made a rasping sound in his throat. "He doesn't give press interviews," he said.

She looked back. Arcott jogging across the stage, arms still flying overhead. The crowd clapping and shouting. He lowered his arms, made a fist, and jabbed at the air before he ran down the steps. The two white men fell in beside him and in an instant the SUV began moving through the crowd, the doors still closing, Arcott barely visible in the rear seat.

She had the picture now. Of course Norman — an Arapaho, a brown face — had to be the public spokesperson demanding justice for his people. And Peter Arcott — the white face — had to stay behind the scenes. If the public was to support the tribes — and wasn't that the idea behind the rally? — it couldn't look as if the whole scheme had been concocted by a white man at the head of a company that built and operated casinos for Indian tribes.

"You can arrange an interview." Catherine watched the crowd flow behind the SUV. It headed toward the parked vehicles, then swerved right, leaving the crowd behind, and tore across the plains. Dust swirled around the tires and rose over the vehicle until it disappeared into a brown cloud.

Catherine waited for Norman to say something. He remained silent, and she said, "You owe me." He kept his gaze in the direction of the SUV, and she studied his profile — the hooked nose, the self-contained expression, like a mask pulled over whatever he was thinking. "You know that I'm going to get to the bottom of this story. I'll find out who's going to benefit from a casino, the tribes or Arcott and whoever he's in bed with. I'm going to give the public the kind of information they'll need to understand what is really going on."

Norman took a step forward, then turned toward her. Something sad in his eyes, she thought, something believing and disbelieving at the same time. "I'll talk to him," he said.

Catherine followed him around the stage,

where the other reporters encircled him. She kept going, past the dancers posing for the television cameras, past the groups of people moving toward the parked trucks and cars, dragging along folded aluminum chairs. She was behind the steering wheel of the convertible when she spotted Marcus Henning yanking his camera bags out of the rear of the *Journal* van. Engines sputtered into life around her. She pulled into the haphazard line of vehicles crawling forward, then turned into the row where Henning was parked and stopped next to the van. "You can still get the dancers in their regalia," she said.

He slammed the rear door and walked over, shouldering the strap on the black case that hung at his side. He squinted against the sun. "Gonna be any problem with taking their pictures?"

She wanted to laugh at that. The rally was all about pictures and newspaper articles and television news. "No problem at all," she said.

She drove down the row and turned into another line of traffic snaking toward the road. She dug her cell out of her bag with one hand and punched in the number for the office. The receptionist's voice sounded muffled and far away: *Journal.* "Hey, it's me," Catherine said. "Let me talk to Violet."

For a moment, she thought the call had been dropped; the cell felt lifeless in her hand. Then Violet Henderson's voice: "Catherine? What's up?"

"Listen, Violet," she said. "There's a 500-acre tract out by the airport, south of I-70." Then she gave Violet her password and told her the map showing the location was attached to an e-mail from Norman White-horse. "Can you get me the name of the owner?"

"I can try," Violet said. "Where can I reach you?"

Catherine let the silence hang between them a moment. God, was there no one she could trust? No one who should know where she was going?

"You have my cell number," she said.

7

Denver Health was a sprawling redbrick fortress in an old part of the city, traffic rushing past on Speer Boulevard, downtown skyscrapers shimmering in the distance. Catherine rode up the escalator in the cavernous atrium and watched people in the lobby below moving about like animated figures in a slow-motion video game, reluctant to head toward whatever destiny might await them.

At the top of the escalator, she walked along the balcony, trailing the tips of her fingers on the icy metal railing, still watching the people below. She felt cold, as though she'd stepped into an invisible blizzard. This was a mistake, coming to the hospital. Erik knew her life; he would know she would come to see Maury. He had only to wait for her here — dressed in green scrubs or a white nurse's uniform or the blue jeans or cutoffs and tee shirts of a hundred visitors. No one would know he was a killer.

She gripped the railing hard and waited a moment until she felt steadier before she headed down the wide corridor to the intensive care unit. A couple of green-clad staff members spilled out of a door and hurried ahead. Faint antiseptic odors hung in the air. There was no one at the desk next to the metal swinging door that led to wherever they had taken Maury. The waiting room on the right was like a cave excavated into the center of the hospital, lit by the dim flare of reading lamps on the little tables arranged among plastic chairs. An elderly woman with white hair and a gray sweater draped over her shoulders occupied one of the chairs. Two men were seated a few feet away, leaning forward, arms propped on thighs, hands dangling between knees, the perfect picture of despair.

She spotted Philip sunk into the chair in the shadows of the far corner. His head was tipped back against the wall, his eyes closed behind wireless glasses tilted to one side. She recognized the couple seated next to him, peering down at magazines: Nancy Jameson, Maury's law partner, and her husband, Don.

Catherine walked over and was about to take the vacant chair on the other side of Philip when he lurched awake and shook his head. His reddish hair looked dark and matted; there were bluish smudges under his eyes. He fiddled with his glasses until they were straight. "Why are you here?" he said.

"I love him, too," she said. She glanced at Nancy and Don, who had closed their magazines and were staring up at her, the stranger crashing a private gathering. They knew what had happened. They had heard the whole story, wrapped up in Philip's bitterness.

"Right," Philip said.

Catherine perched on the chair. "I don't expect you to forgive me," she said. "I'll never forgive myself."

"You should've just called the cops." Philip gave a grunt of dismay. "You didn't have to drag Maury into your problems."

"I know. I'm so sorry." On the drive over to the hospital, she'd been thinking about the hike they'd taken a couple of weeks ago, she and Maury and Philip and the couple that hadn't taken their eyes from her. They'd left their cars in Georgetown, the old mining town with gingerbread houses and wooden sidewalks sprawled in a valley between I-70 and the mountains, and hiked up Argentine Pass through a forest of pines and scrub brush and yellow and lavender wildflowers. Far below, Georgetown looked like a miniature town of dollhouses with sloped roofs and cupolas. Clear Creek shone like a silver ribbon flung along the highway, white caps bursting over the boulders and sparkling in the sun. On the far side of the highway, Rocky Mountain bighorn sheep grazed on the mountain slope.

Maury had climbed ahead, higher and higher, and she had tried to catch up, lungs bursting. She could hear the others groaning and thrashing below, boots scrunching the brush. At one point, Philip had yelled, "Wait up," but she and Maury had kept going, gaining altitude on the others. Then she'd tripped on a rock and slid down slope a little ways, finally grabbing hold of a tree limb to stop herself. In an instant, Maury was there, helping her back to her feet, brushing at her backpack and the torn knees of her jeans, pressing a handkerchief against the scratches on her arm.

And now he might be dying. She squeezed her eyes shut a moment against the tears that were starting.

"They let me see him," Philip said.

"They did?" Catherine shifted toward

112

him, ignoring the couple who had gone back to thumbing through the magazines. The sound of turning pages rustled in the quiet. "How is he?"

Philip shook his head, gulping in air. His Adam's apple bobbed in his thin neck. "I think he's going to leave us."

"They didn't say that, did they?" The knot inside her was so tight, she thought she might throw up.

"They said he's holding his own. It's too early to tell."

"Why don't you go home and get some rest," Catherine said. He looked terrible, shoulders rounded and chest sunken, shirt collar standing out from his neck. He clasped and unclasped his hands as if he weren't sure what to do with them. "I can stay here."

"We didn't think you'd bother to come back." He nodded at Nancy and Don, immersed in the magazines. They wanted no part of this, she thought.

She told him she'd seen Detective Bustamante, and she'd had to go to work. There was a story she was covering.

Philip stared into the middle of the room. "I'm not going anywhere," he said, leaving the rest of it hanging in the air — Maury was here because of her, yet she'd had more important things to do than to stay with him.

"Do you think I can see him?" she said.

"Up to you," he said.

Catherine got to her feet and walked back through the waiting room. A heavyset nurse, encased in white, sat ramrod straight at the desk outside the metal door. Her chest ballooned over the belt cinched at her waist.

"May I help you?" she said. She had short, dark hair and hooded, gray eyes.

"I'd like to see Maury Beekner."

"Your name?"

Catherine gave her name and waited as the nurse ran her index finger down a column of names on a sheet of paper. The finger stopped on the last line. She hesitated a moment, then set both hands against the top of the desk and pushed herself to her feet. "I'll take you to him," she said, brushing past her and pushing through the metal door.

Catherine followed the woman into a corridor suffused in white light that glistened on the cream-colored tile floors and bounced off the beige walls. Detective Bustamante worked faster than she'd expected, she thought. She would have to remember to thank him. There were no sounds apart from a faint electronic buzzing noise somewhere and the clack of their footsteps on the hard floor. Past a series of wide doors: one opened into a darkened, vacant room. Past the nurses' station with TV monitors on the walls between cubicles of file folders. A man with a bald head and the face of a thirty-year-old, wearing the white shirt and pants of a male nurse, rummaged through sheets of paper spread on the counter. He didn't look up. The smell of hot, sudsy water hung in the air, as if the floors had just been scrubbed.

The nurse swung left across the corridor, opened a door, and, flattening herself against it, nodded Catherine into a narrow room with a metal-framed bed in the middle and cabinets lining the walls. "Five minutes," she said.

Catherine stood at the foot of the bed, unable to take her eyes from the figure covered with white sheets. It couldn't be Maury. Maury was full of life, hands and arms flailing the air as he talked, feet dancing about as if there weren't enough space to contain all of him. It was as if Maury had gone somewhere else and left behind a lifeless shape with rubber tubes running into inert arms stretched on top of the sheets, face drained of color, eyelids closed, and lips clamped around a white plastic tube.

"Oh, God," she said, making herself move along the side of the bed. She brushed the tips of her fingers on his arm above the tape that held the needle in his vein. It was like touching dried leather. "I'm so sorry, Maury," she said. "I'm so sorry."

She had to look away for a moment, let her eyes rest on a cabinet door, the shiny metal handle. She wanted it to be yesterday again, when everything was normal and ordinary, because, if it could be that time again, she would change things. Everything would be different.

She looked down at Maury. She felt as if they were underwater, the sheets and tubes and the room blurring together, forming and re-forming into different shapes. She could feel the salty moisture on her cheeks. "Don't leave us, Maury," she said, running both palms across her face. Her hands felt cold and wet. So many people had gone, fallen out of her life. Dad, then Lawrence. Oh, Lawrence reappeared now and then. Still he had gone from her. So many things gone: her marriage, the life that she had thought was hers. And something else, something vague that had slipped away long ago and left nothing in its place except a

116

blank longing.

She bent close to his ear. "Stay, Maury," she whispered.

She straightened herself, aware of the white nurse floating past the little window in the door, hovering outside in the corridor. Catherine brushed Maury's arm again, told him that she loved him — that she and Philip loved him. Then she let herself into the corridor, exchanged a quick glance with the nurse, who darted into Maury's room, leaving her to retrace her steps through the ICU and out into the waiting room.

She intended to tell Philip that Maury was still the same, but Philip was asleep in the chair, head propped against the wall. The coldness hit her again — she was shivering, she realized — as she walked down the corridor to the escalator.

Erik Bolton drummed a pencil on the edge of the steering wheel. He'd folded the section of the *Journal* around the crossword puzzle and set it over the center of the wheel. Four down, six-letter word, "1B Rockies." That had stumped him, but he'd learned to go on, work around the blank spaces until the word became obvious. A bit like life, he thought. Adjust, improvise, remain flexible. Sometimes you had to move sideways in order to go forward.

He'd been parked in the lot next to Denver Health for three hours and sixteen minutes — the branches of an elm offered a little shade in the bloody heat — when she'd finally arrived. Traffic on Speer Boulevard had roared past in a steady stream, the noise punctuated by that of engines throttling down, brakes squealing. He'd finished off a bottle of water and worked three puzzles that he'd saved to hold off the boredom in times such as this. Waiting was part of the job, a minor inconvenience you had to accept because the rest of it was . . . The truth was, the rest of it was damn exciting. It required all of his skills — the ability to read people and understand what made them tick, the expertise to get the most out of a firearm, and, most of all, the timing and physical coordination to handle the job.

He'd seen the silver convertible the moment it had come off Speer Boulevard and turned into the lot. She had driven past the brown Ford as if it were just another random vehicle taking up space and parked about thirty feet away. Oh, it was beautiful. He'd lifted the corner of the *Journal* that he'd laid over the Sig on the passenger seat and tried to contain the eagerness welling inside him, the first rush of adrenaline. "Today is a good day to die," he said out loud. His voice was low, musical, he thought.

He watched Catherine get out of the convertible and make her way across the lot to the covered walkway that reminded him of the cloister he had once seen at a church in Mexico. She walked fast; she was always in a hurry — he'd learned that about her. It had intrigued him, but he hadn't been able to figure out the reason, what it was that drove her on. Now that she was going to die, he realized he would probably never understand, and that bothered him a little. He liked to know the victim's life so well that it gave him the pleasure of thinking that it belonged to him, something that he possessed, before he actually took it.

He didn't take his eyes off her until she'd walked through the glass doors at the entrance and disappeared past the brick wall into the swarm of patients and visitors he'd tracked entering the hospital.

He had a little time. He pulled his cell out of the case on his belt, pressed a key, and listened to the rhythm of the phone ringing on the kitchen wall. Four rings, damn. It would go to the answering machine, and he wasn't sure when he'd be able to call home again. Then Deborah's voice, a half second before the answering machine would have picked up.

"Hey, honey," she said. "I've been worried about you."

"Ran into a little snag yesterday. Meeting had to be postponed."

"That means you won't be home tonight?"

"I'm not sure, sweetheart. Depends upon how the meeting goes today. I'm waiting for it to get under way now. Lot of money riding on this sale. Wish me luck."

"You don't need luck, Steve. You're too good for luck. You'll knock 'em dead."

"Right," he said. He felt a prick of uneasiness at the way her words crowded the truth. "How are the kids?"

"Took Jamie to the doctor today. Strep throat. He was up crying most of the night. I wish you were here."

"Is he okay?"

"Seems better now he's on the antibiotic. Try to wind things up and come home, okay?"

"I'll do my best. I love you, Deborah. Kiss the kids for me." He pressed the end button and watched the word flash in the readout: Disconnected.

He had the plan in place. Erik Bolton would kill her when she came back to her car. Erik Bolton. He liked the name. He liked the way it looked on the driver's license and passport that he'd had his contact in El Paso make before he'd left for Colorado. Erik Bolton, it said on the car rental agreement and the motel registry. Erik Bolton on the credit card he'd applied for and gotten with ease. Of course it was easy; it was perfect. Erik Bolton had lived to be four years old, according to the marker on the gravestone in the big cemetery in Dallas, which meant he had no debts, no bad credit history. But — God love the little fellow — his parents had gotten him a social security number, and he thanked the parents for that, even if the little fellow hadn't gotten around to voicing his gratitude. After he'd obtained a copy of the birth certificate from the Texas Department of Vital Statistics, it had been easy to get the social security number. The little fellow's life was a blank sheet, which he — the new Erik Bolton — intended to fill in. Give the poor kid a life, you might say, filled with adventure, at least for a few months.

The instant she emerged from the building and started down the cloister, he would get out of the Ford, carrying the *Journal* folded around the gun. Ironic, he thought. She'd walk along the front of the parked cars, the way she'd entered the hospital — people were such creatures of habit — while he would walk along the back. He would watch her out of the corner of his eyes without alarming her. Just another hospital visitor heading back to his car with his newspaper. He had to pace his steps to hers — timing was critical in this business. She had to reach the convertible first, open the driver's door, and slide onto the seat. Before she could pull the door closed, he would move between the door and her, his finger curled around the trigger. He would shoot her in the head from maybe six inches away because his client wanted to make certain she was dead — no slipups, no wounds that the hospital emergency doctors could fix. There would be a thud, but not a loud gunshot, thanks to the silencer — nothing that wouldn't meld into the traffic noise and the sound of tires clawing asphalt as cars pulled in and out of the parking lot. He would slip the gun back inside the folded paper, close the door, as if he'd been chatting with an old friend, and walk back. He would be out of the parking lot before anyone noticed the woman's head lolling against the headrest, or the blood trickling across her face.

There she was.

He saw her pushing open the glass door. An older woman, stoop shouldered and leaning on a walking stick, plodded ahead. Then a pregnant woman pushing a stroller, and Catherine McLeod, the Good Samaritan, holding the door for the little parade. She stepped outside and started down the cloister.

Erik Bolton stared in disbelief. She wasn't alone. Walking alongside her, shielding her from the parking lot, was a security guard in a gray uniform with a holstered gun fixed to his wide, black belt. They emerged from the cloister and walked along the front of the cars, just as he had anticipated she would do. In lock step, she and the security guard, a professional, Eric realized, with eyes that took in everything even though his head didn't move. The eyes had taken him in, too, the man behind the steering wheel of a brown Ford sedan, reading the newspaper folded in front of him, waiting for someone. The security guard was still next to her at the car, opening the door, standing aside until she'd settled herself behind the wheel. There was a sharp thwack when he shut the door. Then he stepped away and waited as Catherine McLeod backed out of the space, shifted forward, and drove out of the lot.

Eric waited, too. He waited until the guard had walked back through the cloister and into the hospital before he turned the ignition and drove after the silver convertible.

8

Catherine drove west on I-70 in the rush-hour traffic, the foothills of the mountains turning violet in the shadows, the crush of suburbs, shopping centers, and warehouses falling behind. She passed a truck and settled into the right lane. The wind blew her hair about. She turned the CD up: Coltrane's saxophone, double-time and angry. Rex perched on the backseat, craning over the top of the passenger seat. Sunlight reflected on the cars streaming past. The hood of the Chrysler looked watery in the late-afternoon brightness. On the passenger seat was the brown envelope that Marjorie had handed her earlier.

She'd stopped at the town house to pick up Rex and get enough of her things for two or three days. God, let Bustamante find the shooter by then. The town house had seemed strange and unfamiliar this afternoon, unlike this morning when she had

125

gone home to feed Rex, shower, and sleep a little. She had been still in shock then, she realized, fuzzy headed, stumbling through the aftermath of a bad dream. She had looked away from the blood spattered on the furniture and congealed on the floor. They seemed unreal, not part of her life.

It was different this afternoon, and the difference left her feeling shaky and tense. She had driven around the block several times, waiting for the police officer to arrive and escort her into her own home. In less than fifteen minutes, she'd thrown the slacks and shirts and shoes, the lipsticks and moisturizers into a large backpack, slipped her laptop inside its case, stacked cans of dog food in a paper bag and was back in the convertible with Rex in the backseat. She'd waved a thank-you to the officer — blond crew cut, not more than twenty-five, with sunburned cheeks and the bored impatience of a man eager to be somewhere else.

Bustamante had been right to insist on a police escort. It wasn't just that the shock had begun to wear off. It was all of it: the e-mail from Erik, the warnings that came from everywhere — Bustamante, Lawrence, Marjorie Fennerman — as if everyone else understood the intruder had come for her.

And finally her own reluctant acceptance of the truth. Erik was out there somewhere, watching and waiting.

At the hospital, the sense that he was close had swept over her, leaving her numb, stumbling off the escalator. She'd stood in the atrium and watched the people file past, shaky with the thought that he could be among them. It had taken all of her strength to walk over to the security guard at the entrance. She'd barely begun to explain about the intruder when his eyebrows had come together in a thin, black line and he'd looked as if an apparition had sprung up in front of him. She was *that* woman. Yes, yes, he'd said. He'd heard about it on the radio on his way to work this afternoon. The gunshot victim was upstairs in ICU, might not make it, they say. And if you asked him, she oughtta be careful until the police sorted it all out. You never know these days, all the crackpots out there. Every day victims came to the emergency room, a steady stream of victims. Guy with the gun could have been looking specifically for her. You never know. He would walk her out to her car.

He was a big man, half a head taller than Catherine. Gray uniform, holstered gun. Still she'd felt her muscles tighten as they'd headed down the covered walkway and across the sidewalk that bordered the parking lot. She had glanced at the parked cars — people waiting inside, a man peering down at a newspaper folded on the steering wheel — and at the people coming and going. She was still on edge when she'd reached the town house. If the police escort hadn't arrived, she never would have gone inside. She would have gotten Rex from the side yard, watching the town house all the time, expecting the shooter's hideous face to appear in one of the windows. Then she would have stomped on the gas pedal and driven out of the neighborhood fast.

She pulled around a green pickup lumbering ahead, belching black smoke, and thought about it. She might never be able to go back to the town house, go back home. It was possible that yet another life she had tried to make was over.

She moved into the exit lane, followed the line of traffic through a series of exits — Highway 470 first, then Highway 285 — and headed into the mountains. The slopes looked ragged, dense with boulders and ponderosas. Every few miles, there were vistas of mountain valleys carpeted in golden grasses and purple and red wildflowers. These were the mountains around

Turkey Creek Canyon where the old Denver families had built their ranches — here and in Estes Park. But Estes Park was northwest of Boulder, farther away. "We liked these mountains," Lawrence had explained one evening when they were driving to the ranch, as if he had been part of the family decision more than a hundred years ago.

A large green sign loomed next to the highway, Conifer and Bailey, in big white letters. Sprawling mountain towns that had evolved from little stops for stagecoaches on the dirt road from Denver, according to Lawrence. All part of the history of his own family, and she envied him that. He knew who he was, where he belonged, and no matter where she was, she had always felt that she belonged somewhere else. She had tried to fit in with Marie and Dad, with Lawrence. And she had loved all of them.

The Denver, South Park, and Pacific Railroad had run up here, she remembered Lawrence telling her. And wasn't it his great-grandfather who had helped to finance the railroad? Yes, that's what Lawrence had said. Leland Stern had been involved in so many things — Denver's first water company, first trolley cars, first electrical power company — it was hard to remember all of them. The stage stops had evolved into little towns alongside the train tracks. Every day the trains stopped at the stations to disgorge passengers. Denver families always rode the train, Lawrence said, as if the Sterns and their wealthy friends comprised the entire population of the city. Carriages met them at the Pine Station, which the highway had left stranded, and took them to their ranches in Turkey Creek Canyon.

Everything had changed, of course. The railroad abandoned, tracks torn up and sold for scrap metal, highways and automobiles everywhere. There had been a note of regret in his tone when Lawrence talked about the changes, and she remembered thinking that he had been born too late. He would have preferred to be swaying in the coach of a train, with a carriage waiting at the station, than driving the BMW on Highway 285 with her.

It had been a while since Catherine had been at the Stern ranch — more than a year ago, and so much had changed since then, so many other things crowded into her life — that she wondered if she had passed the turnoff. There were no signs. None of the families had wanted signs directing the public to their ranches. She slowed a little, watching the edge of the highway ahead for the spur of an asphalt road. The dark sedan behind her veered past and honked.

Then she spotted the bridge over the highway and the gray, single-lane road that looped up the mountainside and disappeared. She tapped on the brake pedal. The tires squealed as she banked into the exit. Lawrence would take the exit so fast — odd, the things that came back to her — that she would brace herself against the dashboard and close her eyes, half expecting the BMW to fly off the mountain.

The road was empty, with a lingering sense that other traffic had passed by, like the faint smell of aftershave in the house after Lawrence had left in the mornings. The asphalt gave way to a dirt road that narrowed and switched back on itself as it climbed higher. Every curve opened onto a different view: the highway below threaded between the slopes, the shadows crawling over Denver in the distance, and beyond, the flat, open plains still golden in the sunlight. She spotted a brown sedan taking the asphalt turnoff below.

It was there again as she came around another curve. Starting up the road behind her, the front tires leaning into a turn. The hood and roof looked black in the shadows. The CD had moved on to a slower, darker piece. "People drive up here," she said out

131

loud, as if Rex were a nervous passenger she had to reassure. "The Sterns aren't the only people with homes in the area."

The ranch was close now. She recognized the log fence that had appeared out of nowhere, running through the pines. She shoved away the thought of the brown sedan behind her and hunched over the steering wheel, searching for another dirt road that branched to the right. She spotted the road around the next curve, pulled the steering wheel right, and drove toward the iron gate ahead. She stopped close to the post on the left and waited. The cameras would have already focused on the car. It was only a moment before the intercom came alive: "Who is it?"

"Catherine McLeod." She shouted toward the metal circle in the post.

Another moment passed before the gates started to creak open on the rusty metal hinges. Rex gave a little bark and swung his head back and forth. "It's okay," she said. She eased on the gas pedal and drove onto the Stern ranch. She could hear the gates closing behind as she followed the narrow dirt road, cut through a tunnel of junipers. A short distance beyond the gate, the forest stopped at the edge of a meadow studded with boulders, clumps of wildflowers, and wild golden grass tinged with the blue light of dusk. A creek ran through the center, and little wooden bridges here and there served as walkways from one side to the other.

This was where the residential compound was located, sprawling across the meadow behind the thick wall of junipers and ponderosas, a hushed, private place. The meadow seemed frozen in the nineteenth century. There were no sounds of traffic — no honking horns, no engines gearing down, no tires thrumming on asphalt. The highway she'd been on fifteen minutes ago might have been a million miles away, in a century yet to come. Across the creek ahead was the family ranch house, a façade of stone and logs and a series of peaked roofs that crawled up a slight hill. A tower rose on the front corner, tiny windows cut into stone, and everywhere, around every window and below every roof, was Victorian gingerbread trim. Below the front windows were flower boxes filled with red geraniums and purple and white petunias.

On the other side of the creek was the guest cottage, a smaller version of the main house, with similar peaked roofs and flower-filled window boxes. Farther down the road and out of sight, Catherine knew, were the barns and bunkhouse and cabins for the cowboys and staff. But the house that resembled a guard house — two stories of stone, narrow and rounded like the tower on the main house, with flower boxes beneath the lower-level windows — was directly ahead. It was where Gilly Mason, the ranch manager, lived, and Gilly was out in front now, waving her down.

Catherine stopped in the middle of the road and waited for him to come around the hood. He was the picture of a cowboy — narrow hips, roped arms, and muscular shoulders of a man who wouldn't think twice about throwing a steer. He wore blue jeans, a blue Western shirt with a large silver and turquoise watch protruding from the right cuff, and worn, dirt-smudged cowboy boots. The tan straw cowboy hat sat back on his head so that the V-shaped brim pointed upward. It was hard to guess his age — the bronzed, leathery face, the gray working into his dark hair, and the gray stubble on his chin. Early sixties, probably. He'd been with the family thirty years. Elizabeth Stern had hired him — a Vietnam vet who had stood up to the Viet Cong and taken a bullet in his leg in Da Nang. He always kept a rifle close at hand. Elizabeth trusted Gilly.

"Been expecting you." He had the raspy

voice of a smoker. He set both hands on the ledge of her door and leaned over. Catherine turned off the CD. Odors of tobacco and coffee floated toward her. Deep lines etched his sun-hardened face. His nose was cross-hatched with a network of red veins. "Dial zero if you need anything."

Catherine thanked him and drove forward. She could see him staring after her in the side-view mirror. Knowing Gilly was nearby — a guard with a gun — gave her a sense of relief. She turned onto the one-lane bridge, bounced across the logs, and followed the dirt road around the main house. She parked close to the porch of the guest cottage and took a moment, waiting for the gust of memories to subside. They came to the cottage almost every weekend in the summers, she and Lawrence. They hiked up into the high mountains that surrounded the ranch. They fished for trout in the streams, spread out a blanket and ate the sandwiches they'd carried in their backpacks and made love outdoors in the shade and the sun. They came to the ranch in the winter, strapped on cross-country skis, and glided through the forest, making their own trails in the snow.

It surprised her — she hadn't counted on the force of the memories. She had put it all behind her, the past life with Lawrence. She felt naked and vulnerable and self-conscious, as if she were less than what she had once been. She'd thought she knew who she was, when she had been his wife.

What did it matter! She opened the door, got out, and let Rex out of the back. She had built a new life. Resumed her career and made new friends, like Maury. She felt a little shiver run through her, like the point of a knife scraping her skin.

Rex bounded free, raced to the creek, and lapped up a drink of water. Then he was running about, circling the car, and nosing around the porch. Catherine hauled the backpack, laptop case, and bag of dog food out of the trunk and deposited them in a pile next to the door. The key was in the lock. She let herself inside and, one by one, carried the bags across the threshold. Then she stopped, stunned by the wall of memories rising before her. She felt as if she had stepped into her own past: chintz, over-stuffed sofas and chairs scattered about the large living room, remnants of light filtering through the windows, dark-wood cabinets visible in the kitchen, hallway leading to the bedrooms and baths and the study where Lawrence had moved in his favorite brown leather chair. The cottage had been *theirs,* and Lawrence had gotten his grandmother to agree. Other guests were sent to one of the cabins by the bunkhouse.

Catherine shoved the memories against the back of her mind. Everything was different now; the ranch was a safe place, that was all. She carried the dog food into the kitchen, opened a can, and spooned the red, juicy meat into a bowl that she found in the cabinet. She carried the bowl out to the porch where Rex waited, tail wagging so hard that he was shaking. She set the bowl down and went back to the kitchen. The refrigerator was filled: roasted chicken, cheeses, yogurt, lettuce, tomatoes, green grapes, strawberries and apples, a variety of sauces and salad dressings. Steaks, hamburger, fish fillets were stacked in the freezer, along with extra loaves of bread and ice cream. She checked the pantry — bags of pasta and cans of soup, tomato sauce, olives, pickles, mustard, and ketchup.

She slammed the cabinet door. She could hear Rex pushing the bowl across the porch. They could stay for months. When the food ran out, Gilly would replace it. She would never have to leave. She would be safe. And this was what he had done to her, a man called Erik who intended to kill her. Robbed her of everything she had worked for the

137

past year, stolen whatever was left of her life after Lawrence.

She carried her backpack down the hallway into the large bedroom with the four-poster bed that was so high they had used a stepping stool to climb in and out, and the windows that framed the mountain peaks shining above the forest. She flung the bags on top of the bed and went back down the hallway. She would not allow the memories to come again; she didn't want them.

Outside, Rex lay on the porch, front paws hung over the top step. He looked content. She would be like Rex, she told herself. She got the brown envelope out of the front seat and went back inside.

In the kitchen, she opened the bottle of Chardonnay she found in the refrigerator door, filled a crystal goblet almost to the top, and carried it into the living room. Then she put a Gershwin CD into the player that stood on a table. She remembered the CD: she and Lawrence used to listen to it. She settled into one of the overstuffed chairs — not the one she'd always liked, a different chair, positioned between the sofas — and ripped open the brown envelope. Sipping the wine, she began thumbing through the articles.

Somewhere in the black type that covered

the pages, she understood now, was the reason a man was trying to kill her.

9

Dusk had deepened into the black night that falls over the mountains, and the cottage had turned chilly. Catherine was still curled in the chair, reading in a puddle of light. Rex snored and shook himself in dreams on the rug next to her. A month of her life, unfolding page by page to "Rhapsody in Blue." She had turned over the stack and started from the bottom, reading the stories in the order in which she had written them, then setting them on the coffee table. Odd, the details she'd recalled as she read: the blanched face of the mother of the gang member shot by a Denver police officer when the officer was exonerated; the way the wind flapped the suit jackets of the dignitaries the day ground was broken on the luxury residence and office complex that Lawrence was developing; the waxy mustache of the former state treasurer during his trial in District Court on twenty-six charges of fraud and embezzlement and malfeasance in office.

She'd written earlier articles on the downfall of the state treasurer, beginning with the first hint of irregularities after an accountant had blown the whistle and gone to the governor. Marcy Norton, the governor's press secretary, had alerted her to the story and given her the accountant's name. He had agreed to an interview and she had broken the story. The *Mirror* had piled on, the treasurer resigned, and charges were filed.

But all of that had occurred more than a year ago. The trial took place nearly four weeks ago. The former treasurer was now in the state prison in Canon City. Had he wanted to kill her — and surely, he had reason — why hadn't he sent the killer after her when she had first gotten onto the story? Before the *Journal* had published it?

The stack of papers in her hand was getting smaller. At the beginning of the summer, she had written two or three stories on the lack of requirements for background checks on in-home daycare workers. She had found four people running daycare centers with past convictions of sexual and physical abuse of children. The stories had caused a storm — the paper's telephones

141

jammed with callers wanting to know if their daycare arrangements were safe. There were dozens of e-mails every day. And here was the story she had written two weeks ago on the tougher background checks that the state now required for anyone offering daycare in their homes.

The new regulations would put at least four people out of business, she realized. It was possible one of them blamed her. But that was ridiculous. The *Mirror* and the television news had jumped on the story. Featured the people with prior convictions, blasted their photographs on the front page and the evening news. They had run editorials screaming for tougher regulations to protect children.

She set the daycare story on top of the other stories on the table. The rest of the press had done a better job than she had, that was the truth. Marjorie had even called her into the office, waved the front page of the *Mirror,* and said, "I thought you were on this!"

But by then she'd gotten involved with the story of the Arapaho and Cheyenne land claims. She had written two stories. But the story of the Sand Creek Massacre had touched something inside of her and drawn her in. She'd known she would follow the story wherever it led. She could hear Norman's voice in her head. *You're Arapaho. We brought you the story.*

And maybe that explained the compulsion that had overtaken her, she thought. Made her neglect other stories, not return phone calls, let her e-mail pile up unanswered. Maybe it was her own story, the story she had never been told. She had spent hours — more time than she should have spent — in the Denver Public Library researching the Sand Creek Massacre. She had taken a lot of time writing and rewriting the story about Sand Creek, taking care to shape the sentences and paragraphs so the readers would understand how important they were.

She started rereading the initial story, published two weeks ago. The headline across the top was smudged: "Tribes File Claims to Colorado Lands."

The Arapaho and Cheyenne tribes have filed claims with the Department of the Interior for twenty-seven million acres in Colorado, roughly one-third of the state. The tribes claim the lands belong to them under the Treaty of Fort Laramie, signed in 1851. According to Norman Whitehorse, Arapaho spokesman, the tribes were driven from their ancestral lands following the Sand Creek Massacre, November 29, 1864. He said that the tribes are willing to settle for smaller tracts of land where they could establish tribal ranches and raise hormone-free cattle. "We believe the market for the beef is very strong," he said. "We know how to raise cattle. The ranches will give our people financial security."

Governor Mark Lyle said that the claims have clouded the property titles on most of eastern Colorado. "Property owners will be forced to take legal action to clear titles. The claims will bring a large amount of unwarranted expenses to ordinary Colorado families who will not be able to buy or sell property without extensive litigation."

The governor pointed out that Congress had settled the Arapaho and Cheyenne land claims for $15 million in 1965. He opposes any additional settlement with the tribes.

Catherine slipped the page behind the second article — the interview with the elders. When the elders had described the site of Sand Creek, she had felt as if she had seen it herself. The large black headline ran across two columns: "Tribes Accuse Government of Genocide."

On the plains in southeastern Colorado, not far from La Junta, a dusty wind whips across an expanse of arid land covered with wild grass and broken by clumps of cottonwoods, arroyos, and the dried bed of what had once been Big Sandy Creek. On November 29, 1864, a village of Arapahos and Cheyennes under Chief Left Hand and Chief Black Kettle was camped along the creek. It was freezing cold, but the ground was dry, striped with the white traces of the last snowstorm. At dawn, with the sky turning red in the east, the silence of the plains was broken by the clank of artillery and harnesses and the rustle of horses' hooves as the Third Colorado Cavalry drew up on the bluff overlooking the sleeping camp. The commander, Colonel John M. Chivington, lifted his sword overhead. He exhorted the troops to remember the whites killed by Indians. The Colonel did not believe in taking prisoners. The sword sliced the air. The soldiers spurred their horses and the cavalry swept down on the sleeping village. At the end of the day, one hundred and sixty three Arapahos and Cheyennes — most were women, children, and old men — lay dead. Chief Left Hand was mortally wounded. His family was killed, with the exception of his sister, Mahom, and her young children.

Norman Whitehorse, Arapaho spokesman, called the Sand Creek Massacre "an act of genocide against Indian people who were under the protection of the United States government. Territorial Governor John Evans and other white authorities, including Chivington, had told the chiefs to bring their people to Sand Creek. They had promised to conclude a peace treaty with them. The chiefs had complied with the order."

Whitehorse points out that Left Hand and Black Kettle and White Antelope were known at the time as peace chiefs. "They'd been working very hard to keep peace between the Indians and the white people that had swarmed over their lands." Chief Left Hand had even rescued three white children who had been captured by hostile Indians and turned the children over to Captain Edward Wynkoop at a camp out on the plains, an act that Whitehorse called "brave to the point of recklessness. Not long before he rescued the children, two Cheyennes had ransomed a captured white woman and taken her to safety at Fort Laramie. The fort commander had ordered the Cheyennes hung in chains until they were dead."

"We've never forgotten Sand Creek," said Harold YellowBull, Arapaho elder. "Nobody was expecting an attack. Most of the warriors had gone out hunting. They had six hundred people they had to feed. Women, children, and old men stayed behind." He said that two young girls had gone to the corral at dawn. "They saw the soldiers on top of the bluff. They ran back to the village and shouted, 'The soldiers are coming! The soldiers are coming!' Chief Black Kettle ran out with an American flag so the soldiers could see it was a friendly village. Lots of people ran out of the tipis naked. They didn't have time to get dressed before the soldiers started shooting."

Cheyenne elder James Hunting, a descendant of Cheyenne Chief Black Kettle, told a story passed down in his family. "The Chief called for people to gather around him. He held up his white flag and the people ran to him. Chief

White Antelope did the same, and they shot him. The soldiers galloped through the village and shot everybody they could, even the little children. Shot them in the back, is what I heard."

"People tried to get away from the soldiers," YellowBull said. "They were running about, crazylike. Some of 'em ran up the creek bed. A lot of 'em were shot down, but some got away. Most had been wounded. They ran for miles, carrying children on their backs. When the soldiers stopped coming after them, they made a little camp. It was bitter cold. The ones that were able gathered up dry grass and tried to make fires to keep the wounded and the little children from freezing to death. The children were crying, and people were moaning from their wounds. It was a terrible night."

Hunting said that when Chief Black Kettle saw that the soldiers intended to kill everyone, he yelled for the people to run up the creek bed. "He ran with them," he said. "He thought his wife, Woman-To-Be-Hereafter, was running with him, but when he got to the camp, she was nowhere around. So he ran back! He found her on the ground. She'd been shot pretty bad. He picked her up and carried her miles to the camp. He saved her life, because the soldiers were riding up to the wounded and stabbing them to death."

Whitehorse pointed out that, after the attack, the soldiers mutilated the dead bodies. They took scalps, ears, breasts, and other parts of the bodies as trophies. "There was a big victory parade when they got back to Denver. The soldiers waved their trophies, and the crowds cheered."

He shook his head. "And they said we were savages!"

"Because of Sand Creek," Whitehorse said, "Arapaho and Cheyenne people were forced from their ancestral lands in Colorado. The government had acknowledged the tribal title to the lands in the 1851 Treaty of Fort Laramie. Now we ask Congress to acknowledge the act of genocide, reconsider the reparations that were made in 1965, and give us a just compensation for our lost lands. We have been waiting for justice for one hundred and fifty years."

Congress has designated the site of the Sand Creek Massacre the nation's newest national park. An interpretive center will be built to explain and preserve the history of the event. Visitors will be able to tour the periphery of the battlefield, but will not be allowed onto the actual site of the village. Whitehorse said that the tribes consider the site sacred ground. "It's a place of death," he said. "Sand Creek is the cemetery for many of our ancestors."

Whitehorse said he expects that Congress will finally settle the matter. "It's different now," he says. "The public knows the truth about what happened at Sand Creek, and the public expects Congress to honor the Fort Laramie Treaty."

All of it history, Catherine thought. A story about a massacre that had occurred in the nineteenth century when Denver was nothing more than a collection of log cabins and tents that rose up overnight on the banks of Cherry Creek and the South Platte River. Running beneath the story of the massacre, she knew, was the bigger story of the settlers and the Indians contesting the same lands. She'd found an old photo of that time in the Denver Public Library. Just beyond the town were the tipis of an Arapaho village at the confluence of Cherry Creek and the South Platte River. Not long after the photo had been taken, the Arapaho village had moved.

Nothing in an article on history that would make someone want to kill her.

She slipped a paper clip over the tops of the two articles. Loss and the absence of justice — that was what they were about. She could write similar articles about any group of people. Irish people at the hands of England, Mexicans and South Americans at the hands of generations of oppressive governments, Africans and Middle Easterners, Muslim women — the list was endless. It was the history of the human race.

And yet someone wanted to kill her.

She was missing something. She scanned the pages again, rereading sentences and paragraphs, searching for words that carried more than one meaning and could have been misinterpreted by a crazy man with a gun. She couldn't find anything.

But this evening she would write the story about the Arapaho and Cheyenne plans to settle the claims for five hundred acres where they could build a casino. And casinos were controversial. She felt a new flare of anger. Whitehorse and the elders hadn't told her about the plan to use the land claims as a way of bypassing the state and the people of Colorado to get a casino. There were casinos in Black Hawk, Central City, and Cripple Creek, and on the Ute Reservation in the southwestern corner of the state, but voters had turned down proposals for additional casinos seven times.

She would write about the rally and the announcement of the casino plans. She would quote the developer, Peter Arcott: "We're going to give you a first-rate casino!" The article wouldn't appear until tomorrow morning. And yet, someone wanted her dead now.

She squared all of the articles on the table, stuffed them back into the envelope, and finished off another glass of Chardonnay. Then she went out into the kitchen and refilled the glass. Nothing made sense. She'd gone along with Bustamante's theory — and everyone else's, it seemed — that the intruder had come after her because of something she had written. It made her want to laugh — the classic blame-the-victim theory. It was all her fault — a divorced woman, living alone, walking her dog at night, writing newspaper articles that pissed somebody off. The whole idea was ridiculous.

She gulped the Chardonnay and poured another glass. The bottle was half empty, and she felt a little drunk. She could feel the warmth moving through her, the tenseness draining out of her. And maybe tonight she would sleep. She opened the refrigerator door and looked at the food bulging on the shelves. She wasn't hungry, but she hadn't eaten since last night, except for the nutrition bar she'd gotten out of the vending machine at the newspaper. And she had an article to write tonight. She took out the roasted chicken and set it on the counter. There was a loaf of bread in the cabinets somewhere. She pulled open the doors.

Rex started to growl. Scrambling to his feet in the living room, toenails clawing at the wood floor. He was barking now and emitting low, furious growls that almost drowned out the sound of knocking.

Catherine dropped the loaf of bread she'd lifted out of a cabinet and went into the living room. She felt as though she were walking underwater, legs heavy with the effort. Rex was throwing himself against the door. The sound of his barking reverberated around her. She lifted the lamp off the table as she walked by. The cord stuck for a moment, then ripped free and bounced along the floor. The light went off leaving the light from the kitchen spilling around her. She steered herself toward the window next to the door and peered around the edge.

Beyond the flare of the porch light was an endless stretch of darkness broken by the silvery motion of the pine branches.

The knocking came again. She stepped toward the door, gripping the lamp with both hands. Rex was on his hind legs, front paws pressed against the door, growling. His top lip curled back and strands of saliva drooled out of his mouth.

"Who is it?" she called.

"Catherine, it's me. Can I come in?"

God, Lawrence! She leaned against the door and tried to catch her breath. She felt as if she had been running uphill. Her heart was crashing against her ribs. Her hand slipped over the knob, and it was a moment before she could grip it firmly enough to open the door.

10

"May I come in?" Lawrence Stern stood in the light flaring over the porch, the black night banked around him. He looked a little older than she remembered, Catherine thought. The frown lines a little deeper, the tiny red veins in his face a little more noticeable, the strands of gray in his dark hair more obvious. But then, she always remembered Lawrence as he was when she'd fallen in love with him almost eight years ago. Thirty-three years old then, tall and handsome, as polished as the handcrafted shoes he wore, striding into a restaurant or theater — anyplace they went, even the zoo — with square-shouldered confidence. He had set self-imposed limits back then: no more than one cocktail and two glasses of wine at dinner.

"Catherine?"

"Sorry." She shoved the door open and moved aside. "I wasn't expecting anyone."

Lawrence strode into the living room — hand-tailored striped shirt and expensive trousers and hundred-dollar haircut. "What's with the lamp?" He nodded at the crystal lamp she was gripping with one hand, the shade pitched sideways, the cord strung along the floor.

"You scared me, Lawrence." Catherine slammed the door shut.

He walked over, took the lamp out of her hand and set it on the chest next to the door. "I thought you might like a little company," he said. She felt the slight pressure of his arms around her, drawing her close. His breath smelled minty, traces of whiskey odors breaking through. She leaned into his chest and slipped her own arms around his waist. It was familiar, the safety of his arms.

She had to force herself to step back and look away from the hard set of his jaw and the disappointment in his eyes. She was a little wobbly, the living room moving about her. "Gilly stocked the fridge," she said, making her way past him into the kitchen. "Hungry?"

"Starved," he said. Even the tread of his footsteps behind her was familiar.

They ate in the dining room, a rectangular

space at the far end of the living room, connected to the kitchen through a hallway lined with cabinets and counters, what Lawrence called the "butler's pantry." There were butlers in the guest cottage in the old days. Lawrence had found a pair of bronze-colored place mats somewhere and arranged them on the mahogany table. He had set the table with the china and the silver from the credenza that stood against the dining room wall. He had restarted Gershwin, "American in Paris."

"All this for roasted chicken?" Catherine placed the plate of chicken and a bowl of couscous she'd found in the refrigerator in the center of the table.

"I'd say this calls for a celebration," Lawrence said. He was extracting the cork from another bottle of Chardonnay. He filled two wineglasses at the credenza and handed her one across the table.

"Celebration? What are we celebrating?"

"You're here again. We're at the cottage together." He lifted the glass in a toast. "Here's to old times."

Catherine rolled the stem of the glass between her fingers. "Lawrence . . ."

"Drink up." He saluted her.

"The old times are gone."

"But they were good, weren't they? We

have some good memories. Let's drink to those."

Catherine hesitated. Then she held out the glass. "To the good memories." She took the smallest sip, enough to taste the wine on her lips. She was already drunk. She put the glass on the table and sat down.

"Any word from Detective Bustamante?" Lawrence settled himself across from her and sipped at his wine.

"Not since this morning," she said, shoving the chicken and couscous in his direction.

"He came to see me."

This was interesting. She watched Lawrence help himself to pieces of chicken, a couple of spoonfuls of couscous. Detective Bustamante was working the concentric circle theory: start with the closest people and work out to neighbors, acquaintances, and, finally, strangers. *Most crimes are solved in the inner circles.* She could hear his voice in her head, and her own protests. *Lawrence and I parted on good terms.*

"Asked a lot of questions. Why we got a divorce, that sort of thing. Started me thinking, why the hell did we get a divorce?" Lawrence picked up his knife and fork and sliced absentmindedly at the chicken. "I think about you all the time," he said. "Now your divorce lawyer shot! Ironic, wouldn't you say?"

Catherine slid a piece of chicken onto her own plate, then took a little of the couscous. She felt light-headed and queasy from the wine and the adrenaline that had been pumping all day. The drift of the conversation made her feel even more uneasy. She stopped herself from reminding Lawrence of the reason for the divorce: the secretary that one of Catherine's friends had spotted him having dinner with at the Brown Palace; the other affairs that she'd suspected and that he'd finally admitted one Saturday night after a charity event, when he'd been drunk enough to think he should start confessing.

"Look, I know I didn't play by all the rules." Lawrence lifted his glass again and held it out in a mock toast. He had a crooked smile that had always made her heart turn over. "What I did was wrong and unfair to you, plain and simple. It never meant I didn't love you. You know that, don't you?"

"Let it be," Catherine said. "We've both gone on." She had never blamed him, not totally. He had wanted children. One of the first questions he had asked her — their second date, dinner at a trendy east Denver restaurant that didn't exist anymore — was if she wanted a family. She'd been focused on her career, the stories about the comings and goings of Denver's social elite that appeared in the *Journal* every other day under her byline. She had been hoping for a position as an investigative journalist. She hadn't thought much about a family. "Maybe someday," she'd told him.

But for Lawrence, having a son was his duty. There had been four generations of Stern sons to run the family's businesses and carry on the family name in Colorado. Lawrence's job was to produce the fifth. In the six years of their marriage, there had been only two pregnancies, and both had bled out of her, leaving her feeling depleted and inadequate, as if his grandmother were right: Catherine McLeod wasn't quite up to the Stern standards. The lost babies clamored in the empty space that had opened between them. If they had lived, everything would have been different. How many times she had told herself that.

Lawrence was quiet. He poured himself another glass of wine, took a long sip, then a bite of chicken, giving her time, she realized. Finally, he said, "I'm worried about you. Some nut out there tried to kill you. I suppose that's the risk journalists take. You know, kill the messenger."

"Not really," she said. And yet, she knew it was the truth. She told him she had been reading through a month of stories, looking for something that might have brought last night's intruder.

"The ex-state treasurer?" Lawrence opened his eyes wide. He set his fork down and clasped his hands over his plate. "The bastard got what he deserved," he said. His voice was streaked with vehemence. Public office was a sacred trust in the Stern family. Lawrence's great-grandfather had been one of the first senators from the new state of Colorado. His father had been serving his second term in the Senate when he'd had the heart attack that killed him and left Lawrence, only a few months out of Princeton, virtually an orphan. His parents had divorced when he was still in prep school; his mother had married a man who'd made millions in fiber optics and moved to Scottsdale. His father's death had also left Lawrence in charge of the family businesses — the real estate, the cattle ranches, the stock investments. Elizabeth Stern had never doubted his ability. He was a Stern, after all, and encoded in the DNA was the ability to carry on in the family's interests. She had given him total control.

"You were the reporter who got onto the story first. He could blame you."

"He's in prison," Catherine said. She gave a dismissive shrug.

"So nobody in prison ever ordered a revenge hit on somebody outside?"

"The *Mirror* went at him as hard as we did. Nobody's burst into Dennis Newcomb's home." Catherine took another drink of the Chardonnay. The warmth spread through her; her hands felt tingly. The tension had leaked out of her muscles. "It has something to do with the articles on Sand Creek," she said, surprised at the insistency in her voice, as if she were certain of the truth when she wasn't certain at all.

"Sand Creek took place . . ." Lawrence hesitated. "In 1860 . . ."

"November 29, 1864."

"Ah, you've been doing your research, all right."

"The Arapahos and Cheyennes held a rally this afternoon on undeveloped land out by the airport. They intend to build a casino there."

Lawrence was looking at her. When he didn't say anything, she went on: "They claim that Sand Creek was an act of genocide that negates the reparations paid more than forty years ago and that Congress should return their Colorado lands. At first they were talking about tribal ranches. Now they're willing to settle the land claims for five hundred acres and a casino." She waited a moment. "That's the next story I intend to write."

He looked genuinely worried now. "Maybe you should back off for a while, stop working. If it's money . . ."

She held up her hand. "You don't understand, Lawrence. I have to work. I have to stay in control of some part of my life." She threw a glance toward the kitchen and the living room. Last night she had been in her own townhome. Now she was in a cottage in the mountains behind an iron gate with an armed guard.

She got to her feet, stacked her plate — she'd only managed a few bites — on top of Lawrence's empty plate, and carried them into the kitchen. She still felt light-headed; her legs were wobbly. She was rinsing the plates in the sink when she felt the warmth of Lawrence's arms encircling her waist.

"Let me take care of you, Catherine." He was turning her toward him, and she was helpless to stop the motion. "At least until this is all over."

"No, Lawrence." She wanted to explain that it wasn't necessary; the argument was forming in her mind, the words fitting themselves into place, but he was kissing her, holding her so close her own breath stopped in her lungs, as if he were breathing for both of them. She wanted to pull away, and yet she couldn't seem to summon the strength. "We shouldn't do this," she managed. The protest sounded so feeble she wanted to laugh. She was kissing him back, melting into him, conscious of her nipples responding to the touch of his hands. It was as if time had folded back on itself and everything was the way it had been before. There was no divorce, no stumbling through the last year, no town house where she lived alone, and no bastard bursting through the door. There was no Maury and his friends and her weak attempts to fit into another life. There was only Lawrence, the man she loved, who was kissing her and leading her through the living room. Then they were fumbling their way down the darkened hallway and into the master bedroom.

A telephone was ringing, loud and persistent, breaking through the blackness. Catherine fought her way out of an ocean of sleep and flung her arm across the table next to the bed. There was the sound of something skittering across the floor. She gripped the cold metal of her cell. Rex pushed his wet nose into her neck as she struggled to sit up. "Hello," she muttered.

"You got your interview." The voice was familiar. Still it took her a moment to register that it belonged to Norman White-horse.

"What?" Lawrence's side of the bed was empty; the comforter rolled back. The imprint of his head was still on the pillow. She looked for the alarm clock, then realized that she had knocked it off the table.

"Peter Arcott. You still want the interview?"

"Yes, of course," she said. She felt herself snap back into her own life — the life she had now. It seemed right somehow that Lawrence was no longer beside her. She'd had a story to write last night, and now she wouldn't turn it in until sometime today. But an interview with Arcott would flesh out the story on the rally and scoop whatever Newcomb had written in today's *Mirror.*

"He'll see you at four o'clock, his office. Equitable Building on Seventeenth Street." He swallowed the suite number, and she had to ask him to repeat it. She was fumbling in the night stand drawer for a pen and something to write on.

165

"Arcott operates on white time," White-horse said.

"Meaning?"

"He'll expect you on time."

"Has he talked to anyone else?"

"He doesn't like interviews. He's very reclusive. He likes to conduct his business in private."

"How did you manage . . ."

"You ask a lot of questions for an Arapaho." Then he was gone, the cell a dead thing in her hand. Norman Whitehorse was the only person who had ever called her an Arapaho.

She got out of bed, wrapped herself in an old terrycloth robe that belonged to Lawrence, and went down the hallway looking for him. Rex stayed at her heels, his nails tapping the floor. Lawrence would be in the kitchen, reading a copy of the *Journal* that Gilly would have delivered. The air was filled with the odor of fresh, hot coffee. She let Rex out the front door, then she crossed the living room into the kitchen. There was no sign of Lawrence. The glass coffeepot was almost full.

She poured a mug of coffee and checked the clock on the stove: my God, almost nine o'clock. Of course Lawrence had left for the office. He liked to arrive before the rest of the staff. It was his quiet time, he used to say. The only time he could get some work done.

It was then that her eyes fell on the piece of paper and the thick white envelope at the end of the counter. They hadn't been there last night. Sipping at the hot coffee, she moved along the counter. She spread open the folded paper with one hand and stared at the black words scrawled across the center. She would recognize Lawrence's handwriting anywhere, the odd way that he liked to capitalize important words:

Remember that I Love You.

She set down the mug, picked up the thick envelope, and ran one finger under the sealed flap. She regretted opening the envelope the minute she'd pulled back the flap It was filled with bills, a lot of money. More than a thousand. Five thousand perhaps, maybe ten, and it made her complicit with Lawrence's offer to look after her. Last night was fuzzy; she'd been weak and more than a little drunk and scared. Yes, she was scared, but this wasn't what she wanted. Not this money that she had *taken,* that she held in her hand.

She had the sinking feeling there was more to it than that. If Lawrence had left ten thousand dollars, then he must believe she should stay in hiding for a long time. She shouldn't continue writing for the *Journal*. Maybe she should go somewhere else; with ten thousand dollars cash she could disappear in Phoenix or Los Angeles without ever tapping into her own funds and possibly leaving a trail for Erik. She could be just another face among hordes of people. And when the cash ran short, she could call Lawrence for more.

The realization hit her like a slap in the face. Her situation could be worse than she had allowed herself to imagine.

She went back into the bedroom, pulled on a pair of blue shorts and a tee shirt and her running shoes. Then she retraced her steps to the front door and stepped onto the porch. Before she could call for him, Rex bounded through the pines that stood on the other side of the clearing in front of the cottage.

They started running, a slow lope around the side of the cottage with Rex alongside her. There was an opening in the trees, and she could see the log fence bending through the brush. A brown sedan crawled along the road on the other side of the fence, raising puffs of gray dust. Her heart gave a little lurch. She slowed down and let her eyes follow the sedan until the road wound out of sight behind the stand of trees. No one knew she was here, she told herself. No one that she'd written about. Yet there had been the dark sedan on the road to the ranch yesterday. She'd spotted it every time she'd come around a turn — far below, climbing up the road behind her.

It was ridiculous. How many brown sedans were there in the Denver area? Thousands? So what if one had been on the road yesterday or driving past the ranch this morning? It meant nothing. She broke into an all-out run and the dog sprinted ahead. She knew the trail — she and Lawrence had begun almost every weekend morning at the ranch with a two-mile run. The trail curved at the edge of the trees for a quarter mile, then rose into the trees in a steady uphill climb that started to narrow. The branches scratched at Catherine's arms. The air was hot and dry; her nostrils filled with the smell of pines. Familiar, all of it. She stumbled on a rock and kept going, trying to plot the way ahead. And wasn't that like life, she thought. Stumble and keep going, plot the way ahead?

She was breathing hard when she came out of the trees into a meadow near the top of the mountain, but it was cooler here. Rex was already chasing a wild rabbit that bounded this way and that, as if it were a game the rabbit felt confident of winning. She slowed down and walked toward the dog. The peaks of Mount Stern, named for Lawrence's great-grandfather, lifted above her, steep, bare rock with gullies of last winter's snow. White clouds streamed below the peaks, bifurcating the mountain slopes. They were alone here, she and Rex, and the realization gave her a sense of freedom and determination. She would spend the morning reading through her notes on the rally and writing a rough draft of the story. Then she would drive into downtown Denver and interview Peter Arcott. Tonight she'd finish the story — who knew what twist might come from the interview — and e-mail it into the copy desk at the *Journal.* She would go on.

She swung back across the meadow, calling Rex over one shoulder. It was a moment before he caught up, but then he ran ahead down the narrow path through the trees. She jogged after him, keeping a steady pace until she emerged from the trees into the open stretches of wild grasses around the ranch buildings. She was almost at the cottage — Rex already on the front porch — when the green SUV came down the road alongside the creek. The engine thrummed into the quiet. It swung right, bounced across the log bridge, and skidded to a stop a few feet from her.

The door flew open and Elizabeth Stern stepped out. She was one of those small women who seemed much larger, dressed in white slacks and a blue blouse with silver buttons down the front that glistened in the morning sun. She wore a wide-brimmed tan straw hat that covered most of her curly, reddish hair and threw a shadow across the top part of her face. Her lips were parted in a frozen smile.

"Hello, Catherine," she said. "Lawrence told me you were visiting."

"It's nice to see you again," Catherine heard herself saying. God, if she never saw Elizabeth Stern again it would suit her fine. "Rex and I have just had a run up to the meadow."

"Yes. Well, I'm sure it must seem good to get away after all your trouble."

"The police are investigating," Catherine said. Then she added, "I'm sure it will be over soon."

"Oh, yes. I'm sure it will be. A dreadful experience, no doubt. Wasn't that the lawyer who represented you in the divorce who was shot?"

"Yes."

"I see. Well, he was at your home very late at night."

Catherine didn't say anything. The news stories had explained why Maury came to her home. In any case, what did the woman expect? That she should remain faithful to the man who had divorced her? She wondered what Elizabeth Stern would think if she knew that she and Lawrence had spent last night together.

"I was surprised, I must admit," Elizabeth said.

"About the shooting?"

"That Lawrence invited you here. Of course, he is free to do as he chooses, but I did wonder what Heather might think about Lawrence's ex-wife staying in the cottage."

"I don't understand," Catherine said, but a part of her was beginning to understand. It was like a light slowly turning on in her head. Lawrence hadn't mentioned that he was currently involved with someone else, but then, he had never mentioned the other women.

"Heather Montgomery, his fiancée. It did cross my mind that she might not approve."

Fiancée! The word hit her with the sharp impact of a stone. She recognized the name. Heather's father was a telecommunications billionaire.

"Oh, I'm sure he told you about her," Elizabeth went on, and Catherine knew that *she* knew Lawrence hadn't said anything about his fiancée. "The engagement will be announced in Sunday's *Journal.* The wedding will be September fourteenth."

Catherine turned around and walked over to the cottage. Elizabeth Stern was talking about the reception that would be held at the Denver Country Club when she slammed the door.

11

The Stern Ranch was dense with pines, boulders, and brush penetrated by columns of morning sunlight. Erik had taken the dirt road that looped around the ranch twice last evening before he'd located a funnel through the trees that offered a view of the front door of the guest cottage. He'd parked in a square of meadow across the road and watched the cottage. What he'd seen was unexpected. A gentleman caller, none other than Lawrence Stern the third or something, checking up on his ex-wife. He'd watched until the lights had dimmed in the windows and finally flickered out. A couple of hours, long enough for cocktails and dinner.

He'd gotten a good laugh at what must have come next. He had done his research on Lawrence Stern. Secretaries were such an excellent source. They knew everything about the boss. A few drinks at a bar with a

174

handsome stranger interested in their lives, and they told what they knew. Catherine McLeod either didn't know her ex was engaged to somebody else, or she knew but didn't care. Either way, she seemed more complex and interesting. If she didn't know, it was because she hadn't wanted to know. Whatever was going on in her ex's life hadn't been important enough for her to investigate, which meant she investigated only the subjects she cared about. And once she started, she didn't stop until she had the full story. Erik had read everything she'd written over the last six months. She'd closed down daycare centers. She'd sent the state treasurer to prison.

On the other hand, it was likely she had heard about Lawrence's fiancée and didn't care, and that told him something else. She wasn't as tough as she wanted people to think. She was scared. The little scenario that had played out at her town house had scared her to death and sent her running to the ranch where she had jumped into bed with a man — it could have been any man, he was thinking — who might protect her. This scenario made her seem more vulnerable and helpless, more likely to kick logic aside and act on emotional impulses. He would have to watch her carefully, be prepared for anything. He felt as if he'd found himself facing an unstable opponent in a poker game, one who might jump up and turn the table over and spill the cards across the floor.

He had driven back down the mountain and spent the night in a flat-roofed motel that sloped downhill on the outskirts of Conifer, with red neon lights blinking Vacancy over the dirt parking lot and a few pickups nosed toward the doors along the front of the building. He'd handed forty-eight dollars to the fat man behind the counter who reeked of tobacco and perspiration, and the fat man had pushed a register toward him. It was the kind of place where nobody cared what name you signed — pick your name tonight — but on the other hand, Erik was careful. The name couldn't be obvious. No John Does or Smiths. Nothing that might call out to the fat man, should he get bored with television and decide to read the register, and stick in his memory. He'd signed Matthew Arnold, figuring the fat man wouldn't get it. Inside the seedy room that reeked of cigarette smoke, stale food, and urine, he'd called Deborah, assured her that the business was going well. He would conclude it tomorrow morning and be home by dinner. "Kiss the kids good night for me," he'd said. "A kiss to you, too, sweetheart."

It was starting to get light, the sky in the east layered in crimson and gold, when he had gotten back into the brown sedan and climbed up the mountain. A pair of hawks glided along the high peaks. He'd driven slowly, stopping at the turnouts to study the terrain and the road falling away below. The highway threaded through the canyon, a strip of silvery asphalt in thc half light with a thin line of vehicles flashing past, yellow headlights wobbling ahead. A bridge crossed the highway and bent into the entrance to the eastbound lane. By the time he had parked in the meadow and settled down to wait, he knew how it would come down. Catherine McLeod wouldn't remain at the ranch all day; she was bound to leave. She'd start out for Denver, intending to go to the hospital again, check in at the newspaper, pursue her foolish story, because that was the type of woman she was. An actress playing out her role, choking back her fears.

The air was cool; the outside temperature on the dashboard said fifty-eight degrees. He opened the thermos he'd filled yesterday and sipped at the coffee that was about the same temperature as the air. There was no sign of movement at the guest cottage. The faint morning light shone in the windows.

Waiting is the most important part of the job. He could almost hear the voice of Colonel Walter Blum, as if the man were in the backseat, leaning over his shoulder. *Waiting takes patience. Patience is everything.* How many hours had Blum waited to take out the Viet Cong sniper in 'Nam? Something like forty-eight. Living on drops of water and hardtack and snails, waiting for the sniper to show himself. The bastard had been picking off American patrols. A couple here, a couple there, before he melted back into the jungle. Blum had figured out the area the sniper liked best and had settled in to wait. He'd spotted him coming through the trees, a little guy in baggy black pants and black blouse, rifle slung over one shoulder. Blum had waited until he'd stopped and taken up his shooting position, then he'd walked up behind him and blown his head off.

Walked up behind him, and the gook hadn't heard a thing. But he was good, Blum. One of the best instructors at Yellow Jacket. The place looked like a real college campus three miles outside of a crummy little town in Florida, with buildings and training grounds that sprawled across a filled-in swamp. He'd heard that the town

178

fathers had actually raised the money to fill in the swamp and convinced the founders of Yellow Jacket — three retired Army generals — to build the private training camp close enough to town that the students could spend their money on the crappy restaurants and one-picture movie theater, and far enough away that the town fathers could claim they had no idea what went on at the camp.

Yellow Jacket taught men to kill. There were a few women at the academy, but most of the students were men. "Soldiers of fortune," was how Blum used to refer to them. The term sounded better than "mercenaries," and their skills brought a high price. Erik had earned six hundred dollars a day stalking and killing insurgents in Iraq. The money beat the hell out of what he'd earned in the Army, but it was the Army where he had learned to shoot. Yellow Jacket had just perfected his skills. When he'd gotten out of the Army, one of his Army buddies had called. It had been the middle of the night, Erik remembered, and he had been sound asleep. The ringing phone had pissed him off. He'd been about to tell the guy to go to hell, when he'd mentioned money. Lots of it for doing what he was good at — shooting people. A few months training, getting even better, then time in Iraq as part of a security detail for visiting dignitaries, paid for by the government, and money in the bank, old buddy. Money in the bank.

There were other jobs that came in. Discreet phone calls similar to the discreet ads placed in certain types of magazines. But there was always risk with an advertisement. Any undercover federal agent might answer an ad. On the other hand, a phone call to certain instructors at Yellow Jacket would net the best-trained candidate for the job. Experienced. Professional. Must be willing to travel. Fifty thousand dollars.

Blum had given him the first job a month after he'd returned from Iraq. He wasn't looking forward to going back. He worried about Deborah and the kids. What good was six hundred bucks a day if he was dead? He'd been looking for something else when Blum arranged a meeting at a diner in the crummy town and told him that a Dallas businessman had a domestic problem he wanted solved. Seems his wife liked the next-door neighbor better than she liked him. "Go to Dallas. Follow the neighbor around for a while. Learn his habits. Where he goes to dinner, gets his hair styled, plays golf. Get the layout of the country club he belongs to." He would blend right in, Blum had said. He was the type of man that different people would describe differently, depending upon the moment or the situation where they had seen him. Dark hair, blond, muscular, a little overweight, trim and in shape. Educated and refined, scruffy and hard. Arrogant, friendly. "These kinds of jobs take a chameleon like you," he'd said.

The Dallas job had been easy. Four days of following the bastard around and waiting.

The next job had been in Los Angeles, followed by jobs in Salt Lake City, Evanston, Illinois, St. Louis, and Baltimore. No job the same, all of them interesting, and all of them solving a problem for somebody with a lot of cash. Erik had watched his account in the Cayman Islands climb to a quarter of a million dollars. He had just finished the job in El Paso when Blum had called with the Denver job.

He'd been waiting more than two hours — the coffee gone, his stomach growling, and the temperature rising — when the front door of the cottage opened and Lawrence Stern came outside. He stood in the sunlight on the porch a moment, hands jammed into the pockets of a gray jacket that hung open, glanced around, taking in the ranch, savoring the quiet expanse of it, Erik thought. *All this land, and all of it mine.* God, what was it like to be Lawrence Stern III?

Stern's BMW growled into life, disappeared beyond the trees for a few minutes, then emerged on the dirt road past the gate. It swung east and started into the downhill curves. From the meadow, Erik watched the taillights of the BMW glowing red through the puffs of gray dust.

He waited almost an hour. Sunlight began to penetrate the trees and splash over the meadow. It started to get hot inside the sedan, and he rolled down the front windows. A squirrel or a chipmunk was chattering somewhere nearby. The breeze ruffled the pages of the newspaper on the seat beside him. Beneath the newspaper was the Sig.

The front door of the cottage opened and the dog bounded outside. There was a glimpse of her in the doorway, sleepy and ruffled looking, in a flimsy, short nightgown that the breeze blew around her legs. What he had to do was unfortunate. A woman with a great body like that. He shoved the thought back into the shadows of his mind. He wasn't paid to think about such things.

Too much thinking led to pity, and pity wasn't an emotion he allowed himself to feel. He'd made a mistake the other night. He wouldn't make a mistake again.

The door cracked shut in the mountain quiet; the dog raced into the trees, then circled back onto the driveway, skidded in the gravel, and headed for the trees again. A beautiful creature, he thought, a free thing with no plans or commitments or worries, absorbed in the exhilaration of being alive. "You should be like that," he said out loud, and wondered if he were talking to himself or to the woman inside the cottage.

Here she was again, in blue shorts and white tee shirt, the black hair tucked up into a baseball cap that shaded part of her face. She spent a couple of moments stretching, leaning over and touching the toes of her white running shoes. "Rex," she called. Her voice sounded like the muffled chime of a bell through the trees. The dog leapt across the driveway, and they took off running. Erik watched until they disappeared around the corner of the cottage, the dog darting in and out of the trees along the path.

Erik nosed the sedan across the mossy undergrowth of the meadow and onto the dirt road. He drove carefully, keeping an eye on the thick junipers and ponderosas that ran between the road and the ranch itself. The log fence darted toward the road here and there before losing itself in the tangle of trees and brush. He could see the white shoes flashing through the trees and hear the faint sounds of her running, as if she were running a long ways away.

He could drive ahead, locate a clearing from which he could get off a good shot, and wait for her to run into his line of sight. But he would not do that. He had spotted the cameras mounted on telephone poles when he'd taken the road this morning. The ranch was monitored. Somebody could be watching her. If she went down, a posse of cowboys would be bouncing overland in SUVs. There was only one road down the mountain, and the SUVs would catch him before he could reach the highway. In any case, he had learned at Yellow Jacket to make a good plan and stick with it. A plan considered all possibilities, allowed for the unexpected, and mapped out escape routes ahead of time.

He had deviated from the plan at her town house. He had intended to shoot her while she was out walking the dog, but he'd gotten greedy. He'd wanted more. He'd decided to allow her to return home. He would break into the house and take his time with her. In an instant, he had convinced himself that it was the better plan. It would appear to be the random rape and murder of a single woman alone in her townhome. He had deviated again when her friend arrived. He'd burst through the door, furious that she'd called someone and thrown a monkey wrench into his plan. He'd been consumed with shooting them both and getting the job over. But she had eluded him in the shadows somewhere in the living room, and the sirens had started screaming outside. He had fallen back on the original plan that he'd mapped out on how to make his escape, which he had done through the backyards of the townhomes to the sedan that he'd left in an alley.

She spotted the sedan, he was certain, as she ran past a brush-studded opening between the trees. He saw her head pivot about to get a better look in the instant before he pressed hard on the accelerator and shot ahead, throwing up a wave of dust in the road behind. He kept going, circling the ranch and parking in a spot across from the gate, not wanting to take the chance that she might spot him again and grow suspicious. She was wary, this one. He had learned that about her. She had instincts.

He had been parked for five minutes when

he saw that the ranch was coming alive, waking up. The caretaker slammed out of the cottage near the gate and jumped into a Jeep with a roll bar across the top. The Jeep swung into a U-turn and ground down the road toward the main house where an SUV was backing out of the garage. The two vehicles stopped side by side for a moment — he could see the caretaker leaning over the passenger seat to speak to whoever was under the wide-brimmed straw hat in the driver's seat of the SUV. Then the Jeep spurted past the house and into the vastness of the ranch.

The SUV took its time — backing up, inching forward, and backing up again until it was in the center of the road, heading toward the guest cottage as the dog loped out of the trees. Catherine was close behind, running more slowly, the tee shirt plastered to her skin, as if she had taken a detour through a waterfall. The sight of the SUV took her by surprise because she stopped in mid-step, one foot poised for an instant in the air. Then she seemed to collect herself. She threw her shoulders back and walked over to the woman who had gotten out of the SUV.

Erik pulled a small pair of binoculars out of the glove compartment and focused on the woman. A fringe of red hair poking from the straw hat, eyes hidden behind rounded sunglasses, the skin stretched smooth over sharp cheekbones. An attractive face, no longer young. The jawline was firm, the red painted lips parted in a controlled smile that, he imagined, she had perfected at a thousand gala events. This would be the matriarch of the family, Elizabeth Stern herself, and whatever she was saying caused Catherine to spin around, walk over, and let herself into the cottage. The sound of the door slamming shut rang into the quiet a moment, then the SUV's engine revved, and the vehicle started toward the gate that was already opening. He was able to get a better look at Elizabeth Stern as she drove through the gate and turned onto the downhill road that her grandson had taken two hours ago.

Now he would wait. Something had happened between Catherine and her ex's grandmother. Whatever it was, he had the sense that Catherine would be leaving soon. The way she had stomped away from the SUV, thrown herself into the cottage, as if she had to get away from whatever refuge the ranch was supposed to provide.

Fifteen minutes later, Catherine stomped out of the cottage, pulling a backpack that bounced across the dirt road, black bags hanging off her shoulder, a brown paper bag clutched against her. She'd flung most of it into the trunk and let Rex into the backseat.

Erik turned the ignition. The engine coughed itself awake, and he drove onto the road and started down the mountain. He kept his foot steady on the accelerator, both hands holding the wheel as he turned through the switchbacks. He could feel the rear tires skidding, his own adrenaline pumping, every muscle tensed. He dropped through the last turn and came out on a straight road that ran toward the metal bridge sparkling in the sun ahead.

He drove fast onto the bridge, the tires clumping over the metal slats, then slowed into the entrance to the highway. It was a long entrance that ran downhill a quarter of a mile then gradually flattened into the outside lane. But before the entrance joined the highway — and here was the beauty of the plan he'd formed this morning — it ran past a triangular expanse of bare dirt. Erik tapped on the brake, swung left onto the dirt, and stopped. He left the engine running and slipped the Sig out from beneath the newspaper. Holding it low, he checked to make sure that the silencer was fitted on tight.

The traffic moving toward Denver was heavy, the end of the morning rush hour into the city from the mountain suburbs. There was safety in numbers, he thought, many witnesses always better than one. The motorists passing at the exact moment would all see something different. They would contradict one another, wonder if they had seen what they had actually seen, doubt their own stories, reshape them to fit into what surely must have taken place. By the time the police had sorted through it all, he would be on a plane home, sipping a bourbon and mapping out a tentative plan for the next job.

From where he was parked, he had a clear view across the highway of the road climbing the mountainside. The silver convertible was already in the second switchback. She was driving fast, eager to get away, he thought, rushing toward her destiny. Behind her was a white van with black lettering on the panels. Some kind of service van that kept the appliances and televisions working at the secluded ranches of Denver's oldest families. The van seemed to be crowding her, riding her rear bumper. Another confused witness, in shock and unsure of anything he saw.

He had to smile at the sight of the vehicles

coming down the mountainside, jostling for the road, intent on whatever occupied their thoughts, as if any of it mattered.

12

Catherine pressed down on the accelerator, driving as fast as she dared. In fifteen minutes, she had showered, thrown her things into the backpack, grabbed her laptop and bag. She'd picked up the envelope stuffed with ten thousand dollars, then let it drop. It had thudded against the counter, a thing of consequence. She picked it up again and put it into her bag. She'd set the bag on the front seat and thrown everything else into the trunk. And now the cans of dog food were banging together. Rex had settled into his favorite position in the back-seat, resting his head next to her shoulder. She drove in and out of the sunshine and shadows that striped the road. So this was the way it felt to break out of prison, she thought. Every part of her consumed with the single goal of escaping.

She steered the convertible through an-other switchback and glanced at the rearview mirror. A white van had appeared out of nowhere, coming up fast behind her. Sunshine Cable appeared backward in black letters across the top of the windshield. The dark head of the driver rose over the steering wheel. She banked into another tight curve. Outside her window, the mountainside — boulders, dusty brush, and pine trees — rushed toward her. On the other side, the mountain dropped off into space. Her stomach went into summersaults. The van was still in the rearview mirror as she came out of the curve.

She gripped the steering wheel hard. She felt as if she were rappelling down a cliff. One mistake and she would fall into space. The driver could be *him.* A cable repairman with a white van, waiting for the convertible to pull out of the Stern Ranch. Waiting for her. So this was his new plan — nudge her back bumper and send her careening off the road, crashing down into nothingness. She pressed harder on the accelerator. She could feel the chassis bucking, the wheels skittering.

A coldness gripped her, icy hands moving over her skin. She was aware of the sound of her own breathing, raspy and quick. She turned through a switchback, then another. Still the van in the rearview mirror, the driver — Erik — playing with her, waiting for the right moment. When would it come? The next turn? Her fingers locked around the steering wheel. The road was dropping fast. The faint roar of morning traffic rose from the highway below.

And then the road began to level out across the meadow that divided the highway from the mountainside. She pulled to the right, hoping the van would pass, that it wasn't Erik at the wheel. But the van stayed no more than a couple of feet behind.

Then she understood: the way he tilted his head and stared through the windshield at something other than the road. He was talking on a cell phone attached to the dashboard. This wasn't Erik. This was a cable repairman, checking in with the boss after finishing a job. She tried to relax, but her breath came in shuddering gasps, her fingers stiff around the wheel. A flash of anger moved through the fear. The bastard might have killed her up on the mountain — not paying attention to the road, driving like a fool, engrossed in some stupid conversation.

But that explained only part of the anger, she knew. Would every incident in her life be colored by what had taken place at the town house? Every stranger a possible killer?

Every gas station attendant or waiter, every customer or clerk in a grocery store? Every fool driving down the road? God, what was happening to her life?

She'd been making such headway: building a new career, making new friends. She had gotten over Lawrence; she was going to be fine. Until the night before last, and in an instant — the pop of a gun — everything had changed. Her new life slipping away. Maury clinging to his life in the hospital. The town house and office off-limits. Then Lawrence had appeared again, and this was part of the anger, too. How could she have been so foolish? Falling into his arms, grateful for the smallest sense of the security and comfort she had felt when they were married. Trusting him again. What had she been thinking? That the last year hadn't happened? That she was frozen in time: Mrs. Lawrence Stern III, spending a few days at the family ranch, protected and insulated from a world where someone wanted to kill her.

The tires clattered over the metal overpass that spanned the highway, too narrow for the van to pass. The driver still seemed to be talking, nodding and tilting his head. Catherine could see the disgruntled look on his face; he was arguing with someone. The van wobbled behind her. She came off the overpass and turned left onto the entrance to the highway. Maybe he would pass her here. It was a long entrance that flowed gradually into the outside lane of the highway itself. Between the highway and the entrance was a wide patch of bare ground and — odd, this — a brown sedan parked there. No sign of any trouble. No flat tire. No emergency lights flashing. She was closing on the sedan. The head and shoulders of the driver rose over the front seat.

The driver was waiting.

Catherine pressed the gas pedal to the floor and jerked the steering wheel to the right as the van shot past. And in that instant she heard the sound of glass shattering, tires squealing. The convertible bumped downhill over rocks and brush, clouds of dust rising over the windows. The engine growled, the tires ground into hillocks of dirt. From the highway above came the noise of screeching cars and metal crashing against metal. The seatbelt dug into her chest. She was conscious of Rex on the floor of the front seat, but she had no idea of how he had gotten there.

She managed to ease the convertible into a steady downhill drive, steering around the rocks that poked out of the ground, until

195

she bounced onto the narrow dirt frontage road that ran below the highway. She was shaking. She tightened her hands on the steering wheel to keep them from shaking loose. She felt as if the air had hardened in her lungs; her mouth was like dust.

It was then that she glimpsed the collisions on the highway above: four or five cars scattered over the lanes, spun in different directions, hoods and doors crumpled, windshields smashed. The white van sat sideways in the middle lane, the driver's door hanging open, the driver slumped over the steering wheel. Other cars stopping, and people running toward the van. She had the picture then: The man in the brown sedan had been waiting for her to pull alongside him, but the van had shot ahead. The driver had taken the bullet meant for her, and the van had plunged into the highway traffic.

There was no sign of the brown sedan.

She drove fast along the frontage road. He would know that she had pulled off the entrance. He would know she was on the frontage road, and he would be following her. She spotted the turnoff ahead, and she stepped on the brake pedal and skidded onto the road. Rex had crawled onto the seat and set his muzzle in her lap. She patted his head. "It's okay," she said, but it wasn't okay. She leaned onto the gas pedal and drove upward on a narrow two-track that parted the thick forest. She could feel the tires slipping. In the rearview mirror was nothing except the two-track disappearing past the trees and little clouds of brown dust rolling in the air.

She kept going. The two-track didn't seem to be leading anywhere. There were no signs of homes or ranches, no fences threading the trees. And yet the road had to lead somewhere. A timber camp, perhaps. Still the road could be one of hundreds of old wagon roads that combed the mountains, remnants of the gold rush days. The track was getting rougher, turning into a Jeep road, and she had to slow down to maneuver around the boulders that jutted out of the dirt and threatened the undercarriage of the convertible. She bent into a curve, slammed on the brake, and skidded to a stop. A massive boulder rose ahead, like a piece of cliff broken off in the middle of the track. Pine trees and other boulders crowded close. There was no room to pass.

She started backing down. The road had dissolved in a fog of dust, and she had to twist around and look back to keep the convertible from crashing into a tree. The branch of a ponderosa scraped her arm, and she could feel the warm blood bubbling on her skin. She realized that she had passed a small clearing in the trees. She put the gear into forward, drove into the clearing, and stopped. She left the engine running, rummaged in her bag, and dragged out her cell. Then she went back to rummaging until her fingers found the small, stiff paper of Bustamante's card. She punched in the number. Searching, the readout said. Searching. Searching. The sounds of sirens reverberated around the mountains. And something else: the faintest echo of an engine gearing down. She felt her stomach heave — a dry heave that left her feeling hot and clammy.

Finally, the buzzing noise of a phone at police headquarters, then Bustamante's voice: Detective Bustamante.

"He just tried to kill me." Catherine blurted out the words. She could hear the hysteria in her voice.

"Where are you, Catherine?"

"Do you hear me? He tried to shoot me."

"I hear you. I need you to take a deep breath, try to calm yourself, and tell me where you are."

Catherine gulped at the air, but her lungs had gone hard and inert. She couldn't catch her breath. Rex pushed a cold nose into the palm of her hand. She ran her fingers through his soft fur and managed to tell Bustamante that she was somewhere on a mountainside above Turkey Creek Canyon. She blurted out the rest of it: the brown Ford sedan waiting as she approached the highway, the way she had turned downhill and the white van behind her had shot ahead, the sound of a gunshot, the vehicles colliding on the highway.

"Hold on a minute." His voice was so calm that she wondered if he'd heard anything she'd said. Her chest still felt tight, and her breathing came in shallow, raspy gasps. The cell seemed lifeless in her hand. She was aware of the weight of the dog's head against her thigh. Her heart was doing pirouettes in her chest.

Then Bustamante's voice again, igniting the cell back into life. "State Patrol report is just coming in of a multicar accident on Highway 285, east of Conifer. Looks like one fatality, possibly two. Several people injured. Emergency vehicles are responding now. What kind of car was he driving?"

"I don't know. Brown sedan. Ford, I think. It was nondescript. What difference does it make? He's coming after me."

"Try to tell me exactly where you are."

"I'm at the dead end of a two-track road

199

up the mountain from the frontage road. I don't know where I am!"

"I'll notify the state patrol. They'll send an officer."

"I'll be dead by then. I have to get out of here now." A barrage of ideas tumbled in her head. She could take off walking, she and Rex. They could walk east through the forest for a distance, then downhill to the frontage road. Someone would come by, give them a lift into Denver.

The brown sedan could come by.

"He's looking for me," she said. "He could be waiting somewhere on 285. He could be on the frontage road." She was thinking that she had passed a road before she'd realized that she had to take the next one. Erik would assume she had taken the first road, which meant that he was searching on the mountain slope to the west.

"Okay." Bustamante's voice again. "I've pulled up a map of the area. A few miles east of the collision, there's a road that loops east and connects to Highway 470. You can get it from the frontage road."

"Are you listening to me? He could be waiting on the frontage road."

"I'm notifying the state patrol now to detain the driver of any brown Ford sedan on the frontage road or stopped along the highway. The road is not more than a few miles from you. You've got a chance. I'd advise you to take it."

God. When Erik didn't find her on the first road up the mountain, he'd check the next one. She only had minutes before he drove up here, and she would be trapped.

"I'm on my way to the scene now. I want to see you at police headquarters this afternoon. I'll be waiting for you," Bustamante was saying when she pressed the end key and tossed the cell onto the dashboard. She hunched forward and ran her hands along Rex's flanks and legs. Nothing seemed to be broken. Then she buried her face in his soft fur, a jumble of sensations colliding around her: the weight of tears behind her eyes, the damp sheath of perspiration between her and the dog, the steady thump of his heartbeat.

She pulled herself upright, mopped at the moisture on her cheeks, and backed out onto the road. Then she started downhill, gripping the steering wheel hard, half expecting the brown sedan to appear around the next curve. The rear end shimmied sideways, the tires skidded on the dirt. Through the trees, she could see the empty sections of the frontage road below. Another couple of curves and she was down the mountain. She tapped on the brake as she approached the turnout, scanning the road in both directions. There was no sign of the brown sedan.

She turned onto the frontage road, pressed down on the gas pedal, and drove for the road that Bustamante had said was no more than a few miles ahead. She saw it then, the green sign with white letters that said: Highway 470 Next Right. She slowed into the turn and started winding down a mountain — wide, gentle turns that gave onto occasional views of Denver in the distance, hazy in the heat, and beyond, the sweep of the plains. Still she kept glancing in the rearview mirror. No cars behind her, no sign of the brown sedan. Bustamante was right; this was her chance.

A new realization started over her, like a slow fever. This wasn't about any article she had written. Newcomb and the TV reporters had covered the same stories, but she was the only one targeted by a killer. That brought her back to the questions Bustamante had asked about her personal life. Lawrence? Lawrence had tried to help her; given her ten thousand dollars to help her hide from a killer. She tried to shake away the notion that he could be a killer himself; it made no sense. Still, he'd left the ranch ahead of her; he could have waited for her to come down the mountain, cross the overpass, and turn onto the highway entrance.

The notion was crazy. It defied everything she believed true, contradicted her sense of reality. She forced her thoughts to loop back to her work. There was the Sand Creek story — two articles so far, a story told by the elders about a hundred-and-fifty-year-old massacre combined with history she'd culled out of library books that had been available for years.

The casino was news. But she hadn't yet written the story. She had missed the deadline for today's *Journal,* and the story wouldn't appear until tomorrow. In any case, the story was probably all over last night's news, and Dennis Newcomb would have made certain it was on the front page of this morning's *Mirror.* He would have covered everything: the rally on the plains, the speeches given by Whitehorse and Arcott, all the details about the proposed casino and hotel.

But the other reporters wouldn't have an interview with Peter Arcott. That would be her exclusive piece of the story, if Whitehorse had been straight with her. She shook her head and blinked into the sunshine. Think.

Sand Creek was the story she was working on now. It was her story. Funny how she always knew that the story belonged to her, as if no other reporter could get it right. There had been other stories that had taken hold of her, demanded that she dig out the facts, refused to give her any peace of mind until she had written them. Stories that had shouted: Important. Sand Creek was that kind of story. It was still unfolding — the casino, the claim of genocide, and an old massacre that the Arapahos and Cheyennes had never forgotten.

Someone didn't want her to write the rest of the story.

She wasn't sure when the road had swung around the flank of the mountain, but she was taking gentle turns that swung out over the silvery highway below. Her thigh was numb from the weight of Rex's head. She nudged him onto the passenger seat with one hand. He settled himself around the bulk of her bag and rested his head on the rim of the door, intent on the trees passing outside.

She took the last curve, turned onto the highway, and drove toward the southern edge of Denver. Traffic was light, a broken string of cars and trucks shimmering in the sun. She felt a strange calmness settling over her, a gathering of forces, every part of her focused on what she had to do to stay alive. She reached for the cell on the dashboard and pressed a couple of keys. Three rings, and Marie's voice floated out of nowhere: "Hello?"

"It's me," Catherine said.

"Oh, darling. Are you all right?"

"I'm okay. Listen, I need to see you right away."

"Of course. I'm right here."

"No. I can't come to the house." *He knows everything about me. He will look for me at the house.* "You know the restaurant on Osage where we used to go?" It had been there for more than one hundred years, the walls sagging with photos and mementos of Denver's history. Her parents used to take her there when she was a little girl. It was like visiting a history museum that served delicious hamburgers.

"My goodness. I haven't been there in years." And that was the point, Catherine was thinking. Erik would never look for her there. "You're scaring me."

Catherine glanced at her watch: 11:14 a.m. "Meet me there in thirty minutes," she said.

13

At nine o'clock that morning, Harry Colbert, administrative assistant to Senator George Russell, knocked on the door to the senator's private office. Without waiting for a response, he stepped inside and stood still, arms at his sides. The brown envelope with the printed report brushed against the pant leg of his navy blue suit. The senator lay sprawled on one of the twin sofas arranged in an L-shape in the far corner. His mouth hung open, his snoring was jerky and erratic. A little line of saliva glistened at the corner of his chin. The comb-over of his dyed brown hair had slipped, revealing slices of pink scalp.

Seventy-two years old, the senator's last birthday, and not on top of things the way he used to be — well, who could keep up with everything these days? Legislative papers and folders littered the surface of his desk across the office. It was doubtful that the senator had made his way through any of them. No matter. It was Colbert's job — and he prided himself on doing it well — to read all the bills, steer the senator onto the floor with instructions on how to vote on anything that might either benefit or harm the senator's constituency. Senator Russell had held on to his seat for almost twenty-three years by casting the votes the way his supporters expected.

And the senator's supporters wielded a great deal of influence in the state. Russell hailed from one of the old Colorado families — the oligarchs, as Russell himself referred to them. There was no hint of irony because, as Colbert understood, the old man believed there was still a place in the modern world for oligarchs who understood what was best for everybody else.

Colbert had boned up on Colorado history when he went to work for the senator halfway through his third term. What he'd learned had impressed him. Ethan Russell, the old man's great-grandfather, had arrived in Denver in the 1860s, after pulling a cart with the entirety of his belongings across the plains by hand. Denver was a collection of tents and log cabins, populated by gold prospectors, saloon keepers, ladies of the night, and refugees from the law and normal society. Ethan decided to give the town its first bank. He organized investors among some of the prospectors who had struck gold, opened the bank in a shop on Larimer Street with a safe in the back that a shop-keeper had hauled across the plains and, rather than haul it back when the shop went under, had left in place. Ethan put up flyers around town urging folks to leave their money with him — in the only safe in town — and soon he had enough deposits to make loans to other prospectors heading into the mountains. When the lucky ones struck gold, Ethan paid small dividends to his depositors and large dividends to himself and his investors. Within ten years, Ethan Russell ran the largest bank between the Mississippi and California. Eventually he moved into the Equitable Building on Seventeenth Street, in which he held a silent partnership, along with John Evans and Le-land Stern, and several other oligarchs.

They controlled Colorado for almost a hundred years — transportation, water, electricity, gas, roads, ranches, farms, most of the land and buildings in downtown Denver, and the best real estate throughout the state. And all that control had impressed Harry Colbert, who had grown up in North Dakota on a pig farm with a mortgage that his father had never been able to pay off. After repossessing the farm, the bank had sold it to a large agribusiness company which had dotted the farmlands with metal buildings the size of football fields, where they raised the pigs. Pig farms, they called the buildings.

After World War II, things changed for the Colorado oligarchs. The state's population began to grow beyond anything the oligarchs could have imagined. They no longer had control. Outside money poured in. Entrepreneurs started new businesses that broke the monopolies of the oligarchs. National corporations built factories that employed the newcomers crowding the new suburbs. Everything happened quickly. The oligarchs found they were no longer the wealthiest families in the state; they no longer owned the politicians; they could no longer run things their way. Colbert had wanted to cheer when he'd reached that part of their history — cheer for the ordinary people like his own family. Still the remnants of the old families tried to hang on, like Senator Russell, still looking out for the people that mattered.

Colbert cleared his throat, then cleared his throat again. The senator was as deaf as a post. Finally he walked over and touched the senator's shoulder. Russell shook himself awake and blinked into the office. Then he smoothed his hair back into place across the pink scalp and shifted upright. "Little cat nap, waiting for you," he said.

Colbert smiled down at the man who thought he could snap his fingers and toss Colbert into the cold when, really, it was the other way around. Russell didn't know that, and that was what made it amusing. It was Colbert who kept the old man's reputation intact, placated the supporters, steered the right legislation forward. Without Colbert working behind the scenes, the old man wouldn't have had a prayer of getting reelected to his fourth term.

He sank onto the middle cushion of the sofa across from the senator. "I'm afraid the casino plan has become public knowledge."

"Spill it." Russell planted the heels of his Ferragamos against the sofa and sat up straight. Every once in a while, he showed the spark of his younger years, a hint of formidability, and Colbert realized that, had he known the senator then, he wouldn't have been the one in charge.

"I'm afraid Norman Whitehorse arranged a rally on the land by the airport. My sources say at least three hundred people, most of them Indians, attended. Norman got up and announced that the tribes intended to settle the land claims for a casino. Arcott spoke on how he was going to make it happen."

"Fools, all of them." Russell spit out the words. "Indians are their own worst enemy. Always have been." He shook his head, and his eyes took on a dreamy look, as if he were watching a movie in his head. "God, my granddad used to say that if those Indians had ever gotten together — instead of fighting one another — they could've whupped all the whites coming onto their lands. History would've told a different story. Why the hell did Arcott get involved?"

Colbert blew some air through his teeth. "Haven't been able to reach him yet. I can guess . . ."

"I don't pay you to guess."

Colbert shrugged. Fair enough. He didn't like this side of Russell, but every once in a while the old man reared his back. An annoying habit left over from the old days that usually passed as quickly as it came on. He was aware of the muffled sound of keyboards in the outer office. "Arcott agrees with Whitehorse that the best defense is offense," he said. He was trying to get into Arcott's viewpoint, see things his way. "They think the public will get behind the

211

casino plan now that the tribes are bringing up the genocide at Sand Creek. People will say, 'Let the Indians have whatever they want. They deserve a casino.' "

"It was your job to prevent any public announcements until we had the matter under control." Russell pushed himself to his feet. "This isn't the time for public rallies. What the hell were you doing?"

"Look, Senator," Colbert began, but Russell's hand sliced the air.

"Don't give me excuses. You said Norman Whitehorse was on board with our plans."

"I'm not the first person to lose control of the Indians." Colbert tried for a joking tone, but he could feel the burning in his chest. He had only a handful of people in the Denver office, most of them just out of college and starry-eyed about making a difference in politics, whatever the hell that meant. And how were they expected to handle a bunch of damn Indians with their own ideas on how to do things? Besides, they were up to their asses in phone calls and complaints and requests for tours of the White House from the rest of the senator's constituents.

Senator Russell was glaring at him.

"Whitehorse and Arcott could be right," Colbert said, making an effort to inject the accustomed seriousness into his tone. "The public could be our best ally against the governor, make him look like a heartless bastard for opposing any casino, not wanting to see that the Arapahos and Cheyennes get justice. It could work in our favor."

That seemed to catch the senator's attention. He jammed his hands into the pockets of his gray suit pants and started pacing back and forth in front of the desk. He kept his head bent, his eyes focused on his steps. A long piece of brown hair slid forward again, like a strand of yarn breaking loose from the pink scalp.

"How's the press going to play this?" he said.

"Last evening's TV news and this morning's *Mirror* covered the rally and played the story straight. Looks like the press is willing to give the proposal a chance. Political correctness, you know. They're not going to take a stand against justice for the Arapahos and Cheyennes. Governor Lyle probably went ballistic when he got the news. But we're in the stronger position. We have to hammer the Sand Creek genocide and the need for justice, lean on the public's sense of fairness and political correctness. The governor will start to look like one of the

Third Colorado that marched into Sand Creek."

"You've prepared a press release?"

"It will be ready within the hour. I'll call a few reporters — the ones we might be able to control — and assure them of your concern that the tribes receive overdue justice. I'll fax the others a press release. Should run in tomorrow's papers and go out on the Internet. It won't hurt to get people around the country behind this. Everyone's in favor of justice for Indians."

The senator was still pacing, his hands clasped behind his back now.

"Don't worry," Colbert said. "I'll manage the press. The public will be behind us." He gave the senator a moment to chew on this, then he said, "There may be one . . ." He searched for the right words. ". . . potential problem."

The senator swung around. "Out with it!"

"The *Journal* has been on the story from the beginning. Catherine McLeod's the reporter, a pain in the neck. She's written two articles so far. One of them an interview with tribal elders on the Sand Creek Massacre. She has a reputation for being pretty independent. She may not be easy to keep in line."

"McLeod." The senator had drawn out

the name, as if he were gathering tobacco juice before he spat it. "Ex-wife of Lawrence Stern, is she not? The bitch went after him for five million dollars."

"I believe that was the ex-wife of Jonathan Norton." Also oligarchs, the Norton family, Colbert was thinking. God, they all knew one another's business, looked out for one another.

"And what was she before she married Jonathan? A cocktail waitress?"

"I believe she owned a shop in Cherry Creek."

"She wasn't one of us. Neither was Catherine McLeod, if I recall. Elizabeth Stern was most unhappy when Lawrence married her. Who was she?"

"Denver native. A general assignment reporter at the *Journal* when she met Lawrence."

"Oh, my God. Shopkeeper, reporter. Those boys deserve a whipping, getting mixed up with girls like that. Gold diggers is what they are."

"It's my understanding that Catherine McLeod took a modest settlement. She's not interested in money."

"Not interested in money?" Senator Russell tipped his chin into the folds of his neck and laughed softly. Then he seemed to have another thought. He threw his head back and fixed Colbert with a hard stare. "Independent, you say? A crusading reporter, interested only in the truth? You manage her, Harry. You understand?"

Colbert nodded. "Don't worry."

"Anything else?"

"I suggest we move fast on the proposal. With the press following the story, we don't have the luxury to line up enough votes for legislation to settle the claims."

The senator walked over and sank back onto the sofa. "Go on."

"There are a number of noncontroversial bills moving through Congress at present. They have majority backing and will doubtless be approved. The president is certain to sign them. I suggest we prepare a rider and attach it to one of those bills. Other senators and congressmen have used this tactic to get settlements for tribes in their states. The moment the president affixes his signature, the Arapaho and Cheyenne land claims will be settled. The matter will be out of the governor's hands. The use of land acquired by tribes as part of a federal settlement doesn't fall under state jurisdiction. As long as the secretary of the interior gives the okay, the tribes will be free to construct and operate a casino. We have assurances that the secretary will sign off on the casino."

A smile was working its way across the senator's face. "Prepare the rider," he said.

14

From the parking place across the street, Catherine kept her eyes on the squat, white-bricked building with the green awning fluttering over the entrance and the black-lettered sign next to the parking lot at the side: Hogan's. The branches of an old elm provided a tent of shade, and a cool breeze drifted over the convertible. Traffic hummed on I-25 a couple of blocks away. The lunch hour crowd had started to arrive, cars turning into the asphalt lot and pulling into the available spaces at the curb. A brown sedan came around the corner, and she felt her stomach lurch. The sedan drove past, a young woman at the wheel, the outline of an infant seat in the back. There were so many brown sedans. Still no sign of Marie's Honda.

Catherine felt herself begin to relax. A normal August day with the sky as clear as blue glass, sunlight dappling the strip of

grass along the curb, the temperature drifting into the nineties, but cool here in the
shade. The kind of day she had loved as a
child when she didn't have anywhere to go
and nothing more to do than lie on the grass
in the backyard and listen to the sounds of
summer, a bird chirping, a squirrel rustling
the leaves of a tree, and far away, a dog yapping. She would let herself drift into a kind
of peacefulness and wholeness, almost like
a memory.

It had been years since she had eaten at
Hogan's, not since the days of covering
social events for the *Journal,* stopping for a
sandwich and cup of coffee before heading
out to a gala where the tables were laden
with ice sculptures and gourmet delicacies,
knowing she would be too busy to sample
any of them.

She spotted the Honda stopped at the red
light a half block away, Marie's face backlit
in the brightness. After a moment, the
Honda lurched down the street, made a
wide right turn into the parking lot, and
pulled into a space next to the brick wall of
the restaurant. There was caution in the way
Marie pushed the door halfway open and
lifted herself out from behind the wheel,
still holding on to the edge of the door. She
glanced around the lot, then hurried inside

the restaurant.

Catherine waited almost ten minutes, enough time for the brown sedan to arrive if, by chance, Erik had gone to her mother's house and followed her. Finally she got out of the convertible. Rex scrambled over the top of the seat after her, and she had to push him back before she could close the door. He plopped his head on the edge and stared at her with puzzled eyes. "It'll just be a minute," she said, patting his head.

She crossed the street, making her way between the cars parked at the curb. Waves of heat rose off the asphalt, and the sun was hot on her face and bare arms. A red SUV pulled into the lot and stopped next to the Honda. Both doors flung open. A blond woman with enormous sunglasses and a gray-haired man jumped out and hurried toward the entrance, snatches of conversation trailing behind them. Catherine fed a couple of quarters into the newspaper stand near the entrance, took a copy of the *Mirror,* and followed the couple into the cool interior. Faint odors of hot grease, seared meat, and coffee hung in the air.

Catherine darted around the couple and past the hostess, who was frozen at the podium, gripping two menus and looking out across the crowded restaurant. Her mother was seated in the booth at the rear — the reddish blond hair brushed behind her ears, the little eyeglasses and the bright red lipstick — a familiar face in a sea of faces bobbing over the white tablecloths. And yet, she was struck by how *white* her mother looked. She slid into the booth across from her and set the newspaper and her bag on the seat. "Thanks for coming."

"My God, are you okay?" Her mother took Catherine's hand in both of her own. There was a sense of comfort in the warmth of her small palms, the touch of her fingers. Catherine swallowed hard at the urge to burst into tears, as if she were a child again who had fallen on the playground and her mother had run over, picked her up, and brushed her off. *Are you okay?*

"I need your help," Catherine managed.

"Of course. Anything. What's happened? Has that . . ." She searched for the word. "That thug," she said, "come back?"

Catherine took a moment. She was reluctant to give her any more reason to worry than she already had. Marie was in her early sixties, but she looked younger, skin smooth and tanned from hours on the golf course, blue eyes behind the narrow lenses of her glasses lit with intelligence, little pearls shining in her ears. It was no surprise that she had caught her father's attention — one of the secretaries at the brokerage firm where he had worked. But she hadn't been able to bear children, and she had poured all of her maternal love and instincts over Catherine.

"I think I saw him this morning," Catherine managed. She didn't want to tell her all of it.

"Oh, my —"

Catherine interrupted. "Listen, I'm going to have to . . ." Now it was her turn to search for the right words. "Be careful for a while. Stay away from the town house and office, the usual places."

"You can stay with me. You'll be safe at the house."

"No, that's just it. I can't go anyplace he might expect."

"You should take Dad's gun."

"What?"

"The revolver he taught you to use. Remember? He used to take you target shooting when you were thirteen or fourteen. He always said you were a natural."

"No, no." Catherine waved away the suggestion. What good would a gun have been at the town house? Or this morning? She couldn't shoot every man in a parked brown sedan.

"I wish you would consider it," her mother

222

said. "What are the police doing?" A note of anger sounded in her voice.

"They're trying to find him," Catherine said. "But it has something to do with a story I'm working on, and I'm the one who's going to have to figure it out." She slipped her hand free and patted the top of Marie's hand. She could feel the quivering beneath the smooth, white skin, and she hurried on before Marie could say anything. "I need you to take care of Rex."

"Rex?" She blinked at her, as if somehow they were now discussing the safety of her dog when it was Catherine's safety that concerned her. "Of course you can bring him to the house," she said finally. "He and Macy always have a good time together."

Catherine pulled back against the booth. "He can't stay at the house either. The man who's looking for me . . ." Marie winced at this. Catherine hesitated before she went on: "If he sees Rex in the backyard, he'll think you know where I am." God, this was crazy. Her mother could also be in danger. "I don't want to give him any reason to suspect you know anything."

Marie lifted one hand, but before she could say anything, Catherine said: "I don't want Rex in a kennel. I was thinking about that breeder where you got Macy."

"Lucille?" Marie nodded. "She has the space, long outdoor runs. I'll call and arrange it."

A heavyset waitress in a white blouse with sleeves that dug into the flesh of her arms materialized next to the booth and set a foam box on the table, with a check on top. "What's this?" Catherine said.

"In case you didn't have time for lunch . . ." Marie tried for a smile, but the worry lines kept breaking through. She extracted a couple of bills from her bag and set them on top of the check.

"We'll have a long lunch when this is over," Catherine said. How well her mother knew her, she was thinking. She picked up the foam box and got to her feet. "Rex is in the car. I need you to take him now."

She waited until Marie slid across the vinyl seat and pulled herself upward. Shoulders squared and thrown back, the collar of her pink shirt stiff against her neck, she started for the entrance. Catherine fell in behind, conscious of the way the tap of their footsteps on the vinyl floor cut through the hum of conversations. She found herself glancing around the restaurant, looking for *him.* In one of the booths, sipping soup at the table on the left, reading the menu at the table on the right. She wasn't sure she would know him — a figure blurred in the town house, slouched on the front seat of a brown sedan. He could be anyone.

How long had it taken? she wondered. Two minutes to walk across the street to the convertible. A minute to find the leash in the backseat and slip it over Rex's head. Another minute when she had bent her own head into the soft fur of his neck and told him good-bye. Then three minutes watching as Marie led him across the street to the parking lot, let him into the backseat of the Honda, and drove away. And did she imagine it, or was Rex watching her out the back window until the Honda disappeared through the trees and traffic? Another layer of her life peeled away, she thought, and then a terrible thought that sent a shiver of ice through her: she might never see her mother or Rex again.

She turned the ignition, pulled away from the curb, and wound through the streets toward Speer Boulevard, forcing the thought away. She had to hold herself together, if she were to stay alive. She drove through the traffic-clogged streets until she was on I-70. Heading east, the houses and buildings of the city falling behind and the brown emptiness of the plains opening ahead. She passed the section of undeveloped land where the Arapahos and Cheyennes intended to build the casino and hotel. She could imagine the glass and steel structure spreading across the earth, visible for miles — the new buffalo, Whitehorse had said.

At the airport, Catherine followed the sign that said Long Term Parking. She wedged the convertible between a van and a truck in one of the endless rows jammed with parked vehicles. She put the top up on the convertible, dragged the backpack and the laptop out of the trunk — her bag over one shoulder, the laptop case over the other — and walked away. Another part of her life tossed aside. She rode the airport shuttle, as if she were departing on a trip, a vacation in the Caribbean, a business conference. The shuttle stopped in front of the terminal, and she walked across the lanes of traffic — the honking horns, burr of idling motors, and whiffs of exhaust — divided by asphalt islands and got on another shuttle to the rental car lot. She chose the company with no line at the counter, told the clerk she wanted the rental for a week, and was about to hand over her credit card. She started to put the card back in her wallet. She would pay cash, she said, but the clerk had insisted on taking an imprint of the credit card. Company policy, he said, as Catherine had retrieved the card, lifted several bills out of the envelope in her bag, and pushed them across the counter. She hoped there would be no reason for the rental company to use the card. The man who knew everything might even know how to trace her credit card.

Twenty minutes later, she was heading west on I-70 in a gray Taurus that blended with the asphalt, the downtown skyscrapers shimmering silver against the mountains in the distance. She exited on Colorado Boulevard and drove south. On a busy street past Cherry Creek, she spotted the sign in front of a hair salon that said "Walk-ins Welcome." Inside a girl about eighteen with a tattoo on her neck, a silver ring in her eyebrow, and short, dyed black hair spiked on top, ushered Catherine to a swivel chair, wrapped a pink smock around her shoulders, cut off most of her hair, and turned it the color of sand. Nondescript and almost natural looking. Even her eyebrows had been turned the color of sand.

Catherine had stared in the mirror at the transformation as it was taking place — strands of black hair floating down, littering the floor like a matted rug, the brush painting a yellowish gluelike substance over what was left of her hair, and all the time the girl talking on about how her poker-playing boyfriend was cheating on her. What would you think if you found a lady's lighter in his shirt pocket? And finally, the blessed quiet under the heat lamp that cemented the new color into her hair.

Catherine opened the *Mirror.* Dennis Newcomb's byline jumped out under the first-page headline: "Tribes Demand Land for Casino." She skimmed through the columns. Pretty much the story she should have written last night: rally of three hundred Native Americans on the plains near the Denver International Airport; $300 million Arapaho and Cheyenne casino, hotel, and culture center proposed on five hundred acres.

According to Norman Whitehorse, Arapaho tribal member and rally organizer, the tribes were willing to settle the claim for twenty-seven million acres of Colorado lands in exchange for five hundred acres near the junction of two major highways, I-70 and E-470. Whitehorse said that the five-star hotel and casino would be a destination resort expected to attract thousands of guests each year. "The casino will give our people the economic security that ranches could have provided, had Congress distributed lands a hundred years ago in reparation for the injustices the tribes had suffered," he told the *Mirror.*

Developer for the hotel and casino complex is Peter Arcott Enterprises, a private company located in Denver that has built casinos on Indian reservations in three Western states. Arcott was unavailable for comment.

The article trailed to the inside of the paper, and Catherine turned to page six. Here was something new:

A spokesperson for Colorado's senior senator, George Russell, stated that the senator believes Indian citizens have been neglected long enough. "He supports the land claims settlement and will do everything he can to help right the historic injustices to the Arapahos and Cheyennes."

Catherine realized that the spike-headed stylist had rolled the heat lamp away and was motioning her out of the chair. She folded the newspaper, followed the stylist to the back of the salon, and dropped onto the chair in front of a sink. She leaned back onto the hard knob of porcelain and felt the cool water splashing over her head, the stylist's strong fingers massaging her scalp. Dennis Newcomb was ahead of her on the story with the quote from Senator Russell's office. She had dropped the ball. Worrying about Maury, running to the ranch, looking over her shoulder — and Erik on the highway this morning! She was off her game. There had been no time yesterday to call Russell's office.

She was back in front of the mirror, the sandy hair flying under the dryer. Then her hair was patted into place, and Catherine stumbled out of the chair, thanking the stylist — for what? For erasing the last of her and leaving in place a woman she had never seen before? "Looks really great," the stylist called out as Catherine made her way to the front desk, plucked another bill from the envelope, and paid for her own erasure. She left a tip for the stylist. It wasn't her fault; she'd done what she'd been asked, and she was good at changing people, a magician, really, wielding her magical paints and scissors.

Catherine huddled behind the wheel in the rental car, giving herself a moment to get used to a new reality, this new life flowing over her. The engine purred, the air-conditioning spit out cool air that had a faint smell of dust. Finally she pulled her cell out of her bag. She found the number for Senator Russell's office and asked to speak to Harry Colbert. The voice mail kicked in: "This is Harry Colbert. Leave your name and number."

"Catherine McLeod from the *Journal*," she said. "I'd like to speak with the senator about his support for the Arapaho and Cheyenne land claims." She gave him her number and pressed the end key. Then she scrolled through her messages: three calls from Bustamante, a call from Marjorie, another call from Violet. A call from unknown. She stared at the readout, unable to pull her eyes away. The phone felt slippery in her hand, and she had to tighten her fingers to hold on to it.

She hit the select button and pressed the phone to her ear. Her heart was galloping. "Hello, Catherine." How smooth his voice was, like that of the heartthrob on a soap opera or radio voice selling soap or toothpaste. *No more stains on your clothes; whiten your teeth.*

"Say good-bye, Catherine."

She squeezed her eyes shut and clenched her teeth. For a moment she thought she would vomit, the acid biting her mouth. She swallowed hard. So this was who he was, a sociopath, a stalker. He was enjoying this.

It was another moment before she scrolled past Bustamante's name without listening to the messages and called his office. "Where the hell are you?" His voice was stiff with anger. "I've had an alert out for you. You were supposed to come here a couple of hours ago. What the hell's going on?"

"He called my cell," she heard herself saying, as if her voice were disembodied, floating in the rental car like a wisp of cotton.

"When?"

"An hour ago. He's taunting me. He wants me to crack. I'll be an easier target then."

"And are you?"

"An easier target?"

"Come on, Catherine. I'm trying to help you here. Are you cracking?"

"No," she said. She wasn't sure; it might be true.

"You have to come in. The Jefferson County sheriff needs a statement about this morning."

"He knows everything, don't you get it? He thinks I'll go running to you. He's watching police headquarters."

"We can trace the call. If he used a cell, we can pinpoint where the call came from."

"Look outside! A brown sedan, Nick. It's parked somewhere on the street or in the lot. He's out there. I can't go anywhere he might be."

"All right, all right. Listen to me, Catherine. I'm going to talk to the district attorney about putting you in the witness protection program until we get this figured out. You have to trust me."

"Witness protection program? You don't get it. I'm the only one who can figure out why he's trying to kill me."

"What?"

"What do you know about the Sand Creek Massacre?"

"What makes you think that's why he wants to kill you?"

"You don't know anything about Sand Creek, and that's why you can't help me." Catherine could hear the sound of her breathing mingling with the hiss of the air conditioner. She had a profound sense of being alone, cut off from everyone and everything familiar, as if she'd been transported to a different planet. "I'll call you when I figure out the rest of it," she said, and hit the end key, cutting off Bustamante's voice in midsentence — something about recognizing the danger she was in. A sense of angry impatience hung in the silence.

She called the office and listened to the

sound of the ringing, broken by Bustamante's attempts to call her back. When the
receptionist picked up, she asked for Violet.

"Hey, Catherine." Catherine could hear
the forced cheerfulness in Violet's voice. "I
have the name of the company that owns
the five hundred acres. Denver Land Company."

"Any names of principals?"

"That's all I could find. Just the name of
the company. Is everything okay?"

Everything was fine, Catherine said. She
asked to speak to Marjorie.

The cell went dead for a moment, then
Marjorie's voice: "It's about time you called.
Where was our story on the rally?"

"I'm fine, Marjorie. Thanks for asking,
and yes, I read the *Mirror.*"

"Newcomb got to Senator Russell. Tell
me you'll have a new angle. An interview
with Peter Arcott, I hope."

"How did you know?"

"His office called this morning to confirm."

His office called. "Man? Woman? Who
called, Marjorie?"

"I don't know. Does it matter?"

"Yes, it matters. Did you give out my cell
number?"

"Hold on a minute." The hum of the air-conditioning rushed into the quiet, then Marjorie's voice again: "It was a man, and yes, we gave him your number. I hadn't had any luck in reaching you, but I was hoping he would. We're going to need that interview for your story."

Catherine took the cell from her ear. Her thumb found the end button and pushed hard. He knew everything about her, even the fact that she had an interview at four o'clock — twenty minutes from now, by the dashboard clock — with Peter Arcott at his office in the Equitable Building.

He was there now, waiting for her.

Catherine left the Taurus in a parking lot and nudged her way onto the Sixteenth Street shuttle with the crowd of suits and briefcases and tight-lipped faces that had started spilling out of the skyscrapers at five o'clock. She got off at Stout Street, elbowing her way to the door — excuse me, excuse me — and walked the block to Seventeenth Street, glancing around as she went, keeping an eye on the traffic moving past, half expecting the brown sedan to draw close to the curb, the shadowy profile of the gunman at the wheel.

The sun washed over the mauve stone of the Equitable Building sitting squat and imperious on the corner, much like the city's founders who had occupied the building in the 1890s. The Equitable Life Assurance Company, an eastern company, had financed the building, in a display of financial confidence for a western city with dusty roads and cows grazing in the yards. It was the city founders who had convinced easterners to bring their money west. David Moffat had brought the First National Bank to the main floor of the Equitable. Companies owned by the other founders had occupied the upper floors, including SR Associates, the real estate and development enterprise started by Leland Stern and Ethan Russell. Everything about the Equitable exuded confidence and permanence and tradition, as well as a serene privacy, like a private club that admitted only select members.

Catherine stepped past the double doors into a lobby of beige marble floors and walls, with sunlight streaming red, blue, and yellow through the Tiffany glass windows. The bronze elevator clanked to a stop, and lawyers and business types shouldered through the parting doors. Footsteps pounded across the marble to the exit. She slid between the closing elevator doors. Peter Arcott's office was on the third floor.

The elevator rose slowly, the relic of a slower time, Catherine thought. She leaned against the brass railing and tried to ignore the funhouse-mirror image of the woman with short, dark-blond hair floating in one of the brass panels. A freak, this figure, a construct made from bits and pieces of the woman she had once been. She didn't recognize this new woman, running and hiding, looking over her shoulder. She'd found a business hotel not too far from downtown, wedged between office buildings and a restaurant. She'd signed in as Mary Fitzpatrick. It was odd how Fitzpatrick had bubbled up out of some deep recess in her mind. And Mary. Mary could be anyone. She peeled several more bills from the envelope, enough for one night, and pushed them across the counter to the red-cheeked, pimply faced clerk in a black suit and white shirt with a collar that stood out around his skinny neck. He had asked for a credit card for incidentals. A precaution. Of course it wouldn't be used. Reluctantly she had pushed the card toward him and explained that she was recently divorced, had changed her name, and hadn't yet received the credit card with her new name. This was who she was now, she thought, a woman with sandy hair and a backpack with a story to explain everything, who preferred to use cash. In town for business, she'd told the clerk.

The elevator jerked to a stop, and Catherine made her way down the wide corridor to the pebbly glass door with black lettering: Arcott Enterprises. The bronze door handle jammed in her hand. She felt her heart lurch. She had deliberately waited until Erik concluded she had no intention of keeping the appointment. She'd timed her arrival with the precision of the hunted: late enough for the gunman to have left, early enough for Peter Arcott to still be in the office.

The handle moved downward, giving her a jolt of surprise. She stepped into an office the size of a small ballroom, the sweep of polished wood floor interrupted by plush Persian carpets and mahogany paneling that ran halfway up the walls. On the cream-colored walls above the paneling were large photographs of buildings that looked like hotels and casinos, blocks of steel and brick and stone, the names on discreet plaques. There was no one in the office, but the brown leather sofa and chairs on the left still held rumpled imprints and the uphol-stered chairs around the table on the right were pushed back, as if a meeting had just adjourned. At the far side of the office, across from the entrance, a mahogany desk stretched in front of a bank of beveled glass windows that fractured the daylight. Through the glass, the images of the build-ing across the street looked wavy and blurred.

"May I help you?" A trim woman in a navy blue suit, tall with fashionably cut dark hair, came through the door on the other side of the table and chairs. Before she could close the door behind her, Catherine caught a glimpse of a long corridor, the blue carpet and gray walls receding into the shadows.

"Catherine McLeod from the *Journal* to see Peter Arcott." Catherine strove for a professional, confident tone meant to send the message that she expected a positive response.

"You're very late," the woman said. She stood in place a moment, gripping a stack of file folders close to her chest, allowing her gaze to travel over Catherine. In the woman's eyes, Catherine could almost see the short, sandy hair, the white blouse and dark slacks that she had pulled on in the hotel room, and the flat, black shoes she'd worn because she hadn't put any heels in the backpack.

"I have an appointment for five thirty," Catherine said, still the steady, confident voice.

The woman made a wide arc around her to the desk. She dropped the file folders onto the polished surface. "Your appointment was for four o'clock."

"There must be some misunderstanding." Catherine tried for a conciliatory smile. This was going to take some persuading. "I'm working on a story about the proposed Arapaho and Cheyenne casino. Mr. Arcott has agreed to speak with me. I need only a few minutes."

"There's no misunderstanding." The woman opened the top folder, and Catherine watched her eyes move from side to side. "Mr. Arcott never makes appointments past four thirty," she said without looking up. "In any case, I'm afraid he's already left the office."

There was a chance of this. Still the revelation gave Catherine a sinking feeling. "I know he wants to speak with me for tomorrow's paper," she said. "Where can I reach him?"

"You can't." The woman lifted her eyes and gave Catherine a frank look. "He has an important meeting this evening."

"Oh, yes." Catherine could feel herself recovering. "I was hoping Mr. Arcott would be at the meeting."

The woman tilted her dark head to one side and gave Catherine a puzzled look. Before she could say anything, Catherine hurried on: "I'll be covering the meeting for the *Journal.*" She could feel the smile smashed against her face like a mask, as if the matter were settled, the awkward problem of a missed appointment solved. "I'm sure we'll find a few minutes to chat at the Hyatt." She was guessing here. A man who built hotels and casinos would take meetings at one of Denver's plush hotels, but there were so many hotels, so many places for meetings. It was a wild guess, a stab in the dark.

Catherine waited for the woman to say something, and when she didn't, Catherine turned and started back across the wood floor and the Persian carpets. She'd gambled and lost. She would have to get a hold of Whitehorse and hope that he could set up another meeting with Arcott, but it would be too late for tomorrow's paper. And Newcomb might manage to track down Arcott and get his own interviews. The scoop she'd counted on was flowing past like a fast-moving creek.

She was about to step into the corridor when the woman's voice rang like a bell behind her: "Hyatt? You mean the Brown."

Catherine swung around. "Yes, of course, I meant to say the Brown Palace." She should have guessed that a man with an office in the Equitable Building, a sense of Denver's past still clinging to the marble and the plaster, would prefer meetings at the Brown Palace Hotel. Leland Stern and Ethan Russell and the other city founders had probably met at the Brown Palace, and wouldn't Arcott have gotten on well with them? A man from somewhere else, bringing enough capital into the city to build a hotel and casino? She gave the woman another smile, easy and genuine this time, closed the door, and retraced her steps back to the elevator.

"I'm here to meet Peter Arcott," Catherine told the concierge at the desk in the lobby of the Brown Palace Hotel. Bellmen in dark uniforms and round, beaked hats hurried among the smartly dressed and coiffured guests milling about. The hum of conversations and scuff of footsteps on thick carpets were muffled in the immensity of the lobby atrium rising seven stories overhead, brass railings marking each floor and the cream-colored glass ceiling muting the afternoon light. A chandelier the size of a small room hung over the center of the lobby, crystals sparkling like a million fireflies.

"I don't believe Mr. Arcott is a guest at present," the concierge said. He looked distinguished in a blue blazer, with dark hair running to gray, tiny wrinkles in his face, and a tan that gave him the same patina as the fine old wood furniture arranged around the lobby.

Catherine told him that Arcott was at the Brown for a meeting, and that he was expecting her. The concierge snapped his fingers and beckoned one of the bellboys. Within a moment, the bellman was strolling through the lobby, around the tables in the center where groups of men in dark suits and women — some in suits, others in backless summer dresses and dangling earrings — were sipping cocktails. Then the bellman strolled out of the lobby and down the wide corridor toward the Ship Tavern.

Three or four minutes passed before Catherine saw the bellman walking back, Peter Arcott a few feet behind, looking annoyed and interrupted, his gaze darting among the knots of people in the lobby. He wore a dark, pin-striped suit that made him seem more formidable and less friendly than the image he had portrayed at the rally — an ordinary guy in slacks and pink shirt. He had sandy-colored hair — not unlike the color of her own now — cut short over his ears, and a long nose that dipped over lips as thin as a pencil line.

Then his eyes fell on her: "You paged me?" A mixture of impatience and curiosity cut through the question.

"Catherine McLeod from the *Journal.*" Catherine held out her hand. It was a half second before Arcott squeezed her hand hard against his palm.

"You were supposed to be at my office at four."

"I'm sorry. There was a misunderstanding. Do you have a few minutes now?"

"How did you find me?" He wasn't amused.

Catherine hesitated, then she said, "What matters is that I have a deadline for tomorrow's paper. I'm writing about the tribal land claims and the plan to build a casino. There are several things I believe you can clear up. I'm sure you would want the correct information published."

She could see the way he was mulling this over, moving his eyes from her to the lobby and back. "Five minutes," he said finally. "Then I have a dinner meeting." He swung out one arm, ushering her forward. "We'll talk in the tavern."

The light was low in the Ship Tavern, little globes of light hanging over the dark wood tables and shining on the leather chairs, mood lighting along the back of the bar, people seated here and there, and sounds of conversations floating in the air like a jazz melody. Catherine took a second in the doorway to let her eyes adjust to the dimness, the way she'd stopped in a hundred movie theaters before starting down the aisle. She was aware of Arcott behind her, the touch of his hand on her arm urging her forward. Then she was following him across the tavern to a table with a half-empty martini glass and a cocktail napkin on one side.

Catherine sat down on the other side. Arcott resumed his seat and pointed to the glass. "Martini?"

She shook her head. Yes, she was thinking. She wanted a martini or a whiskey or whatever kind of wine the waiter cared to deliver, but a killer was looking for her. She'd been lucky this morning, hungover and foggy. She was surprised that she'd summoned the sense to swerve off the entrance road. She had to stay clearheaded.

She took out her notepad and pen. "Tell me about yourself . . ."

Arcott cut in: "I don't give interviews to the press, because they always mess up the facts and put their own spin on things. This is your one and only interview, so take your best shot."

"Why did you agree to this interview?"

"That's your best shot?" He tilted his head

back and gave a snort of laughter. "Let's just say I owed Whitehorse." He shrugged. "You have five minutes."

"Arcott Enterprises constructs and operates casinos for Native American tribes in several states, is that correct?" Catherine wrote the date and Arcott's name on the top page.

"Three western states," Arcott said. His fingers did a drum roll on the table. "Alaska, Nevada, California."

"Were the casinos built on land acquired by the tribes as part of land settlements?"

"That's how it works," Arcott said, still looking annoyed, but now something else was working its way into his eyes. She'd felt him studying her — sipping at the martini, appraising her — since they had sat down, and what he had found, she could see, met with his approval, even caught his interest. "A lot of tribes across the country are still waiting for Congress to settle land claims." He tapped his fingers on the table again. "Indian gaming law says that Indian casinos can only be built on lands acquired by tribes prior to 1988. Exception is for land that is part of congressional reparations for land claims."

"You expect the tribes to give up claims to twenty-seven million acres for five hundred acres? Some might say it doesn't make sense."

"On the contrary." Arcott took another sip of the martini and stared at her over the rim. "It makes economic sense. Five hundred acres is enough land for a five-star resort hotel and a first-class Las Vegas–style casino that will generate two hundred million dollars a year. That's capital the tribes can use to develop other business ventures. Senator Russell is behind the proposal one hundred percent."

"Governor Lyle has opposed any settlement at all. He'll certainly oppose a settlement that would bring another casino."

Arcott spread his hands on the table. "The governor has to live with the terms of the Indian gaming law. When Congress settles the Arapaho and Cheyenne land claims, the matter will be out of the governor's hands. The tribes have every right to claim all of eastern Colorado. They've filed the notice of a land claim with the Interior Department. It could take years to settle . . ." He gave a little shrug. "In the meantime, land title companies will be informed that the tribes had claimed the land. The claim will tie up real estate deals, affect real estate prices, probably bring real estate transactions to a standstill. I suspect the governor will see the wisdom in backing the settlement."

"Some people might call that extortion. They might say you went reservation shopping." Catherine snapped the end of the pen.

"Extortion? Reservation shopping?" Arcott had just taken a sip of the martini, and she thought for a moment that he would start choking. He set the glass down hard on the table. "Very ugly words. Your words, not mine. We are talking facts here. The facts are that the tribes are within their rights to file the land claim. If you use those words, I will sue both you and your paper for slander, libel, and everything else that my lawyers can come up with. I assure you they are very good at coming up with a great many things."

He let the threat hang between them for a moment, then his face cracked into a smile, as if that pesky matter had been disposed of. "The governor can't deny that Coloradans love to gamble. Go to Blackhawk, Central City, or Cripple Creek and check out the crowds. He'll be doing the people a favor by getting behind a casino closer to Denver."

He drained the rest of the martini, lifted one hand, and beckoned the waiter, who appeared in an instant, as if he'd been transported on a conveyor belt, head bowed, arms straight at his sides.

"Another martini, sir? Right away. And for the lady?"

"A glass of water," Catherine said. She scribbled some notes on the pad, waiting for the waiter to turn away before she said, "What about the Arapahos and Cheyennes in Wyoming and Montana? Have they agreed to this settlement?"

"Don't worry about them," he said. "They understand the benefits."

"How will the project be financed?"

"Financial institutions, of course."

"Names?" she said.

Arcott seemed to find this amusing, his lips working into a half smile. "When the arrangements are finalized, I'll make an announcement. Until then, the names must be kept private."

"Denver Land Company owns the five hundred acres," she said. A mixture of surprise and admiration worked into his expression. "What if the owners don't want to sell?"

The waiter had brought another martini, and Arcott picked up the glass and took a long drink. He rubbed his lips together. "The company is in complete agreement with the proposal."

Catherine sipped at the cold water the waiter had set in front of her. The ice clinked against the glass. Everything seemed to be in place, had been in place when she'd written the first stories, but she hadn't known. No one had told her — not White-horse, not the elders. And here was the thing — they had used her, and she had let them use her in exchange for an exclusive interview.

Arcott gulped the rest of the martini and swayed to his feet. Catherine stuffed her notebook into her bag and stood up beside him. "I know who you are now," he said. He was a little drunk, his voice slurred, red veins blossoming in the whites of his eyes. "I've been trying to place you. Lawrence Stern's ex-wife, right? Some nut job broke into your townhome and tried to kill you a couple of nights ago." He went on without waiting for a confirmation. "So now you're a reporter pretending to care about all of this. Tell me, why should you care if a couple of tribes want to build a casino?"

"My readers care," Catherine said. A phone started ringing, an odd sound, close yet muffled. She dug in her bag and pulled out her cell, aware that Peter Arcott had also extracted a cell from somewhere, then dropped it into his jacket pocket. The name Philip Case flashed in the readout. Maury, Catherine thought. God, let him be okay.

"Hello," she said, trying to keep her voice calm.

"It's Maury. His heart stopped."

"Oh, God, no! I'll be right there." She jammed the cell back into her bag and, saying something about having to go, brushed past Arcott and made for the door. She ran down the wide corridor and plunged through the revolving glass door, only half aware of the sound of her shoes pounding the hard floor.

16

Shimmering in the early evening sun that moved toward the mountains in the distance, Denver Health was caught in time, unchanged from yesterday, visitors and patients and staff in green scrubs moving in slow motion along the front walkway. Everything the same, except that inside, Maury was dying. Catherine rammed the Taurus into a too-small space between two vans, and took off at a run, past the blurred figures of people coming and going. She slowed to a half run through the lobby, then raced up the escalator, pushing past visitors on the steps.

She was hurrying down the corridor when she saw Philip, shoulders bent toward the nurse seated at the desk, the tail of his short-sleeve shirt hanging out. He swung around as she approached, clumps of reddish hair springing upward, face blotched and eyes rimmed in red. He stared at her a moment, lack of recognition finally giving way to a look of surprise. Catherine stopped and dug her hands past the soft leather and into the hard outlines of objects in her bag, struggling to keep herself from flying apart. Then Philip was moving toward her, arms outstretched, and somehow she propelled herself toward him. "Is he . . ." She swallowed the rest of it.

"They got his heart started," Philip said. His voice was barely a whisper.

"He's okay?" The sense of relief poured over her like a cold sweat. She felt the weight of Philip's arm snake across her shoulders.

"He's still alive," Philip said. "They used everything — paddles, electrical shock. Oh, God, Catherine." He folded against her, and she found herself comforting him, patting his back. "He's resting now, they said. No visitors tonight."

"Maury's alive. He's alive," she said, but he shouldn't have been here, shouldn't have been shot. She should never have called him, and she felt all of this running like a river beneath the surface of the man she was holding. She could sense it in the deliberate way in which Philip finally stepped back, the frank way in which he looked at her.

"What did you do to yourself? Your hair?" he said, his mouth forming a round O.

Catherine pulled her fingers through the stiff clumps of hair. She hesitated, not knowing how much to tell him, not wanting to relive all of it. Finally she said, "He's looking for me. He wants to kill me."

"What?" Philip threw a glance down the corridor toward the escalator, as if the killer might be ascending from the atrium. "You think he's after you? How do you know? He could've been a gang member, happened into your neighborhood looking for some cheap thrills."

"He . . ." she began, then stopped. She did not want to recount what had happened this morning, the brown sedan waiting for her at the highway, the white van spinning onto the highway. Two people killed. God, they might have brought them here, wheeled them into the emergency room where they had taken Maury, then wheeled them to the morgue. "Until they arrest him, I have to be careful."

"What about Maury? That crazy man could be looking for him, too." Philip was swinging his arms back and forth, swinging his head and shoulders between her and the double steel doors leading into the ICU. "Shouldn't there be a police guard here?"

"No. No." Catherine tried to set her hand on his bare arm — the light bristle of hair on his skin — but he pulled away. "It doesn't have anything to do with Maury. It's about my job, a story I've been working on." She made herself hurry on: "Detective Bustamante is investigating the case full time. He'll have him in custody in a couple of days, I'm certain." She wasn't certain of anything, but — odd this — saying the words seemed to give her a momentary shot of courage.

And that seemed to flow into Philip, because he straightened his shoulders and drew in a deep breath. She could see his chest expand beneath the cream-colored shirt. Still his eyes were dull with exhaustion, white worry lines embedded in his forehead. "Thanks for coming by," he said.

As he started to turn around, Catherine caught his arm. "I can stay here if you'd like to go home and rest for a while."

He turned back. "I called you because . . ." His lips moved around the soundless words a moment before he plunged on: "I thought Maury was dying, and I thought you should know. But he made it, and I'm going to stay in case he needs me. I really don't want company."

Catherine let her hand drop. "Will you

call me . . . ?" She let the rest of it hang between them, until Philip nodded and walked off. She waited until he had passed the desk and disappeared around the corner into the waiting area. Waiting still, staring at the swinging double doors that led down a corridor, the air thick with antiseptic, to the cubicle-sized room where Maury lay stretched under white sheets. She had a sickening feeling that she would never see him again.

Somehow Catherine made her way back to the escalator, riding it down, clinging to the rubber handhold, the atrium below swimming under the fluorescent lights. He had changed everything, the man named Erik, following her in the dark, bursting into her home, shooting Maury. She could feel the anger sputtering inside her like live wires. She stepped off the escalator and started across the lobby. A different guard stood near the entrance this evening, tall and pimply faced, Adam's apple popping in his throat. She walked past and let herself through the double glass doors. Down the walkway — she was invisible, wasn't she? A woman with short, sandy hair like thousands of other women, head high, shoulders thrown back. She would not fear him.

But he should fear her, because of what

he had done to Maury.

Erik lay on top of the scratchy bedspread in the motel room, hands clasped behind his head, watching the mute, flickering images on the television against the wall. A highway, mountain slopes all around, and a white van and three, four — no, there were five — cars spun about, and police vehicles, ambulances parked across the lanes. The remote lay on the bedspread next to him, but he didn't have the energy or the desire to listen to the inane comments. Besides, the words in white block letters floated across the bottom of the screen on a black band. He didn't try to follow them. He could have given the running commentary himself, all of it true — the van plunging onto the highway, colliding with two cars, and other cars piling on, brakes screeching, metal crashing into metal. How the driver of the van was declared dead at the scene, a bullet hole in the head. How the injured were airlifted to St. Anthony Central where two men were declared dead. All identities withheld until families could be notified.

He could describe exactly what had happened, even the *alleged* part. *Several drivers claim to have seen a vehicle parked near the site of the accident. The police are looking for a brown sedan allegedly driven by a white male. They believe the man may have fired a weapon that struck the driver of the white van.*

Oh, yes, he had fired the weapon all right, the Sig 226 Tactical that put the bastard in the van permanently out of his misery, caused a six-car wreck, and missed Catherine McLeod. A foolish mistake, and not one he would make again. But it meant he'd had to turn in the brown sedan, now that she had seen it, and rent a nondescript light-colored Pontiac. Now he understood who the enemy was. He hadn't fully understood before. Always give the enemy credit for being intelligent, the first lesson he'd learned at Yellow Jacket. He hadn't forgotten it. What he'd forgotten was how wily, how street-smart the enemy could be. She was like a guerilla in the jungle, senses on the alert — she could *feel* things — ready to leap from side to side, swing from a branch, fade into the shadows. In a guerilla war, you had to consider different tactics.

The cell phone lay on his chest, a light weight pressing against his heart. The ringing was like the gong of an alarm. He half expected the client's voice on the other end, shouting that he was incompetent, threatening to terminate him — an ironic term. Wasn't it the man with the gun who might terminate the client? A fact the client must have understood, because it wasn't the client calling. It was Deborah, barely concealed impatience running through her voice. Was he coming home tonight?

No, he was not. He spent twenty minutes explaining. No, the deal wasn't finished yet. One of the principals had balked at the terms; they were going to have to meet again tomorrow and hammer things out. But you promised . . . Yes, he knew he'd promised, but he couldn't control everything. He'd made an effort to soften his voice then and told her that it may take a little longer than he had expected. How much longer? Longer was all he could say. A day or two, whatever it took. He'd try to wrap it up as fast as possible, but there was a sonofabitch involved that was going to take some persuading. You're very good at that, Erik. Yes, he was good at that.

He said good night, told her he loved her, told her not to worry, get a good night's sleep, kiss the kids. He'd call tomorrow. Then he picked up the remote, turned off the TV, and stared into the shadows. Headlights flashed through the blue drapes. An engine was revving up outside, and he had to force back the urge to jump off the bed, fling open the door, and shout at the driver to get the hell out of here. Finally, the vehicle — a pickup, most likely, in this neighborhood, a place for losers and loners and people who wanted to be left alone — started to move out of the parking lot. He listened to the engine turning onto the street, popping and sputtering.

He knew Catherine McLeod. She would continue writing her foolish stories, attempting to live her foolish life. He would be her most faithful reader, and the stories would tell him where to find her next. But even if they didn't, sooner or later she would make a mistake and use a credit card. His contact would call, and he would have her.

Catherine finished writing the article on the laptop positioned on the desk in front of the window. She'd worked on the interview with Arcott and the press releases from Senator Russell's office and the governor's office that Marjorie had e-mailed her. Headlights below flitted across the gauzy curtains. The bleep of a car horn and the sound of an engine turning over broke through the hotel quiet. She had finished half of the club sandwich room service had delivered, and the bottle of Chardonnay she'd bought on the way back to the hotel was nearly empty. There was still a film of

261

liquid on the glass next to the laptop.

She refilled the glass, took another sip, and scrolled to the top of the article.

The Arapahos and Cheyennes plan a major homecoming to the plains of Colorado where they once lived. The tribes have announced plans to build a Las Vegas–style casino and five-star resort hotel on five hundred acres thirty miles east of Denver. Peter Arcott, head of Arcott Enterprises, will develop and manage the casino complex. The plan is contingent, however, on a complicated land exchange settlement that will require congressional action.

In a press release issued today, Senator George Russell stated that he believed the time had come for the Arapahos and Cheyennes to be compensated for the unjust loss of their lands. "They have waited for justice long enough. It is time the people of Colorado rallied behind their demand for a small part of the lands taken from them. I believe that when the voters understand the genocidal acts committed in 1864 at the Sand Creek Massacre, they will support and applaud any attempt to right such terrible wrongs."

Governor Mark Lyle has rejected any land settlement with the Native American tribes that would take Colorado lands. In a statement issued today, he called the tribal proposal to relinquish claims on lands in exchange for five hundred acres near Denver an outrageous attempt to circumvent the state constitution, which stipulates that gaming can only be approved by a vote of the people. Colorado voters have turned down the expansion of gaming seven times. He called upon the state's congressional representatives to block any settlement agreement that would allow the tribes to build a casino.

Before writing the article, she had spent an hour on the Internet, and the research had paid off. She'd confirmed what Arcott had said about bypassing the governor, as long as the casino was built on land the tribes acquired after 1988 in a reparations settlement.

And she had found something else:

Arcott Enterprises developed casinos for tribes in Alaska, Nevada, and California after Congress had agreed to land settlements. The settlements had been authorized through riders attached to other bills, approved by Congress and signed by the president. Governors of the three states had complained that the riders bypassed the states by allowing casinos without the approval of voters.

She had written a side article about the Sand Creek Homecoming Run set for a week from Saturday, quoting Norman on how the Arapaho kids would run across the ancestral lands to the Wind River Reservation in Wyoming in memory of the Arapahos and Cheyennes who had been killed at Sand Creek.

All in all, the articles weren't too bad, but not the in-depth reporting she was known for — the direct quotes from unlikely sources, the truth hidden in smiling faces and obscure documents. Still the article would run in tomorrow's paper. A biding of time, a stab at the revelations sure to come. And she hadn't seen anything in the *Mirror* about the scheduled Sand Creek run or about how other land settlements had gone through Congress on riders attached to other bills. She highlighted the articles and sent them to Marjorie. The black numerals in the upper corner of the screen said: 12:01 a.m.

She found her cell on the nightstand and checked the messages, her thumb curved stiffly over the delete key, wanting to wipe away any black letters that spelled Unknown. Yet she could not delete a message from Erik. She would have to listen to the oily, sickening voice and call Bustamante. The message wasn't there. Instead, a message from Marjorie. Would she make the deadline? They were holding the front right column. "Yes, Marjorie," she said out loud. "I made the deadline." Three calls from Lawrence. She felt her stomach muscles tighten: she didn't want to hear his voice and listen to the excuses, whatever they would be this time.

Catherine deleted the messages, took another gulp of the Chardonnay, and listened to the night quietly moving through the downtown streets. She had the sense of things flying away, that they could never be retrieved. When she had finished the bottle of wine, she opened the hotel refrigerator and poured the small bottle of whiskey into her wine glass.

17

A bright morning, light glowing through the gauzy curtains, the walls of the hotel room a soft golden color, and the sound of the telephone screeching through the muffled noise of traffic on the street below. Catherine stared into the room and tried to recall where she was, every part of her heavy with sleep. A dull ache crept through her head. She reached for the cell on the nightstand.

Bustamante's voice burst into her ear, jarring her wide-awake. "We may have some good news," he said. "How soon can you get here?"

"What are you talking about?" She sat up and pushed the pillow between the headboard and her spine.

"We may have the gunman in custody. I need you to come down here right away."

The cell felt cool and inert in her hand. Whoever had wanted to kill her was in police custody, and for a moment, the possibility of normality flashed in front of her. She could return to the town house, go to the newsroom every day, walk Rex whenever she felt like it. But not yet, she realized. Not until she was certain. She told Bustamante she would meet him at police headquarters in forty minutes.

Catherine parked in the garage near Civic Center, and walked along 13th Avenue. A block away was the city and county building, a great expanse of white stone and columns that looked over Civic Center Park. A couple of blocks ahead was the beige brick building of the Denver Police Headquarters that resembled a fortress abutting the sidewalk. It was already hot, the morning sun bathing the pavement and reflecting off the brick, and the heat added to her sense of queasiness and the persistent aching in her head.

Inside the lobby, she waited at the counter while the policewoman tried to calm a Hispanic woman weeping into a wad of tissue and clutching the hand of a little girl with black braids and scared, brown eyes. After several minutes, the woman wandered over to the blue plastic chairs in the waiting area, pulling the little girl behind her, and Catherine told the policewoman that she was there to see Detective Bustamante.

Catherine took the last vacant chair. The Hispanic woman sat across from her, face buried in the black hair of the little girl gathered on her lap. There were several other women with children, but most of the people waiting were men — young men and older men, black and brown and white men — sprawled on the chairs, staring into space, arms crossed over their chests. Others sat hunched forward, elbows propped on thighs, studying the floor. The air was filled with odors of perspiration, tobacco, and the sense of hopelessness.

In the alcove behind the counter, the elevator doors parted and Nick Bustamante stepped out. Catherine watched him scan the waiting area before his eyes settled on her. She got to her feet and walked over. "I didn't recognize you at first." He stuck an arm between the sliding doors and ushered her into the elevator.

"But then you did," she said. She felt the pull of gravity as the elevator rose and wondered what else she ought to do. A pair of black framed glasses, perhaps, the floppy clothes of an older woman. She would keep changing if she had to, keep peeling away until there was nothing left of her.

The elevator bell clanged. The doors

parted and they stepped out into a wide corridor. "This way," Bustamante said, nodding her ahead. A pair of uniformed officers stepped to one side to give them room. They passed a succession of closed doors before Bustamante stopped in front of one. The knob made a clicking noise when he turned it. He pushed the door open, and Catherine walked into a small cubicle similar to the one where he had interviewed her two days ago. A table with chairs on either side filled up most of the space. A thin stack of folders had been arranged in the center of the table.

Bustamante walked around and dropped into the chair beneath the window. Daylight streamed past the tan window shade and shone in his black hair. Lines of fatigue fanned his eyes, and she wondered if he had been awake all night. She sat down across from him.

"Jefferson County sheriff needs your statement about the shooting on the highway yesterday. We'll be videotaping you" — a nod toward the one-way mirror — "same as before."

"Is that why you brought me here? You said you'd arrested the bastard." She was thinking that he'd expected her at headquarters yesterday, but she'd had no intention of going to a place where the gunman might be waiting outside. "I told you what happened on the phone," she said.

"Tell me again." He gave her a little smile that lingered a moment longer than it should have, she thought. "For the record," he said.

She looked away. Nick Bustamante was altogether too good-looking and too — what was it about him? — trustworthy, as if he was the man he appeared to be, a man who said what he meant. She wasn't used to that. She had never known when Lawrence was saying what he meant. The night at the ranch had only confirmed that fact. And she was a reporter, for godssakes. Accustomed to people saying what they wanted to read in the paper, trying to project an appearance of who they wanted to be. She was always trying to get below the surface, to strip away the pretense.

"Tell me exactly what you saw."

"I saw a brown sedan parked between the entrance road and the highway." She hesitated, watching the scene play out again in her mind. How strange for it to be parked there, she had thought. But there was something else she'd seen, or maybe she was just seeing it now. "I saw the flash of metal," she said. "I jerked the steering wheel to the right. It was instinct."

"The van was right behind you."

"On my tail, trying to pass all the way down the mountain. Who was he?"

"Twenty-two-year-old cable installer, name of Bryan Murphy. In a hurry to get to another job, his boss said. Survived by his widowed mother."

"Oh, God."

"It wasn't your fault."

"The others?"

"A fifty-eight-year-old grandfather in a red sedan that crashed into the van. A forty-two-year-old father of two from Kansas, on vacation."

Catherine leaned back against the chair and clasped her hands together hard. For a moment, she thought she might be sick.

"Can I get you anything?" Bustamante said, concern moving into his face. "A glass of water?"

She shook her head.

"Anything else you remember? Did you get a glimpse of the gunman?"

Catherine lifted her hands to her mouth and bit at a thumbnail. Maybe, she thought. But she couldn't be sure. What had happened, and what did she later think had happened? She shook her head again.

"We arrested the man we believe to be the Washington Park rapist. Seven women in two years. It's possible he intended you to be the next victim."

"He had a gun."

"That was the way he operated. Held a gun on his victims, threatened to shoot if they fought him. Do you think you're up to seeing him?" He picked up the file folders. "There might be something about him that you recognize. Two of the victims have given a positive ID, and with the DNA evidence we have, we'll nail him. It would be good to know if he's the man who came after you."

"You think he tried to kill me on the highway?"

"When things didn't work out at your town house the way he had planned? It's possible. We intend to find out."

She nodded. She was thinking that her own theory seemed to be crumbling into pieces around her feet. Someone wanting to kill her for what she *might* write about a casino and an act of genocide at Sand Creek? It seemed preposterous with a rapist sitting in custody somewhere close by, listening to the faint clank and whir of the air-conditioning system.

"I'll see him," she heard herself say.

Another corridor, then past other closed doors, down the elevator in the rear of the building, and through an underground parking garage to another elevator that took them up into a room inside the jail. About twelve feet wide, Catherine guessed, and twenty feet deep with chairs arranged in front of a platform. Bustamante said something to the two officers inside the door, then nodded her to one of the chairs. "Ready?" he said.

Catherine dropped onto the hard chair. The room darkened, then a bright light beamed on the platform and seven men walked out, like actors making an entrance from stage right. They stood in a line and blinked out into the darkness. On the white wall behind were black lines that measured height. They were all about six feet, all wearing the same baggy jail uniforms. Catherine realized that she could see them, but they could not see her.

Bustamante stood with the other officers next to the door. Even from three feet away, she could sense that he was waiting, that anything she might recognize could be important — the mole on the side of one of the men's neck, perhaps, except that she had never seen it before. The sharp knobs on another man's hands, but Erik had worn gloves at the town house. He had been dressed in black.

There was nothing familiar about any of the men on the platform. She shook her head toward Bustamante, and he gave some inaudible command and the men began a slow, lumbering exit to stage right.

"Everything happened so fast," she said.

Bustamante sat down beside her. "What about yesterday?"

Catherine turned toward him. "He was inside the sedan. Just *somebody*. I couldn't make out his face." The ceiling lights had come up, and Catherine could see the patience in Bustamante's eyes. She looked back at the vacant platform, in shadows now, and remembering now. Remembering the flash of metal inside the sedan — and something else. A moving blur of color.

She had seen something.

She could feel Bustamante waiting, but she took her time before she said, "It's not the rapist. The man in the sedan had blond hair. Yellowish blond hair. I caught a glimpse. And the night at the town house, I think I saw blond hair at his neck when his cap slipped."

He's still out there. He's still out there. The words drummed inside her head in rhythm to their footsteps as they took the elevator down into the underground garage and rode

274

the other elevator back up into the corridors of the police building. "Where are you staying?" Bustamante said.

"Where I feel safe."

"I can't help you if you won't trust me."

When she didn't say anything, he said, "I intend to have another talk with your ex-husband."

"I told you, this has something to do with the Sand Creek Massacre and the plan to build a casino," she said.

"What makes you so sure?"

Catherine was quiet again. So many gaps in the story, so many anonymous, shadowy figures behind the scenes. Investors and landowners who might stand to benefit from an Arapaho and Cheyenne casino. But something else was hovering in the background — a hundred-and-fifty-year-old massacre.

Bustamante pushed the button for the elevator to the main lobby. There was a ding, and the doors opened. Catherine moved inside and swung back toward the man still in the corridor. "I'll call you when I figure it out," she said into the closing doors. She wasn't sure whether he said that she should be careful, or whether she had just imagined it.

She felt the downward pull and with it, a

kind of excitement that always came over her when she realized that she was on to a bigger story than she had thought, that she had only started to explore the dark, hidden places.

Outside in the shade falling over the building, Catherine pulled out her cell and pressed the numbers for Philip's cell. It rang a long time. When the ringing finally stopped, she felt her muscles tense, waiting for the recorded voice — *leave your name and number* — but it was Philip himself on the other end, weary sounding and sleep drugged. "Hello," he said.

"How's Maury doing?"

"Holding his own when I left the hospital this morning." He paused a moment, swallowing back tears, Catherine thought. "Maury's strong. I have to believe he'll be okay."

"You must be exhausted."

"Don't worry about me," Philip said, the old edginess returning, the reminder that she was the one responsible. The guilt rubbed at her like sandpaper.

"I'll call you later," she said, but she realized that the connection had been dropped and she was speaking into an inert piece of plastic.

There was a text message from Marcy Norton, the governor's press secretary. "10:30. Gov office."

Catherine glanced at her watch. She had twenty minutes to get to the capitol. Then she checked her voice mail. A call from Marie. Catherine called her back and assured her everything was fine. She shouldn't worry. Marie said that Rex was doing okay at the breeder's house, but he missed her. He didn't have much appetite. Catherine squeezed her eyes shut at this and fought against the idea that her life was gone forever, that things would never be the same, she and Rex out for a walk in the coolness of the evenings, moonlight washing the sidewalks.

She said she would call tomorrow and pressed the end key.

There was another voice mail. She realized her hand was shaking as she pressed the phone against her ear and waited for the low, familiar voice: "I look forward to our next rendezvous. Say good-bye, Catherine."

Catherine pressed the keys that sent the message on to Bustamante. Then she slipped the phone inside her bag, her hand still shaking. She hurried down the concrete steps and started toward Colfax Avenue, checking the faces of the lawyers and bail bondsmen and other pedestrians coming and going, wondering if Erik were *that* straw-haired man, or the lanky, blond-headed fellow approaching, or *that* blond man across the street. She could see the golden dome of the capitol gleaming against the sky. She started running.

The granite-slabbed, neoclassical capitol building occupied the hilltop above Civic Center Park, an expanse of lawn and shade and stone walkways. Adjacent to the park was a collection of official-looking buildings, state offices, and museums, the Denver Public Library and the Denver Art Museum. The whole area exuded a sense of history, Catherine thought. Even the trees in the park. The black walnuts, she'd read somewhere, descended from saplings transplanted a century ago from Lincoln's home in Illinois.

She walked up the sidewalk that bordered the park, scanning the groups of tourists and homeless men milling about. The yellow-haired man was still out there somewhere. The thought sent a shiver rippling through her. Cars and buses churned past on Colfax, depositing faint smells of exhaust in their wake. The sun was warm on her bare arms. Ahead, the golden dome of the capitol seemed to sway with the clouds floating through the blue sky.

She entered the capitol on the west side and went through security — place bag in the plastic tub, please; step through here, please — and then she was in the lower level. She hurried up the staircase, heels ringing on the marble steps. Light glinted on the brass railings. Everything about the building summoned the past — the paintings and sculpture, the pink marble walls, the marble floors polished and worn by the footsteps of Colorado's founding fathers. She could almost imagine the voices from the past blending into the conversations of the tourists grouped in the rotunda, heads tilted back, eyes fixed on the interior of the dome shining overhead.

She headed down a wide corridor, pushed open the heavy oak door with "Governor" in black lettering on the pebbled glass, and stepped into a large, paneled waiting room. The redheaded receptionist glanced up over the computer on the desk inside the door, and Catherine told her that she had an appointment with the governor. "I'll get Marcy," the receptionist said, picking up the phone.

In a moment, Marcy Norton was in the doorway on the far side of the waiting room, motioning her forward. About thirty, stylish blond hair, an air of efficiency about her, Marcy Norton had taken the job of press secretary about the same time that Catherine had gone back to work at the *Journal*. They had stumbled through the first weeks of their jobs together, which had created a kind of bond. More than once, Marcy had squeezed out a few minutes from the governor's schedule for an interview that gave Catherine a scoop ahead of the rest of the press.

"Changed our hair?" Marcy said. Little motes of surprise danced in her eyes. "You don't look like yourself. Is everything okay?"

Catherine tried for a dismissive smile. My God, nothing was okay.

They were walking down a corridor past a warren of cubicles, people moving about and phones ringing. Marcy stopped at the door beyond the cubicles. She knocked once, then pushed the door open. "Catherine McLeod's here," she said, leaning inside. "Sorry, Catherine. Ten minutes is all."

Catherine walked into the spacious office with a desk that curved in a half circle, light sweeping over the surface, and Governor Mark Lyle, a large man with black curly hair and glasses perched partway down his nose, hunched over the papers spread in front of him. It was a long moment before he glanced over the top of the glasses and motioned her toward a vacant chair.

"Nice to see you again." He gave her a practiced smile. Always a politician, Catherine thought, on the campaign trail, shaking hands with the voters. He had on a white shirt, sleeves rolled over thick forearms, red tie loosened around the open collar. A dark blue suit jacket was draped over the back of his chair. The cowboy, Lawrence and his friends called the governor, from out in the state somewhere. A nobody who had bumbled into the governor's seat and had the temerity to aspire to Russell's seat in the Senate. "We'll get to the cowboy," she'd heard Lawrence say on the phone one evening when it looked like a business deal was about to stall, but as far as she could tell, they had never been able to get to the cowboy. Governor Lyle had a reputation for not bending the rules or caving in to the demands of any interest group.

"Any more leads on this cockamamie casino proposal?" he said.

"Leads?"

He pulled a folded copy of this morning's *Journal* from under a stack of papers and waved it across the desk. "You exposed Arcott's technique. Get in bed with a senator and see that he attaches a rider to some innocuous bill so that Congress ends up settling the land claims for various tribes. And what do you know, the tribes build casinos on their newfound land, Arcott being the builder and operator. Reservation shopping is what I call it. Worked in other states and now he's hoping it will work in Colorado."

Catherine smoothed the top page of the notebook that she had pulled out of her bag. "What about Senator Russell? Does he intend to attach a rider that will push the settlement through Congress?"

"He's stated publicly that he supports the proposal. What has he told you?"

"His office hasn't returned my calls."

Governor Lyle gave a cough of laughter. "Maybe he thinks you're not the friendly press." He folded his arms over the papers strewn in front of him and leaned toward her. "I have no intention of leaving the matter to Senator Russell. I've asked Bill Adkins to schedule a briefing before the Senate Indian Affairs Committee. Russell won't be able to make any moves before the briefing."

Well, well. This was news. Catherine jotted down: Senator William Adkins, committee briefing. "Date's not set yet. Russell will be foaming at the mouth. That's off the record. I intend to be at the briefing, along with the entire Colorado delegation. Everyone except Russell opposes another casino in this state."

He sat back and regarded her a moment. "I read your interview with the elders," he said finally. "Who sold them on this scheme? Arcott or the company that owns the land?"

"I'm trying to chase that down," she said.

"Well, seems to me, the people of this state have a right to know who's behind the proposal. You can quote me on that."

Catherine stopped writing. "As soon as Congress hears about the atrocities committed at Sand Creek, there could be a rush to settle the claims. Isn't it true the hearing could work against your position?"

A slow smile crossed the governor's face. "The Arapaho and Cheyenne land claims have long been settled," he said. He waited a moment, allowing the words to hang in the air. "We'll simply remind Congress that, in 1965, the government paid the Arapahos and Cheyennes $15 million for their ancestral lands. State attorney says the agreement is final. End of the matter."

The governor held up one hand, something else still on his mind. "Only reason Russell's behind this is because he thinks it will be good for business. He's always favored the businesses of this state, whether it comes to easing environmental restrictions or pushing through tax breaks. Check his voting record."

There was a knock on the door, and Marcy stepped into the office. "You're due at the legislature, Governor," she said.

Catherine got to her feet. She was thinking of Russell's record. The *Journal* had been the only newspaper to expose the economic consequences for ordinary families of the bills he'd muscled through Congress. Even if he had planned to run for office again, she doubted he would be re-elected.

She thanked the governor, who was lifting himself out of his chair and smoothing down his shirt sleeves at the same time. Then she retraced her route through the office, across the marble floors, and down the staircase, checking the text messages and voice mail on her cell. Nothing more from *him*. She made her way past the security station and out the door. It was cool in the shade of the building, a little breeze stirring the air, the leaves rustling on the trees. For the briefest moment, everything seemed almost normal. She thought about the land claims and the plan for the casino. And the entire plan based on what Norman and the elders claimed to be an act of genocide committed at Sand Creek.

After a moment she started walking down the hill toward the Denver Public Library.

18

Western History occupied most of the fifth
floor of the library. Hushed and solemn as a
cathedral. A dozen people at long oak
library tables, serious scholars, Catherine
thought, heads bent over stacks of documents and opened books, brows wrinkled
in concentration. She waited at the counter
next to a blond-haired woman a little older
than Catherine, but attractive and well
dressed, gripping a yellow legal pad like her
own. All bags had to be deposited in lockers
inside the Western History entrance. Only
notepads and pencils allowed inside.

She would need the 1851 Fort Laramie
treaty, she was thinking. She wanted to read
whatever legal jargon had been used in the
nineteenth century to acknowledge the
Arapaho and Cheyenne ownership of one-
third of Colorado.

The librarian who assisted her every time
she did research here — Andy Mays —

emerged from the stacks and handed the woman a leather volume frayed at the corners. "An excellent account of the Ku Klux Klan in Colorado," he said, his voice low. He was slightly built and tall, with wispy black hair and dark eyes that looked outsized behind the thick, rimless glasses. The woman thanked him and carried the book over to the nearest table where it dropped on the surface with a loud thud, like a clap of thunder, that lifted eyebrows around the reading room.

"How may I assist you?" He turned to Catherine.

"It's me, Andy," Catherine said.

The man blinked and took a step backward, as if he needed more distance to bring her into focus. "My goodness," he said. "I didn't recognize you." He took a couple of seconds, running the words over his lips before he went on: "Are you in trouble? I read about the intruder."

"Let's just say I shouldn't look too much like myself for a while." Catherine tried for a reassuring smile. "I'm still working on the Sand Creek story," she said.

"You're doing a fine job. I read your articles. Tribal elders don't usually talk to outsiders. They must accept you."

She stopped herself from saying, They

think I'm Arapaho. What difference did her ethnicity make, whatever it was? She was a reporter, and a yellow-haired man was trying to kill her before she reported something that she didn't even know. She asked to see a copy of the Fort Laramie Treaty and any other documents that might refer to Sand Creek.

He headed across the reading room into a row of stacks, and she understood she was supposed to follow. He walked down the shelves, tapping a pencil in the palm of his hand. The faint smell of dust and old leather permeated the air. Finally he stopped and withdrew a four-inch-thick volume. She caught a glimpse of the title: *Indian Treaties.* He located two other volumes and stacked them in the crook of his arm. "You might want to look at statements from early settlers," he said, throwing the comment over one shoulder as they walked to the end of the row and emerged in the reading room. He set the volumes on a table off by itself.

Catherine slid onto the hard wood seat, conscious of the soft padding of Andy's footsteps back through the stacks. Daylight streamed through the windows overhead. It was one of the features that she loved about the design of the library, a mixture of beige and reddish towers and vertical rectangles and windows that invited the daylight and the outdoors into every area.

She opened the top volume, *Indian Treaties,* ran her finger down the table of contents, and turned to the Fort Laramie Treaty. The pages were thin, almost glued together from age and disuse. She skimmed through the introduction, the backstory to the treaty itself:

Thomas Fitzpatrick, the government agent, traveled around the plains in the spring and summer of 1851 instructing the Arapaho, Cheyenne, Sioux, Assiniboine, Arikara, Gros Ventre, Crow, and Shoshone tribes to assemble at Fort Laramie on the Platte River for a treaty council with representatives of the Great White Father in Washington. By the end of the summer, ten thousand Indians were camped near the fort with thousands and thousands of horses. So many that in a short time, the horses had depleted the wild grasses and Fitzpatrick had been forced to move the council site to Horse Creek, thirty-seven miles away, where the wild grasses were plentiful.

She stared at the name Fitzpatrick. She had used the same name to register at the hotel. A name from history, and yet she'd had the odd sense of connection. She pushed away the notion. Mary Fitzpatrick happened to be the woman with sandy-colored hair who drove a rental car and stayed at a hotel. That was all.

She read through the treaty itself.

The Treaty Council began on September 8, 1851. The tribal chiefs and the government commissioners assembled in the shade of a canopy erected by the Indian women. Before the talks began, the calumet was passed around. As each chief accepted the red stone pipe, decorated with beads and feathers and filled with a mixture of plants, tobacco, and the bark of red willow, he drew an invisible line with his hand from the bowl to his throat as a sign that everything he said would be sincere and truthful.

The council lasted a week, and on September 15, the first treaty between the federal government and the Plains Indians was signed. The treaty acknowledged Indian ownership of the Great Plains. Tribes were guaranteed the legal rights to their traditional lands. Fitzpatrick and several traders huddled with the chiefs and wrote out the boundary descriptions for the land owned by each tribe. The government acknowledged that the sweep of land between the

Platte River and the Arkansas River, from the Continental Divide eastward across the plains of Colorado, belonged to the Arapaho and Cheyenne.

Catherine carefully wrote down the description and added her own notes: Eastern half of Colorado. Twenty-seven million acres. All the towns, ranches, settlements, stage coach stops, and army forts when Sand Creek occurred in 1864 were IL-LEGAL. She slashed a black line under illegal, nearly cutting though the page. No governor or territorial legislature could change that fact. United States treaties took precedence over other legislation.

But there was another way to take control of the land: the tribes had to be eliminated.

She lifted the next volume off the stack. The title was embossed in gold: *A Compilation of Our Times. 1858–1870.* Edited by M. C. Johnson. Little motes of dust rose off the spine as she opened the cover. The pages were brittle. Carefully she went to the table of contents, and bless M. Johnson, whoever he was, he'd had the foresight to gather accounts from people who had lived in Colorado in the early 1860s. Some accounts were secondhand, others speculations. She dismissed them. The eyewitness accounts were what mattered. She noted the pages for the sections she intended to read and settled into the task, allowing herself to be transported into the strange country of the past.

I was roundin' up some strays when I seen the Indians lined up on the bluff, sittin' on their ponies all painted, like they do. They had on feathered head-dresses, and they was naked as jaybirds, except for them breechcloths they wear, and they had themselves all painted. Chests and faces smeared with red, blue, and yellow paint. They was a sight, I tell you, and I took off runnin' back to the house where the wife and kids was. I got my rifle, and went out on the porch, ready for 'em. They come whooping and hollering down the bluff. Headed straight for my herd. Some of 'em rode for the corral. They was the ones that took my horses, all six of 'em. They had guns, and soon's they got close enough, they started shooting at the house. They weren't gonna take me alive, I knew that to be a fact. They wasn't gonna get the kids and the wife. You know what they do to women? I don't wanna talk about it. They take kids and turn 'em into Indians. I was ready to kill any of 'em that rode up to the house. Guess they knew that, 'cause after they fired off the first shots, they just went about getting the cattle and the horses. Next thing I know, they're herding my cows back up the bluff. Couple them braves was taking the horses. I watched them go off with everything I'd been building up the last four years. Everything was gone, just like that. — Lucas Weatherbee, Rancher, South Platte.

We saddled up soon's Major Jacob Downing give the orders. We got word them Arapahos and Cheyennes were marauding on the South Platte. They was hittin' ranches, stealing horses and cattle, and getting away with it. What rights they have to be doin' that? They needed to be punished and feel the whip of the white man. We rode out first light of dawn. There was Cheyenne villages near the river, and the major was certain those marauding thieves was in those villages. We rode into the first village we come to. It was nothin' but a bunch of buffalo-skin tipis, and they looked pretty ratty, like a good wind would've knocked 'em over. We shot them redskins, and good riddance, I say. We did our best to

293

put an end to their murderous ways. Killed several old bucks that come walkin' out with their hands in the air, the way they always do, like they was innocent and wasn't harboring no thieves. Shot 'em down, like they deserved. There was some warriors in the village, and we got them, too, before they could get their weapons and do their dastardly deeds. It was self-defense for us troops, you ask anybody that was there. There was some squaws and younguns' that got in the line of fire, but like the major says, you gotta expect that in war. Soon's we left the village burning, we rode on to two other villages and did the same.
— Private Luke Handy, Camp Weld.

I was the first to come upon the mutilated bodies of the most unfortunate Nathan Hundgate and his family. There were a great many shells scattered over the grounds not far from the ranch house. I saw with my own eyes what had taken place. A band of marauding Indians had intended to drive off the stock. From the way that Mr. Hungate lay on the hard ground, not far from the house, it was obvious that he had heard the commotion and run out with his gun firing. We found Mrs. Hungate and the children a farther distance from the house. All the bodies had been mutilated in a horrible manner. I believe it was correct for Governor Evans to order the bodies brought into Denver and put on display so that Denver citizens could see with their own eyes what our command saw. I believe we are confronted with a terrible and ruthless enemy that will stop at nothing to drive settlers from this area. — Sergeant Marcus Hitchens, Camp Weld.

I worked closely with Governor John Evans during the violent years of 1863 and 1864 that led to the battle at Sand Creek. Arapahos and Cheyennes had been raiding the outlying ranches for months. One of the leaders, an imposing-looking Arapaho by the name of Chief Left Hand, came to see the governor. It is a fact that this Indian brave spoke English better than some of the prospectors in the area. I wrote down the record of the meeting. The brave told the governor that his people were hungry. He said the whites had killed a great many buffalo and dispersed the herds so that their warriors had to ride great distances to find food for their villages. He said that 1863 was a year of hunger. His people wanted peace with the whites.

The governor said, if you want peace, why do your warriors attack our ranches? The chief said they needed food. They weren't looking to kill the ranchers. He said it was the ranchers that fired on the warriors. Later the troops came and destroyed three villages. He claimed that the warriors who raided the ranches weren't from those villages. The people killed there were innocent.

The governor said that he couldn't expect the troops to distinguish guilty Indians from innocent, that they were all guilty if they accepted stolen cattle or harbored hostile warriors.

Chief Left Hand assured the governor that he and the other so-called "peace chief," Chief Black Kettle of the Cheyennes, were working hard to keep their young men under control, but that the provocations were mighty. They want only to be allowed to live in peace.

If you care so much about peace, the governor told him, then why didn't the chiefs come to the meeting on the plains as they had promised. He had waited for two weeks, but no Cheyenne or Arapaho came.

The chief said that they had wanted to come, but the villages were in mourning over the deaths of many children from strange sicknesses and hunger. They had sent a messenger to tell the governor they could not meet with him.

Governor Evans said he never received any such messenger. He advised the chief to go back to his people and stop the atrocities against whites.

After the chief left, the governor poured us each a glass of sherry and we sat in his parlor discussing the present worrisome situation. We were still talking after the sun had disappeared behind the mountains and the parlor walls turned a dull red with the dusk. I remember hearing horse carts passing outside on Fourteenth Street. The governor opened his soul to me. He said he carried a great burden to protect Colorado settlers, in light of the Sioux uprising almost two years ago in Minnesota. The Sioux went on a rampage and slaughtered seven hundred white settlers. The governor said he could not allow that to happen in Colorado. The settlers were getting nervous, he said.

Bands of hostiles had cut off the Overland Trail and stopped all commerce for three weeks. Our settlements depended upon supplies coming from the east, and he reckoned we could hold out against an Indian blockade of the trail for only a short time.

Another thing making the settlers nervous, he said, was the lack of title to the lands they were ranching and farming. The Treaty of Fort Laramie said that most of Colorado belonged to the Arapahos and Cheyennes. Settlers are unable to acquire a clear title to their lands. This is highly detrimental for the development of the territory, he said, which, in his view, offers great opportunity for the accumulation of wealth for its citizens. He called Colorado, with the vast deposits of gold, silver, and other metals, the nation's treasure house. We must build a transcontinental railroad into Colorado to connect the mines with the rest of the country. He reiterated that a railroad could not be built without title to the land, and he said that he would not allow the advancement of civilization to be halted by primitive, uncivilized Indians.

Catherine worked through the pages again, jotting down some of the quotes: *The people killed there were innocent. The children were dying from strange sicknesses and hunger. The settlers were getting nervous . . . he would not allow the advancement of civilization to be halted by primitive, uncivilized Indians.*

Strange the way events had unfolded then, she thought, as if they had just happened, and yet moving like a shadow beneath the surface, faceless and inexorable, were forces that pushed the events into their appointed places. She scribbled more notes, writing quickly before the connections, as fragile as air, evaporated.

Camp Weld Council, Denver, late September 1864. Governor John Evans, Colonel John M. Chivington, Arapaho and Cheyenne leaders. Governor and Colonel instruct tribal leaders to place their people under the protection of the troops at Fort Lyon until a peace agreement is reached. October and November, 1864. Chiefs Black Kettle and White Antelope, Cheyenne, and Chief Left Hand, Arapaho, move their villages to Sand Creek, forty miles north of Fort Lyon.

The voices of the elders drummed in her head. *They told us to go to Sand Creek. They said the people would be safe.* She kept thumbing through the brittle pages, looking for what? Confirmation? Evidence that Evans and Chivington and the other white leaders had deliberately misled the tribes by sending them to Sand Creek? No longer would the troops have to hunt Arapahos and Cheyennes across the plains, they would know exactly where the Indians were.

And here it was: Major Scott J. Anthony meets with Chief Black Kettle and Chief Left Hand at Fort Lyon. The chiefs inform the major that six hundred Cheyennes and Arapahos are now camped at Sand Creek. More bands are on the way. A large band of Arapahos under Chief Little Raven was expected soon. They had complied with the instructions, and they are eager to surrender their people to the safety of the fort. Anthony dispatches a report to the district commander at the Army headquarters in Kansas. "They appear to want peace, and want someone authorized to make a permanent settlement of all troubles with them to meet them and agree upon terms. They cannot understand why I will not make peace with them."

After the massacre, Lieutenant Silas Soule

testifies before the congressional committee that had investigated Sand Creek. "Anthony was for killing all Indians, and was only acting friendly until he had a force large enough for the job."

Chivington makes a public speech in Denver: "My intention is to scalp all Indians, little and big . . . nits make lice."

And the chilling idea running through it all: Governor Evans and Colonel Chivington had corralled the Indians at Sand Creek.

Catherine sat back and stared at the motes of dust suspended in a shaft of daylight. Odd how the voices from so long ago reverberated around her. The air was close and stuffy. Still she stayed at the table for a long while before she finally made her way back through the library to the outdoors.

19

Catherine awoke in a haze of daylight filtering through the curtains, coffee odors floating from somewhere. She blinked into the light a moment. The elevator dinged in the corridor, and there was a murmuring of voices outside her door. She felt groggy and thick-headed. Cellophane from the sandwich room service had delivered last night glistened on top of the desk next to the glass tinged red with Merlot. Light shone through the wine bottle that she had bought on the way back to the hotel. There was still half a glass in the bottom.

She'd worked late writing the interview with Governor Lyle, the Dave Brubeck Quartet playing on the little radio on the bedside table. Another scoop, and the realization gave her a distinct sense of pleasure. She was the first to report that the governor had asked Senator Adkins to schedule a briefing with the Senate Indian

Affairs Committee. When she had finished the article on the interview, she'd written a side story on Sand Creek. Quoting the first-person accounts, the fear and tension that had rippled through the white settlements, the hunger and desperation of the Indians, the decision on the part of Governor Evans and Colonel Chivington to settle the matter once and for all.

She managed to lift herself out of bed and stumble into the shower. After a good ten minutes of steaming water pounding her skin, her head began to clear. Still the thought of breakfast sent her stomach into spasms. She pulled on the slacks from yesterday, found a clean blouse in the backpack, ran a brush through the sandy hair. Then she called Philip. Still no change. Maury was holding his own. She rode the elevator to the lobby and waited for the valet to bring the gray Taurus. She stared at it a moment, reminding herself that it was the car driven by the sandy-haired woman who had stared back at her in the mirror a few minutes ago.

Catherine parked again in the Civic Center garage next to the Denver Art Museum. She crossed the plaza in front of the museum and headed north across the park to the black-glass skyscraper where the secretary of state's office was located. The office had once been in the capitol, she knew, but a number of offices had outgrown the capitol even before 1906 when construction on the building was completed. Construction had taken twenty-two years, and in that time Colorado's population had doubled and tripled. Denver had gone from a loose collection of log cabins and dirt roads with cattle grazing on the prairie that was now Civic Center to a metropolitan city with trolleys running up and down paved streets, electric lights shining in brick homes, and fresh water pumped in from the mountains. All of which — Lawrence had liked to boast — had been brought about by the founding fathers — the Evanses and the Russells and the Sterns. A handful of founding families known as the "Sacred 36."

Colorado would have grown up without them, which was the nature of things, she used to remind Lawrence. Sometimes he'd smile and shake his head. Sometimes he'd pour them each a glass of wine and say, "Let's drink to their accomplishments." One time, she remembered, he had stomped off, slammed the door, and shouted through the closed door, his voice muffled and shaky, "You'll never understand!"

Now Catherine made her way through the cool atrium of the skyscraper and found the bank of elevators that went to the first ten floors. She got out on the second floor and let herself through the doors on the left: the business center. The entry was small — a counter in front of two vacant desks and, behind the desks, people moving about a warren of offices with glass walls. A man and two women huddled together in front of the counter, waiting.

Catherine glanced into the computer room on the right. Tables lining the walls, and a half dozen people hunched over monitors. At the far end was Dennis Newcomb. His gray ponytail trailed halfway down the back of a red shirt. She had the sinking feeling that he was ahead of her, already on to the names of people behind Arcott Enterprises and Denver Land Company. *They're willing to sell the five hundred acres,* Arcott had said.

Catherine kept her face turned away as she went into the room and sat in front of the computer down from Newcomb. It would be like him to glance around and spot her. "Newshound" was coined for reporters like him, she thought. He could sniff changes in the atmosphere. She didn't want to get into a conversation while he probed for what she might know that he hadn't yet found out.

She had just pulled up the home page for the Colorado secretary of state's office when Ramona Sanchez led the couple from the counter to a computer a couple of stations away. Catherine had known Ramona since she'd gone back to the *Journal.* "Go see Ramona," Marjorie would say, and she had to admit there were times when she was working on tight deadlines that she had said to Violet: "Get that from Ramona, will you?" Ramona had worked in the office through the tenure of several secretaries of state. A little overweight and more competent than some of the state secretaries, she knew where to find the most obscure information on Colorado businesses, an expertise that had allowed Catherine to follow trails of fraud that had led to furious e-mails and phone calls to Marjorie. They had also led to indictments.

Catherine typed Arcott Enterprises in the search box and waited for a document to materialize on the screen. Company address was Arcott's office in the Equitable Building. Registered agent, Peter Arcott. On the next page was the name of the individual causing the document to be delivered for filing: Peter Arcott. There was no third page, no lists of officers and directors, no other names.

Out of the corner of her eye, she could see Ramona leaning sideways toward the computer while the man sat down and stared at the blank screen. The woman rested her hand on his shoulder and leaned in close, as if she expected something miraculous to appear as Ramona pressed the keys. She was giving them the same instructions she probably gave a hundred times every day. All of the records were on-line. They had only to type in the names of the companies they were looking for. Yes, they could print anything they wished. The printer was over there, she said, nodding past Catherine.

Then she was walking over, eyes wide with incredulity. Her face was round, her cheeks flushed, as if she'd been climbing stairs. Catherine lay a finger against her own mouth and threw a glance at Newcomb. "It's me." Her voice was barely a whisper.

"What have you done to yourself?" Ramona kept her own voice low. There was the lilt of Spanish in her accent. She pulled back the chair next to Catherine and plopped down. The hem of her black skirt dragged onto the floor; her hips overran the edges of the chair. Strands of gray shone in her black hair, and a silver chain and tiny silver cross sparkled against her red blouse.

"I'm looking for information on private companies."

"You did this because of that guy that broke into your house and shot Maury Beekner?"

"I just need to lie low for a while."

"He's still after you? I mean, he didn't just break into a house at random?"

"Look, Ramona . . ."

"Is Maury going to be okay? I mean, he's such a nice guy. Comes in here from time to time."

"The doctors don't know."

Ramona lifted her eyes, as if she were uttering an internal prayer. Then she said, "What are you working on to make somebody come after you?"

Catherine stared at the woman, the words she'd been about to say jammed behind her teeth. Ramona had cut through the other possible scenarios to what they both knew was the truth: because of something she might write, a man intended to kill her. She tried for a little shrug, but couldn't manage it. "I need to know who's involved in Arcott Enterprises and Denver Land Company."

"You and everybody else." Ramona tilted her head in Newcomb's direction. "You know how it is with private companies. The law doesn't require a lot of information, especially if they were formed after 2000. Address, name of registered agent, and name of person who files the incorporation, that's it. Holler if I can help with anything."

Ramona lifted herself off the chair and Catherine felt the woman's hand drop onto her shoulder for a moment. "Take care of yourself."

Catherine nodded and typed Denver Land Company in the search box. In a half second another document appeared. The company had been formed in 1983. She could feel her heart speeding up, and she leaned closer. Jordan Rummage was the registered agent, which meant that tax bills and other official documents went to him. Catherine knew the name. Nelson and Rummage was one of the oldest law firms in Denver. It had handled numerous real estate deals she had covered — renovation of several historic Denver buildings transposed into high-priced condominiums.

The law firm had also filed the incorporation documents. She scrolled to the next page and no surprise there: Officers were James Nelson and Jordan Rummage. The company's address was the same as the law firm's — an historic house converted into an office building on the other side of down-town.

She sat back and stared at the screen. What she had was nothing, and yet it was something. She had the name of the law firm that was the public face of Denver Land Company.

"Well, well, if we aren't following the same tracks."

Catherine spun around. She wondered how long Dennis Newcomb had been stand-ing behind her. He wore a startled look, like that of a runner who'd glanced around and seen another runner closing his lead. "Wasn't sure it was you for a few minutes. So tell me, who's pulling Senator Russell's strings? Arcott?" He put up the palm of one hand before Catherine could say anything. "I've been following your articles. The governor thinks he can block the whole proposal with a briefing. You ask me, he's taking the chance that Congress will go along with the genocide theory and give Ar-cott what he wants."

"It was genocide," Catherine said.

"A hundred and fifty years ago! Not relevant, I say. What else did Arcott tell you? Where's he getting his financial backing?" Newcomb leaned down. His face was pit-ted, as if it had been sandblasted. The stale odor of cigarettes floated between them.

"Find out for yourself," Catherine said. But she was looking for answers to the same questions. She turned back, pushed the print key, and closed the screen.

"We can help each other, save a lot of time and energy." Newcomb moved in closer. "This is a big story. Tribes willing to trade twenty-seven million acres for five hundred acres and a three-hundred-million-dollar casino? Who came up with that idea? The tribal elders? I don't buy that, and neither do you. There's big money in a casino like that and, you ask me, there's big money behind it. You with me?"

"What do you want from me?" Catherine got to her feet and Newcomb took a step back. They were on the same track. Arcott could have local investors eager to bypass state voters who didn't want any more casinos. The silent partners in an Indian casino could reap millions every year. She hadn't asked Arcott the right questions, and answers were always in direct relation to questions. Wasn't that the first rule of journalism? Ask different questions and get different answers?

"We should cooperate, Catherine. We're both trying to run down the truth about what's really going on here."

"I'm running down my own story," she said.

"Okay, okay." Newcomb waved his hand in a gesture of truce. "Have it your way, but the day will come when it'll be the press against whoever's trying to force a casino on the state. There's millions of dollars riding on the deal. Governor might be against it, but Senator Russell's on the side of Arcott and the tribes."

He waited a moment, as if he expected her to respond, and when she didn't say anything, he gave her a mirthless smile. "Stay cool." He spun around and walked into the entry. There was a sense of expectation in the way he stopped at the door, as if he hadn't given up the possibility that she might come to her senses and call him back. Then he flung the door open and let it slam behind him.

Catherine gathered up the pages that the printer had spit out and walked back to the counter. She waited until Ramona looked up from the desk. "The only names for Denver Land Company are lawyers," she said.

Ramona gave one of those sympathetic nods that meant she understood and wasn't it a shame. "Not unusual for lawyers to be listed on the articles of incorporation for private companies. Maintains privacy for the investors." She ran her tongue over her lips, considering something before she went on: "I couldn't help overhearing Newcomb. I mean, nobody wants a big casino near Denver. If the deal goes through, there'll be a major uproar."

"That's just it, Ramona. If Congress approves the deal, the people of Colorado can protest all they want. There won't be anything anybody can do about it."

She left her with that, Ramona nodding and sighing as if it were all out of their hands and what could they do?

Outside Catherine walked in the rectangle of shade next to the buildings and checked the messages on her cell. Traffic sputtered and whined along Colfax Avenue. No text messages. No voice mail. She glanced at the pedestrians moving along the sidewalk, the cars flowing past. She felt the tension start to melt away, and realized she had been holding her breath.

She scrolled to the number for Senator Russell's office and pressed the call key. A man's voice came on after the first ring. "Office of Senator Russell."

Catherine held the cell tight against the wheezing noise of a bus that had just disgorged a group of kids in red tee shirts. She gave her name and asked to speak to Harry Colbert.

"Sorry, Mr. Colbert is unavailable." No hesitation in the voice, no hint that the man was lying. "Leave your number and someone will return your call."

"I've left my number, and no one has returned my call."

"Sorry, Ms. McLeod." The tone of his voice said that the people in Senator Russell's office knew who she was. What was it that *Denver Magazine* had written last January in the annual "Best of the West" issue? *The* Journal *publishes the stories behind the stories. Reporter Catherine McLeod is relentless. Must reading for anyone who wants to know what's really going on in our region.*

Someone had given instructions to the effect that Senator Russell and his assistant were permanently unavailable to Catherine McLeod. She said that she wanted to leave another message for Mr. Colbert.

"Hold, please, while I transfer you to his voice mail."

Catherine counted the seconds . . . nineteen, twenty. The traffic noise ground in her ear. Then the recorded voice of Harry Colbert cutting through the noise: "Senator Russell is eager to hear your comments. Please leave your name and number."

"Catherine McLeod, the *Journal*," she said. "My sources . . ." Sources? Speculation was all she had, along with a gut feeling that something was wrong. She kept her voice firm and deliberate and started again. "My sources tell me that Senator Russell plans to take action to settle the tribal claims and make the casino possible. I'd like to confirm that," she said, still the determined tone meant to let Colbert know that she intended to run the story whether or not she heard from him, which in itself would be a confirmation.

She pressed the end key, then called information and got the number for Nelson and Rummage. A group of businessmen passed by, talking all at once, waving their arms. The sounds of their voices mingled with the noise of a string of buses heaving themselves through the intersection.

A blond man was on the other side of the street, waiting to cross. She felt her heart jump. Then he was crossing the street, coming closer, and she was in a half spin toward the direction in which she'd come. There was a security guard in the skyscraper lobby, she was certain she'd spotted one.

But it wasn't him. The man walking toward her was probably in his sixties, with fading blond hair and the beginnings of a blond beard. She had to take a moment before she called the law firm. A woman answered on the first ring, as if her hand had been on the phone. She delivered the name of the firm so quickly that the names ran together like a verbal stew laced with impatience. Every second counted at a law firm like Nelson and Rummage. Seconds were money.

She gave her name and said she was with the *Journal.* Preparing a story on the Indian casino. Wanting to confirm information with Jordan Rummage.

"Mr. Rummage is with a client at the moment," the woman said, speaking more slowly now, deliberately. She had the woman's attention, Catherine thought. "Let me check his schedule." The line went dead. A woman who looked like a runner herded three small children down the sidewalk.

"Ms. McLeod?" The woman was back on the line: "Mr. Rummage will be available in thirty minutes. I suggest you call back then."

"I'll be in your office in twenty minutes," Catherine said.

20

Erik waited until the gangly man with thick glasses and the name plate on his shirt that said "Andy" finished directing a pink-haired woman to the genealogical department of the library. "Oh, I'm sure my family would be in Western History." She held up a mottled hand in protest. "We've been in Colorado so long, you see. Dear me, a century at least." She should start in genealogy, Andy was saying, tossing a glance past her shoulder toward Erik, as if to say that he would answer his questions next.

Finally the woman began moving away, and Andy walked down the counter. "How may I help you?"

"I'm looking for Catherine McLeod." Erik pulled the business card that he'd had printed this morning from his shirt pocket. "I'm a colleague. I was supposed to meet her here."

"I'm afraid she hasn't come in yet." The

man pulled a sour face that made it seem he was genuinely sorry he couldn't be of help. "She was here yesterday."

It was a long shot, Erik was thinking. After the article she had written for this morning's paper, he'd taken the chance she would want to do even more research on Sand Creek and the genocide looming behind the settlement proposal. He should have gotten here yesterday. A perfect place for their meeting, this reading room with rows of stacked books and papers, and tables set here and there, and all the heads dropped into leather-bound volumes or a thick wad of documents, oblivious to anything going on around them. He could have ushered her into the stacks and left her there. He could feel the weight of the Sig in his pocket.

"Did she happen to mention any other research she intended to do? Wouldn't surprise me if she were elsewhere in the library."

Andy nodded, as if the possibility had also crossed his mind. Then he said, "I'm afraid she didn't say. She's a very thorough researcher. You might want to look around."

"Appreciate your time," Erik said.

He'd started for the door when the man behind the counter said, "I hardly recognized her myself."

"Excuse me?" Erik turned back.

"Well, the color of her hair now. Almost blond, I'd say, and a lot shorter. Doesn't look like herself. But you know how women are . . ." He let the half thought hang between them, a little man-to-man joke.

"Yeah, always wanting to look different." Erik tried for a laugh and thanked the man again because, after all, he had just told him something useful.

"I assume you're the reporter from the *Journal*." A black-haired woman, all angles and sharp edges, turned away from the computer on the polished walnut desk. Reluctance was stamped on her narrow face. Everything about her seemed defined by black and white and slashes of red: the shiny black hair smoothed back like a tight-fitting cap and the tiny ruby earrings; the powdered white face and bright red lipstick; the large white collar flattened over the lapels of the black jacket and the ruby pin dancing near the shoulder. She made a pyramid under her chin out of long white fingers tipped with red.

"Catherine McLeod." Catherine pushed a business card across the desk. The reflection of her hand shone in the smooth surface. The sound of traffic burrowed through the brick walls of the two-story Victorian house a few blocks from the capitol. She had spotted the house when she'd reached the corner. Halfway down a block lined with metal and steel buildings, ten or twelve stories high, sunbursts reflecting in the bluish windows. Behind the buildings, downtown skyscrapers rose like silvery steps into the blue sky. She'd crossed on the diagonal with the suits and briefcases and high heels, the army of lawyers, brokers, secretaries, and business people, still glancing around for the blond-headed man and, at the same time, watching the brick house, so out of place, wedged between two modern buildings. A remnant of the past, rectangular windows marching across the front with flower boxes stuffed with petunias. Nelson and Rummage had won an award from the Denver Historical Society last year for preserving a piece of Denver's history, and the *Journal* had devoted two pages of text and color photographs to the house.

The receptionist rose out of her chair. She was taller than Catherine by several inches, and she swayed forward, as if the wind were at her back. "Mr. Rummage is a very busy man. Out of necessity, his policy is not to see anyone without an appointment, which can take weeks to secure, I might add.

However, he has agreed to make a one-time exception in your case. He can give you five minutes."

And those were the ground rules, punctuated by the woman's hard-eyed stare.

Catherine spread her hands. *Of course.* Then she was following the woman across the light blue carpet and down a narrow hallway past two closed doors that had probably led to bedrooms a hundred years ago. The air had a fruity chemical odor, like that of an air freshener blowing through the air vents. The woman stopped at the third door, gave a sharp rap, and pushed the door open. "Mr. Rummage is waiting for you," she said, stepping to the side.

Catherine moved past the woman into a spacious room that spread across the rear of the house. A wide-shouldered man in a gray pin-striped suit with a white shirt and a red tie knotted against his thick neck rose from behind the walnut desk. With the exception of a neat stack of folders, the surface was clear. Filtered daylight glowed in the bank of windows behind the desk. Outside was a small courtyard with a flagstone floor and pots of flowers and metal chairs scattered about, walled in by the smooth glass and metal surfaces of the adjoining buildings.

Catherine walked over and shook the

fleshy hand that Rummage held out. He looked like an aging athlete, tanned face and hands, gray hair trimmed close, a little too much weight around the midsection.

"What can I confirm for the *Journal,* Ms. McLeod?" he said.

"I'm doing a story on the proposed Arapaho and Cheyenne casino," Catherine began.

Rummage waved away the preliminaries. He was still on his feet, and he hadn't invited her to take one of the brown leather chairs arranged around the room. "As soon as Congress settles the land claims with the tribes, the casino will be constructed on five hundred acres currently owned by Denver Land Company. I assume that is the confirmation you require," he said, and Catherine understood then that Peter Arcott had tipped him off that she would be coming around.

"A few things I'm not clear about," Catherine said.

Rummage drummed his fingers on the edge of the desk a moment, weighing various scenarios in his head. Finally he nodded her toward a leather chair. "Five minutes," he said, "and you've already used two." He dropped into the leather chair behind him.

"Who are the principals in the company?"

Rummage gave her a crooked smile. "Privileged information, as I'm sure you know. If the investors wanted their names public, they would have placed them on the articles of incorporation, which I'm sure you've already pulled."

"Why the five hundred acres owned by Denver Land?" Catherine pushed on. "There's a lot of undeveloped land around the airport, valuable land that will only become more valuable. Eventually the area will be developed into hotels, restaurants, warehouses . . ." She threw out both hands with the endless possibilities of what the future might hold. "I'm curious as to why the company would want to sell so early."

Rummage was shaking his head. Amusement flooded his eyes. "Buy. Sell. Denver Land makes buy-sell decisions every day. In this situation, the company's sense of public responsibility determined the decision."

"I don't understand," Catherine said.

Rummage leaned forward and flattened his hands on the desk. "Let me make it as clear as I can. Denver Land has operated since 1983. The company has always been a good citizen, and we are aware of our public responsibilities. After a hundred and fifty years, the Arapaho and Cheyenne tribes deserve a fair settlement to legitimate land claims. I'm sure you agree. I've been following your stories." He paused for the briefest moment, as if he expected her to thank him, then went on. "The company is proud to be part of the settlement. Our parcel of land near the airport is a perfect location for a casino. It will draw thousands" — he lifted his hands and spread his fingers — "of visitors and generate a flow of capital for the tribes. We believe this is a worthy venture, and we're convinced the people of Colorado will also agree when they know the facts."

"So the company has no problem with selling to the government?"

"We expect to trade the land."

"Trade?"

Rummage sat back in his chair. He clasped his hands across his middle and began swiveling side to side. "The usual accommodation in agreements such as this. The federal government owns a lot of this country. National forests, BLM land. The tribes will receive title to five hundred acres of ancestral lands, and we'll receive five hundred acres of BLM land in Colorado."

"Where?"

Rummage pursed his lips together a moment, considering. "I'm afraid the exact location hasn't been finalized."

"Pitkin County? Eagle County?" She was guessing, a stab in the dark. But if she was right, the Indian settlement could be a lucrative deal for Denver Land Company. The two mountain counties comprised some of the state's most valuable land. Aspen was located in Pitkin County; Vail was in Eagle County.

Rummage gave an exaggerated shrug.

"So it's possible."

"The federal government owns lands across the state, including Pitkin and Eagle counties." He pushed away from the desk and stood up. "I'm afraid you've exceeded your five minutes. I'm expecting a client."

Catherine got to her feet. "Who initiated the proposal for a tribal land settlement that included a casino? Denver Land? Arcott Enterprises? The tribes?"

A slow smile burned through his features. "Justice for the Arapahos and Cheyennes has been delayed too long, Ms. McLeod," he said, sounding like a public relations flack. She could have written down the next statement before he'd mouthed the words: "All the parties agreed to the proposed settlement."

Catherine pushed on: "Whose idea was it, Mr. Rummage?"

"You've interviewed Norman Whitehorse.

I'm certain he told you it was the tribes' idea. The company has joined the proposal as a public service."

"Are you working with Senator Russell?"

"Enough, Ms. McLeod." Rummage hauled himself around the desk, walked over to the door, and snapped it open. "I believe you have everything you need. The interview is over."

Catherine stepped across the room. A curious choice of words, she was thinking. *Everything you need.* Did he really believe that he could determine what she needed, that he was in control of the story? She stopped in front of him. "Shall I say that you refused to comment on whether Denver Land Company is working with Senator Russell?"

Rummage drew in a long breath of exasperation. "Senator Russell is a great friend of the Indians," he said. "Naturally all the parties interested in justice for the Arapahos and Cheyennes are working together for the settlement."

"What about Governor Lyle? He opposes the settlement. Does that mean he isn't a friend of the Indians?"

"Ms. McLeod, please." Catherine felt the weight of Rummage's hand on her shoulder, nudging her through the door. "You'll have to take that up with the governor."

Catherine took a different route back toward the garage, operating on instinct. Walk on the other side of the street, two blocks out of the way to Sixteenth Street, hop on the shuttle and ride a short distance to the end of the line. It was good to vary her routine; she had to remember that. *Erik* couldn't expect her to do anything or be anywhere. She couldn't become reliable. She got off the shuttle into crowds milling around the corner of Colfax and Broadway. A bus pulled alongside the curb, doors wheezed open, and passengers shouldered their way to the sidewalk. A crowd waited to board. Traffic churned past, drivers downshifting and revving the engines. Then the bus started off, followed by a long exhalation of exhaust that blended in to the cacophony of city noise.

The light changed, traffic squealed to a halt, and she stepped into the stream of people crossing Colfax. The golden dome of the capitol shone in the sun. She could feel the heat of the pavement working through the soles of her shoes. The sun was hot on her arms and face, her blouse was damp with perspiration. She glanced about: the Hispanic woman pulling two young children along; the three men in dark business suits, intent on some conversation; another man in a lawyer suit, a cell pressed to his ear; several families in the tourist attire of shorts and tee shirts; a group of young women in flowing skirts and open-toed sandals. Across the street, on the lawn that swept down the hill in front of the capitol, knots of homeless lounging in the pockets of shade beneath the trees. There was no sign of *him,* no man with yellowish blond hair anywhere about.

She headed for the red cart on the corner, with Hot Dogs painted in white letters on the side, and waited while a middle-aged black woman in a red apron handed out chips and soda and hot dogs to a group of teenagers. The heat from the grill radiated around the sidewalk. Catherine bought a hot dog wrapped in aluminum foil and a lukewarm can of Coke and started toward a wrought-iron bench in a slice of shade.

Then she saw him.

21

Blond hair that looked dyed, too yellow to be natural, walking along Broadway. Tan shirt, khaki slacks, blending into the sidewalk. He had just left the library. Of course, that was it. He had assumed she would go back to the library to do more research. How long had he sat in the main corridor, watching patrons passing by, or hung around in the Western History Department? He would have posed as a patron, thumbing through who knew how many historical documents, keeping an eye on the entrance, studying every woman who walked in.

He was on the other side of the street, less than a half block away, looking around, a hunter searching for his prey. He slowed down, studied the small group of women coming toward him, then sped up.

Catherine swung about and started up Colfax, keeping a steady even pace. She dropped the can of Coke into her bag and tried to blend into the small crowd of tourists that had just disembarked from the bus next to the curb. Elderly looking, gray heads and thick middles, but they moved right along, determination in the way they propelled themselves up the slight incline toward the west door of the capitol. She walked next to a large, white-haired man; she was his wife. *He* would think she was one of the tourists!

He was behind them somewhere, and he knew how to find her. She tried to think how he knew, flipping through images from the last two days as if they were a deck of cards. Keeping one image, discarding the next. She'd interacted with dozens of people. Dozens had seen her disguise. Most didn't count. The shuttle driver and the black woman at the red hot dog cart, the clerk at the police station, the bellman at the Brown Palace. They didn't know who she used to be. But Newcomb knew, and Ramona at the secretary of state's office. And the secretary in Arcott's office would remember her, the way she'd tricked her into saying that Peter Arcott was at the Brown. Rummage's secretary this morning, and Arcott and Rummage themselves. They could all describe her: short sandy-colored hair, plain looking with no makeup, wearing casual tan slacks and a cream-colored, nondescript blouse. No one would ever pick her out of a crowd.

Except that yellow hair would know how to pick her out of a crowd, despite the cheap hairdo. He had known everything about her: where she worked and where she lived, phone number, e-mail address, how she walked Rex in the evenings, how she might turn to her ex-husband and try to hide at the Stern Ranch. Everything. He could recognize the way she walked and held her shoulders and tilted her head to one side, pretending to be part of a conversation that wasn't taking place with the elderly man beside her.

The tourists veered toward the capitol, and Catherine fell in beside a group of young women, secretaries on a late lunch break, giggling and teasing one another. Now she was one of them. She stayed with them, past the statue of the Civil War soldier. A woman with a black ponytail shook a cigarette out of a pack, then offered the pack to the others. They turned onto the grass and headed toward a wrought-iron bench. Catherine kept going.

She waited for a break in the traffic on Fourteenth Avenue, then dashed across, feeling exposed, the lone duck in a shooting gallery. She headed downhill toward Broadway. Past the corner of the Colorado History Museum, she could see the garage across the plaza a block away. She had to reach the garage, get to the second floor, and drive off in the Taurus. There was some kind of construction going on at the corner — a new pipe being laid in the street — and a man in a yellow hat held up a stop sign. She bunched with the other pedestrians, waited for the sign to drop, and crossed Broadway, staying with a couple of women. She kept looking up Broadway where she'd spotted him, but he'd disappeared. He might have spotted her walking toward the capitol. He could be inside the capitol now; he could be anywhere.

She turned left and hurried past the grassy area next to the library. Then she was walking along the front of the library, the afternoon sun bathing the stone façade and radiating from the sidewalk. She felt nauseated from the fear and heat and the emptiness in the pit of her stomach. The aluminum-wrapped hot dog felt clammy and mashed in her hand. She took a few diagonal steps across the sidewalk and dropped the hot dog into a trash can. And she saw him again.

In the corner of her eye, retracing his steps

down Broadway, and he had spotted her, too, because he picked up his pace. Half walking, half jogging, he was not even a block away, and he was coming toward her.

Catherine ran for the library entrance and threw herself past the doors. There was always a guard at the desk just inside the door. Sometimes he was white with white hair and the bored expectation of retirement in his expression, and sometimes he was black with short, cropped hair and a friendly "hello," and sometimes he was fat and out of shape, and sometimes he looked like a Bronco. He was always there! But he wasn't there now. There was nothing but the worn-looking desk that had probably been moved out of some storeroom, and the vacant chair pushed sideways, as if he'd gotten up in a hurry to tend to some emergency.

She darted past the inner doors and ran down the wide corridor that divided the resource room from the stacks and reading rooms, past the table with the sign that said "Library Picks" and the books on display; past the teenagers hovering outside the reading room, and the sixtyish woman standing next to the table covered with brochures — "Help you?" she called — and past the line forming in front of the machines that automatically checked out books. She glanced around only once, and he hadn't yet come through the entrance, but he would. He'd seen where she'd gone.

The doors at the end of the corridor led onto the brick plaza that connected the library with the plaza in front of the art museum and the garage. The bricks spilled into a walkway across Thirteenth Avenue, and Catherine was still running as she crossed the street. She headed for the entrance to the garage, then veered right, operating on instinct, her heart pounding against her ribs. He hadn't come into the library behind her. He was running when she saw him; he could have run a block and entered the library before she reached the other exit, but he hadn't. Because he knew where she was heading. He expected her to go to the garage. There was only one entrance, a concrete box with glass doors to the first parking level and an elevator and a metal and concrete stairway to the next levels. He would be waiting for her there.

She flung open the heavy glass door that led into the Denver Art Museum. "Tickets Ahead" said the sign teetering next to the black ropes meant to control the crowds, but there were no crowds today, just small groups of visitors milling about in front of the ticket counter. The agents were busy, heads bent into their tasks. Catherine turned to the left and started upstairs, through a canyon rising into the high, open spaces of the atrium. Little white paper birds fluttered on the walls. She felt as if she were ascending into a vacuum, the sounds of footsteps and conversations muffled far below. She looked around. No sign of him yet.

She walked on the far side of the railing where he couldn't see her when he entered — and he would enter the museum, she was certain. He would wait for her in the garage only a few moments before he understood that she wasn't coming. He might even have seen her run into the museum.

She walked hurriedly and with purpose. She knew the layout of the museum; she'd spent a day wandering through the slanting halls and galleries, climbing up and down the stairs, and she'd written a long article about the Hamilton addition that made no attempt to contain the thrill of experiencing it. The white walls slanted at various angles, the galleries were like giant cubes tossed together, and there were visitors who said the walls gave them vertigo. How can you enjoy paintings hanging on walls that jut toward you or threaten to fall on you? But the walls didn't fall, and people kept coming, drawn, she thought, by the collections and the architecture and the way the architecture shook visitors out of their complacencies and maybe allowed them to experience the art differently, all preconceptions wiped away.

She hurried through the galleries until she came to the steel and glass walkway over Thirteenth Avenue that connected the new addition to the old museum, a gray castle that rose over Civic Center. The windows in the walkway were wedged between steel pillars. She stopped at the edge of the first window and peered down. Traffic hummed underneath. She could feel the faint vibrations in the glass. A busload of tourists must have arrived, because there was a large group of kids gathering at the museum entrance. Just past the kids, she watched two girls in shorts and tee shirts enter the garage. The sun glinted in the glass when they closed the door behind them.

The door opened again, and he walked out. He looked across Thirteenth toward the library, then his eyes searched the brick apron in front of the museum. He took a moment to decide before he walked past the kids. She lost him behind the roof that crept out over the entrance. She spun around and ran along the walkway into the galleries of the castle, the voice of the guide who had taken her through the complex that day sounding in her head. *The space flows harmoniously, as you can see, from the Hamilton to the old museum, which is still a fine building housing many of the museum's collections. That was the goal, of course, to tie everything into a first-class complex. Truly worthy of a major city like Denver, wouldn't you agree?*

And of course she had agreed. It had all flowed harmoniously, and the stairs were over there somewhere. She remembered traipsing after the guide, following her downstairs into the large entry of the old building. She took the steps fast — it felt like hopping — crossed the entry and went outside into the heat that rolled like waves through the noise of traffic on Colfax. The light at the corner was green, and she hurried to get across before it could change and leave her stationary and helpless waiting for the cycle of yellow, red, and finally green again. And all the time, he would be gaining on her.

She ran along the sidewalk, cutting past the other pedestrians, knocking into a man in a dark suit, almost stumbling, then righting herself — excuse me, excuse me — and running on. She turned a corner and ran another block to Sixteenth Street where she hopped on the shuttle. The seats were taken, and she leaned into a metal pole to steady herself. She could hear her heart hammering in her ears; she was breathing hard and her blouse felt wet and clingy. The shuttle lumbered ten blocks, and she got off. She'd gone farther than necessary, but that meant she could come at the hotel from a different direction.

She pulled her cell out of her bag, walking fast — half running — weaving through knots of pedestrians, trying to put as much space as possible between herself and a man with yellow hair named Erik. She managed to press the keys for Bustamante. It took a moment before he picked up. "Detective Bustamante." His voice sounded distracted, far away.

"He spotted me," Catherine said.

"What? Where are you?"

"Downtown."

"Where did you see him?"

"He came out of the library. I walked up to the capitol, came down Fourteenth, and ran through the library and art museum. My rental car's in the garage."

"God, Catherine. The capitol is swarming with state patrol officers. All you had to do was go inside and find one."

"Well, there's always a guard inside the library, too, but he wasn't there." She heard herself shouting. A couple of women passing by glanced at her. She lowered her voice. "I was scared. I ran."

"Okay. Okay. Where'd you last see him?"

"He followed me into the museum."

"How's he dressed?"

"Tan shirt, khaki slacks. Yellow hair. For godssakes, you've got to get him."

"Where are you now?"

"Just get him, damn it." She pressed the end key.

The three blocks to the hotel stretched ahead in a hazy blur of heat. She was still walking fast, glancing over her shoulder every few minutes, watching the people coming toward her, the pedestrians on the other side of the street, half expecting a brown sedan to pull alongside the curb. Then the hotel was in front of her. She crossed the street, hurried past the two uniformed doormen at the entrance, and pushed through the double glass doors before either of them could grab the handle. The air in the lobby hit her like an arctic blast that made her suck in her breath. For a second she thought she might faint. She made herself take a couple of deep breaths before she headed for the elevator.

"Ms. McLeod?"

She turned toward the registration desk. She could feel the hair bristling on the back of her neck. The woman in the black uniform blazer with dark, curly hair waved a white envelope across the desk. No one knew where she was staying, not Marie or Marjorie or Philip. Not even Bustamante. But she had let the desk clerk take an imprint of her credit card — "for additional expenses" — and she understood with a cold certainty she had made a mistake. The kind of mistake that could get her killed. The clerk had assured her the charges wouldn't be put through until she checked out, and she intended to pay in cash when she checked out. But she had ordered room service last night and the night before — club sandwich, turkey sandwich. Catherine felt as if she were moving through water as she walked over and took the envelope.

She waited until she was in the elevator, the motor humming around her, before she tore open the flap and pulled out the folded piece of paper. Generic envelope, generic paper, the kind you could buy in the office supplies aisle of any grocery store. Her fingers felt stiff and clumsy as she unfolded the paper.

Scrolled across the fold in large black letters were the words: *I look forward to seeing you soon. We will want to say good-bye.* She had the sense that the floor was rising toward her as the elevator came to a stop and the doors slid open. They were starting to close when she managed to push herself off the brass railing on the back wall and stumble into the corridor.

22

Ten minutes later, Catherine was in a cab crawling down the center lane of a one-way street, lines of cars and trucks flashing past. "Colorado Boulevard," she'd told the driver. She'd heard the tremor in her voice. She'd stuffed her clothes and makeup kit into the backpack, grabbed her laptop case, and run down the corridor to the elevator, the backpack in her arms, squashed against her chest, laptop case and bag banging against her back. She'd confirmed with the clerk that, yes, a mistake had been made in charging the credit card. Not hotel policy. So sorry, but if there was anything they might do to persuade her to stay — dinner in the restaurant this evening, perhaps?

Catherine had shoved the credit card across the counter. What difference if the card was processed again? He already knew where she was staying. Except that now, he would know she had checked out. She snatched the credit card away and pulled several bills out of the white envelope. The clerk's eyebrows had swooped upward, but she hadn't said anything. Just waited while the printer whirred out the receipt, which Catherine stuffed in her bag. Then she gathered up everything and waited inside the door while the doorman summoned a cab. It wasn't until he had placed her backpack and laptop in the trunk and opened the rear door that she had darted across the sidewalk and into the backseat, her skin prickly with the sense that she was being watched, that he was out there somewhere — in the parking lot across the street, on the sidewalk, at one of the windows of the nearby buildings. Looking down, waiting.

"Colorado Boulevard's a long street." The cabdriver tossed a half glance over his shoulder, then jerked the steering wheel to avoid a pickup that cut ahead. "What address you want?" His jaw didn't move. His voice bounced off the back of his teeth.

Catherine watched the passing traffic and the people on the sidewalks. Is that what she had become? A watcher? Always watching and waiting for him? She leaned forward. "Make sure we're not being followed," she said.

And that seemed to flip some switch inside him. He straightened his shoulders and looked back at her. "What is this, lady, the movies? I got a wife and four kids. I don't need any trouble. You better get out." He was already changing lanes, pulling toward the curb.

"You don't understand," Catherine said. She felt clammy at the thought of being ejected onto the sidewalk again, exposed like a naked woman in the afternoon heat. "It won't be any trouble for you. All you have to do is take the side roads to Colorado Boulevard. I'll double your fare."

He seemed to consider this a moment. The cab slowed down, then lurched forward and turned onto another one-way street. Traffic on Speer Boulevard shimmered in the hazy heat ahead. They crossed the boulevard and began weaving through residential neighborhoods with lines of cars parked at the curbs and little patches of dried lawns crawling out from brick bungalows. Every couple of blocks, Catherine made herself look out the rear window, half expecting to see a brown sedan or some other vehicle with a yellow-haired driver. She felt her jaw clench. He would have a different car now, she realized. He would know that she had spotted the brown sedan.

He could be in *any* vehicle behind them.

The cabdriver was looking, too. She could see him glancing in the rearview mirror and checking the side mirrors.

"Okay, where to now?" he said. They turned into the whir of traffic moving south on Colorado Boulevard. Cars and trucks switching lanes, jockeying for space. There was the thrum of engines, the whine of tires on asphalt. The air inside the cab smelled of exhaust. Sirens were wailing in the distance. A horn blasted behind them, a white sedan sped past and pulled in ahead. The driver jammed on the brakes, rocking her forward against the seatbelt.

"Pull in at the first grocery store, Kmart, or Target you see," she told him. What she needed was time to focus on what to do next, where to go, without the fear of the yellow-haired man jamming all of her thoughts. There was a boutique hotel not far from where they were now, but wouldn't he think of that first? He would expect her to seek out a small, quiet hotel. Close to downtown where she was researching the story — the capitol, the library. My God, he could have already left a message there. That was what she had to focus on — what he was thinking. She had to tap into his thoughts and make decisions he didn't expect, if she was going to stay alive.

She realized they'd made a sharp right turn into a strip mall and were slowing toward the supermarket ahead. They swung into a loading lane directly across from the entrance with an automatic door that swooshed open each time a customer approached. "Wait here." She opened the door and got out.

"Wait?" The trunk popped and started to lift. The cabbie was out his door and heading to the rear of the cab, shoulders hunched around his head. "I got enough crime on TV, lady. You can get yourself another cab."

"Please," she said. "I'll only be a few minutes. I want you to take me to the Tech Center." Because she realized now that was where she should go, away from the center of town. She gave him the name of one of the major hotels that served the high-tech and financial businesses in the southern part of the city. "There's a big tip on top of the double fare, all right?"

He brought a fist down hard on the trunk and slammed it shut. Then he walked back to the driver's door, taking her in across the roof as he went. It gave her an uncomfortable, edgy feeling, and in that moment, a new plan formed in her head. As far as he would know, he had taken her to the major hotel.

She swung around and went through the automatic door. It took a moment to get her bearings — bakery over there, deli on the right — but within ten minutes she was back in the cab, clutching a plastic bag of hair dye with an auburn-haired model on the front and a turkey sandwich probably made in the deli sometime this morning, the two halves stacked together and wrapped in plastic.

"One more stop, over there," she said. The cab was moving along the front of the supermarket. She leaned forward and pointed across the mall toward the shop with Liquor spelled in red letters on the plate glass window.

"Jesus, lady," he said, but he pulled out of the left turn he was making and shot forward across the mall, weaving past a family sauntering toward an SUV, licking at ice cream cones. The tires gave a little squeal as he pulled up in front of the shop. Catherine went inside and selected an expensive bottle of Merlot. Dinner would be a turkey sandwich and Merlot. Perfect, she thought, wondering who she was now, this woman who ate deli sandwiches and drank wine alone.

Traffic seemed heavier on Colorado Boulevard, and heavier yet on I-25, rush hour in full swing, lanes filled with cars pouring out of downtown and heading to the southern suburbs. She still found herself looking around, checking the other drivers and passengers. Yellow hair wasn't there, and she told herself to relax. She'd lost him for the moment, and that meant she might be able to sink into her past life for a little while. Odd, she thought, that she considered it past, as if what had once been normal, everyday routine, would never come again.

She fished her cell out of the bag and checked the messages. Marie's voice: "I'm so worried about you, dear. Call me right away." Violet at the newspaper: "I think I have something for you. I'm e-mailing you." Lawrence: "How're things going, sweetheart? Been thinking about you. Let me know you're okay." Philip: "You better call me."

She pressed the key for Philip's number. It was a moment before the connection clicked and the ringing started, muffled and far away sounding. Finally, Philip's recorded voice: "I'm not here. Leave a message."

"How's Maury doing?" she said. God, she hadn't called since this morning. Anything could have happened since then.

They had taken an exit and joined the stream of traffic on the elevated road that crossed the highway. Traffic roared like a cauldron below. A left turn and they were curving through what might have been a residential neighborhood, except that the manicured lawns, flower beds, and sidewalks wound around glass and concrete skyscrapers. They made another turn and pulled into the shade of the hotel portico. The driver was out of the cab, it seemed to Catherine, while it was still rolling to a stop. He lifted her backpack and laptop out of the trunk before she'd counted out the bills to cover the double fare and the tip and gotten out of the backseat. She held out the money, which he snapped from her hand before hurling himself around the cab and getting behind the steering wheel. The cab squealed out of the portico.

Catherine stepped through the revolving door and emerged into a hollowed-out lobby, marble and glass with crystal chandeliers dangling from the ceiling high overhead. The registration desk was across the lobby: two clerks bent over computer screens, a group of men in dark suits leaning on the counter. There was the soft padding of footsteps as another group of businessmen moved through the lobby, subdued

349

tones of conversation floating past. She'd attended several conferences here in the last couple of years, and for a brief moment, a sense of normality came over her, as if she had just arrived for another conference, an ordinary assignment for the *Journal,* here to cover the keynote address of some celebrity.

She had to swallow hard against the lump rising in her throat. This was not an ordinary day. Nothing would ever again be ordinary. She jammed the wine and hair dye into the backpack, slung the backpack and laptop case over her shoulders and, gripping her bag in one hand, walked over to the marble column on the far side of the plate glass window that bordered the revolving door. From there, she had a clear view of the portico and the drive into the hotel. There were no other vehicles, no sign of anyone. A line of trees had been planted along the street. She waited a moment, looking past the trees for the flash of an oncoming vehicle. Still nothing.

The conference rooms were down the wide corridor on the right, she remembered, and that was where she headed. Moving casually, no need to hurry. She was simply another guest going to her room, except that the elevator to the rooms was down the corridor on the left. Still she might be heading to a conference room. She could see that none of the business people she passed gave her a second thought. A quick once-over from most of the men, but she was used to that, and that's all it was — a glance — because they were deep in conversations about whatever lecture or meeting they had just attended.

She passed two conference rooms, doors flung open, white-clothed tables in the corridor covered with cans of soda, silver coffee servers, and trays of cookies. Inside the rooms, groups of people were standing about. Others wandered past the doors into the corridor. Oh, she knew how it went. The breaks before the next speakers.

She kept going until she reached the end of the corridor, and here, just as she remembered, were double glass doors that exited into the parking lot in back. She hurried through the doors and walked across the lot and through the trees out onto a street that ran parallel to the street in front of the hotel. It took longer than she'd expected to walk to the small bed-and-breakfast that stood on the corner of a residential street at the edge of the Tech Center, and when she arrived, she was damp with perspiration. Her throat was dry, and the backpack and laptop felt like sacks of bricks.

The bed-and-breakfast might have been a small shop at one time, she thought. It had that look about it: flat-faced brick front, the wide windows on either side of the door. She'd never stayed here, but the *Journal* had run a feature on the place a few months ago. She remembered the headline: "Executives Step Off Fast Track." And the story about a married couple who ditched the corporate life and bought a bed-and-breakfast for executives tired of impersonal hotels, looking for a taste of home when they traveled.

And when he found the cabdriver — and he would find him somehow, she was certain. He knew how to do things. He would think she had gone to the hotel. He wouldn't know about the bed-and-breakfast.

"Guest check-in 3:00 p.m." said the engraved letters on the bronze plaque on the door. Catherine tried the knob, but it wouldn't turn. She pressed a gray button next to the door. A jingling noise, like wind chimes, came from inside, then the clack of footsteps on hard floors, and finally, the door opened. A woman about Catherine's age, tall and fit looking, with brown hair swept behind her ears and intense brown eyes stood in the opening.

"Yes?" she said, a note of surprise sounding in her voice.

"I was hoping you'd have an available room," Catherine said.

The brown eyes traveled over her: backpack, casual slacks, and blouse and everything about her casual, from the short, dyed sandy hair to the sandals. Hardly a business woman.

Catherine hurried on, trying to block the objections moving through the woman's expression: "An unexpected trip to Denver." She shrugged, as if making unexpected trips were part of her routine. "I'm a writer, and the opportunity for an interview came up that I hadn't expected. A friend . . ." She hesitated. Who was the reporter on the bed-and-breakfast story? "Carey Lewis," she said, taking a chance, "recommended your place."

The brown eyes softened. "Oh, yes," the woman said, hints of recollection and pride moving through her expression. "Great article. Increased our business thirty percent." She took a step backward, still holding on to the edge of the door. "We're booked for tonight," she said, "but one of our regular clients had to cancel. I can let you have his room." Another step backward, and this time she pulled the door open and waved Catherine inside.

The entry was small and homey — round

table and credenza with vases of flowers, silver candlesticks, and tall, tapered candles. Oil paintings of mountain landscapes displayed against the cream-colored wallpaper. The woman leaned over a polished desk across from the door and thumbed through the pages of a small guest book. Next to the book was a silver dish of mints. "One night?" she said.

"I may want to stay longer."

The woman flipped to another page. "I think I can arrange that." She glanced up. "Name?"

Catherine tried not to flinch. Had she flinched? Her name was who she was, and who was she? She wasn't sure anymore, so much of her had fallen away, like water evaporating from her skin when she came out of a pool. "Mary Fitzpatrick," she said, forcing a steadiness into her voice, as if this was who she would be now, someone with a name out of history.

The woman was scribbling the name. "From San Francisco," Catherine added. Then she gave what she hoped was the correct address of a college friend who lived in San Francisco.

The woman set the pen into a crystal holder, closed the guest book, and motioned Catherine toward the carpeted stairway on the right. "I hope you'll be comfortable here," she said. "Our clientele appreciate the quiet. They're always able to work here."

Catherine followed the woman up the stairs and down a narrow corridor to a room that was an expanded version of the entry — polished wood chests and tables with vases of flowers, upholstered chair and otto- man, four-poster bed with white comforter and pillows, and chair and desk beneath the window. Silky white curtains filtered the late afternoon sun and trailed along the back of the desk. Through the curtains, the moun- tains looked like an impressionistic paint- ing, a blue haze bathed in golden sunlight. The outside seemed remote and unimpor- tant. She could relax here, she thought. Relax and think and work. Reclaim some part of herself.

Erik sat behind the wheel of the black Pon- tiac he had rented this morning. He had parked in the garage at Civic Center, sure he would find her in the library. She wasn't there, but then he'd seen her at Colfax and Broadway. A stroke of luck, and yet — not really. He had known she would be in the vicinity of Civic Center. The sources for her stories were in the neighborhood.

But she had eluded him. Foolish and

counterproductive, he thought, to waste resources tracking the guerilla fighter into the jungle. She would only draw you in farther and farther, until you were on her turf, in her line of sight, and she would kill you. *Never allow the enemy to take control.* He could hear the voice of Colonel Blum booming in his head.

Catherine McLeod was taking control, and that was unacceptable. He'd played her game. Followed her to the ranch, found the exact spot for the assassination, waited for her to drive past. But all the time, she operated on instincts that had nothing to do with logic, nothing to do with what should have happened. She'd disappeared somewhere in the maze of galleries inside the art museum, and he had lost her.

Lost her in the jungle. But he wouldn't track her through the jungle again. A fool's game for inexperienced, pink-cheeked, nineteen-year-old privates with a few months of rifle training, not for skilled snipers, accustomed to picking off masked insurgents from the rooftops of Baghdad. The winning game was to bring the insurgents to the sniper, set up a place where they would want to be, give them a reason to come.

He would have to devise a new plan, and

that would take a little time. He would have to cajole Deborah, dangle the $50,000 payoff in front of her, but that would be easy. It was the idea of his client getting nervous, doubting his ability, that gave him a stab of worry. He had to work out the plan tonight; this had to be over fast.

23

After the woman's footsteps had padded back down the hall, Catherine set up her office: laptop on the desk, notepad squared to one side of the laptop, cell on the other. Silence engulfed the whole place, as if she'd wandered into a vacuum. She walked over to the bedside table, turned on the radio, and found the jazz station. A trumpeter imitating Miles Davis. She left the volume low, went back to the desk, and tapped out the number on the cell for the Victorian house high on a hill across the city. One ring and Marie picked up, as if she had been sitting by the phone, staring at it, willing it to ring. The familiar voice brought the knot to Catherine's throat again. She swallowed it back, and — odd, this — felt a sense of relief. There were still parts of her old life that remained. There was still Marie.

She was working hard, she told her, everything was going to be fine. She shouldn't worry. Catherine could feel herself forcing the words, willing them to be true. She could sense in the hush at the other end that Marie knew the real truth.

"All right, dear. If you say so." Both putting on an act, and what good actresses they had become, Catherine thought. She was getting to be an expert at being someone else, and so was Marie, the relaxed, unconcerned mother.

"How's Rex?" Catherine said, still digging back into that other life.

"Getting along okay. He misses you."

Catherine winced at the sharp pain that stabbed her, as if she'd touched a hot iron. She was about to end the call when another thought bubbled up out of somewhere: "Did you ever know anything about my . . ." She hesitated a moment. ". . . natural parents?"

Marie took a moment. Catherine could hear the sharp intakes of her breathing, followed by the quiet sound of resignation. "What do you mean?"

"I found the name Fitzpatrick while I was researching Sand Creek. It sounded familiar. I was wondering . . ."

"It was your birth mother's name," Marie said. Catherine wondered at the cost to her of uttering the word *mother.* "She was part

Arapaho. I'm sorry, but we never knew much about your father. You never seemed to want to know about them."

Part Arapaho, Catherine was thinking. She knew how it had worked. Lawrence used to talk about the half-breeds in the early days of Denver. A lot of white men on the plains back then and not many white women. Often white men took Indian wives. Squaws, they were called. Thomas Fitzpatrick might have married an Arapaho woman. If so, they could be her ancestors. She closed her eyes and tried to picture her mother — a dark-skinned woman leaning toward her, wisps of long black hair brushing her face. She tried to recall the sound of her mother's voice, but it was like trying to catch the melody of a song that she hadn't heard in a long time.

"There's the box of your mother's things in the attic," Marie said. "I haven't gone through it in years. I can pull it out for you."

"It's not important now." It was a moment, that was all, the faintest sense of connection to her own past when she had picked the name Fitzpatrick to hide under and had then come across the name of Thomas Fitzpatrick. She smiled at the irony. In her old life, she had always had a sense of disconnection, and now it was as if the

360

past were trying to reach out and touch this new woman she was becoming. She told Marie again not to worry and pressed the end key.

She checked the other messages. Nothing from Unknown. She could almost picture his expression when he learned she had checked out of the hotel. Talking to the doormen, trying to figure out which cab had picked her up — dark-blond hair, five feet six or so, slim, backpack, couple of bags. Surely you remember? It would take him a while. She shook off the safe feeling that had begun to wrap itself around her. She would never be safe until he was arrested.

Lawrence had called, but she had no intention of returning the call. He was a part of the old life that had broken into pieces, and the pieces could never be put back together.

She turned on the laptop. Twenty-nine messages in her e-mail box, and most of them junk. She scrolled down, clicked on the message from Violet, and glanced down through the black typed lines:

Checked on Arcott Enterprises in Alaska, California, and Nevada. Arcott has been very busy the last four years. The company built five casinos. All operating and making a lot of money for the tribes. But I did confirm that the company raised money to build the casinos from numerous financial institutions. Alaska — Northern Investment and Global Financial Services. California — Majority Finances, Centurion Investments. Nevada State Financial Corporation. All of the financial institutions are located within the respective states. Arcott's company manages the casinos, although that wasn't public information. I had to make a few calls to some local newspapers. Here is where it gets interesting. I was not able to confirm that the tribes are the sole owners of the casinos.

Catherine read through the message again. It could mean nothing, and yet it might mean everything. Arcott Enterprises depended on borrowed money to build the casinos, and Arcott worked with local institutions. What kind of deal had he struck with the tribes and the financial backers? Repayment from the tribal profits or an ownership stake in tribal casinos that the institutions would have been unable to build on their own? What kind of deal had Arcott struck for himself? And what side agreement had he made with the Arapahos and Cheyennes? There was so much Arcott had left out in the interview. But she hadn't asked the right questions.

She found Arcott's number in her cell and pressed the dial key. The automated voice came on after two rings. *Please leave a message. Someone will return your call during regular business hours.*

"Mr. Arcott, Catherine McLeod of the *Journal*." She could feel a little rush of excitement that came every time she knew she had finally figured out the right questions that would cause whoever she was interviewing to blanch and stammer; every time she pulled up a page on the Internet or found a document in some dusty archive that some official had hoped would stay hidden. She could sense when she had stumbled onto the right track. "My sources say you relied on local financial backers to build the casinos in other states. Will the financial institutions you're working with here have a silent partnership in the casinos? Will you have a silent partnership? My information will run in tomorrow's story. I'd appreciate your comments."

She hit the end button and went back to the e-mail messages. Similar messages from several readers: She should keep up the good work. Nobody wants another casino in the state. Why are the tribes able to go against the people's wishes? Who's really going to make money if the casino is built? Well, those were the questions, and she intended to find the answers.

She understood then. Erik, whoever he was, intended to kill her before she could find the answers.

And yet, Newcomb and the TV reporters were also following the story. They would pick up the leads and follow them to the end, just as she was doing. Did Erik intend to kill every reporter covering the proposed casino? It didn't make sense. Unless there was something she knew that they would never find out.

Here was something unusual. A message from someone named Sam Morrow: The Truth of Sand Creek. She hesitated a moment before opening the message. *He* could be Sam Morrow. "I'm a professor of history at the University of Colorado in Denver," the message began. "I've been following your stories on the Sand Creek Massacre and the proposal to build an Arapaho and Cheyenne casino near Denver. You have neglected several important aspects, or perhaps you yourself have decided they are not important enough to include. In the interests of accuracy in history, I believe we should have a talk. I will be in my office tomorrow at 3:00 p.m." Beneath the message was a telephone number and the address of an office on the third floor of the North Building on the Auraria campus.

Something not important enough to include? As if she made decisions about what mattered and what didn't. She felt a little sting of annoyance. She was a reporter. She reported the news, she didn't make it. She hit the reply button and typed: "I will see you then."

She scrolled down to the message from Marcy at the governor's office: "Briefing set for Monday, 3:00 p.m., Senate Office Building, Washington."

She would be there.

Finally she dug the carton of hair color out of the plastic bag. Then she found a pair of scissors in the desk drawer, went into the bathroom, laid out the coloring bottles and tubes, and went to work cutting her hair even shorter until it spiked around her head and changing the color to dark auburn, becoming someone else again, someone she hardly recognized in the mirror after she'd finished the process. Medium height, thin-looking woman still in her thirties, but barely — God, she was getting gaunt — with dark reddish hair cut above her ears, a boy's haircut.

She went back to the desk and laid out her dinner next to the laptop. She pried the plastic wrap from the sandwich and poured a little wine into one of the crystal glasses from the tray on top of the dresser. The smell of hair dye invaded the room, and she flung open the window. It was getting dark outside, a soft grayness settling over the street and lawn. Yellowish lights glowed in the street lamps. Apart from the distant hum of traffic and a dog yapping somewhere, the evening was quiet. She settled back into the chair and glanced through the notes she'd made today, underlining certain parts she intended to emphasize for tomorrow's article. Just as she was about to start writing, the cell rang. Unknown appeared in the readout.

She felt her muscles freeze, her joints lock into place. She wanted to drop the cell, but her fingers remained stuck around it. Then another feeling started through her, like a slow-burning flame. She had to hear the sound of his voice again, listen beyond the words to what he was thinking. It seemed as if this were required. She pressed the key and waited.

"Catherine? Peter Arcott." Arcott's voice boomed in her ear. She felt her fingers relax, her body sink against the back of the chair.

"What do you want?"

"Clarification of a few things in our interview," she said, using the most businesslike tone she could muster. She pulled over her notepad. "My sources . . ."

"Your sources? Who else have you talked to?"

"I'm running down a story, Mr. Arcott. My paper's contacted numerous sources. Is it true that you built the other casinos with local financial partners?"

"If you're asking if I raised investments to build the casinos, I've already told you that."

"Does that mean you intend to have local partners in the proposed Arapaho-Cheyenne casino?" The sandwich was already starting to dry out. She smoothed the plastic over the top.

"I told you, the financial plans aren't finalized."

"So you don't deny that the financial backers may be local institutions or investment companies?"

"Depends upon the terms." She was scribbling everything he said in her own brand of shorthand that she'd developed through countless interviews. "I intend to secure the best terms to make the casino as economically attractive as possible for the tribes."

"Will the financial backers have a stake in

the casino?"

"Methods of repayment have not yet been worked out."

"You'll take a finder's fee for raising the capital, correct? Another fee for handling construction. You'll also step into a lucrative position of operating the casino."

Arcott didn't say anything for a moment. She could hear the air blowing through his teeth. "I don't like what you're insinuating."

"What am I insinuating, Mr. Arcott? That you and the owners of the land and the financial backers will make a great deal of money from an Indian casino?"

"Last I heard from my lawyers, there's no law against businesses making profits in legitimate business arrangements."

"Whose idea was it to trade Arapaho and Cheyenne settlement claims for five hundred acres?"

"You already have the answer, but looks like it's not the answer you're after. Doesn't fit in with your preconceived ideas that, somehow, the Indians are being conned. Nonsense. The tribes know what's in their own best interests. My company is in the business of helping them to a better life. If you print anything else . . ." He waited a couple of beats before he went on. "I promise to sue you for defamation of character and slander. Are you sure you want to get into a lawsuit with me?"

"I intend to publish the facts surrounding the casino proposal, Mr. Arcott. No matter what they are." Before she could thank him for his time, she realized he'd hung up.

She unwrapped the sandwich again, took a bite, and washed it down with a gulp of wine. Her whole system seemed to pounce on the food, and she realized she hadn't eaten since the muffin and coffee she'd grabbed this morning. She hadn't had a decent meal since *he* had burst into her town house. She finished half the sandwich and went to work.

It took almost two hours to finish the article — writing, rewriting, checking her notes. Nibbling at the sandwich. Finishing off the glass of wine and pouring another. The faint smell of chemicals rose out of the empty bottle of hair coloring in the waste-paper basket near her feet. She'd been careful to stick with the facts, not cast any shadows on Arcott Enterprises, Denver Land Company, or anyone involved with the casino proposal:

According to reliable sources, Peter Arcott raised financial capital from local businesses to build casinos in other states.

Arcott declined to comment on the source of financing to build the proposed $300 million casino in Colorado. He did not deny that financing may come from local sources. Arcott Enterprises expects to operate the casino.

Jordan Rummage, spokesman for Denver Land Company, owner of the proposed 500-acre casino site, said that the company expects to trade the land for Bureau of Land Management acreage in another part of the state. He declined to name the company owners.

Senator Charles Russell's office did not return the *Journal*'s call.

She pressed the send key, feeling limp with frustration. Arcott Enterprises and Denver Land Company stood to make a lot of money if Congress approved a land settlement. But the tribes also stood to make a great deal of money. Who had initiated the whole idea in the first place? Arcott? Rummage? The tribes? Still so many holes to fill in, so much to learn before she could write the entire story.

The ringing noise punctuated the quiet. Catherine picked up the cell and glanced at the readout. Philip Case. She jammed her thumb against a key. "Philip," she said, and they were both talking at once. "How's Maury?" "It's about Maury." "Is he okay?" And "He's gone, Catherine."

Then she heard the sobs and the strangled gulps of air coming through the phone. She felt herself falling forward. Her elbow struck the edge of the desk. "No, Philip," she heard herself saying. "No! No!" And in between the sobs, Philip saying, "His heart stopped. They tried to start it again. They tried. They tried, but it just wouldn't start." Then Philip's voice, choked and muffled, coming from somewhere far away, "I can't talk anymore." The cell silent against her ear, and she was still saying, "No! No!" and sliding off the chair, the cell clacking against the surface of the desk, and the floor coming toward her, her knees scraping the carpet.

Not Maury! It could not be true. How could it be true? How could the world be without Maury? Biking ahead on the path along the Platte River, and she, trying to pump as hard as she could to stay with him, and Philip shouting behind, "Wait up!" And just last Saturday night, Maury walking across the grass at City Park, hauling the wicker hamper filled with the gourmet dinner and two bottles of good wine, Philip hurrying beside him. They'd spread out the blanket she'd brought, eaten the dinner, sipped the wine, and listened to the jazz concert. Watched the sun set behind the mountains and the long streaks of orange and fuchsia spread through the sky. She'd understood then that Maury was kind. He'd taken pity on her, the recent divorcée, still getting her bearings, trying to figure out who she was and where she belonged. Let's ask her along, he'd said to Philip, and Philip had plastered on the resigned expression that he wore all evening.

She managed to crawl into the corner next to the desk. It seemed the noise of her sobs filled up the whole room, burst out the window, and filled up the outdoors. She clamped her knees to her chest, rested her head against the wall, and gave in to the sobbing and to the wall of grief crashing over her.

24

Harry Colbert waited as Senator Russell folded his bulky frame into the rear seat. The door closed with a soft thud, the driver got in behind the wheel, and the town car slipped back into the narrow street that wound past the lawns in front of the flat-faced brick mansions. The morning sun twinkled in the upstairs windows.

"Give me the bad news." The senator spit out the order, managing to cough and growl at the same time. He was in a foul mood, Harry thought, not unlike his mood most mornings before he'd had the requisite half pot of black coffee. "You wouldn't be here otherwise."

Colbert pulled a thin stack of papers out of the briefcase balanced on his lap. He'd gotten to the office by 5:00 a.m. as usual. He liked to be ahead of the day, collect the messages that had come in during the night, read the *Post* and *New York Times* for whatever damaging statements they might have attributed to Senator Russell, some of which the senator himself had most likely given to some reporter who had cornered him in the corridors of the Senate Office Building when Colbert wasn't around to run interference. It was getting so that Colbert couldn't let the man out of his sight.

"Fax came in two hours ago." Colbert drummed his fingers on the top page. "Your esteemed colleague Senator Adkins has scheduled the briefing for the Indian Affairs Committee."

"Bastard!" Senator Russell barked out the word, and Colbert watched him tighten and release both fists, as if he were working a pair of worry balls. "So Governor Lyle got to him. Wants to stand up in front of a bunch of politicians who couldn't find Colorado on a map with a magnifying glass, never heard of Arapahos and Cheyennes, and don't give a rat's ass whether the state gets another casino. Make Lyle and Adkins both look like geniuses, plotting to keep more casinos out of the state."

"The voters have rejected other casinos," Colbert said.

"What do they know? Whipped up by a lot of do-gooders running ads about the social ills of gambling. Christ, let people spend their money any way they want. Little recreational gambling never hurt anybody. They sure weren't thinking about the economic impact and all those lost jobs when they cast those ballets. Christ, it's a crummy business we're in. Try to give the state a multimillion-dollar windfall every year and do a good deed for a poor bunch of Indians and what d'ya get? Nothing but opposition from liberals always shouting about how they're gonna help the poor people. Well, this here's the chance, and what do Adkins and Lyle do? Try to flush the whole project down the toilet. Why the hell haven't we attached a rider to a bill and settled this thing?"

"The bill we had decided was appropriate was postponed, remember?"

"Adkins's doing?"

"Most likely. I'm trying to confirm what happened. My guess is that Lyle called Adkins's office, asked him to do whatever he could to stall the bill in committee."

"That newspaper reporter . . ." Russell drew in his lower lip, as if he were drawing on a cigar. "What's her name?"

"Catherine McLeod at the *Journal.*"

"Oh, yes. Lawrence Stern's ex-wife. He never could control her. Should've taught her the way things are. She wrote that article about the riders that got the Indian casinos in other states. Tipped off Lyle that we might try the same maneuver, the bitch. We would've had this matter settled before he knew what had happened."

"It could have backfired on us," Colbert said.

Russell was quiet, but he'd shifted sideways, and Colbert could feel the old man's gaze burning into his skin. He hurried on. "McLeod's been talking to Arcott and Rummage, asking questions about who will be making money on the casino deal. She would have made it look as if the only reason you attached a rider that approved the settlement was to benefit certain business interests."

"Nonsense. Arcott Enterprises and Denver Land are engaged in legitimate business transactions."

"Made possible by your actions," Colbert said. He stopped himself from saying that the briefing was the best thing that could have happened and Russell should have called it himself. He didn't want to remind the senator that he hadn't suggested the briefing to him. They were weaving through the traffic into the city, the Potomac rippling in the morning light. "In any case, Lyle's only concerned about his own standing in the polls," he said, taking a concilia-tory tone. "He thinks that if Congress ap-proves the settlement and the Indians build a casino, voters'll crucify him. Throw him out of office, and that would be the end of his starry-eyed visions of succeeding you."

Senator Russell threw his head back and squared his shoulders. He shouldn't have said that, Colbert realized. The senator never liked being reminded that four years ago, Lyle — "that assistant district attorney nobody ever heard of," Russell called him — had come within a few percentage points of defeating him. Two years later, Lyle was elected governor, but it was no secret that he was only biding his time in the governor's mansion until the next Senate election. It was a topic not to be discussed openly, as if the possibility that a man like Lyle, who'd come to the state only ten years ago, might take over the Senate seat held by the found-ing fathers and their sons was too incompre-hensible to discuss.

And yet it hovered over every discussion they had. Russell would be seventy-three his next birthday. He was from another generation, another time when there was a certain order to things, certain ways in which events should unfold, certain people who were in charge. He could hardly speak the language of his constituents. Environment? Health care? Better schools and roads? He had no idea what they were talking about. But that was *his* job, Colbert thought. Translate the twenty-first century for the old man. Steer him around like a fin-tailed Cadillac out for a drive across the state on I-25. Tell him what to say, what to do, how to vote. Keep the Cadillac on the highway.

The truth was time was running out and Russell knew it. It wasn't as if the old man didn't have an agenda. He meant to preserve as much of the old ways as he could, cement them in place, make it impossible for any newcomer like Lyle to change them. There were certain things he meant to accomplish before he left the Senate. Settling the Arapaho and Cheyenne claims in exchange for a casino was at the top of the list, and Colbert intended to make certain that happened.

"I've given the briefing some thought," he said.

"Oh, yes, I'm sure you have. How are we going to stop it?"

"We're not."

"I'm in no mood for your levity."

"We'll turn it to our advantage. The governor can say anything he wants about the so-called will of the people. We'll have Norman Whitehorse and a few of those old Indians talk about the Sand Creek Massacre, all the atrocities. The U.S. military scalping Indians and chopping off women's breasts and parading their trophies through the streets of Denver. We'll have them talk about how Governor Evans and Colonel Chivington sent the tribes to Sand Creek to wait for a peace agreement, and how as soon as the tribes set up their camps, Chivington launched a surprise attack. We'll read an excerpt from the Fort Laramie Treaty that says the land belonged to the Indians. We'll have the elders plead with Congress to honor the treaty. Lyle will look like he opposes justice for the Indians. Senator Adkins and Governor Lyle just made the settlement a certainty."

"Get 'em here," Russell said. "All of them. Whitehorse, the elders, and anybody else you can think of. I want this done, Colbert. You understand. We have to finish this."

The jangling noise cut through the blackness. Catherine struggled upward into consciousness and tried to open her eyes. The shaft of sunlight streaming past the curtains burned into her pupils. She was curled on the floor, the carpet rough against her cheek. The empty wine bottle lay a foot away. Red wine had trickled onto the carpet. Her head pounded in an erratic rhythm to the noise of the cell. The radio was still playing, a soft jazz number that she didn't recognize. She managed to lift herself upright and grabbed the cell off the desk. Then she curled herself back against the carpet. "Who's there?" she said. Her voice sounded thick and groggy bursting out of the drum that was her head.

"Catherine?" She blinked around the sound of the voice that broke through the pounding, unsure of her own judgment, conscious only of the nausea foaming inside her. "It's Nick Bustamante. Are you all right?"

"Maury's dead," she said. The awful reality crashed over her again, sweeping her back into the surge of grief. She tried to sit up along the wall and squeezed her eyes shut against the tears rolling down her cheeks, tasting of salt and musty carpet fibers.

"I know." Bustamante sounded calm, an anchor in the storm, and yet there was something in his voice that allowed for her own grief. "I'm very sorry," he said. She jabbed her fist against her mouth and bit her knuckles to stifle the sobbing that threatened to overtake her again. "Where are you, Catherine?"

It was a moment before she felt in enough control to respond. "Hiding," she said.

"I have to see you. There's something I have to talk to you about."

For a moment, she had an image of herself behind the wheel of the rental car, plunging through the rush-hour traffic on I-25 to downtown, watching everything — the passing cars, the cars in front and in the rear — but that was the woman she had been yesterday, with a friend named Maury, and that woman didn't exist anymore. "I can't," she said. Then she added, as if to make sense of something, "I left the rental car in the garage by the art museum when I ran."

"I'm sorry," he said again. "We missed him. The officers had him in sight but he spotted them and turned into one of the galleries. By the time they got there, he was gone." He was quiet a long moment before he said, "We will get him, Catherine. That's why I have to see you. We'll talk wherever you are. I'll have a couple of men bring the rental car to you. Where are you?"

She gave him the address then, the small bed-and-breakfast on the northern edge of the Tech Center, far enough from the highway that the sound was no more than a background buzz. "I'll need a little time," she said. The pounding in her head seemed calmer, and the room was no longer spinning. Still she had to swallow back the nausea.

They agreed on forty-five minutes, and she managed to pull herself to her feet. She had to stand over the desk a long moment, holding on to the edge to steady herself, before she found the courage to walk to the bed, dig some clean underwear out of the backpack, and head for the shower.

Catherine waited inside the entry next to the window that framed views of the street and the intersection. The coffee smells coming from the kitchen stirred up the nausea again. No, thank you, she'd told the owner who had materialized from somewhere deep inside the house and invited her to the dining room for breakfast as Catherine had come down the stairs. The thought of scrambled eggs, sausage, and apple fritters had made her stomach lurch. The owner had retreated to wherever she'd come from, heels clacking on the wood floors, and Catherine had turned back to the window. Surely Bustamante wouldn't arrive in a police car. He was a detective, for godssakes. The owner would never forget a writer who had dyed her hair bloodred in the upstairs bathroom and waited for a policeman in the entry.

She saw the gray Taurus coming through the intersection first, followed by a blue sedan a few feet behind. The Taurus was at the curb, the sedan pulling in behind when a squad car appeared. The switch-off was smooth, she had to give Bustamante that. An officer got out of the rental, tossed the keys to Bustamante as he was climbing out of the sedan, then slid into the squad car that had barely slowed down.

Catherine watched Bustamante come up the sidewalk. Tan slacks flapping against his legs, an open-collared white shirt under a summery-looking sport coat, and a holstered gun, she suspected, somewhere under the sport coat. He looked handsome, all that black hair and the strong-looking face — her handsome knight coming to save her. She had to stifle a laugh, because she knew that she would start crying and she wasn't sure if she could stop. She fished her sunglasses out of her bag, opened the door, and went to meet him. "We can't talk here," she said.

"There's a place nearby." He pressed the keys into her hand. She could feel his eyes moving over her, taking her in — she might have been a woman he'd never seen before, and yet something was familiar about her. "I'm very sorry about Maury," he said again, as if he'd glimpsed the grief curled inside of her like a wounded animal and caught the sound of the drumming in her head. She felt the slight pressure of his hand on her elbow, guiding her back down the walk and into the front seat of the blue sedan.

In a moment, he was behind the wheel and they were driving through the Tech Center, the morning sunshine slicing past the office buildings and rippling over the stretches of lawn. Knots of people hurried up the walks, briefcases banging against their skirts and pant legs. She should be hurrying into the newspaper office, Catherine thought. An ordinary activity — going to work in the morning. She had never thought about it, how extraordinary it was.

"Are you sure you're going to be all right?" Bustamante glanced at her, and when she met his eyes, he gave her a little smile — a flash of white teeth in a dark face, the mixture of sympathy and understanding in the brown eyes.

"I don't think I'll ever be all right," she said. "I'll just be different."

He was quiet a moment, his eyes back on

384

the traffic. They had turned onto Belleview and were heading west, the sun bursting through the rear window and flooding the sedan with a welcome warmth. Catherine realized how chilled she'd been since the ringing had drawn her out of the wine-induced coma this morning. The floor had been chilly, she guessed. She hadn't cared. She'd wanted only to lose herself in forgetfulness.

"That's how it is," Bustamante said, glancing her way again. "After a terrible loss, the kind of trauma you've been through. It changes people." She caught his eye again for the briefest moment, and wondered what this police detective might have been through and who he might have been before.

He turned into a shopping center and drove across the parking lot. Only a few cars scattered about. The shops wouldn't open for another hour and a half. He pulled into one of the vacant spaces close to the flat-fronted brick buildings and got out. Catherine was out of the sedan before he got around to her side. A coffee shop was located in the corner, metal tables and chairs arranged around the sidewalk, and that was where they were headed, she knew. She liked the idea that there was no one around, no one seated at the tables, no brown sedans parked anywhere. She liked the sound of Bustamante's footsteps behind her as she started for the coffee shop.

Through the plate glass window, Catherine could see the blurred figures at the tables inside. She sat down at one of the outside tables. She had a sideways view of the front door and a clear view of the parking lot and the street beyond.

"Coffee?" Bustamante said, standing over the table like a waiter, a big silver watch visible below the cuff of his sport coat. She must have flinched at the idea. The smells of coffee seeping through the brick wall and the plate glass window had set her stomach to churning again. He started toward the front door. "Some tea might help," he said over his shoulder.

A few moments later, he emerged from the shop carrying two paper cups with white lids. Behind him was a leggy twenty-year-old girl in a short skirt and tight tee shirt, with clumps of long, blond hair dropping over her shoulders. He stepped aside as the girl set a plate of toast on the table. "Enjoy," she said, the blond hair swinging around.

Bustamante set a cup in front of her, then sat down beside her, which also gave him an unobstructed view of the lot, she realized. "I asked her to make you some toast," he said, fishing in his side pocket for something. He drew out a small white package and pushed it toward her. "Toast and aspirin," he said. "Washed down with a little tea. Always works for my hangovers." He gave her a quick smile, then he said, "We may have found something."

25

"We've gotten reports of similar shootings around the country." Bustamante wrapped his fingers around the coffee cup.

When Catherine didn't say anything, he went on: "We sent out a BOLO to detective bureaus in major cities."

"BOLO?"

"Be on the lookout," he said. "Asked if anybody had any similar cases. Blond-haired man stalking and trying to kill somebody. Using a Sig 226 Tactical with a silencer. Six bureaus responded. All fatal cases and all unsolved. The bullets match the ones we found in your town house and the bullet recovered from the man shot on Highway 285. This Erik chose an accurate, reliable gun. He's a professional."

Catherine sipped at the tea, half expecting it to come back up, and stared at the man next to her, trying to make sense of it. "A serial killer," she said finally.

"Serial assassin." Bustamante sat back and tapped the edge of the table with his index finger. He didn't take his eyes from her. "He moves around the country. L.A., Salt Lake City, Dallas, St. Louis, Baltimore, El Paso. Covers his tracks wherever he goes, uses cheap cells that he tosses, steals what he needs, like BlackBerries. Previous victims included a dentist most likely having an affair with his assistant, owner of a hardware store, owner of a plumbing company, wealthy developer, wealthy lawyer, bankrupt entrepreneur with nothing left other than a big life insurance policy with his wife's name on the front. All the suspects are close to the victims — spouses, business partners — but there's no evidence to tie them to the killer."

He took a couple of moments before he went on. "I'm going to ask your ex-husband to come downtown for more questioning."

Catherine gave a little laugh, low and sarcastic. Lawrence Stern appearing at police headquarters for questioning was like an image out of a bad science fiction film, unrelated to reality. "There isn't a Stern who even knows where police headquarters are located," she said. "He won't like it."

"Exactly. It might unnerve him, rattle him a little. We'll see what he has to say."

"He'll bring a lawyer. He doesn't go to any meeting without a lawyer." She took another long sip of tea. It was tepid now. "Why would Lawrence hire someone to kill me?" she said.

"That's what I intend to ask him."

"Come on, Bustamante."

"Nick."

"None of this is making sense. Professional shooters can hit the target. The bastard hit Maury instead of me. He hit that poor guy in the cable van instead of me."

"The rifling on the bullets is the same," Bustamante said. "It's the same man." He leaned across the table, coming closer. "Ever heard of the Drake Wake?"

"I'm sure you're going to tell me."

"When I was a kid, Dad took me and my brother Donnie to Boulder for the University of Colorado–Drake football game. CU had an awesome team. They were beating everybody. Drake was going nowhere that season. Of course CU was favored to win."

"But Drake won." She had the faintest memory of Dad talking about that game. She took a small bite of the toast and willed it to stay down.

"Drake won because the CU team got overconfident and lazy and didn't play their best game. They didn't believe they had to.

They let down, but the Drake team didn't let down for a minute. The CU campus and the whole town went into mourning."

He sat back and took a long drink of coffee. "Female reporter at a major newspaper, regular routine. Walks her dog every night. A bit like a plastic duck in a shooting gallery. He could have taken you out on the street. Why didn't he? It was so easy, he wanted to make it more interesting, so he followed you home, intending to break into the town house. But Maury showed up, which was more than he could have hoped for. He would have shot both of you, and we would have been chasing our tails trying to figure out which one of you had been the target, or whether the killer had randomly picked your house. But he wasn't at the top of his game. I mean, who was the opponent? Drake? And that was his mistake, not giving you enough credit. Before he broke in, he gave you enough time to call Maury and the police. Out on the highway, he was set to pull the trigger when you veered off the road and the van sped ahead. He underestimated you."

He put up his hand before she could say anything. "I've talked to the detectives working the other cases. They have an FBI profile on this guy. Probably came out of the military, some kind of special forces. Possibly trained as a sniper. Found civilian life boring, so he joined one of the security companies with government contracts in places like Iraq. Call them mercenaries or rent-a-cops, it doesn't matter. The men are highly trained professional shooters." He took another sip of coffee, studying the table a moment. "Profile says he probably got tired of dodging car bombs in Baghdad and became a private contractor. How he finds clients, we don't know. We can only surmise that clients have figured out a way to find people like him, possibly through some rogue guy at one of the security companies. Somebody hired him to kill you."

"It's not Lawrence," Catherine said. "How would he find somebody like that? I know, I know," she hurried on before he could interrupt. "That's another question you intend to ask. I told you before. This has to do with the story I'm working on. Somebody wants me dead before I can fill in the gaps and write the whole story."

She started to tell him about the windfall coming to Arcott Enterprises and Denver Land Company if Congress settled the Arapaho and Cheyenne land claims. He raised his hand again. "I read your articles. Arcott Enterprises plans to construct and operate a casino for a fee. Perfectly legitimate. Denver Land can trade the acres to the government for more valuable land somewhere else. That's up to Congress."

He waited a couple of beats. "What are they afraid you might find? And why you? Other reporters are also covering the proposal."

"I don't know," she said.

"Have you heard from him again?"

She fished through her bag, pulled out the note Erik had left at the hotel, and pushed it along the table.

Bustamante read it, then he said, "I've spoken to the district attorney. Since you're the witness to a murder, you are eligible for the witness protection program. You'll be sent to another city until we make an arrest."

"He'd find me," Catherine said. "He found me at the hotel. He can find me anywhere. I can't spend the rest of my life running." She pushed away the plate with half a slice of toast still left. Nausea had invaded her stomach again. "He's trying to take everything from me. Maury. My home. My dog. My job. I'm trying to hold on, Nick. Don't you see? I'm trying to hold on to something. I have to stay with this story. He can't take everything."

"He wants to take your life, Catherine."

"I'm not sure of who I am anymore."

"What do you mean? So you cut your hair and dyed it. It can grow back to the way it was." He tilted his head sideways and looked at her a moment. She could feel his eyes burning into her. "What is it?"

"Nothing," she said and she gave a little wave. He was still watching her. "Something I found in my research into Sand Creek. A white man on the plains named Thomas Fitzpatrick could have married an Arapaho woman. My natural mother was Arapaho and her name had been Fitzpatrick."

"So you came across an ancestor."

"Maybe. I don't know. I don't know anything about my mother's family. I don't know where I came from. I don't know my own heritage."

"Is that what this is all about? You're determined to stay with the story to find out about your own heritage?"

That was it, she realized, and the calm way in which Nick Bustamante had phrased it, dissolved the whole craziness and left in its place something that seemed obvious. If she could sort out the past, then maybe she could find the strength to hold on to the present. No matter the color or length of her hair, no matter how much was lost, she would know for certain who she was.

"He won't drive me away," she said. "We have to lure him to someplace where I'll be. You can arrest him then."

"Do you know what you're saying? He's a professional shooter, a sniper. He can pick you off a block away. From a rooftop or a second-floor window, if he knows where you are."

"So I keep running and hiding and waiting for him to find me?"

"There might be another way." Bustamante let his eyes roam over the parking lot for a long moment.

"Tell me, Nick."

She locked her eyes on his, and he went on: "Think like he thinks. His other plans didn't work. He's tired of chasing you around the city. What would you do in his place?"

Catherine was quiet a moment. "Try to get me to come to him."

"Exactly. He'll set up a meeting. You'll think you're going to meet someone you know and trust, but it will be him."

"He could shoot me from a block away, like you said."

"But he'll be off his guard. He won't think you suspect anything. Instead of shooting you when you were walking the dog, he decided to indulge his sadistic streak. I think he'll do that again. He'll want to get up close and personal. We'll have plainclothes all around when you go to the meeting. I won't be more than a few feet away. You think you could do it?"

Catherine nodded. "He killed Maury."

"Okay. Anybody called to set up a meeting with you?"

She told him about meeting this afternoon with Professor Morrow at CU-Denver.

"Call the school," he said. "Don't use the callback number."

Catherine dragged the cell out of her bag, found the number for CU-Denver in her phone book, and pressed the key. She went through two automatic voices before a male voice came on the other end. "Professor Morrow?" she said.

"Yes. Who's calling?"

"Catherine McLeod," she said. "I'm calling to confirm our meeting this afternoon at three."

"Yes, Ms. McLeod. I'm looking forward to talking with you."

She said she would see him then and pressed the end key. "I think it's legitimate," she said.

Bustamante was nodding and half smiling, the corners of his mouth barely turning up. "You're a very brave woman, Catherine McLeod," he said.

"You're wrong," she said.

The B&B was quiet, apart from the soft burr of the air-conditioning and the creak of the stairs under her footsteps. Catherine let herself into her room and sat down at the desk. The sun streamed slantwise through the curtains, a hazy column of light falling over the carpet. She took her cell out of her bag and placed it next to the laptop. She placed her hands over them — the cool, hard metal. Cell and laptop. The last connections to her life.

She opened the laptop and clicked on mail. She realized she was holding her breath, and she licked her lips. They tasted faintly of tea. The usual e-mails materialized on the screen, nothing from *him,* whoever he was. A professional killer, Bustamante said. An assassin. She forced herself to take in a long breath.

Bustamante had dropped her at the bed-and-breakfast ten minutes ago. The owner had been waiting in the entry, all eagerness and smiles. "Coffee?" "No, thank you." "Interview go well?" "Very well, thank you." The woman had seen everything, Catherine realized — the police car, the blue sedan,

Bustamante coming up the walk. She was like a caged animal, stuck in a B&B every day, far away from her normal environment, eager to pick up any scraps about what it was like out there. Not unlike herself, Catherine thought. Hiding from her own life, pushed farther and farther back into a cage.

She glanced through the messages. At least two dozen comments from readers following the casino story. Most had read between the lines and gotten the point she'd hoped to make: two companies positioned to make windfall profits if Congress approved a settlement with the tribes. "Who's behind this casino plan, anyway? The Indians or the companies?" "Looks like the tribes are about to be cheated again. Is this a bad, nineteenth-century joke?"

All the comments echoed one another. She could hear the voice of one of her journalism professors, a hardened veteran of the newspaper business, booming in her ears. *Give the readers information. They'll reach their own conclusions. Maybe they'll agree with yours, maybe they won't. Doesn't matter. Just make sure you give them all the information and you get it right.*

But she didn't have all the information. She picked up the cell and pressed the number for Norman Whitehorse. His voice mail clicked on, and she said, "We need to talk. Where can I meet you?"

She ended the call and tapped out the number for the *Journal.* Three, four rings, and finally, the receptionist's familiar voice: "Catherine, is that you?"

"It's me. I need to speak to Violet."

"We're all worried about you. It's terrible about your friend."

Catherine was quiet a moment. "Yes, terrible," she managed. "Is Violet in today?"

"Think I saw her come in," she said, notes of disappointment ringing through her tone, as if she'd wanted to go on about Maury and the killer and how Catherine still couldn't come to the office. "Hold on," she said.

The cell went dead for a moment, then Violet was on, her voice as clear and crisp as if she were in the room. "It's terrible about Maury. Everybody's really sad. You said he was a great guy."

"He was."

"You shouldn't blame yourself. I mean, it wasn't your fault."

"Listen, Violet," Catherine said, not wanting to be sucked down again into the well of guilt and grief. "I need the title records for the five hundred acres owned by Denver

Land Company." Title records could have the names of the owners, she was thinking.

"I don't know about today. It's Saturday. County clerk offices are closed."

"As soon as you can get them," Catherine said.

She started to thank her, moving her finger to the end key, when Violet said: "Marjorie's been trying to reach you. So has Jason. He's doing a follow-up to your story. You checked your voice mail?"

Catherine closed her eyes a moment and tilted her head back against the chair. She hadn't wanted to check her voice mail this morning. She hadn't wanted the sound of *his* voice cutting through the blur of pain and nausea.

"Catherine?"

"I'll call her later," Catherine said, wanting now only to end the call. She had no intention of returning any of Jason's calls. And she knew what Marjorie would say. The killer was still walking around. She should back off the story, go visit a friend in L.A. or New York or Timbuktu, go into the witness protection program. Give up. Let the killer rob her of what was left of her life and turn her into a ghost of herself, a walking and breathing ghost.

And Maury's killer would go on. She

pressed the end key and listened for a second to the deadened silence before she spun the cell across the desk.

26

Catherine waited for the walk light on the other side of Speer Boulevard. Through the traffic, she could see a few weekend students walking along the sidewalks of the grassy campus. The light changed, tires squealed, and she set off with several students, backpacks bouncing on their backs.

She had parked in a lot a few blocks away and walked through Larimer Square, slightly out of breath, her mouth dry and the headache crouching like a beast ready to pounce again. She had always liked Larimer Square, the oldest buildings in the city lining the street, two stories high and bricked with the irregular bricks from the city's first kilns. A sense of the past floated like a ghost around the traffic and the crowds heading into the trendy restaurants and shops. And somewhere she had read that Chief Left Hand had gone to the Apollo Theater on Larimer Street, watched a performance, then jumped onto the stage and given a speech. He had told the audience to take their gold and leave the Arapaho lands. He spoke fluent English. The newcomers knew him and respected him.

They killed him at Sand Creek.

Catherine thought about that as she made her way down the empty Saturday corridors of the North Building and up the stairs to the fifth floor. She found the King Center. The door was locked. This was a bad idea, she was thinking. Almost no one around, apart from the few students emerging out of the stairwell and disappearing around a corner, voices echoing into the silence.

She walked down the hall past the closed doors, checking the names printed on white cards below the pebbled glass windows and knocked on the door with Professor Morrow's name on the card. Silence. She kept going to the end of the corridor and flattened herself into a corner next to the window. The traffic on Speer Boulevard streamed below. A scattering of students moved through campus. He'll try to lure you somewhere, Bustamante had said, and he'll be waiting.

There was nothing unusual below: brown sedans driving past now and then, but they kept going. And what did it matter? He would no longer be driving a brown sedan. He could be in any of the vehicles. He could be anywhere. But there was no one with yellow hair walking about the campus or coming down the corridor. Still, she held her bag against her stomach and worked her fingers into the leather.

A middle-aged man stepped off the elevator and headed toward the door down from the History Department. Black, straight hair that brushed the collar of a blue shirt, blue jeans, and boots that clumped on the hard floor. Except for the stack of books and folders clutched at his side, he could play the role of a cowboy on any stage. Or an Indian, she thought. She watched as he fished a key out of his jeans pocket and let himself into the office. A couple of students were getting off the elevator now, but they walked around a corner. No one else heading for the office.

Catherine pushed herself off the wall, walked over, and knocked on the closed door.

"Come in." The voice inside was low pitched and smooth, the bass voice of a singer. She stepped into the small office and left the door ajar behind her. It was like wandering into a cave of books: books filed on the shelves against the walls, stacked on the floor and the pair of chairs, stacked across one side of the desk, and only the smallest window letting in a slice of daylight. Sam Morrow stood between the desk and a worn, leather chair, peering down at the pages of an opened book.

"I'm Catherine McLeod," she said. "We have an appointment."

"Yes, yes." He waved at one of the chairs covered with books, not lifting his eyes from the pages. Catherine picked up the books, laid them on the floor next to another stack, and sat down. She took her notepad and pen from her bag and waited. He was in his forties, she guessed, dark complexion and black eyebrows running together in concentration, hard-set jaw. A couple of seconds passed before he straightened his back and turned toward her. "Rechecking a few facts before we talk," he said. "You've taken on a controversial subject."

"I don't understand," Catherine said.

"The Sand Creek Massacre?" He sank into the chair behind him. "There are scholars who disagree with the term."

Catherine waited for him to go on. "They cite certain evidence — reports and documents, oral histories." He set a fist in the spine of the opened book. "The early 1860s were a tumultuous time here," he said, tilting his head toward the window and the city beyond. "Cheyennes, Arapahos, even Sioux, attacking settlements and wagon trains. In August of 1864, Indians shut down the Platte River Road. Imagine what that must have been like for the settlers camped along Cherry Creek. No farms, no ranches for beef. Everything had to be brought by wagon from Omaha or St. Louis. Flour, sugar, fruits, vegetables, meat. Tools of all kinds, bolts of cloth for shirts and pants, leather for boots. Horses and mules and wagons. All coming from far away, and the flow of supplies stopped by bands of hostile Indians."

"They were being driven off their own lands." Catherine could see the stories unfolding across the pages she had read. "The newcomers were slaughtering the buffalo, driving off what was left of the herds so that the warriors had to ride for days to get food for the villages." She leaned forward. "The people were hungry, the children were sick. The soldiers attacked villages indiscriminately and killed people who had nothing to do with the hostiles. They killed families of Arapahos and Cheyennes at Sand Creek who were there with the peace chiefs."

"A tumultuous time." The professor

crossed his hands over his stomach and gave her a smile. "Some believe the Indians got what they deserved."

"Is that what you believe?" She was oddly aware of the pressure of the pen in her hand.

For a moment, she thought he was about to say yes, that he would cite some document as evidence. She was a reporter. She would have to include the document in her story. And she didn't know how she could then look into the eyes of the elders.

"The historical records speak for themselves," Morrow said. "Sand Creek was a horrific attack on Indians who believed themselves safe. The atrocities were unconscionable. Nevertheless, there are scholars who will oppose additional settlements for the tribes," he said. "Quite apart from any consideration of a casino."

"Is that why you called me?" she said, scribbling notes on the pad.

He shook his head. "Those scholars are entitled to their opinions. The academy does not agree, and in my opinion, neither will Congress. In the Treaty of the Little Arkansas and the Treaty of Medicine Lodge, both held after Sand Creek, the government acknowledged the injustices against the tribes. We can be reasonably sure the transcriptions are accurate. The translator was

Margaret Fitzpatrick —"

Catherine cut in: "Margaret Fitzpatrick? Who was she?"

"The widow of the government agent, Thomas Fitzpatrick. Actually her name was Wilmarth. Fitzpatrick had died and she'd remarried by the time of the treaties. The tribes respected her because she was the oldest daughter of Mahom, Chief Left Hand's sister. And because she was Fitzpatrick's widow. He had been a good friend to the Indians."

And these were her Arapaho ancestors, Catherine was thinking. Mahom, the sister of Chief Left Hand. And her daughter, Margaret Fitzpatrick. "She was a squaw," she said.

"Fitzpatrick never treated her like a squaw. The historical record shows that he treated her with respect. Sent her to St. Louis to be educated. She used her education to help her people. Too often the interpreters interpreted agreements with the Indians the way the whites wanted. The Arapahos insisted on Margaret as the official interpreter for the treaties. They knew she would speak the truth."

She could feel him watching her. There was so much she would have liked to ask about Margaret Fitzpatrick. But that was *her* story, not the story she was covering. When she didn't say anything, he said, "The point is, the government acknowledged the injustices and the loss of lands shortly after Sand Creek. Three government commissions investigated the attack, and all condemned it. People cheered Chivington and his troops in the streets of Denver, but around the country, people were outraged. Nevertheless, people who believe Sand Creek was justified will line up with the governor to oppose any additional settlement."

"The elders say that Sand Creek was an act of genocide. Do you agree?"

"I believe the bulk of historical evidence supports that claim. But what happened at Sand Creek shouldn't be confused with any claims the tribes make on their ancestral lands. The loss of their lands and the massacre are separate events. The descendants of people killed at Sand Creek are entitled to pursue their own land claims as reparations, but that's a different matter. The tribes have already been compensated for the loss of their lands. It may have taken Congress a hundred years to approve a settlement, but the Arapahos and Cheyennes received $15 million in 1965."

■ ■ ■ ■

Catherine felt slightly dizzy as she made her way down the stairs, through the glass doors, and into the heat rising off the concrete walkways. The headache crouched like a mountain lion in her head, ready to pounce. This was new, everything that Professor Morrow had said. The claim of genocide and the claim on the tribal lands were separate issues, and yet the tribes had linked them together, counting on Sand Creek to make the casino a reality. Maybe Arcott had hit upon the scheme, but Norman Whitehorse and the elders had gone along.

She hurried down the sidewalk, shading the cell with her hand, forcing herself to skim the list of messages. Traffic streamed past — the hum of tires and the faint odors of exhaust and boiling asphalt. For a second, she had to close her eyes against the earth heaving around her and the white clouds tumbling through the sky. She bent her head closer to the cell. A text message from Norman. "Nd talk private. Confluence Park. 4:00 p.m."

She tapped out the keys: C U Th.

Then she went into her voice mail. Another message from Lawrence: "Call me. We have to talk." And a message from Marjorie. "Stop avoiding me, Catherine. Get back to me immediately."

She forced herself to call Lawrence. He would never stop calling until she returned his calls. It surprised her how quickly he answered. "For Christ's sake, Catherine, what the hell's going on?"

She knew then that Bustamante had asked Lawrence Stern to come to police headquarters with the courthouses nearby and every chance of one of his attorney friends taking in the whole charade. "Someone's trying to kill me," she said.

"I understand that." She could hear the incredulity in his voice, imagine the way he was shaking his head. "Surely there's some explanation for . . ." He hesitated. "This craziness. Listen, I want to see you. I'm worried about you, and I want to talk with you. Have dinner with me tonight, Catherine."

Before she could say anything, he went on: "I'm not taking no for an answer. We have to talk." Then he was giving her the name of a restaurant — "Just opened, quaint little place, excellent food, quiet street off Thirteenth Avenue" — and telling her he'd made reservations for eight o'clock. She heard herself agree. She'd meet him there, she said, and they would sit at a quiet table near the back where they could talk privately.

She crossed Speer Boulevard and headed down Larimer Street, tapping Marjorie's number as she went.

27

"Listen, Catherine." A sharpness cut through Marjorie's voice. "It's not safe for you out there. Maury Beekner's dead. The cops have been here all morning asking the same questions — who's trying to kill you and why?"

Catherine pressed the cell hard against her ear and dodged past the couple window shopping on Larimer Street. "I can take care of myself, Marjorie." A horn blasted, and a sedan took a sharp right into the outside lane. "Don't worry about me."

"Don't worry about you? My God, you're a journalist and somebody wants you dead? This is news, Catherine. Jason needs to talk to you. He's been trying to reach you all day. I can put him on now. We're running the story on the front page of tomorrow's paper."

"Don't do that! The killer doesn't know!" Catherine heard herself shouting. She pushed ahead of the crowd at the corner and crossed Fifteenth Street on the red light, slowing for an oncoming pickup, running ahead of the sedan that screamed toward her, brakes squealing, horn honking. "If you run the story, he'll know that I know he's trying to kill me because of what I'm writing."

"Well, what the hell are you writing? I haven't seen anything in the casino stories that would make someone want to kill you. Certainly not for anything you've written about the Sand Creek Massacre. Please, it happened in the nineteenth century, for godssakes."

Catherine dodged the thick black wire that ran around the parking lot and wove past the parked vehicles toward the rental car on the far side. "I'm on to something," Catherine said. "He's trying to stop me from making it public."

"What? What are you on to?"

"I don't know yet, but I'm getting close. I can feel it." She fumbled inside the bag for the keys and pressed the unlock button. "Listen, Marjorie," she said. "There's a briefing Monday in Washington. I have to be there." She started the engine and turned on the air-conditioning. A stream of cool air blasted through the heat inside the car.

"What? No way. You'd be too exposed, too vulnerable. The man who's trying to kill you could be there, too."

"He doesn't know what I look like now," Catherine said. She hoped that was true. "This is my story."

"I'll send Jason. You can get him up to speed on the story."

"No! Marjorie, this is my story. I'm on my way to see Norman Whitehorse. I intend to find out how the tribes got involved in the first place. I want to know if the Northern Arapahos and Cheyennes are in agreement with the tribes in Oklahoma. I want to know what kind of deal Arcott and Denver Land Company have cut for themselves in the casino. You'll have the story in time for tomorrow's paper."

"We have to be careful," Marjorie said. "Arcott and the lawyer for the company —"

"Jordan Rummage."

"— will sue if we run anything that casts an unfavorable light on them. You'd better have the evidence."

"I'm working on it," Catherine said. "I'll fly to Washington first thing Monday, cover the briefing, and fly back that night."

"I don't know . . ."

"Marjorie, I have to do this." Catherine pressed her thumb on the end key and steered the car across the lot and out into the traffic heading west. The numbers glowed yellow in the dashboard: 3:50 p.m. Ten minutes before the meeting with Norman. She took the viaduct across the Platte River and swung left. As she circled back toward the park where Cherry Creek flowed into the Platte, she could see kayakers paddling the rapids, bicyclists, and runners on the river walk, kids tossing Frisbees on the grassy slopes, a family spreading a blanket for a picnic. This place, this spit of land between the creek and the river, close to the log cabins and tents that the gold seekers had pitched on a rutted dirt path that would become Larimer Street, was once the site of an Arapaho village. Her people had lived here, she thought, her own people. She blinked at the salty tears stinging her eyes and blurring the road that curved ahead. She had never thought that she had her own people.

She drove past two small parking lots — both full — and kept going. The trolley that ran along the South Platte clanged past, faces of the passengers framed in the open windows. She found a space in the strip lot wedged between the walkway and the trolley tracks and started walking toward the park. The sun was still hot, a yellow glow in the sky that made the mountains loom closer, as if she might walk a little farther and lose herself among the rocky slopes. She reached the concrete landing above the steps that led down to the confluence of the rivers. The sounds of children — laughter and squealing — floated toward her from the grassy slopes. On a platform adjacent to the banks of the South Platte, men were setting up microphones and speakers. There would be a concert this evening, crowds of people would be here. Already more picnickers were staking out places on the slope. It would be a lovely summer evening, she thought. The sun would set, the sky would turn crimson, and coolness would invade the air. A normal evening, people doing normal things.

She stood on the landing and searched the faces of the kayakers and runners passing below, the men hauling coolers toward blankets spread on the slope. She couldn't spot Norman anywhere.

She moved back along the metal railing and folded herself into the shade near one of the posts, still watching people moving about, but watching them differently now, she realized, the way the hunted watch the hunter. She pulled her shoulder bag around, found her cell, and tapped out Norman's number. She hadn't talked to Norman, hadn't heard his voice setting up the meeting. God. She'd relied on a text message! She listened to the ringing, frozen in space. The voice mail kicked in: Sorry, you've missed me. Leave your name and number. She hit the end key and slipped the cell back into her bag. She kept the bag in front of her. And that made her give a gasp of laughter, as if the thin leather bag could stop a bullet. He was down there somewhere, pulling the oars in a kayak, locking his bicycle to a stairway railing. He was the one waiting for her, not Norman Whitehorse.

She realized the phone was jingling, and she dug into the bag again until her fingers curled around the familiar metal shape. YellowBull, the readout said. She opened the phone and cradled it against her ear. "This is Catherine," she said. She waited for the sound of the elder's voice.

There was a long pause, then Norman's voice came on: "Sorry I couldn't get back to you earlier today."

"Why are you using Harold YellowBull's cell?" She could feel the knot tightening in her stomach.

"Listen, Catherine. It's been hectic as hell. Along with everything else, somebody lifted my cell out of the car this afternoon. Everything's moving pretty fast. Congress has scheduled a briefing Monday. We're heading to Washington. Meet with some congressmen tomorrow. Try to get their support."

"Where are you now?" Her own voice sounded strained and breathless, far away, as if it belonged to someone else.

"Airport. Plane leaves in a little while. I intended to call you, Catherine. Sorry . . ."

She snapped the phone shut, spun around, and headed back along the concrete walkway. The trolley rumbled behind her. She dodged the families heading toward the park, the baby strollers and dogs on leashes and toddlers dawdling behind, the sound of Bustamante's voice in her ear. *He can pick you off a block away. From a rooftop or a second-floor window. You'll never hear the shot.* There were buildings around, windows that looked out over the park. He could be crouched in one of the windows waiting until she came into view. My God, he could try to shoot her here, with families strolling by. He'd missed before, and he'd killed Maury. He'd killed the cable van driver. He might kill one of the children.

She veered off the sidewalk, crossed the strip of grass, and darted across the tracks in front of the trolley. The bell clanged,

419

brakes squealed. Out of the corner of her eye, she saw orange sparks sprinkling the air. The trolley grinding to a halt. The momentum propelled her down a little slope, and then she was sliding sideways, grasping at the bushes and clumps of grass that pricked her hands. A sharp pain exploded in her knee as she came down hard on the sidewalk. She pushed herself to her feet, rubbed at the pain circling cyclonelike down her calf and up into her thigh, then made herself hurry on. The trolley screamed in outrage on the track above, but it had started moving again. She could feel the hard stares of the passengers peering down on her.

She kept going. As soon as the trolley passed, she dragged herself up the slope and across the tracks into the parking lot. Hunched over, one hand gripping her knee, she hobbled between the parked cars toward the Taurus. Then she was plunging around the curve, back out onto Speer and heading west up the hill into Highlands. She wove through the traffic, changing lanes, steering with one hand, rubbing her knee with the other. Knowing only one thing: she had to get away from Confluence Park.

He could be behind her. Oh, he was clever, Erik the professional killer. He had known she would agree to a meeting with Norman. He had found a way to get Norman's cell. But he didn't know which lot she would park in, from which direction she would approach the park. And that had been a mistake, she realized. He could have text messaged her to meet him in a specific lot and shot her there. But he hadn't.

He was still playing with her. The Drake Wake, Bustamante had called it. A certain attitude that kept him from admitting she was his equal, that she could sense his presence — as real as if she had reached out and touched the dried texture of his skin. He hadn't known, he hadn't understood, and neither had she, she realized, that her people had been hunted before, hiding in the villages with troops bearing down, sabers and rifles flashing in the sun, artillery clanking. And whatever had allowed them to survive — some instinct, some fierce and implacable force to live — that was in her.

She turned right into a residential neighborhood and drove around several blocks, up and down alleys, all the time watching the rearview mirror and the side mirrors. An occasional car lumbered into view, then disappeared. There was no one following her. She was in a maze of bungalows, oak trees, groomed lawns, and parked cars, like the people fleeing Sand Creek, running up the creek bed, darting through a maze of dried brush and rocks and little caves dug out by hand in the sandy slopes where they sheltered for a moment before running on. They had survived. Her ancestors had been among the survivors.

She pulled against the curb ahead of a pickup and ran the palms of her hands across her cheeks. Her palms were wet, as if she'd held them under a running faucet. Oh, she was so brave, telling herself she would survive. What a bunch of crap. So many hadn't survived. Chief Left Hand, savvy and smart and on to white people. Hadn't he visited their ranches, sat at their kitchen tables and drunk their coffee, given interviews to their newspaper reporters? They had killed him. But his sister, Mahom, and her young children had survived. It was her oldest daughter, Margaret, who had been married to Thomas Fitzpatrick.

She turned off the air-conditioning. She was trembling with cold, and yet the sun shimmered on the hood and burst past the windshield. She could barely feel the brief waves of warmth lapping toward the cubes of ice that her arms and legs had become. Her knee felt numb with cold, and for that she was grateful. She found her cell and called Bustamante, holding her breath, half expecting the voice of an answering machine.

"What's happened?" It was Bustamante's voice over the hum of the engine and the air conditioner.

"He was at Confluence Park," she said. Then she blurted out the whole story, the text message and the way she had followed directions. Stupid. Stupid.

"Where are you?"

She closed her eyes and tried to picture the street signs when she'd come around the corner. Thirty-sixth Avenue. Perry? Osceola? Somewhere along the street.

"Stay where you are," he said. "Unless . . ." He broke off, but the unspoken message was as loud as if he'd shouted into her ear. *Unless you spot him.*

She kept the engine running, her eyes darting from the windows to the mirrors, taking in everything. The blue sedan pulling up across the street, the man hoisting a briefcase out of the backseat, slamming the doors and — a quick glance her way — heading up the sidewalk and disappearing inside the redbrick bungalow. The woman pushing a stroller along the sidewalk, bumping it over the curb and crossing the street.

The sound of a dog yapping in a yard somewhere far away.

There was a tapping noise on the passenger window. Catherine felt her heart leap into her throat, her hands crash against the edge of the steering wheel. Bustamante was outside, and when had he arrived? He *could arrive just as unexpectedly,* she thought. She hit the unlock button and watched the detective slide onto the seat and pull the door shut behind him.

"I didn't see your car," she said.

"Parked back there." He tilted his head toward the pickup behind them. "A plain-clothes team is scouring Confluence Park, plus a couple of uniforms. Not too many. I didn't want to scare him off."

"Let me guess. No sign of him anywhere."

Bustamante nodded and looked straight ahead, and she understood that he was watching, too, studying the street and sidewalks, the fronts of the houses for anything out of the ordinary. He had a strong profile — an actual Roman nose, she thought, the long, black eyelashes, the prominent jaw. She trusted him, and there were so few people left now that she could trust with her life. Marie, certainly, Marjorie and Violet at the paper, but that was it. A small remnant that cared whether she lived

424

or died. And now there was Bustamante.

"We will get him," he said, looking back at her. He had dark eyes, set back beneath the cleft of his forehead. Little pinpricks of light shone in his pupils. "Trust me," he said. Then he told her that he had brought in Lawrence this morning for an interview. And how had that gone? As well as they might expect. He looked shocked, stunned, when Bustamante had told him that a hired killer was trying to kill her. "Either he's a very good actor, or he doesn't know anything about it," he said.

Catherine set her elbow on the rim of the wheel and dipped her forehead into her hand. What was it? Four nights ago? She had lain in Lawrence's arms while he'd told her how they should be together, they never should have separated, and she had drifted along with him, believing, believing.

"He's a very good actor," she said. "He wants to meet me tonight for dinner."

"Where?"

Catherine told him the name of the restaurant.

"There will be an unmarked police car out front," Bustamante said. "Dark sedan, nondescript, okay? It'll follow you back to the bed-and-breakfast." He took a moment before he said, "I assume that's where you'll

425

be going."

She nodded. Where else would she go? Not with Lawrence. That was over now, finally over, another part of her life swept away. She said that she had to go to the town house to get clothes for Monday. She intended to go to Washington for a congressional briefing.

"You think that's wise?"

"The town house or Washington?" She kept her eyes straight ahead, but she could glimpse him in her peripheral vision.

"Either," he said. "The killer could expect you to go to Washington. We can't protect you there."

"You can't protect me here," she said, turning toward him. She was immediately sorry. They both knew it was the truth, but the truth could be hurtful. She hurried on, wanting to get past the hurt in his expression. "He doesn't know about the hearing," she said.

"What makes you think so?"

"He would have used someone other than Norman to lure me to Confluence Park, if he'd known Norman was on his way to Washington. He would have assumed I knew Norman would be leaving." The hurt was still there, impressed in the lines fanning from his eyes, the little frown on his forehead. She heard herself yammering on about how the hearing was a big part of her story and how she had to cover it. She told him she planned to fly back Monday night. Tomorrow she'd stay in the room at the B&B.

"Call me the minute you land Monday." He didn't take his eyes from hers. It occurred to her then that he would be watching her closely, that he would be in the unmarked car at the restaurant tonight, and he would follow her to the B&B. She was beginning to feel warm, wrapped in the safety of the car, the sun blazing over the mountains.

Bustamante opened the door. In a nanosecond he was outside, changing places with the agility of a gymnast. He leaned back into the car. "I'm going to the town house with you. Ten minutes, that's it."

28

She saw Lawrence the minute she stepped inside the restaurant. Seated at a small table beyond the stainless steel counter that separated the dining area from the open kitchen. He had spotted her, too, because he was getting to his feet, the edges of the white tablecloth clinging to the dark trousers of his suit. He brushed the tablecloth away and stood ramrod straight while she walked past the other tables. The noise of clattering pans and dishes drifted around the conversations at the tables as she passed.

"You look tired." He came around the table and held out the chair for her. "I had no idea of what you've been going through." He waited until she'd sat down before he went back to his own chair. "You probably know that Detective Bustamante has come to the office a couple of times. Today he requested I come to his." He spread both hands over the white plate glistening in the dim light in front of him. "Saturday morning, golf day. But it wasn't a request. More a summons, I would say, not legally binding, of course, but very suspicious if I refused to go."

Catherine stopped herself from saying that Bustamante had been talking to everyone she knew. She would not make this easier for him. "What did you tell him?" she said.

"I know nothing about this, Catherine." He sat back and waited while the waiter, a woman in her twenties with dark hair pulled back from sharp cheekbones, set the menus on top of the plates. Would Catherine like a drink? Yes, she would like a drink. A gin martini, like the one that Lawrence had half consumed. And he would have another, Lawrence said. When she had moved away, he leaned over the table. In the flickering candlelight, he looked five years older, the lines at his mouth deeper, the vertical line above his nose permanently carved in stone. "You do believe me," he said.

"Is that why you insisted I meet you for dinner? To convince me you have nothing to do with the professional killer trying to take my life?"

"Catherine, please. You know I'll always . . ."

"Stop, Lawrence." She raised one hand,

palm outward, like a traffic cop trying to stop a speeding car and prevent a wreck. "It's really quite simple. Someone doesn't like what I've been writing about a tribal settlement that would allow a casino. Someone wants me to stop."

Lawrence sat and waited while the waitress placed the martinis at the edges of the plates. Then he started to give their orders. "I'll have the filet." Pointing to an item on the menu. "The lady will have . . ." He hesitated, deciding.

An old habit, Catherine thought. He had always ordered for both of them. He had known her then, known her preferences. But that woman no longer existed, and someone else now inhabited her skin. "The lady will have the pasta," she said, watching Lawrence's head snap backward, as if she'd landed an unexpected blow to his solar plexus. He managed a smile, then handed up the menu and waited until the waitress glided to another table.

"It's that job of yours, isn't it?" Lawrence was leaning toward her again, his voice so low that she had to come toward him in order to hear. "You never had to work, Catherine. I told you that when we were married. You still don't have to work. I can make a financial arrangement . . ."

"What are you talking about? This is what I do, Lawrence. I'm an investigative reporter. I have a great job that I love."

"Your great job is about to get you killed." He glanced around the dining room, running his tongue over his lips, collecting his thoughts. "Let me help you, for Christ's sake." He slipped a hand inside his suit coat and extracted a thick white envelope. "You must be getting low on cash. Take this and go away somewhere. I can arrange for you to stay with my cousin in Los Angeles. You remember Brian? He'll look after you. I'll have my lawyer draw up the bank papers. You'll get $10,000 each month and I'll make certain it's tax free. You should be okay."

"And all I have to do is quit my job, stop writing about the casino and the Sand Creek Massacre and whatever else somebody wants to kill me over?" She stared at him for a long moment, until he looked away. A wave of nausea rushed over her, so strong that she thought she might slip off the chair. He was trying to buy her off. The thick envelope he'd left at the ranch had been the down payment, but she hadn't understood the part she should play. Now another envelope, and $10,000 each month. All she had to do was stop writing.

"I care about you," he said. "I'll always love you."

She swallowed back the nausea and waited a long moment before she took a drink of the martini. She needed the drink. "You're engaged to Heather Montgomery," she said.

"That has nothing to do . . ." He broke off and gulped the rest of the martini. Then he lifted the new glass and took another long sip. "You have to understand," he said. "Things aren't what they seem. The Stern companies look great on the outside." He leaned close again, his voice not much more than a whisper. "But cash flow has been tight lately."

"The family owns land and properties all over Denver and you just offered me ten thousand a month."

He lifted his shoulders in a halfhearted shrug — What could he say? "We just broke ground on a forty-million-dollar residential and office complex. We hoped to have leases in place in advance, but we overestimated the demand. Do you know how long we project it will take for the place to lease fully? Five years, maybe ten. And that is only one of our developments that are leasing out at a slower rate than we expected. In the meantime, we're shoveling money to the banks. Ten thousand dollars?" He grasped the stem of the glass and took another drink. "A small drop in a flood."

The waitress was back, delivering salads, turning the pepper grinder. Catherine watched the little black dots blossoming on the lettuce. When the waitress was gone, she said, "You could sell your interest in the complex."

He lifted the glass again and drained half of the martini. "You should know the family better than that. We have never backed down. How would it look?" He glanced around, as if he wanted to check on the way he appeared to the other diners. "We have our reputation to uphold. We own this town," he said, and she understood that he was talking about all of the old families, the founding fathers. "No one's going to come in here from someplace and buy us out and take it over."

Catherine picked at the salad, conscious of the pepper biting the inside of her throat. She took another sip of the martini. She could feel the headache creeping into the center of her head again. She shouldn't be drinking, but she needed the drink, the way alcohol glued together all the rough pieces into a smooth whole. "So you're marrying the daughter of a telecommunications billionaire." She could still picture Heather's parents glittering for the *Journal* photographer at some social gala she had covered in a past life, before Lawrence. It was pitiful, when you thought about it. She wondered if the only rebellious action Lawrence Stern had ever taken was to marry her. But he had divorced her, just as his grandmother had expected. "You're marrying an outsider," she said.

"She'll be a Stern."

"I see. And did that happen in the past? The Stern men looking for wealthy brides in the east who came with enough money to ease the cash flow?"

"You never understood business."

"I write about business deals all the time."

"The kind of business like ours. Yes, we own property all over the state. Yes, we have a billion dollars' worth of assets, but it's all on paper. We'd have to liquidate assets to get enough cash to service the debts on the various complexes we've built."

"You could do that. There are probably buyers lining up, ready to buy."

He shook his head. "You'll never understand."

But she did understand, she was thinking. She understood that selling the lands and the properties would be tantamount to selling the family legacy, that without them the

Sterns would dissolve into the past, like other families with names that appeared in history books and nowhere else.

The waitress had removed the salad plates and replaced them with the entrees. A plate of pasta with steam rising over the creamy sauce; a filet and baked potato. Catherine ate a couple spoonfuls of pasta, but the nausea was gathering force. She pushed the plate away.

"Was there anything else?" she said.

Lawrence sliced off a corner of the filet and looked up. "What?"

"Anything else you wanted me to understand, other than the reason you're marrying Heather? I have to go."

"No." He reached over and took her hand into his. "Don't go now. I thought we could spend the evening together. The other night at the ranch . . ."

"Don't, Lawrence."

"Was wonderful. You felt it, and so did I. We belong together."

"You want me to be your mistress?"

He winced, then studied the filet a moment, the red juices spreading over the plate and leaking into the potato. "No one uses that word anymore. We could still be together, that's all. You could go to L.A. until the police arrest the crazy killer running

435

loose, then you can come back here." He leaned closer, squeezing her hand. "Listen. You don't even have to leave town. Go to the ranch and stay there. Gilly will watch over you. No one will get past Gilly."

Catherine ripped her hand free. "I don't believe this," she said.

"I love you, Catherine. It's very simple."

"You're wrong. It's very complicated."

"I have to do what's best for —"

"Right. I've got it." Catherine threw her napkin onto the table and got to her feet. "You and Heather, you both know what you're getting, don't you? She's getting the name and the prestige of an old family; you're getting the money. Maybe you're right after all. It really is simple." She unhooked her bag from the chair and walked back through the tables and the clattering of dishes and pans, the snatches of conversation. Outside the evening was cool, deep shadows spreading down the front of the restaurant and out onto the street. There was the sudden surge of traffic as the light changed at the corner. She glanced at the cars parked along the curb. The black sedan was across the street. Beyond the tinted glass, she could make out the shadowy figure of Nick Bustamante behind the wheel.

■ ■ ■ ■

Catherine slipped into the quiet of the bed-and-breakfast and wrote the story for tomorrow's paper, the bottle of Chardonnay she'd gotten at a liquor store half gone. The Dave Brubeck Quartet played in the background. The clothes she'd gotten at the town house lay strewn over the bed: the suit she intended to wear Monday, an array of underwear, another pair of jeans and a pair of khakis, a couple of blouses, a sack of makeup. She had felt like a stranger in the townhome, a burglar rifling the dresser drawers, yanking clothes off the hangers, helping herself to things that belonged to someone else, another woman who had lived there once upon a time and had gone away. In less than ten minutes, she'd gathered what she needed, stuffed everything into a suitcase, and reappeared in the entry where Bustamante had stood guard. He had followed her to the restaurant and waited in his car until she had parked and gone inside. And he had waited while she sipped the martini and marveled at the way Lawrence could so easily slide around the past they had shared. And yet, it made sense. The woman seated across from him was not the woman who had loved him.

It took a little more than an hour to write up the story. Then she typed in a possible head: Professor Says Genocide Separate from Land Claims.

She sat back, read through the story again, and finished off the glass of wine, wishing she had bought a bottle for tomorrow and glad she hadn't. She would have drunk all of it. And Monday she needed to be clear-headed, not foggy and half-dizzy, the way she had been today when she had agreed to a meeting based on a text message. My God, she could have been dead.

She ran the spell check and sent the article to Marjorie. Still two hours before deadline. Then she checked her messages — Marie again, and a message from Philip. She tapped out Marie's number and felt herself sinking into a soft blanket of safety and well-being at the sound of her mother's voice. Was Rex okay? Catherine asked. Rex was fine. Marie had taken him for a good romp at Sloan's Lake Park today.

Then Marie said, "I found your mother's box in the attic. It's downstairs on the dining room table waiting for you."

"Thank you," Catherine said. She would like to go through the box now. It was as if whatever had been stored inside had finally become hers, pieces of her own life that she needed to fit together to make herself whole again.

She told Marie good night and called Philip. His voice was ragged with grief, and her own grief imploded inside her again, leaking from her eyes and nose, distorting the sound of her voice. Maury's memorial service would be held next week. Small and private, his sister and brother-in-law from New Orleans, a few friends. He'd hesitated then. "We agree it would be best if you don't come," he said.

Catherine hung up, feeling at once drained and heavy with guilt. Of course they did not want her — and with her the reminder that Maury had died in her place, that she was still alive.

She had to force herself to focus on the e-mail messages. Comments from as far away as Florida and Virginia from readers who had read her articles online and were concerned that the Arapahos and Cheyennes should finally see justice for their stolen lands. She skimmed through the messages, deleted the junk, and opened the message from Violet: "I expect to have the title report Monday. When will you be back from Washington?"

Catherine typed in the reply. "Not until

late evening. Meet me first thing Tuesday morning." She gave the address of a coffee shop on South Pearl, a place she never went to.

29

Washington was hot and muggy, a gray sky pressing down over the city. Traffic clogged the streets and tourists jostled the serious-looking bureaucratic types on the sidewalks. Catherine leaned against the window in the backseat of the cab to catch a glimpse of the Lincoln Memorial, the tip of the Washington Memorial riding in the clouds, the dome of the Capitol looming on a hill. The Potomac shimmered in the muted afternoon light. She had always liked the city. She had pounced on every opportunity to visit, looked for the angle in an article — an interview with a senator or congressman or department bureaucrat — that might take her to Washington.

There was power in Washington, a sense that problems could be solved. That was what the Arapahos and every other tribe had always believed. She had read about the delegations they always sent to Washington to talk to the Great White Father who would solve all the problems, stop the injustices. Dozens of delegations, dozens of chiefs on horseback, bouncing over dirt roads in flimsy wooden wagons, riding the swaying coaches behind smoke-belching locomotives, and all of them certain that when the Great White Father knew what was happening to his Indian children, he would see that they had justice.

And the tribes were still coming. She smiled at that, the way the myth had survived for two centuries.

She got out of the cab at the corner of the Russell Senate Building and joined the groups of people filing through the entrance. The security station gave her a feeling of safety, the same safety she'd felt after passing through security at the airport. During the flight, she had fallen into the first deep and restful sleep since Maury had been shot. Even if Erik were following, even if somehow he had managed to book a seat on the same plane — the gun riding in the belly — he would not be able to bring the gun inside the building.

She followed the corridor to an elevator, rode to the fourth floor, and joined the crowd moving down another corridor and into a conference room with chairs around the walls and a long table in the center. Everything about the room was purposeful and serious — paneled walls and thick carpeting, upholstered chairs, and chandeliers dangling from a molded ceiling.

The room was already crowded. Still people were pouring through the doors and clambering toward the vacant chairs. She recognized some of the senators and congressmen taking the front-row seats that seemed to have been reserved for them. Staff people with briefcases and file folders moved into the row behind, leaning over their shoulders and whispering quick messages before finally settling onto the chairs.

Senator Adkins emerged through the crowd jammed near the door across the room and sat down at the end of the table, a big man still in his forties, with rounded shoulders that strained the dark jacket of his suit, blondish Marine-cropped hair, and the nose and alert eyes of a prize fighter. Then she spotted Senator Russell making his way to one of the last front-row seats. He looked tired and haggard, worn down by years of trailing the Capitol corridors, muscling through the kind of legislation expected by the corporations and businesses that had always assured his reelection. Last spring, he'd announced he would not run again. Time to retire to the family ranch in Turkey Creek Canyon, he'd said, an old horse heading back to the corral.

Still, Senator Russell had been around so long that he'd endeared himself to the other senators, like a piece of furniture in the Capitol, a remnant from another time, highly polished and still usable. There was every chance he could ram through a rider that would settle tribal land claims and bring a major casino to Colorado.

The hum of conversations, scuff of footsteps, and rustle of papers filled the room. Catherine walked along the rows of chairs toward the section beyond the black metal stand with the sign that said "Press." Dennis Newcomb sat in the second row, head bent over a notepad, the long gray braid curled over the shoulder of his white shirt. She had to slide past two other reporters that she didn't recognize to reach the seat next to Newcomb.

"Didn't expect to see you here," he said as she sat down.

"Oh? I'm covering this story." The rows were tight, and Catherine had to turn slightly sideways to fish her notepad and pen out of her bag before she dropped the bag onto the floor. In the seats directly across from her were Norman Whitehorse,

Harold YellowBull, and Peter Arcott. Governor Lyle sat in the middle, staff members on either side. At the end of the row were two Indian people she hadn't seen before: a beefy-looking man with gray hair pulled into a ponytail, dressed in a red cowboy shirt, blue jeans, and boots. He might have just ridden in from the plains, she thought. Beside him was an attractive woman — shoulder-length black hair, dark complexion, and black, intense eyes surveying the room. A briefcase stood at her feet.

"You're also being stalked by a killer," Dennis said. Catherine turned toward him, and he shrugged. The pockmarks on his cheeks looked as if they had been dug out by a spoon. "That's the rumor going 'round. You deny it?"

"Are you interviewing me?"

"After the briefing? Outside in the corridor? Anywhere you say. We can go to the cafeteria and talk over coffee."

"There's no story."

"Bullshit!" he said. The heads of two congresswomen in the front row swiveled around. The women glared at Dennis a moment, then turned back and stared at the polished table.

"Look, all I get from Marjorie is 'no comment, no comment.' Ironic, wouldn't you

445

say? Intruder breaks into a journalist's home and shoots her friend by mistake. The friend dies. The killer still wants to kill the journalist for doing her job, and the editor — and the journalist — pretend it's not a major news story that strikes at the heart of the First Amendment and all that shit. Kind of thing goes on in Afghanistan and Iraq and countries in Africa and South America run by tin-pot dictators. But never happens in the good old US of A. Right?" He clamped his arm to the armrest and leaned in close. "I'm going with the rumors. I'm gonna write everything I've heard, attribute it to reliable sources, and say that you and your editor refuse to comment."

"Listen, Dennis." The two women in front were straining backward, heads cocked at awkward angles. Catherine lowered her voice to almost a whisper. "Sit on it for a while, will you?"

"Why should I?"

"You'll give him more than he knows."

"Such as?"

Catherine stared straight ahead a moment, past the dark heads of the women, past the stragglers still making their way toward the remaining vacant seats. Senator Adkins was nodding at the staff member whispering in his ear. "Look, I know more

446

— the police know more — than he does. That gives us an advantage, okay?" She leaned sideways toward him. The faint odors of shampoo and stale coffee filled her nostrils. "I'd like to stay alive, okay?"

"Two, three days, that's the best I can do, Catherine. I'm not walking away from a story like this."

"I've called this briefing . . ." Senator Adkins shouted over the humming noise. "All right! Everyone!" The noise started to fall like a gust of wind passing through, and the senator began again: "I've called this informal briefing for the purpose of gathering information on the claims of the Arapaho and Cheyenne tribes for lands lost to them in the nineteenth century." He cleared his throat and glanced down the row of senators and congressmen to the right, then the left. Catherine held her pen over the pad. The instant he started speaking again, she started writing. "Congress is aware of the many injustices the Indian people have suffered. Today we will consider a proposal to address those injustices." He bent his head over the papers in a file folder opened in front of him. "We need information on whether it is a fair proposal that would satisfy a legitimate claim or whether it is simply a scheme to build and operate another casino in the state of Colorado. I believe Mr. Harold YellowBull is here to speak on behalf of the tribes."

He looked over at the elder who was getting to his feet, the chair scraping the floor. He walked with a little hop to the microphone that stood at the opposite end of the table. "I am here for my people, the Arapahos," he said, leaning into the mic. There was the whooshing noise of his breathing. He pulled back. "Cheyenne people in Oklahoma also asked me to speak on their behalf. Terrible thing occurred at Sand Creek, Colorado, on November 29, 1864. Our people were massacred there by United States troops. You may say, 'That was a long time ago,' but to Arapahos and Cheyennes, it was yesterday. Many of our people died there. Women, children, entire families. We do not forget them. We think of the children they might have had, even the grandchildren down to the present day, and we say, many of our people are not here because of Sand Creek."

Catherine wrote down everything, word for word. The page was filling up with black scribbles. She flipped to the next page and kept writing. "Our people had gone to Sand Creek to wait for the peace agreement they had been promised by Governor John Evans and Colonel John Chivington." He paused and glanced along the rows of legislators. Everyone was staring at him except for Senator Russell, who was slumped in his seat, his gaze fixed on the edge of the table. Catherine wrote that down.

YellowBull went on: "This is very hard for us. Cheyenne Chief Black Kettle ran out of his lodge and planted a pole with the American flag on it. He believed the flag would show the troops they were friendly Indians. Our chief, Left Hand, ran toward the troops and put up his hands to show that he had no weapons and was peaceful. They shot him. They shot everybody they saw. They wanted to kill all our people. It was genocide. After the killing stopped, the soldiers went about the dead bodies and took trophies. Ears and breasts, the private parts of men and women. They took their trophies back to Denver and paraded through the streets and waved them on high. The people cheered."

The elder turned away from the microphone. He took a long moment, a fist clenched against his mouth, before he returned to his chair. The room was still, the senators along the table, the staff behind them, everyone frozen in place. Catherine felt a kind of panic rising inside of her, shutting off her breath. She had the urge to leap out of the seat and run, but her legs and arms were heavy and numb. She couldn't move.

Senator Adkins cleared his throat and leaned forward. "Thank you, Mr. Yellow-Bull. I'm sure we're all moved by this," he said. "But we are not here to discuss genocide and hundred-and-fifty-year-old atrocities. We are here to learn about a proposal to settle tribal land claims. I believe Mr. Norman Whitehorse has also asked to speak."

Catherine was still scribbling as Norman walked to the table. Professor Morrow had reached the governor, she was thinking, and the governor had informed Senator Adkins: the land claims and genocide were separate issues.

Norman took a moment, swaying in front of the mic. "Arapahos and Cheyennes have filed a claim with the Department of the Interior for twenty-seven million acres of our ancestral lands in Colorado. After Sand Creek, we were forced off our lands. We are willing to settle our claims for five hundred acres on the plains near the DIA airport. We will then build a destination resort and casino, allowed under the Indian Gaming Act."

"Thank you," Senator Adkins said.

"Senator." Peter Arcott was on his feet approaching the microphone. Norman stepped backward and sat down. "I'd like to elaborate on the proposal, if I may." He grabbed the stem of the mic and shouted that he was Peter Arcott of Arcott Enterprises. The names boomed around the room. "This proposal will be of immense benefit to the Arapahos and Cheyennes, who — may I point out — are among the poorest people in this country. The destination resort hotel and casino will give the tribes an annual income of $200 million. They will have economic security for the first time. They intend to build an Arapaho-Cheyenne cultural center adjacent to the hotel and casino. The center will reaffirm the presence of these two great tribes on their ancestral lands. It will represent a true homecoming."

Senator Adkins cleared his throat, and Arcott held up one hand. "May I continue? The hotel and casino will also contribute $1 billion in direct revenues and other economic benefits to the state of Colorado. The resort will employ hundreds. This is a win-win proposal for everyone — the tribes and the state. I urge Congress to support legislation that will make the resort possible and permanently settle Arapaho and Cheyenne land claims."

"Hold on just one moment." Adkins drove a fist onto the top of the table, scattering the little pile of papers in front of him. "I want to make sure I have this straight. The tribes are offering to give up claims to twenty-seven million acres for five hundred acres?"

Oh, this was good, Catherine thought. She flipped to the next page of the notepad.

"We believe the claim is realistic."

"Your claim isn't real," the senator said. He resembled a stone statue, eyes narrowed on Arcott.

The room went quiet for a moment. Arcott seemed to hesitate, as if he weren't certain that Adkins had understood and there was more he might say to persuade him. Finally he dropped back and took his seat. Then the woman with black hair and intense eyes was on her feet. The Indian man stood up beside her. "Senator, may we be heard?" the woman said. Without waiting for a response, she stepped over to the mic, the Indian behind her, like a bodyguard, Catherine thought, watchful and alert.

"My name is Vicky Holden. I am Arapaho," she said.

Catherine felt her heart skip a beat. She felt a pang of envy toward this woman she had never seen before. Vicky Holden, Arapaho. A woman who knew who she was.

All the eyes were turned on her, and she went on: "I'm an attorney representing the Arapaho people on the Wind River Reservation. With me is Wesley Iron Shirt from the Cheyenne reservation at Lame Deer. I want to remind the committee that the Treaty of Fort Laramie was made with the Arapaho and Cheyenne nations. Any further consideration of the $15 million settlement made in 1965 would have to be made with the entire nations, not just the people represented by Mr. Whitehorse. Our people oppose the proposal offered by Mr. Arcott and Mr. Whitehorse." She paused and threw a glance in the direction of Senator Russell. "In our opinion the proposal is nothing more than a wedge that would allow businesses to build a casino in Colorado. We consider it a crass exploitation of the pain and suffering of our people at Sand Creek. We will never agree to any further settlement based on the proposal."

The pain and suffering of our people at Sand Creek. Catherine jotted down the words. All for a casino? For the first time, the proposal — the story she had been following —

seemed small and insignificant against something so enormous as Sand Creek.

Wesley Iron Shirt leaned over the microphone now. "I speak for the Cheyenne people in Montana," he said. "We have studied Mr. Arcott's proposal, and we have rejected it. Norman Whitehorse does not speak for the entire tribe. We will not be party to a settlement that exploits the painful history of our people."

"We appreciate your input," Senator Adkins was saying as they both returned to their seats. "We'll hear from Governor Lyle now."

The governor strode to the mic, file folder clutched in his hand. He opened the folder and held up a sheet of paper. "Let me begin by thanking the attorney from the Wind River Reservation for reminding everyone that the Arapahos and Cheyennes have already been compensated for their ancestral lands."

Arcott jumped up. "Governor," he shouted. "Would you accept two point seven cents per acre for land in Colorado? We're asking Congress to declare the so-called settlement null and void. Genocide was committed upon these people. I am confident that the entire nations of Arapahos and Cheyennes will eventually understand that genocide must be addressed. The 1965 settlement was nothing but extortion to silence the tribes about the act of genocide."

"Extortion?" Governor Lyle kept his gaze on Senator Adkins. "The tribes have filed land claims with the Bureau of Indian Affairs for one-third of the state. Property owners in eastern Colorado no longer have clear title to their lands. Now Mr. Arcott wants to settle the claim in exchange for five hundred acres on which to build a casino. That is extortion!"

Governor Lyle shifted sideways a little and fixed his gaze on Senator Russell. "I ask you, Senator, who do you represent?"

Russell seemed to snap awake. He blinked around the room, then squinted toward the governor. "Indians got a rough deal. You heard what the elder and Mr. Whitehorse said. They deserve to get a casino, give 'em jobs with steady money coming in every month."

"Who do you represent, Senator?"

The room went quiet. Catherine was aware of the sound of her pen scratching the notepad. She had filled three pages, and she was starting the fourth.

The man behind Russell leaned forward and whispered in the senator's ear. Harry Colbert, the bald circle spreading on top of his scalp, the unflappable expression pasted on his face. He was like an appendage of Russell, Catherine thought, the right hand the senator could never leave behind. She had met Colbert a number of times, spoken with him on the phone for other stories, but he hadn't returned her calls on this story.

"People of my state, of course." Senator Russell straightened his shoulders and blinked several times, as if he'd just found the path he was supposed to take to a destination of which he wasn't sure. "This casino proposal will be best for everyone."

"I call on you, Senator Russell, to pledge that you will not offer a rider on any legislation that will approve a casino against the wishes of the people of Colorado. Will you make that pledge, Senator?"

Harry Colbert was leaning so far forward that, for a moment, Catherine expected him to slip off his chair. The sound of whispering was loud and insistent. Finally he sat back.

"I am not prepared at this moment to make any pledge that could harm the people and the economy of the state I have served for many years." He pulled himself up in the chair, as if a rod had been attached to his backbone. Something changed in his expression, and for an instant, Catherine recognized the man she had watched on television from the time she was a kid. The Old Man, her dad had called Russell. Always looking out for his folks, making sure nothing's gonna stop the money train.

She wrote down everything he had said. Suddenly the proposal seemed to have shifted away from the Arapahos and Cheyennes to the economy of Colorado.

"I call on you . . ." the governor began.

Senator Adkins interrupted. "I'll pledge to do everything in my power to make certain that any such rider does not leave the Congress."

"I'll make the same pledge." The voice came from the group of senators next to Russell. Other senators were glancing at one another and nodding.

"This briefing is over." Senator Adkins rose from his chair and started for the rear door, but the other senators were circling around, patting him on the back. Russell remained seated for several moments before he got to his feet, Colbert lunging forward to support his arm. He guided the old man out the door past the knots of senators and staff.

"Well, I'm disappointed." Dennis Newcomb shouldered next to Catherine in the corridor. "Frankly, I was looking forward to a real classy resort and casino close to home. Governor never asked me."

Catherine stopped and turned toward him. She waited until two of the senators, trailed by staff, had walked by. "Who do you think would benefit most?"

"The tribes, of course."

"Read my story tomorrow, Dennis. You might learn something."

30

Catherine carried the steaming latte through the coffee shop and out onto the sidewalk. She sat down at a table in front of the plate glass window and took a sip of the foamy milk floating on top of the coffee. Most of the other tables were occupied. A couple of young mothers, strollers pulled in close; a realtor or banker or investments counselor poring over papers with a worried-looking man and woman gripping their coffee cups; some kind of businessman working at a laptop, a couple of other people chatting on cell phones.

From her table, she could see anyone entering or leaving the shop and still keep an eye on the street and the sidewalk. The need to watch had come over her the minute the plane had landed in Denver. It was like an armor she'd left at the gate and had to take up again. Erik would be here waiting for her, she was certain of that. She was close now. She was close to the end of the story that somebody didn't want her to write.

She'd written today's story on the plane, quoting Whitehorse and YellowBull and Arcott, Senator Russell and Governor Lyle, and the Arapaho attorney from the Wind River Reservation. "I'm confident we have stopped this attempt to override the wishes of our people in its tracks," the governor had said outside the briefing room. He was grinning; there was a bounce in his step when he'd walked away. It had made sense, the entire complicated proposal nothing more than an excuse to bring a casino into a state that didn't want it. Still Senator Russell had been around long enough to know how to cajole and arm-twist and cash in favors. Even as she had typed "end," she'd understood that the ending still waited to be written.

Catherine took another sip of latte and watched Violet steer a white sedan alongside the curb. Then she was coming across the street, her bag tight under one arm, as if she had just come from an ATM where she had withdrawn her life's savings. There was a little breeze, a coolness that promised to cut through today's heat, and her blond hair streamed backward over her shoulders. She looked pale in the sunshine. Big round sunglasses shielded her eyes.

She was almost to the front door when her head snapped around. "There you are," she said, walking over and setting the bag on the table. "You'll find the title report in the inside pocket. Frankly, I don't see how it will prove anything. I'm going to get some coffee."

She disappeared inside the shop as Catherine opened the bag and pulled out a folded sheaf of white pages. She flattened them on the table. She recognized Violet's handwriting on the note attached to the first page: Title Record, followed by the legal description of the five hundred acres. Arcott might have chosen any parcel of land in the vast emptiness of the plains, she thought, but this was the land he wanted.

She glanced down the top page. Title transferred to Denver Land Company in 1992. Previous owner: West Associates. Nelson Rummage, agent of record. Title transferred via quick claim deed. Whoever owned the land had simply transferred the title into a different company.

She began flipping through the other pages, running her eyes down the lines of black type. A series of transfers from one company to another — 1958, 1932, 1901

— all by quick claim deeds with agents' names that she didn't recognize.

Here was something. At the top of the page, in black cursive, were the words: The United States of America. Then came a dense paragraph of nineteenth-century legal jargon describing the northwest quarter of a section of land in Colorado Territory containing five hundred acres. *Now, know ye, that the United States of America, in consideration of the premises and in conformity with several Acts of Congress Do Give and Grant unto SR Associates.* At the bottom was the signature: Ulysses S. Grant, President of the United States of America. The date was the tenth day of May, 1876.

SR Associates. The company name in black type, as innocuous as all the other company names. Catherine shut her eyes and summoned the image of the sepia photograph hanging on the wall of the study in the Stern Mansion. Leland Stern and Ethan Russell posing in front of a two-story brick building, faded white shirts and black string ties and wide-lapelled jackets, grins on their faces, the black letters painted over the door: SR Associates. The original real estate partnership between the Stern and Russell families, Lawrence had told her on the first night he had brought her to dinner at the mansion. Even then — Lawrence walking her up and down the hallways, in and out of the library and living room and sun room, identifying all the serious faces of his ancestors that peered down from the portraits on the walls — even then she had sensed Elizabeth Stern's disapproval, standing apart, watching from the end of a corridor.

Lawrence had talked on and on: SR Associates, one of the first companies formed in the year Colorado became a state. Offices in the building that his great-grandfather and Ethan Russell had constructed on Market Street. *New office building's on the site now,* he'd said. *You've seen it, haven't you? Beautiful building. Almost fully leased.*

"So? Was I right?"

Catherine opened her eyes as Violet slipped into the chair across from her. "I looked up the names of the agents. All attorneys. So the title record doesn't really prove anything. We still don't know who owns the five hundred acres."

That wasn't true, Catherine was thinking. Lawrence and his grandmother and Senator Russell owned the land. She moved the cup of latte halfway across the table. Still the odor floated back; her stomach was churning. She was afraid she would be sick.

"You okay?" Violet leaned over the table. "Maybe you should eat something. Shall I get you something?"

"No. No," Catherine said. "I don't want anything."

"Wait a minute." Violet removed her sunglasses and folded them. She reached out and tapped the title record. "You recognize one of the companies or the name of one of the attorneys, don't you? Tell me, Catherine. Who is it?"

Catherine looked away. The nausea was rising in her throat, and everything seemed blurry — the people at the other tables, the cars parked at the curb, the red sedan crawling past. The breeze had died back and the air was hot, suffocating. She forced herself to turn back. "The Sterns and the Russells own the land," she managed. "My ex-husband owns the land."

"You mean . . ." Violet slumped in the chair. "Why, Catherine? Why would he hire someone to kill you? Any reporter could have found out who the owners are. I mean, what about Newcomb at the *Mirror*?"

"He would have to dig through a lot of historical records, make a lot of connections," Catherine said. "It could take time. Congress might have approved the settlement claim and the casino could be halfway built before he stumbled onto the owners." She hurried on, trying to make sense of it. "Maybe they just wanted the deal done before anyone found out who was behind it. It would look bad when the truth came out. Senator Russell would have pushed through a deal that let him exchange land that he and his old friends own for even more valuable land. But Russell would be out of office. Eventually the whole matter would just fade away."

And yet something felt odd, not quite right. They had so much to lose! The respect accorded the old families, the reputations, the traditions, and the legacy. All in the hope of acquiring more valuable land. Catherine had the sense that she was circling a mine shaft sunk into the depths of a mountain. She could see the entrance, but she couldn't see down into the darkness.

There had to be something else.

She folded the pages of the title record and got to her feet. "Listen, Violet," she said. "Don't mention this to anyone."

"Marjorie?"

"Not yet. This doesn't prove anything."

She waved the wad of pages over the table, stuck them in her bag, and started to walk away, Violet's voice trailing behind her. "Be careful." Not until she got into the Taurus that she'd left near the corner of a parking lot, hidden from the street by a red delivery truck, did she open her cell and tap out Norman's number. The engine came alive when she turned the ignition, the low hum blended into the ringing noise in her ear. Then Norman's voice: "What is it, Catherine?"

"I'm on my way to the Indian Center," she said. "I think you'd better meet me there."

"Well, that's a problem."

"What shall I write, Norman? That you cut a deal with Lawrence Stern and Senator Russell? A 500-acre parcel of land, in exchange for what? More valuable land? Or was there more to it than that?"

"I'll see you there."

The white numbers on the dashboard clock read 10:27 a.m. She would be at the Indian Center in twenty minutes.

Catherine expected him to be late. She would arrive, pour a cup of coffee in the cafeteria, and station herself at a table where she could see the entrance. She would have a few minutes to untangle the thoughts that jumbled together, the craziness of them. She'd spent six years as Mrs. Lawrence

Stern, trying to cocoon herself in his world, as if she belonged, and yet she didn't know him at all. He was a man of risks, that was true. He'd taken a big risk to develop large buildings, and he'd taken a big risk to marry her. But when the buildings didn't pay off, he'd divorced her. Which had left him free to marry the daughter of a billionaire.

As for Senator Russell — there was a man she knew nothing about. Exchanged a few nice-to-see-yous at the country club or some gala fund-raiser, and always the old man was looking past her, expecting a more appropriate woman to materialize beside Lawrence. And his office had not returned her calls.

Still the idea that Lawrence or Senator Russell would hire a professional killer to stop her from reporting that they owned the five hundred acres and had made some kind of private deal with the tribes seemed so out of the way of things, so big and dense that she couldn't reduce it to something she could comprehend. Still, a killer who called himself Erik, with yellow hair and narrow shoulders, had come for her. He had killed Maury.

She spotted Norman as she came through the front door of the Indian Center. At the far end of the cafeteria, seated at a table

467

apart from the other tables clustered in the center of the room. A handful of people were working behind the lunch counter. Sounds of a faucet running, plates scraping together. A couple of kids sat at one table over plates of sandwiches. The odors of peanut butter drifted toward her as she walked past.

Norman was half to his feet, leaning forward, balancing himself against the edge of the table. He watched her with hooded eyes, shadowed under bushy black eyebrows. She sat down across from him, plopped her bag on the table, and took out the title records. She pushed the folded pages across the table.

"The names of the owners of the land will be in tomorrow's paper," she said.

Norman made no move to pick up the pages. They lay like road kill between them. "Tell me the rest of it, because . . ." She bit at her bottom lip; she could taste the blood. "Because I need to know whose idea this was."

He clasped his hands together and looked down, appealing to the table, the floor. "They came to us, all right?"

"Who?" Catherine set her notepad on the table and started writing.

"Your ex. Colbert from Senator Russell's

office." Norman glanced up. "Said they had a surefire deal, get us a casino, a lot of money coming in every month. All we had to do was go along, file a new claim with the BIA for all the land stolen from us. Said we'd be working with Arcott Enterprises. Peter Arcott had gotten lands for tribes in other states." He smiled to himself and nodded, as if this were amusing. "He'd already talked to Senator Russell, made sure Congress would give us five hundred acres for a first-rate hotel and casino. Everything was legitimate. Hell, I never questioned whether it was legitimate. Colbert was sitting right there, laying it all out. The senator's right-hand man."

"So you went along? Willing to exploit what had happened to our people at Sand Creek." She stopped writing and looked at the man across from her. The word "our" still clung to her tongue. It had felt natural. "How did you convince the elders?"

"You know how poor our people are? You know how most of 'em live every day? Lucky to get some food to feed the kids, a little gas to get to some low-paying job that's gonna lay 'em off tomorrow, and that's if they're lucky enough to get the damn job in the first place. Wanting more, you know, for the kids. Wanting things to be better." He shoved his clenched hands into the middle of the table and leaned toward her. She started writing again. "You want to know the truth? I wanted the casino more than I ever wanted anything in my life. It was like a dream, and I wanted it to come true. There'd be jobs for any Arapaho or Cheyenne that wanted 'em. We'd get millions of dollars every year from our share."

He snapped backward and, folding his arms across his chest, focused on some point across the room. There was the sound of footsteps behind her, people coming in for lunch. "Our share," she said. And this was it, she knew, this was what was hidden in the darkness. "Who else would share the casino profits?"

"Stern and Russell. They'd put up the land."

"They planned to trade the five hundred acres for even more valuable land."

"Make it easy that way, your ex told us. No landowner to fight Congress over condemning the land. They'd offer the land for a trade. Just lookin' out for the poor Indians, he said, and I admit that got my dander up, 'cause they were lookin' out for themselves."

Perfect, Catherine was thinking. She finished jotting down what he had just said and added her own thoughts: Casino spitting out millions every year, cash flow no longer a problem. Lawrence could continue developing large commercial and residential complexes, independent of his new wife's finances, and Senator Russell could retire to his ranch, a man assured of wealth.

Norman was saying something about how he and the elders had gone along, kept quiet, because it was good for the tribes. Everything was gonna work out, he said, until she had come along.

"You were the one who called me," Catherine said. "Alerted me to the story, arranged for the exclusive with the elders."

"You're one of us."

"You don't know that."

"We knew by looking at you. We figured we could trust you. You'd write the truth about Sand Creek and soon as people in this state knew about the genocide, they'd get behind the settlement. You'd help us get the casino."

Catherine set her pen down and dropped her head into her hands. She had the picture now, all the little pieces snapped into their proper places. She could feel the little waves of nausea rippling through her, and the headache hovering like a cloud. Her mouth felt dry. She would give a hundred dollars for a glass of wine. She wondered how it had happened, each step of the process. Had Lawrence hired the assassin on his own? That seemed unlikely. More likely, he had consulted with Colbert, who would know these things, wouldn't he? A man about Washington with all kinds of connections, even to professional killers.

She was going to be sick now. She got out of the chair and ran past the tables filling up with grandmothers and little kids, past the brown startled eyes of the Indians lining up at the lunch counter. She pushed through the door to the bathroom and sank onto the floor of a stall. There was a moment when she felt as if she were watching all that was left of whoever she had tried to be, all the wretched lies she had told herself swirling down the white porcelain toilet.

Harold YellowBull was at the table when she got back. She pulled up the chair that she'd kicked backward as she'd jumped up and sat down. Norman had already told the elder, she knew. He sat blank-faced, cowboy hat tipped low, eyes peering at her from the shadow of the brim.

"There is something else I have to know." She looked from the elder to Norman. "Why did you let them hire an assassin to kill me?"

It was Harold who said, "We don't know

nothing about that, daughter." The old man's face was patched with weariness, as if he'd just understood the rest of the deal that Arcott and Lawrence and Colbert had offered, the part that would have stopped everything, the part that white men never told Indians. "We never thought they was gonna harm you. Soon's Norman here got to thinkin' that one of 'em sent a killer after you, he went to see Stern. Stern wasn't happy to see you, that right, Norman?" Without moving his eyes from her, he tilted his head toward the man next to him.

"Told me I shouldn't ever come to his office again," Norman said. "Couldn't ever be seen with him. He didn't want anybody putting two and two together now that the stories were coming out." He ran his tongue over his lips. "Lawrence swore to me he didn't know anything about anybody trying to kill you. He said he was worried about you, tried to help you. I came away thinking that somebody else wanted you dead for some other reason. Maybe I shouldn't've believed him."

Catherine waited a moment before she said, "Detective Bustamante will want to interview you. You'll have to tell him everything."

Norman glanced sideways at the elder,

then nodded.

"Everything," Catherine said. "The killer's still out there."

31

The elevator bell dinged, and Catherine got to her feet, knowing instinctively that Bustamante would appear through the parting doors. She was halfway across the lobby at Denver Police Headquarters when he stepped out. White oxford shirt with opened collar and sleeves rolled up over brown, muscular forearms; khaki slacks with sit creases, and brown, polished loafers. She could sense the certainty in the way he came to meet her, drawing her into his orbit. The kind of certainty that came from having seen everything, from no longer being capable of surprise. Nothing she would tell Nick Bustamante would surprise him. "We'll go upstairs and talk," he said.

Another detective had come through the entrance and crossed the lobby. Tall and on the heavy side, the same kind of certainty about him. There were low mutterings of "how's it going" and "same as usual," he and Bustamante nodding as the elevator doors slid open again and they stepped inside. She could feel the other detective's eyes on her as the elevator pulled upward. Witness to some crime, no doubt. Wife, girlfriend. Maybe she was an accomplice.

The elevator rocked to a stop, the doors slid open, and they stepped out. The other detective veered to the left. Bustamante ushered her down the corridor to the right. The sound of their footsteps on the tiled floor was like the riff and counter riff of a jazz tune. He stepped sideways and nodded her into the big office that the detectives shared, cubicles arranged around the perimeter. She felt the slight pressure of his hand on her arm, steering her over to his cubicle where she sat down on a plastic chair.

"So what do you have?" He perched on the chair on the other side of the desk, not taking his eyes from her. She'd called him as she'd driven away from the Indian Center, her hand shaking, her index finger sliding off the keys. "I know the truth," she'd stammered. Her stomach was still churning. He'd told her to come to headquarters right away.

Catherine pulled the title report from her bag and handed it across the desk. "The Stern and Russell families own the land in the settlement proposal," she said. She hurried on, explaining how the land had been transferred to different companies over a century, always by quick claim deeds for no significant amount of money. The owners had never really sold the land.

"Okay." Bustamante hunched over the desk, his eyes scouring the pages. "So Senator Russell is behind a settlement claim that will benefit him personally, along with your ex-in-laws."

"That's only part of it," Catherine said. "Both families will be silent partners in the casino. They're looking at millions in profits every year."

"Why you, Catherine? Other journalists could have gotten onto this. They couldn't have the entire press corps killed."

She told him then the way she had figured it out: They had hoped to have the casino operating before anyone got onto the truth. The truth wouldn't matter then; the deal would be done. Norman Whitehorse had brought her into the story, got her an exclusive interview with the elders. Counted on her to write the truth about their people, how they had been driven from their lands, how they had been ambushed at Sand Creek. Counted on her to get the people of Colorado behind the casino.

Bustamante was nodding. "So what went wrong?"

"Lawrence . . ." She stopped, then began again. "My ex-husband, maybe Senator Russell, knew that I would try to find out who owned the land. Lawrence knows how I work. 'Why do you care about all of the details?' he used to say. Well, the truth is in the details. He was afraid I would recognize one of the companies and realize that the Sterns and Russells owned the land. They couldn't take that chance. A land settlement with the Arapahos and Cheyennes was the only way they could get a casino."

"How do you know all this?" A flat note of skepticism sounded in Bustamante's voice. He sat back, waiting, she knew, for the kind of incontrovertible evidence that detectives placed their bets on.

"Norman Whitehorse and Harold Yellow-Bull told me everything. They'll give you a statement."

Bustamante set his elbow on the armrest and ran the palm of his hand over his mouth. "Okay," he said. "Senator Russell's going to bring in a five-hundred-dollar-an-hour lawyer from Washington who will point out that the senator's private holdings have been in a blind trust since he took office and that the senator had no idea what his partner — that would be your ex-husband — was up to. He'll claim the senator wasn't even aware that land held in the trust was in play."

He leaned forward and placed his palms together over the title record. "If Congress allowed the settlement, the Arapahos and Cheyennes could bring any partners into the casino that they wanted. They need financial backing, so they hired Arcott to raise the money. They need land, so they got into bed with Stern and Russell, who agreed to provide five hundred acres that Congress would exchange for federal land somewhere else. In return for their co-operation, they would get a piece of the casino. The lawyers are going to cite a lot of statutes that prove no crime has been com-mitted. The Senate ethics committee might get involved, look into the senator's affairs. But he's on his way out of office. He doesn't give a hoot about the ethics committee." He waited a couple of seconds. "There's no crime, Catherine."

"Maury murdered! That's not a crime? Some poor guy who happened to follow me down the mountain, shot to death. Not a crime? A freak killer following me around."

"Take it easy," Bustamante said. "That's a whole other matter. If Lawrence Stern and

Senator Russell hired a killer to take your life, they're looking at the rest of their lives in prison. If we can prove it."

And that was the problem. Catherine slumped against the chair. Her bag slid off her lap and landed on the floor with a soft thud, like the sound of a ball bouncing once. There was no connection between Lawrence or Russell and the assassin. No evidence, only a theory about motivation that the expensive lawyers would demolish in a heartbeat.

"Look," Bustamante said. "We might've gotten lucky. FBI sent us photos and bios on a few mercenaries they suspect might be responsible for the other killings around the country." He fished a folder from beneath a stack and opened it. A brown official-looking envelope lay inside on top of some papers. He took six photos from the envelope — headshots of men — and slapped them down in front of her, as if he were dealing her a hand of cards. "Recognize anybody?"

Catherine saw the photo right away — second from the left. The shape of the face, the large nose, and something about the eyes. His hair was short — military cut — and brown. But it was Erik.

She set her index finger on the photo.

"That's him."

Bustamante was shuffling through the papers in the folder now. He pulled out a sheet and began reading: "Name is Steve Hitchens, four years in the Army Special Services, trained sniper. Honorable discharge. Signed on with Yellow Jacket, private company that contracts with the government to supply security in foreign countries. Spent eighteen months in Iraq on a security detail for visiting diplomats. Took part in special assignments, classified, of course. Left the company and disappeared."

He laid the page back in place and closed the file. "Went into business for himself. We can be sure he's using an assumed name. As soon as we find him . . ."

"When's that going to be?" Catherine scooped her bag off the floor and stood up.

"When we find him," Bustamante said, pushing himself to his feet now, "we'll know who hired him."

"I'm going to see Lawrence," she said.

"And do what? Confront him? Tell him you know the truth that he was trying to hide? If he hired Hitchens . . ."

"Oh, he hired him all right."

"It's too dangerous. You can't do that."

She swung around and started for the door.

"Wait, Catherine." Bustamante's voice was like a punch between the shoulders.

She turned back.

"It's dangerous," he said again.

"He's already trying to have me killed. How can it get any more dangerous than that?"

"So you intend to confront him. You expect him to tell you the truth so you can publish it in tomorrow's paper?"

"He'll be surprised. I don't know what he might say."

"We can fit you with a wire," he said.

"Great. Fit me with a wire. Let's get this over with."

"I want you to understand that it will increase the danger." He waited a moment, reconsidering. "You don't have to do it."

"Did you hear what I said? I want this to end."

"I'm going with you. I'll be right outside in a van listening."

"Okay," she said, and it surprised her, the confidence coming over her, as if she'd caught a virus from him and now it was invading her own body.

"Call him." Bustamante tilted his head toward the bag in her hand.

She slipped out her cell and tapped out Lawrence's number. The drill was familiar:

receptionist, private secretary, and finally Lawrence on the other end. "Catherine? What's up?"

"I have to talk to you," she said. "I've uncovered everything . . ." She caught Bustamante's eye for a moment, a look of urging her on. "I want to confirm the facts with you before the story runs in tomorrow's paper."

The cell went quiet, deadlike. She could hear the hushed in and out of his breathing, the sounds he made when he was asleep or lost in thought. "I don't know what you're talking about," he said finally.

"Oh, I think you do, Lawrence. I owe you the chance to confirm or deny the story."

"Not the office." He blurted out the words. "I'm having dinner with Grandmother at the mansion tonight. You can come by later. Ten o'clock." Then the little click as Lawrence ended the call.

"Tonight," she said.

So many memories, Catherine thought. The brick walkway that curved from the street to the stone steps in front of the mansion. The dark-wood door with the grilled rectangular window and the brass knocker. How many times had she and Lawrence come up this walkway, the soles of their shoes squishing the red leaves in the fall or slipping on the skin of new snow in the winter? Spring was always filled with the smells of blossoming trees and moist dirt as the gardener trimmed and planted. And summer evenings were like this, coolness invading the heat leftover from the day, shadows falling through the trees and bushes and the air filled with the pungent odor of roses, lavender, and nicotiana.

The brass knocker was heavy in her hand. She let it fall against the door, listening to the low thud reverberate through the high-ceilinged entry inside. Footsteps, then, just as all the times she had stood waiting with Lawrence, who had a key in his pocket. But it wasn't polite, you see, to let oneself in when one no longer lived there.

So they had waited as the footsteps came closer and the big wooden door swung open. "Come in, sir. Madam," Lewis would say, just as now he said: "Please come in. Mr. Stern is waiting for you in the library."

Catherine thanked the old man and brushed aside his offer to lead her up the stairway. He had been with the Stern family when Elizabeth had married into the family. He was probably older than she was, almost like a member of the family, Catherine thought, or one of the polished newels that she gripped as she made her way up the staircase curving into the floor above.

She found Lawrence seated in an upholstered chair in the library — two doors down the wide corridor on the right. She could have found the place with her eyes closed. He made no effort to get to his feet as she crossed the wood floor and stepped onto the oriental rug that anchored the leather sofa and chairs in the center of the room. Bookcases were stacked around the walls, and in between the stacks were the old photographs of Stern ancestors and Denver buildings designed for another era. The library itself seemed to emerge out of another era, trailing musty smells and faded draperies that let in a half light from the streetlamps.

Lawrence peered at her over a crystal glass half-full of coppery liquid. "Help yourself," he said, "if you need a drink."

Catherine turned left and went over to the table under one of the photographs. Oh, she needed a drink for this. The tape holding the wire down between her breasts was itchy; she had to force herself not to lift her hand and rub at her skin. The ice cubes made a tinkling sound as she dropped them into a crystal glass. She watched the bourbon run out of the decanter and float around the mounds of ice, then she walked back.

"The casino plan is dead, Lawrence." She sat down across from him. "Half of the Arapahos and Cheyennes oppose the settlement. Governor Lyle, Senator Adkins, and the entire Colorado delegation except for Russell are opposed. And when my story appears in tomorrow's paper, Senator Russell will be forced to resign from office. I've spoken with Norman," she said. "He's admitted that you and Russell were behind the settlement claim so that you could get a piece of a $300 million casino."

"So what do you want from me?" Lawrence spoke quietly, as if he had been asking the question before she'd arrived and hadn't yet come up with the answer.

"The story will run in tomorrow's paper. Do you deny that it's true?" She held her breath. Deny, Lawrence. Deny that it was all true, because then there would be no reason for him to want her dead.

"You don't have to write that part of the story." He held the glass with both hands under the tip of his nose. "The casino would have been good for everybody, have you thought about that? So what if it would have been good for our business? It would have benefited the Arapahos and Cheyennes. I would think you would want that."

"You used the tribes."

"They wanted to be used. They hoped Congress would overlook the fact that reparations had already been paid. After all, they weren't asking for much, were they? Five hundred more acres. Didn't the tribes deserve that?"

"Whose idea was it, Lawrence? Yours or Senator Russell's?"

"What difference does it make?"

"Senator Russell will deny everything. He'll shift the blame onto you. It will look as if you were the one who wanted to ram another casino down the throats of the people of this state. The reputation of the Stern family will suffer."

"Don't write the story," he said. "You said yourself the proposal is dead. Congress is not going to approve any settlement. The story will only hurt Grandmother. You don't have to write it."

"Is that why you hired a professional to kill me? To make sure Elizabeth never learned the truth?"

Lawrence balanced the glass on one thigh and stared at her, as if everything about her had become incomprehensible. As if he had never before seen the woman sitting across from him, chopped red hair, fingers kneading the leather of her bag, stomach churning. "You can't believe that," he said.

"You wanted the casino built and operating before the truth had a chance of coming out. I was the only journalist in your way."

"Truth!" He spit out the word. "You think that's the truth?"

"I think you came to the ranch to persuade me not to follow the story. You thought I'd agree. I'd be so scared after the killer broke into my town house and shot Maury that I'd agree to whatever you asked. Take the ten thousand and run and hide. And you were only thinking of my safety, thinking of me?"

Lawrence stood up. He loomed over her, blocking the faint light in the window. There were pinpricks of light in his eyes. "I swear to you, Catherine, on my family's name, on all that is sacred to me, it is not true. I have no idea why anyone would want to kill you. I've loved you from the day we met. I would never harm you. You have to believe me."

"The trouble is, I could never tell when you were lying." Catherine got to her feet and faced him. "The police believe you hired the sonofabitch that killed Maury and is still trying to kill me. So do I. That's the story I intend to write. That the police suspect you of hiring a killer."

There was the almost imperceptible noise of a door creaking open, followed by the soft sound of footsteps on the carpet. Catherine watched Elizabeth Stern moving through the gloomy space. The silver revolver glinted in her hand.

"Have you no sense of honor or decency?" She lifted the gun. Catherine could see the blackness of the muzzle, like the blackness of a tunnel that went forever into the earth.

"Grandmother!" Lawrence swung around and stared at the old woman.

"You would ruin my grandson's reputation." She kept coming forward, the tunnel growing wider and deeper. A clock ticked somewhere. "Besmirch the legacy of this family with a vicious lie. Destroy our position in this city. Lawrence knows nothing about any attempt on your life. He never understood that events must transpire according to their natural order."

"My God, Grandmother. What have you done?"

"Shut up." She lurched forward. Gripping the gun in one hand, she reached up and whipped the palm of her other hand across Lawrence's face. He flinched backward, blinking hard, moving his lips around soundless words.

"You brought this about, you and your

nonsense," Elizabeth said. "Developing building after building, overextending at the banks with no idea of how to cover the loans until the buildings were leased, overestimating the demand for office space and luxurious condominiums. There are no excuses for such stupidity. Any first-year business student could have done better. You put this family in jeopardy. The good, solid Stern name that has always stood for probity and sound financial judgment and for . . ." She stopped and drew in a shuddering breath. "We have always stood for something. But you were willing to throw away a hundred and fifty years of accomplishments. When Leland Stern came here, there was nobody. Nobody."

"The Arapahos and Cheyennes were here," Lawrence said.

"Indians! The Stern family brought industry and modern ways. They brought civilization. None of this would have happened if you hadn't . . ." She stumbled, searching for the words. "Brought an Indian into the family. How inappropriate of you, Lawrence. How unforgivable. Allowed her access to our family history, our ways. A journalist, no less. What did you expect she would do when she got onto your stupid scheme to get the cash flow you needed? You didn't think it through. I had to think for you."

"My God, Grandmother!" Lawrence took a step toward her, eyes hard with comprehension. "You hired someone to kill Catherine?"

Elizabeth Stern gave a raw-throated laugh. "I did what was necessary for this family, and Gilly took care of the details. He understands more of what it means to be a Stern than you do. You're a disgrace." She turned slightly, leveling the gun again.

Catherine felt numb and immobile, an image carved into a rock. Her legs were drilled into the floor. Her voice strangled in her throat.

"I have no intention of shooting you in the Stern mansion, unless I am forced to do so," Elizabeth said. "You will walk out of here and drive away. He will be close behind. You won't make it far. You won't know anything. It will be a merciful death, better than you deserve."

"Please, Grandmother . . ."

"Shut up! Stay out of this."

There was the sharp crack of a door bursting open, then Bustamante's voice behind them: "Drop the gun, Mrs. Stern." Out of the corner of her eye, Catherine saw Bustamante coming up. Crouched over, the gun gripped in both hands. Across the study, two other men had come through the other door, guns extended, approaching the old woman. "Don't make me shoot you," Bustamante said.

Afterward, when Catherine tried to piece together the sequence of events, she couldn't be sure of what had happened first. Her eyes had been locked onto the muzzle of the gun rising in the old woman's hands. Odd, how she had remembered the way her hands had looked, liver spotted and gnarled and shaking a little. And for the briefest moment, the time it took to snap a photograph, she had known that she was about to die.

Then Lawrence's arm thrust in front of her, crashing against his grandmother, and the gun flying into the air and hanging there, it seemed, for a long time before it crashed and skidded along the carpet. Bustamante had rushed forward and taken hold of one of the old woman's arms, then the other. He'd pulled them behind her back and Catherine had heard the click of handcuffs. The other policemen were moving about, a blur of blue uniforms, ordering Lawrence to lie on the ground.

But Lawrence was holding her, sobbing into her neck. "I didn't know. I swear I didn't know." He was still sobbing when he

was ripped away from her and sent sprawling facedown on the carpet.

32

"What the hell is this?" Erik tapped on the brake and slowed past the pulsing stream of red, blue, and yellow lights from the police cars parked in front of the Stern mansion. Shadowy figures moved across the yard and around the other police cars in the driveway. The whole mansion was lit up like a Christmas tree, lights blazing in the windows, spotlights washing down the front walls. A group of men stood inside the opened front door, backlit by the lights in the entry. Catherine was probably there somewhere, but she'd be looking for a brown sedan, not the Pontiac he was driving.

He drove to the end of the block, turned the corner, and sped toward Speer Boulevard. People were out on the sidewalks, coming and going toward the commotion, he guessed. Not the kind of commotion expected in a neighborhood of gnarled old trees and sprawling slate-roofed mansions that practically oozed old money. He laughed at that, the surprise and consternation caused by all those police cars screaming by.

He turned into the traffic heading west on Speer and settled into the outrage burning through him. He was flashing back now — and he hated the flashbacks, the images more real than the boulevard and the red taillights glowing ahead. He was in Baghdad when the call came. Escort a group of congressmen out of the green zone and show off the progress in a suburb with stuttering electricity and water dripping out of faucets an hour a day. Rolling along in the convoy one minute, looking past the shouting and jeering people on the streets, and the next minute the SUV ahead blasted into the air, doors and bumpers and arms and legs and a human head — he could still see the surprise in the bulging eyes — frozen in the air before fluttering over the street like confetti. He'd decided then that there were people who deserved to die, that he would use his skills for justice. He'd also vowed he would never be set up again.

Gilly had set him up this evening.

He turned onto Broadway and drove south toward the motel, steering with one thumb, pushing in Gilly's number on the cell with the other. Something new stirred in his consciousness now, another possibility. The phone was ringing. He could picture the phone in the gatehouse at the ranch where Gilly had handed him the envelope with fifty thousand dollars — because he always demanded payment in advance; he was a professional — and another envelope with photos of Catherine McLeod. A wedding photo, for Christ's sake, white gown and pearl necklace, as if he needed that image! And snapshots of the town house and car and even a picture of the side door she used at the newspaper building. Everything he had needed to take care of the job.

There was no answer, no machine voice telling him to leave his name and number. Erik hit the end key, dropped the cell on the seat beside him, and tried to grasp the sense of what had happened this evening. Gilly must have known the target had stumbled onto the truth. Why else would she have gone to the mansion, except to confront Lawrence? But that didn't mean Gilly knew the target would bring the police. He could have been on the level when he'd called this afternoon — he'd give him that, he decided. And if he ever did find the proof that Gilly had set him up, he would kill the man.

He thought of the police at the Stern Mansion. They had probably arrested Lawrence — it was logical, the head of the Stern companies, the man with the most to lose. He wondered if Catherine McLeod had figured out the old lady's part.

He intended to fulfill his contract with the old lady. He always fulfilled his contract. He picked up the cell again, scrolled to Catherine's name, and pressed the redial key. After three long rings, he connected to her voice mail.

"Say good-bye," he said. He slowly pushed in the end key.

Catherine slumped against the planter on the stone porch, petunias and geraniums licking at her arms. An airplane hummed overhead, a white slash of light that cut through the black sky. Police cars had pulled into the driveway and stopped at the curb, lights flashing, radios crackling. She had watched Bustamante and the blue uniforms hustle Elizabeth Stern and Lawrence across the porch, down the brick walkway and into squad cars that had peeled away. The neighbors huddled in the shadows had disappeared.

Her cell had rung in the muffled depths of her bag. She'd waited a moment before dragging it out and checking the voice mail. The sound of his voice had made her go cold, as if a blizzard had blown into the evening. Now the cell lay opened on the lip of the column. The light in the readout had shut off ten minutes ago. Her legs felt like rubber beneath her. If she pushed away from the column, she would dissolve into the stone floor.

Bustamante came through the front door and across the porch. "You did good," he said. He was backlit by the house lights, his face in shadow, smiling at her. "Jefferson County sheriff arrested Gilly Mason a few minutes ago. He and Mrs. Stern will be charged with conspiracy to commit homicide."

She picked up the cell and handed it to Bustamante. "He called me," she said.

Bustamante swung around, said something to one of the officers, and pressed the cell into his hand. The officer disappeared into the house. "We'll see if we can pinpoint where the call came from," he said.

"What about Lawrence?" Catherine heard herself say. He had saved her life. She could still see the black tunnel aimed at her. She had gone perfectly still — she remembered that now — simply waiting to die because there was nothing else to do, no words to utter, no actions to take.

"We'll separate Lawrence and Mrs. Stern, interrogate them, and make sure their stories check."

"I believe him," Catherine said. "He wasn't involved with the killer."

Bustamante was quiet a moment. He turned away and glanced out across the yard. She could see the resolve in the set of his jaw. "I hope you're right," he said. "Sometimes in cases like this, the conspirators start spilling the beans on one another to cut a better deal for themselves. We'll see what Gilly Mason wants to tell us." He looked back at her. "You should go back to the B&B and get some sleep."

Sleep? That was funny. The idea of the empty room at the B&B with odds and ends of clothes she had dragged from her old life, the laptop on the desk waiting for her to write tomorrow's story — the story of her career — the bed that the owner would have tightened like an Army cot — all of it made her want to laugh out loud. It seemed likely that she would never sleep again.

"I was hoping we could go somewhere and have a drink first," she said.

This seemed to take him by surprise. He turned his head a little, as if he hadn't heard correctly and might still catch the words hanging between them. Then something else came into his expression, a kind of amusement, as if he were entertaining the idea.

"Some other time, Catherine. I'd like that. Right now I've got to deal with this." He tossed his head in the direction of the front door. "I'll have an officer follow you to the B&B, make sure everything's okay."

"Will this ever end?"

"We're close, Catherine. Gilly may be eager enough to make a deal that he'll tell us where to find the killer." He jammed his hands into the pockets of his khakis and gave a little shrug, as if it were all he had to offer and he was aware that it wasn't enough. "You still have to be careful for a while."

Catherine drove through Sloan's Lake Park until she found a lot with several parked cars near the tennis courts. It was still early in the morning — not yet eight o'clock, she guessed, although the dashboard clock looked bleached out in the sunlight. Even with the dark sunglasses, she had to squint into the brightness reflected in the windshield. She wedged the Taurus between two other nondescript sedans; it would have been conspicuous in one of the vacant lots. Here it would look as if it belonged to a tennis player.

She slid her bag off the passenger seat and picked up the yellow long-stemmed rose with the plastic water container at the end of the stem and started walking across the grass and down the hill to the lake. Halfway there, she stopped and took off her sandals. The feel of the grass in her toes, cushioning the soles of her feet, gave her a sense of calmness, she thought, as if this were natural, touching the earth this way.

She hadn't slept last night, although she'd curled up on top of the bed after she'd finished the articles and sent the text to Marjorie. An hour late, she knew, but Marjorie had held the first page. The headline in this morning's paper was an inch-high: "Prominent Family Arrested." And beneath the headline, in bold, black type: "Murder-for-Hire Scheme Discovered." Running beside the article was the story she had written on the briefing held in Washington, with the explanation of the way in which the Stern family and Senator Russell had hoped to be silent partners in the casino. Inside on page two was another article on the Sand Creek run scheduled for tomorrow — the real homecoming, Norman had called it.

"You sure you want to write about all of

this?" Marjorie asked when Catherine had called to tell her what happened. "Maybe I'd better put Jason on the story."

"It's my story," Catherine had said. *My story and my life,* she was thinking. "I was there. No one else knows this story." Still, she suspected that Marjorie had brought in Jason to tidy up her prose, cut down on the emotional aspects — the black tunnel of the gun rising toward her and that sort of thing that she hadn't been able to resist adding. The deletions didn't matter. Erik would have read the paper, and he knew by now that he had failed. He had not prevented her from writing the truth. The realization gave her more satisfaction than she had anticipated. It was possible he would leave town, give up his mission to kill her, now that Elizabeth Stern was in custody. It would be the sensible thing to do, and yet a part of her knew he would not give up.

She reached the lake shore, clamored over the rocks, and stepped into the water. Runoff from the snow on the high peaks of the mountains. The cold sent spears of shock up her legs. Maury's memorial service would be held sometime this morning. Philip hadn't mentioned the time or the place, making certain that she didn't show up. No matter. She would have her own service. You were supposed to pray at these things, she supposed, but she hadn't prayed since she was a child. She remembered praying that her mother — the woman with long, black hair, leaning over her, smiling — wouldn't be sick anymore. Such a faint memory, pulled out of the shadows of her mind. But her mother had gone off in an ambulance and had never come back, and Catherine had stopped praying. She had gone to live with people she didn't know — a lot of people she didn't know — until Dad and Marie had taken her home.

She rolled up her capris and took a couple more steps into the water that lapped around her calves. She flexed her toes in the cold, soft mud and tossed the rosebud like a Frisbee. It rode on the surface, moving away, a streak of yellow on the blue water. "Go with the spirits, my friend," she said, and that seemed right somehow. Something her mother used to say: go in harmony, go in beauty, go with the spirits. She watched the rose until it slid under a small wave and disappeared.

She saw Rex bounding over the grass as she climbed back over the rocks, Marie behind him, dragging the leash and balancing a large carton in both arms. Everything about the dog was familiar, the way he ran with his ears back and his head stretched forward, the funny way his back legs splayed sideways. She ran up the hill to meet him, and then he was jumping on her, barking and howling. She dropped down onto her knees and pulled him against her, but the weight of him pushed her over sideways. She heard herself laughing out loud, rolling with the dog, tugging at his fur until finally, he settled down and crawled onto her lap and licked at her hands.

Marie was still a little ways up the hill. She had stopped, Catherine realized, giving her a moment with Rex, but now she came toward them. She set the carton down, then let herself down on the grass next to Catherine. "He missed you," she said.

"I've missed him." Catherine glanced back at the lake. She tried not to start crying. She'd called Marie last night after she'd gotten back to the B&B and asked her to bring Rex to Sloan's Lake. It was a risk, she knew. The old Victorian house was only a few blocks away. She wanted to say good-bye to Maury, and she wanted to see Rex. "Thank you for bringing him," she said. Then, "I've missed you, too."

"Oh, Catherine." She felt herself pressed against Marie's chest, her arms warm and soft against her blouse. "I read the newspaper this morning. Is it over now?"

"Detective Bustamante hopes to learn the killer's whereabouts from Gilly Mason."

"Until then . . ." Marie let her go.

"I'll be careful." Catherine tried for the most reassuring smile she could muster. "I promise."

"I've brought your birth mother's box of things," Marie said, pulling the box over between them. "I thought you'd like to see them now."

Catherine lifted off the lid and stared at the necklace and earrings strung with what looked like old glass beads, chipped a little, but still shiny and bright, a rainbow of colors. They sat on top of the loose pile of papers. So little for a lifetime, she thought. She picked up the necklace and let the beads run like water through her fingers. She'd seen beads like this in old photographs. She wondered if Margaret Fitzpatrick had worn a necklace like this at the treaty councils.

She curled the necklace into the little cushion in her lap and lifted out a stack of papers, yellowed with age, brittle in her hands, the edges frayed and torn. The first page was smaller than the others, with a thin border around the edges and large black type across the top that said, "Marriage

Certificate." Catherine glanced down the page: Mary Fitzpatrick and Thomas Perry. United in marriage on June 3, 1968, St. Elizabeth Church, Denver, Colorado. Father Michael Byrne, witness.

Then, stuck to the back of the certificate, as if they belonged together — the beginning and the ending — was a three-inch newspaper clipping, the type smeared, the lines in the folds faded. The small headline read: "Worker Killed." In the margin above the headline, someone had penciled, October 20, 1970.

Catherine read through the article slowly, absorbing the news as if it had occurred yesterday. She knew so little about her parents. The vaguest memories of her mother, the silky black hair, the quietness about her, the easy smiles. Her father — a remote figure in history who no longer existed, except that he seemed to exist now, in his marriage and in his death. Somewhere along the line, someone — she supposed it had been Marie or Dad — had told her that her father had been killed shortly before her mother had died. "You're our little girl now," they had always told her.

Catherine turned away a moment. The lake, and the mountains in the distance, looked blurred and shimmering. Rex had fallen asleep, nuzzled against her leg, snoring into the morning quiet. This was who she was, she was thinking, before she tried to become everyone else.

"I'm sorry," Marie said, reaching out and touching her shoulder. "I thought you were ready."

"I am ready." Catherine patted at the moisture on her cheeks and went back to thumbing through the other papers. A collection of childish drawings and colorings, all stick figures and circles and wobbly stars with the name "Catherine" scrawled in the corners. Her mother had kept these, she realized. They had meant something to her.

Beneath the drawings was a bundle of thin pages held together by an old rubber band that broke in half when she tried to pull it off. She spread the pages in a fan on the grass. Lines of beautiful and precise handwriting — the kind of penmanship taught in another age when important records had to be written by hand. There was no name on the first page, but on the last line of the last page was a signature: Margaret Fitzpatrick. 1867.

She slid the pages into a neat stack and began reading:

My mother was Mahom. She came from

a leading family of our people. She was the sister of Niwot, who was called Left Hand by the whites. He was a great chief and the people trusted him. He was also a peace chief. He worked with the Cheyenne chiefs, Black Kettle and White Antelope, to make peace on the plains. The chiefs told everyone to go to Sand Creek where the people would be safe until a peace agreement was made. My mother and her other children went with Chief Left Hand. They camped a little apart from the Cheyennes. There were only about fifty Arapahos in the camp when the soldiers came. Chief Little Raven and the other Arapahos were still on the way. Some boys were able to run away from the soldiers. They found ponies and rode to warn Little Raven. The old chief told his people to cross the Arkansas River and go to Oklahoma. They never returned to Colorado.

My mother said that the camp at Sand Creek was like all our camps. We had a camp pattern that we always used. We always put up our tipis in a circle, with the openings facing the east and the rising sun. The tipis of the chiefs were in the middle. She said that when the soldiers came, Chief Left Hand ran from his tipi toward the soldiers with his arms extended, his palms out, which was our sign of peace. The white soldiers knew him. He used to visit their ranches in the Boulder area. It was the soldiers from Boulder who shot him. My mother was able to run away with her children. They were the only Arapahos at Sand Creek who survived.

I heard that Chief Black Kettle and Chief White Antelope did the same for their people. They grabbed white flags and ran out to the soldiers and shouted for them to stop. But the soldiers kept coming. They killed White Antelope. Then Black Kettle shouted to the people to run. It was terrible. The soldiers kept shooting, and people were running around, trying to get away. They killed everybody they saw, even little children. I heard they shot a tiny girl who was toddling around.

Afterward many warriors joined the Sioux and went on a rampage along the Platte River. They cut off the overland roads into Colorado. They were enraged at what had happened at Sand Creek, and they were inconsolable at the deaths of their families. Finally the government offered to make a new peace treaty that would give us reparations for all we had lost. Chief Little Raven asked me to interpret the words of the white commissioners.

There were many Indian people at the treaty meeting. There were many relatives of the old people and the women and the children who had been killed, and some Cheyennes who had survived Sand Creek. Many of them were still sick from gunshot wounds. Everyone was sad. "It is very hard for us," Chief Little Raven said. "Many of our people lie at Sand Creek."

The commissioners said that a great injustice had been done to our people. They promised to make reparations. Medicine Lodge Treaty Council, 1867. Margaret Fitzpatrick.

Catherine gathered all the papers together, smoothing the edges of the little stack, trying to grasp the full extent of the meaning. She was aware of Marie's eyes watching her, filled with questions she didn't know how to ask. Whatever was written on the pages belonged to Catherine.

Finally Catherine said, "There's more to the story. Leland Stern and Ethan Russell and most likely many of the other founding fathers probably helped themselves to the Arapaho and Cheyenne lands after Sand Creek. They were here, and the Indians were gone. The government promised to make reparations, but if the Arapahos and Cheyennes had tried to come back and take possession of any of their lands, they would have been killed. It was a hundred years before the government made reparations."

Catherine was about to drop the stack of papers into the carton when she saw another carton at the bottom. She set the papers on the grass and pried it out. "What's this?" she said. But she knew the answer, even before she had lifted the lid.

Inside, wrapped in a soft white cotton, would be her father's revolver. She pulled back the cotton and stared at the K-38 Special, the blued, double-action revolver with a six-inch barrel that she had learned to shoot when she was twelve years old. What she saw was a girl with black braids and braces, gangly and awkward and lost between two worlds, and the kind man who had become her dad, on Saturday afternoons in the summer at a shooting range, taking aim at the targets stapled to the target board.

"I think you should take it," Marie said.

"I don't need it." What help would the

revolver have been last night? In the bottom of her bag, and the bag on the floor two feet away. Elizabeth Stern would have shot her if she had even glanced toward the bag.

"Take it anyway," Marie said. "For me."

Catherine closed the lid, wedged the box back into the carton, and set the papers on top. Rex was awake now, shaking himself and watching her, as if he were waiting for her to say they were going home.

"Not yet, buddy," Catherine said, patting the top of his head, scratching the hard knobs behind his ears. "Soon, I hope."

She stood up and waited while Marie pulled herself to her feet. "Would you like to come to Sand Creek with me tomorrow?" Catherine said. She wondered why she'd asked. He was still out there, and she didn't want to put Marie in danger. But Marie looked so . . . bereft, as if she felt that Catherine had gone away from her. It was true, but not the whole truth. She finally had herself, but she would always love Marie. She told her about the homecoming run, how Arapaho kids would leave Sand Creek and run in relays across the ancestral lands in Colorado all the way to the Wind River Reservation in Wyoming. There would be a ceremony, blessings of the elders, drumming and singing in memory of the dead at Sand Creek.

"Yes," Marie said. "I would love to go with you."

33

Catherine could hear the drumming when she pulled into a vacant space on the dirt lot filled with pickups and dust-spattered sedans. A crowd of three hundred or four hundred people, she guessed, stood on the bluff on the far side of the lot. Groups of Indians — women with small children in tow, other kids running ahead, and men lugging ice chests and folding chairs — crossed the lot and headed up the dirt incline. Dust balls scattered around their boots. The air was hot; the brown earth dried and burned, the stubby patches of sagebrush blistered. There was a hushed solemnity to the place, like the solemnity of a cemetery, with only the steady, muffled sound of the drums.

Marie had slept for the last thirty miles over the dirt roads, and now she yawned, rubbed at her eyes, and combed her fingers through her hair. It had been a four-hour drive from Denver, and they had left early, driving into the rising sun, the sky ablaze in streaks of pink and red and vermilion. Even the rolling brown plains had turned pink. They talked about the Arapahos, Catherine's people, Marie had called them. They had lived here, Catherine had said, reassuring herself. Along the streams, in the shade of the cottonwoods. It was like a game that she and Marie had played, nodding toward the occasional cluster of trees. "Could have been over there. Chief Left Hand's village, possibly. Margaret Fitzpatrick could have lived over there." She was starting to learn about herself. It would be a long process. Maybe she would go to the Wind River Reservation and see if anyone remembered her mother.

The sun burrowed into her like a laser beam when she got out of the car. She stuffed the keys into her jeans pocket, opened the trunk, and set her bag inside. Then she pulled out the blue fabric chairs, folded into narrow bags, that Marie had brought. She slammed the lid and waited for Marie to put on the straw cowboy hat that cast a line of shadow above her nose. *Odd,* Catherine thought, as they set off for the bluff. She had deliberately left her own hat on the backseat, and Marie hadn't said anything, as if she'd guessed that Catherine would welcome the sun washing over her, warming parts of her that had always seemed cold.

She could feel the dark eyes following them as they reached the top of the bluff and started through the haphazard groups of people seated in folding chairs and standing about. A trail of smoke rose from a small campfire at the edge of the crowd. The sweet smell of sage wafted through the air. She found a bare spot where they opened the chairs and sat down. The runners gathered near the campfire, kids, most of them, with black hair and bronze skin, dressed in shorts and tee shirts with "Sand Creek Memorial Run" printed on the backs. Beyond the runners, she could see the dirt path down a gradual slope toward a platform with an iron railing. And beyond the railing, she knew, was the site of the massacre, a stretch of bare plains broken by scrub brush and stands of cottonwoods along the dried creek bed. She felt an uneasiness prickling her, a queasiness in her stomach. The people had run up the creek bed.

"So you have finally come to Sand Creek." Norman Whitehorse appeared beside her. She nodded, then introduced Marie. "Sometimes people feel a little sick the first time." He had hooked his hands into the pockets of his blue jeans and was peering down at her, as if he expected her to bolt out of the chair and run for a bush. "Soon's the elders give the blessing, the first relay of runners will get started. They'll run ten miles, then the next relay team will take over. They run so people won't forget the terrible thing that was done here."

"My ancestors were here," Catherine said. "Most of them were killed."

"I know," Norman said. He nudged a webbed folding chair across a foot of dirt with his boot and sat down. "At least we would've gotten some of our land back with a settlement."

"Maybe someday we'll get a better settlement, land for ranches and homes." She doubted that was true. The people had already agreed to a settlement for the lost lands. She knew that Norman knew the truth: the land was gone.

The crowd started moving like a giant organism shifting sideways. A group of elders came through the opening, Harold YellowBull and James Hunting among them. They circled the runners, then turned and faced them. Harold stooped over and lifted a pan off the campfire. Gripping the handle with both hands, he held out the pan like an offering and began speaking in Arapaho. The sound was melodious, a rising and falling with points and counterpoints, like the mournful sound of a jazz saxophone. Smoke poured out of the pan, drifting and curling through the crowd.

Norman leaned over the armrest. "He says the people that got away from here always remembered and carried the memory with them the rest of their lives. He says that now we gotta keep the memory, so the people that died here won't be with the forgotten people. He says it's our duty to remember. The running and the remembering will help our people heal."

The kids stood quietly, heads bowed, sunk into themselves, Catherine thought, summoning the strength for the long run ahead. The drumming started again, a low thudding noise that reverberated in the quiet vastness. The other elders raised their hands toward the kids, palms outward in the sign of peace, and muttered something in Arapaho: wishing them well, she guessed, wishing them Godspeed. The kids turned and started running, a long line snaking down the dirt path toward the railing, veering onto a side path, disappearing for a moment then reappearing out on the plains where the villages had stood. Still running, a long line of black-haired kids weaving up the creek bed. Catherine was on her feet now and so were Marie and Norman. Everyone was standing, watching the runners until they looked like a white line drawn across the brown plains.

The crowd had begun to thin out, and the sound of engines coughing into life and tires squealing punctuated the quiet. Some of the families had eaten sandwiches and drunk cans of soda from the ice chests, but they now had packed up everything and were making their way down the slope to the parking lot. There were a few families still finishing picnics. Norman and the elders had left. They were to be in the vans with the relay teams, driving down the dirt roads beside the runners. Every ten miles, the sweat-soaked kids would climb into the vans and pour water over their heads and down their throats. Eat a little. Sleep a little. The next team would be running. The same routine for almost six hundred miles, across Colorado and part of Wyoming.

Catherine had walked back to the car for the small ice chest that Marie had set in the trunk along with the chairs. They had pretended they were having a picnic, but the smell of mayonnaise and turkey sandwiches had made her stomach turn. She'd sipped on a can of Coke, but she had no appetite. Neither did Marie, she realized. Marie had taken a few bites of her sandwich, then slipped it back into a plastic bag and dropped it into the cooler.

"I want to see the site," Catherine said. She had been thinking about walking to the platform and looking out over the railing since the blessing had ended and the runners headed out, but she wasn't sure how she could summon the courage.

"I can go with you," Marie said.

Catherine shook her head. "It's okay. I'd like to go alone." She pushed herself out of the chair and walked past the last knots of people folding chairs and packing ice chests, past the campfire with embers flickering and the odors of sage still in the air. She went down the path and crossed to the railing.

The site spread below, even more beautiful and serene from the overlook. The sound of the breeze riffling the cottonwoods drifted toward her. Out toward the northeast, she knew, was the site of the Arapaho camp. A cluster of tipis, a small group of people, not more than sixty, and all of them part of Chief Left Hand's band. His family, her ancestors. Spread north and west was the large Cheyenne camp, six hundred people, a few warriors, but mostly women, children, and old people. The soldiers had stopped on the bluff and looked down onto the sleeping camp, just as she was looking down now. Then the noise had started: the clanking of sabers and harnesses, the whinnying of the horses, the churning of the wagons that hauled the howitzers over the dirt. And Colonel Chivington lifting his rifle and shouting: Remember your dead on the plains!

She turned around and walked back. A few people were still milling about, and Marie had struck up a conversation with two women near the edge of the bluff. Catherine picked up the ice chest and started for the car. She had to catch herself from sliding down the incline into the parking lot. She felt slightly numb, drained. The sun was blazing in a perfect, blue sky. A pickup pulled out of a space and downshifted past her, the tires spitting out a cloud of dust. She passed several sedans lined up next to the rental car. She opened the trunk.

It was then, out of the corner of her eye, that she saw the yellow head emerging from the dark-colored Pontiac sedan two cars away. She froze for an instant, and in that instant her eyes took in the rest of her surroundings: the tan sedan next to her, a pickup at the end of the row. No one else in the lot. She was alone with the killer.

She had one thought. Everything must appear normal. He must not know that she had seen him. Normal. She leaned down as she set the ice chest into the trunk, and in that instant, she slipped her hand into her bag and slid out the revolver that Marie had insisted she bring along. She gripped it in her right hand, a smallish thing. Strange how familiar it seemed, as if she were a kid again, fixing her fingers around the handle, her thumb barely brushing the trigger. Dad standing beside her saying, "Don't take your eyes away from the target, Catherine. You can hit the bull's-eye."

She slammed the lid and turned slowly, her arms straight at her sides, the gun in her right hand a little behind her. The killer was about ten feet away, moving past the trunk of the tan sedan. In his hand was a black revolver with a long silencer. Everything about him seemed big, larger than life, a phantom figure from a nightmare. The yellow hair like the crazy wig of a clown, the dark tee shirt and blue jeans, the cowboy boots. He was smiling in a way that only involved his lips. His eyes were dark and dead.

He could shoot her in an instant.

He likes to have his fun. She could hear Bustamante's voice. You're an easy target. He's overconfident.

"Haven't you heard that it's over?" she said. Start a conversation, she was thinking. Distract him. "The story has already run. Elizabeth Stern and Gilly Mason are in custody. The police know who you are and how to find you."

"Wrong, Catherine." He turned his head slightly and spat out a wad of saliva. "If they knew how to find me, I wouldn't be here. They don't know shit."

"There are people on the bluff." She could see Marie still talking to the women, and a couple of men folding chairs. "You'll never get away with this."

"Oh, I'll get away all right. By the time anybody notices you sprawled in the dirt, I'll be a half mile down the road. Nobody's gonna find me out here in all this emptiness." He worked his jaw for a moment, then spat again. "You surprised me, Catherine, and very few people surprise me. Calling your friend to come rescue you. Running your car off the highway in the mountains. Oh, there's lots of other times I could've taken you out. Nights out walking your dog. Parking lot at the hospital. I was there waiting for you. Up at the ranch, I saw you out running. But I was waiting for the right moment. I wanted to see your face, watch the fear light up in your eyes. You're prettier up close than I thought. But I made a contract. I always fulfill my contracts. It's a shame, Catherine, but I believe you're gonna have to say good-bye."

Something shifted in his mouth, his lips twisted. He turned his head a quarter inch and started to spit again, and in that instant she raised the revolver and pulled the trigger. The gunshot blasted the air. He staggered backward, eyes bulging, saliva draining out of the corners of his mouth, a string of saliva hanging off his chin. His hand was shaking on the gun that rose toward her.

She fired again, and this time he fell backward, dropping onto the dirt, legs bent like the legs of a plastic robot. In her line of vision, coming off the bluff, running down the slope, sprinting across the lot — a blur of dark faces and black hair, blue jeans pumping and tee shirts heaving, and running ahead of everyone else, Marie. Her mouth opened in a round O, arms outstretched. There were sounds of screaming a long way away.

Catherine looked at the man with yellow hair sprawled in front of her.

"Good-bye," she said.

ABOUT THE AUTHOR

Margaret Coel is the *New York Times* bestselling, award-winning author of the acclaimed novels featuring Father John O'Malley and Vicky Holden, as well as several works of nonfiction. Originally a historian by trade, she is considered an expert on the Arapaho Indians. A native of Colorado, she resides in Boulder. Her website address is www.margaretcoel.com.